The Catfish Man

Other Books by Jerome Charyn

The Catfish Man

A Conjured Life

by Jerome Charyn

ARBOR HOUSE

NEW YORK

For Robert Patten and Max Apple

ONE

Catfish and the Crotona Y

I.

THE Bronx River is a wormy little stream famous for its catfish and the color of its mud; the Bronx catfish can swallow a tin can and slap a child off a mudbank with their long whiskers and bands of powerful teeth. Such fish live in the yellow mud on both sides of the river, scooping trails in the mud with their noses and nesting with their fins in the air.

The catfish has nothing to do with the sculpted terraces and middleclass appetites of Parkchester village, east of the river. But to the enclave of Polish Jews that once dominated the west bank, from Longfellow Avenue to Crotona Park, the catfish was a creature to be reckoned with; playmate, garbage can (the catfish swallowed paper, steel wool, and rubber soles as well as tin), and muddy water god, it was worshiped, derided, and slaughtered for food. The catfish would have been inedible to the grocers and diamond merchants of Parkchester, Riverdale, and the Grand Concourse; it's a fish without scales, swinelike in its habits, a mudcrawler, pugnacious, evil to look at, strictly unclean. But the poor Jews of Longfellow Avenue understood no such dietary laws. They were a special breed.

Stuck between a shallow river and a skimpy park, they were

isolated from the rest of the world. The wives sat home with their babies, the husbands nearby. They were superintendents, draymen, butchers' assistants, ragpickers, tanners, deliverers of eggs. Whoever needed a workhorse could always find a Polish Jew from Crotona Park. Their children were profoundly dumb. They dreamed of becoming nurses and firemen, rather than doctors, kindergarten teachers, and business tycoons. And they ate catfish, raw or cooked in the mud, over a fire of twigs.

I was born into this enclave of Poles in 1937. A second child, I was called "baby" until I got beyond the age of ten. My brother Harvey had the rickets, and my mother kept him in the sun, summer and winter, his skin baking to a fine crust of blueish red while it lapped up vitamin D. He drank out of a bottle up to his sixth or seventh birthday. Neither of us learned to eat with a fork and a spoon. My mother would run around the kitchen table stuffing bananas and prunes into our mouths. There was nothing sissified about bananas and prunes. My rickety brother destroyed the Porasoff twins, notorious bullies, eight years old, banging their foreheads together with his permanently sunbaked hands.

We moved from the enclave in 1943, to the worldly Art Deco landscape of the West Bronx. We arrived on Sheridan Avenue, one block east of the Grand Concourse, the mecca of middle-class German and Russian Jews, with its great interior courtyards, its savings banks, synagogues with stained-glass windows (called "temples" on the Grand Concourse), and little parks with stone statuettes. My father was out of his element. We had bedbugs in the walls that stained pillows, sheets, and furniture legs with snatches of our own blood. I suffered calamities at school because I was unable to keep up with those aggressive, smart Concourse brats. My teachers threatened to hold me in the first grade forever unless my brain could absorb some of the intelligence that was rampant in the West Bronx. My brother joined the Sea Scouts. We saw Franklin Delano

Roosevelt in a motorcade. We moved back to Crotona Park.

The Grand Concourse had corrupted me. My head was filled with idle bits of knowledge that an East Bronx child shouldn't have known. The dummies of Crotona Park glared at me from their inkpots in sullen, brave ignorance when I began to jabber about Ferdinand Magellan and the Battle of Waterloo, or the cruel maneuverings of compound interest that had been whipped into me, since most first and second graders in the West Bronx had their own small bank accounts. Curried by my new teachers as a wonderboy who had fallen into their laps from a different part of the country, I was loathed by the rest of the class.

I survived. Once you've rubbed the whiskers of a catfish, you never lose the smell. I had the natural cunning of a child who stepped in yellow mud. Remembering how the catfish would burrow under the riverbank to hide from its enemies, I played dead. Stammering, limping over the syllables of Magellan, I managed to become dumb Jerome. Meantime I grew. I dwarfed my mother by the age of seven. I peeked over my father's bald spot before I was nine. I had a moustache in the fifth grade.

My reckoning came inside of a year. I got into a scuffle with a friend of mine. Her name was Gloria. A black girl from Boston Road with all the private wisdom of Crotona Park Jews, and her own store of grace, she was around six feet tall. There was little malice in Gloria. She meant me no real harm. She simply drummed the sides of my skull with her long elbows whenever I prepared to attack. Mortified, I crawled home with my moustache in my mouth.

Overpowered by a girl in the halls of P.S. 61. Who could outlive such a smear to his reputation? Polish Jews were supposed to be stronger than the Siberian mule. I began lugging bureaus through the house. I dipped my body between two weakbacked chairs until my face had the puffy look of a catfish out of water. How could I ever frighten Gloria? Moustaches weren't made for war. I had bumps on my shoulders and a hollow design in the middle of my chest. I peeked at the veins on my brother's arms. He had been lifting weights at the Crotona Y for almost two years. I said, "Harvey, I'm going with you."

It was a YMHA, for working class Christians and Polish Jews, at the northern end of Crotona Park. You crossed this park at your own risk. It was a battle zone, inhabited by the Irish Eagles of Clay Avenue and the Black Barons of Boston Road, who set aside their hatred from one another to seek out a common enemy: the catfish-loving Sammies who lived south of Crotona Park. Carrying the stalks of ruined umbrellas, my brother and I sneaked into the park. We could hear the taunting whisper of "Sammy, Sammy boy" from every second bush. I couldn't understand why my brother would expose himself to such rotten music for the sake of pumping up his arms.

With judicious pokes in the grass from our umbrella stalks, we reached the Crotona Y, a dour building with a façade of crumbling bricks and a pair of shredded green awnings that must have been leftovers from the Civil War, they were so crusted down with grime and ancient pigeonshit. My brother shoved me through a side entrance, and we climbed six flights of savage, twisting stairs. We arrived in a locker room that couldn't accommodate two boys standing up; we had to crawl our way onto a basketball court in the midst of a skirmish involving men and boys in colored jerseys and shorts, who shouted and pushed with a rawness on their faces and a wet stink running down their backs. Husky people, they leered at us, scratching under their kneebraces in contempt of me and my brother. "Dumb weightlifters," they said. "The fairy corps." And they hurled the basketball at us, aiming for our eyes.

My brother took the brunt of the ball. He stuck me inside his shoulder, twirled me around, and offered up one of his wings to be hit. The ball crashed into Harvey with a gruesome bark that rippled through his neck and catapulted us into the wall. It was no time to feel a swollen cheek. Harvey scooped me up, and we went through an opening in the wall, climbed more stairs, and came out on a track above the basketball court. The track had a floor that curved under your feet like the inside of a bowl; it was slippery up there. You walked pigeontoed, or couldn't walk at all.

We endured a brutal twentieth of a mile, hobbling with our hands on the rail. The basketballers despised us from below, cursing our choppy labors across the track. We entered the weightlifting room on our knees, sliding off the rail. I chewed my moustache to stifle any cries of bitterness towards my brother. We'd landed in a closet, a hump of a room, without a window or a decent air duct. The closet was crowded with torture machines, bars and pulleys stretching from the ceiling and the walls that could have wrapped around your neck, and strangled the ribs of a schoolboy. My brother ordered me to undress. We stood in our underpants, wearing jockstraps Harvey had brought to protect us from falling barbells and a tear in our groins. I saw the evil red mark the basketball had left on my brother's wing. I wiped my moustache with my wrist.

These weightlifters were a peculiar lot. They sat among the torture machines gobbling raisins, with honey jars between their thighs, or else they floated towards the mirrors on the rear wall with the laziest motion I'd ever seen, their hips swinging in syncopation with their arms, their chests rising under their jaws, their knees dipping perfectly. They would pose in front of the mirrors, following the track of a muscle, sneeze, touch a calf, make their abdominals hop, and float back to the honey jars.

When they put their fingers in the honey for a lick, it became serious business. They would get up, pinch their jockstraps, snort, stare at a particular barbell with a mad concentration that shut out mirrors and superfluous machines, snort again, and grip the barbell with an agility you couldn't believe. Before you had the chance to look into their eyes, the barbell would be resting on their shoulders. They would snort for a third time and shove the barbell up into the ceiling until their elbows locked out. Others would grab a dumbbell, or stick their necks into the bowels of a machine, working pulleys with their legs. They'd show contempt for a barbell or a dumbbell soon as they completed an individual lift, letting it smash to the floor. The room would shiver, and if you put your head outside, you could watch the whole track go buckling in the air and listen to the basketballers groan.

My brother taught me how to use all the wires, frames, and pulleys: the dipping bars that could give you broader "pecs" than Linda Darnell; the squatting rack to fatten your thighs; the "lat" machine, a pulley with weights on the end, to provide you with a decent pair of wings; the abdominal board to put striations in your belly; the leg-pressing machine, a windy tunnel you entered with your rump on the floor, while you wished to God and the Bronx catfish that the weights you were throwing up with your knees in your chest wouldn't come down on your head.

I sampled the abdominal board. The wires of the lat machine nicked my ear. I did squats with a hundred pounds on my back, waiting for my belly to rip. I crawled out of the leg-pressing machine with enough grease on me to keep my sideburns in slick shape for a month. I borrowed licks of honey. I fell into the quiet mood of the weightlifters. I walked from mirror to mirror staring into the hollows of my breastbone. I joined the Crotona Y.

2.

THERE was no rematch with Gloria of Boston Road. Weight-lifters didn't fight girls. We were a gentle breed, lost in our honey jars, unless provoked. Don't be fooled by any talk of musclebound freaks. The strutting we did, the "weightlifter's trot" with your wings spread wide, was only a lure; it alarmed your enemies and alerted your friends, allowing you to tuck in your hips in front of strangers, possible rivals, and neighbor-hood girls. Removed from his honey jar, my brother could still wrestle both Porasoff twins to the ground, race an Irish gang across the park, duel with an umbrella stalk, lay down killers in a handball game, and pop a walnut without splintering the shell.

Most of our strutting took place in the summer, on lot 13 of Orchard Beach. We scorned Coney Island and Jacob Riis Park. We weren't gypsies running to another borough. We had our own "muscle beach." This was an innocent time, before Korea. The men wore skimpy bathing suits on lot 13, not the girls. We shaved our thighs up to the crotch, plucking stubborn hairs with a tweezer, so we could wiggle into a strip of velvet cut to the sleek dimensions of a jockstrap. Our girlfriends had to wear clumsy bandannas on their chests, and go around in shorts that cluttered a good deal of their legs.

We couldn't throw non-weightlifters out of lot 13. But we could prevent them from pestering any of the girls who drifted over from different parts of the beach to admire our velvet pants and watch us sip banana drinks, play chess with our biceps flexed, and tumble in and out of headstands. The Crotona Y had its own contingent of bodybuilders at Orchard Beach, with territorial rights, blanket space, and a direct route to the water. Our numbers included Triceps Charley, Mambo Red, Buster, who had a flair for doing handstands off the edge of a roof and had already survived one fall, Abie, a wild child who came to the beach in farmer's overalls and wouldn't strip, Marcus, who would leave the flock in a few years to open a chiropractor's school on Freeman Street and become a millionaire, Al Berman, who walked away with the Mr. Eastern America title before turning into a Bronx junkie, Marty Shine, who would go from professional wrestling to post office work, Burt, the artist, George, the fireman, Miles, who had the best abdominals among us, Stan, with the pretty face, Little Dave, Gregor, Morris Wigstein, Harvey, me, and the girlfriends, Marilyn, the three Annettes, the five Wasserman sisters, and more (at twelve I was entitled to the skinniest girl on the beach).

It wasn't all trumpery and poses, velvet briefs, and sand in your eyes. I loved to work out, to train in that closet above the basketball court, sometimes with a partner who could get you to squat with an additional fifty pounds on your back, sometimes alone. The seasons didn't matter at the Crotona Y: the weightlifting room always stank of rosin, honey, metal, grease, moldy jockstraps, and unwashed skin. Walking home, with your arms, back, and chest flushed from three hours of exercise, there was an exhilaration you could hardly find on a handball court, in the water, or even at the movies with one of the Wasserman sisters: it was an intimacy with your body that went beyond simple narcissism. Weightlifters love to feel themselves up, but so do pregnant women. Is it kinesthesia, the ability of a muscle to "think," the awareness of a body engendering its own power, a kind of witchery? Who knows? At Shimkin's delicatessen on Prospect Avenue, where I worked scrubbing potatoes and guarding the sauerkraut barrel, I was called the crazy Polish kid who looks at his tits in the mirror. Crazy or not, when a drunk wandered into the delicatessen, demanding frankfurters on the house, Shimkin came to me.

Conditions grew complex at the Crotona Y. Doc Sanchez, a Brazilian hospital orderly who trained with us, got himself into trouble. The basketball players swore Sanchez was a thief; they claimed he had picked their wallets out of the locker room while they were heaving the ball. Unless we surrendered Doc, they would destroy our closet and ban all weightlifters from the Y. They stood outside the weightlifting room, imponderable in their jerseys, twelve big men with little, raucous eyes and rancor in their mouths. We wouldn't give Doc over to them. They charged into the closet. No one was shy. We threw ourselves at the jerseys. I remember grabbing a kneebrace, twisting under the rubber foam to bite a hairy leg, while shoulders smacked above my widow's peak.

Lunging in our underwear, our biceps flashing back at us from the mirrors, we drove the jerseys out of our closet. They hobbled along the track, with puffs under their eyes and pieces missing from their fancy gym suits. We had our share of casualties. Mambo Red lost his jockstrap in the scuffle. Abie bloodied the bib of his overalls. Little Dave sacrificed a tooth. The lat machine was demolished. My brother walked with a noticeable limp. Miles scratched his beautiful abdominals saving Doc Sanchez. I had hair in my mouth from the leg I'd been chewing.

I caught my brother whispering to Doc. Harvey put on his clothes. He sneaked down to the locker room. Then he came upstairs. The basketball players stood under the track with sheepish faces. They began serenading us. "Screwy," they said. "Aint it weird?" Rummaging through the lockers, they'd found their wallets stuffed inside their street shoes.

3.

DON'T think of us as boys with narrow intellects. Our minds didn't crumble under the strain of squatting with our asses near the ground. We had our hobbies and our moral truths. It was 1949. We talked of creeping Stalinism, air-raid drills, food for the beleaguered citizens of West Berlin, the latest chess prodigy (a kid from Brooklyn with a pointy skull), and whether Steve Reeves would be the next Mr. Universe. We worried a lot about Hollywood. We couldn't name one legitimate weightlifter among the stars. Still, we compiled a list of actors with passable physiques, awarding points in the following way.

Best Arms: Robert Mitchum
Best Chest: Sonny Tufts
Best Back: Burt Lancaster
Best Midsection: Sabu
Best Legs: Victor Mature

We got little satisfaction from our list. We knew that Burt Lancaster had once been an acrobat, but walking on your head in a circus isn't the same as sitting under the shaky platform of a leg-pressing machine. Then stories came back from Little Dave, who had moved to Santa Monica because he was tired of Orchard Beach and winters in the Bronx. "There's a lifter out here," Dave wrote. "His arms are so-so, like Harvey's kid brother, but he has pretty good definition. He'll be in a picture soon." Little Dave couldn't quite remember the actor's name. "Bregner, Bragner, something like that."

We perked up our noses. We sniffed for Davey's "picture." We had to wait six months until it arrived at the Loew's Boston, a film in black and white, called *The Men*. Little Dave had scouted well for us. The hook in Marlon Brando's biceps was unmistakable. He wasn't a scarecrow off the street. He had the pecs and wings of a bodybuilder. He mumbled like a Bronx child. He slouched like any patron of the Crotona Y. He played a paraplegic, so we never saw his legs. The hell with that. We'd appraise his calves another time. The one thing that troubled us was his name. There were no Marlons in the East Bronx. It had to be a phony, picked by a Hollywood tycoon. We wrote to Little Dave. He answered us with rotten news. He tried to tell us Marlon was a Nebraska name. "Bullshit," we said. We could smell the Bronx River on Brando, even from a movie screen. He was a boy who had chased catfish through the mud. Stymied, we grabbed for a perfect lie. "Marvin Brendel," we muttered. "That's what they called him on Crotona Park."

Marvin Brendel wasn't our only preoccupation. A new craze struck the Crotona Y. It was the "super set," a theory of working out with barbells and dumbbells that revolutionized bodybuilding in America, and the Bronx. Hitherto we had been told to exercise with the heaviest weight possible, to do three short sets of curls, benchpresses, squats, lateral raises, and such, resting between each set, so we could lick honey and recover our strength. Now *Muscle Power,* our primer, training manual, and gossip magazine, warned us that we were straining our muscles, hurting their elasticity, under the old method. We had to disband the notion of heavy weights, train with light dumb-bells, increase the number of repetitions, curl for an hour, with little rest. The catchword was concentration. Doing curls, with your elbow against your knee, you were meant to stare at both peaks of your biceps while you accomplished thirty to forty "reps."

We live in an age of twenty-one-inch biceps and fifty-six-inch chests; these things would have been impossible without the "super set." In the primitive days of 1949, you couldn't have found a pair of eighteen-inch biceps on Orchard Beach. Only Marvin Eder, that wonderboy from Gowanus Bay, had biceps measured by Mambo Red himself at a full eighteen, with a quarter of an inch to spare. My brother was the great hope of the Crotona Y. He brought his right arm up to seventeen and a half. I didn't take after Harvey. I couldn't get my biceps much over fifteen.

We trained and trained, until our tape measures grew raw rubbing against our skin. What can I tell you about those yellow tapes? They stretched on us; perspiration made them worthless. They curled along the inch lines and tore. Measuring your biceps was a religious affair; no one wanted an unearned sixteenth of an inch. We had problems in addition to the grubbiness of our tapes. My father was unemployed during most of '49 (workhorses were less valuable in a general recession). So my mother had to ration the milk. She carved our initials into the wax of a milk container, H for Harvey, J for me. It would have been a disgusting act to drink from my brother's container, and deprive him of his milk. We abided by the H's and the J's.

Marvin Eder was no longer a threat. The Army grabbed hold of him; he'd been swallowed up by the draft. It was a peacetime Army, but for any bodybuilder induction was a special curse. You couldn't work out. You couldn't snort wheat germ and honey. You had to watch your body shrink. What does the Army know about the need to pump up a muscle? Bodybuilders would go berserk. They'd come home to the Crotona Y on a weekend pass, with two ears sticking out of a shaved skull, and drag their scrawny bodies around. Zombies, they didn't have the patience to sit under the leg-pressing machine. They would toy with a dumbbell, hunch in a corner, and talk to themselves. We pitied Marvin Eder, and continued to curl.

It was an evil year; a month before the Mr. New York City contest, my brother tripped over a dead wire hanging from the lat machine and pulled his groin. He couldn't grab a dumbbell without feeling a twitch in his obliques. His name had to be scratched off the Mr. New York City lists. The Crotona Y considered entering me; but stringy calves, ordinary lats, and biceps with shallow peaks would have disgraced us all. The best we could hope was that I wouldn't place last: there had to be another "lifter" at the contest with stringier calves than mine. We couldn't take the chance. So I never got to wear my posing briefs at the Mr. New York City of 1949.

We would have boycotted the whole affair, kept away from

the Roosevelt Auditorium, but the backers of the contest had promised us Steve Reeves. Mr. America was scheduled to give a posing exhibition before the winners were announced. Six Crotona boys arrived at the auditorium, my brother, Mambo Red, Triceps Charlie, Burt, Gregor, and myself. We sat in a middle row, surrounded by gay photographers, boys in muscle tee shirts, girls with startling bosoms under blouses with open necks: they'd come for Steve Reeves. Mambo Red pinched my earlobe, forcing me to turn sideways; Marvin Eder was two rows behind us, dressed in khaki, with a girlfriend nuzzling either shoulder. Had he lost his biceps? Who can say? His arms seemed snug in an Eisenhower jacket. We'd heard reports that he'd be out of uniform soon enough. A mythology had sprung up around Marvin Eder. Was it true that he'd broken every bed in his barracks at Fort Dix in a weightlifter's rage?

It was a humdrum Mr. New York City; we slept through most of the contest. The Crotona Y had slighted my build; I couldn't have placed last against such turkeys. I swear I had better pecs than anyone in that skimpy field of bodybuilders on-stage. After the first round of poses the announcer shuffled out in his blue tuxedo to tell us Steve Reeves wasn't coming. He had to jump behind the curtain to escape our wrath. We flung apples and shoes at him, and hi-protein honey bars. Some of us ripped the arms off our chairs. The announcer promised us a substitute: George Paine. He didn't dare leave his curtain.

We knew about George Paine, a black weightlifter from the Harlem Y. He had placed third at the last Mr. America and had been named Most Muscular Man, a kind of consolation prize given to contestants with washboard abdominals and other signs of amazing definition. Most Muscular Man usually meant you had some flaw in your body that didn't allow you to win a contest outright. We hadn't paid two dollars a head to see George Paine in little pink underpants.

He climbed the posing blocks to a thick squall of jeers. The announcer fluttered about picking debris off the stage. George

Paine didn't have to frown at the audience. He quieted us with one wiggle of his arms. You could have stuffed apples and cheese into the triceps of George Paine. I looked and looked. Long, miraculous worms crawled under the chunks of muscle in George Paine's back. Al Berman had the biggest lats in the Bronx; George Paine could have fit all of him into his left wing. The clefts between his major and minor pectorals were like huge, blinking eyes. We shivered, clasped our hands, and begged him to pose. Most Muscular Man? Who could speak of a consolation prize? We didn't want to hear about Mr. Americas. George Paine had been robbed.

4.

WE were savaged by Communism and the Korean War. The Crotona Y fell to pieces. The draft board on Arthur Avenue bit into our necks. We began receiving induction notices in the summer of 1950. We devised schemes for failing the Army physical. We bathed in chicken blood. We swilled castor oil. We prayed to our Bronx ancestors, the catfish. We stepped in yellow mud. We practiced walking like a hunchback. Our schemes rarely worked. Gregor ran to the Coast Guard enlistment booth on Fordham Road. Marcus jumped to Panama. Miles stood near the walls of Rockland State without his clothes on; no one let him in. Mambo Red picked dust out of his belly, his mailbox filled with inquiries from his local board.

A few of us were lucky; we sat out the year, crouched through 1951, unable to do concentration curls. The tape measures lay in our drawers. We didn't need a yellow tape to remind us what it meant to dangle. Inching towards our separate fates, we tried to breathe without making any noise. Harvey would be serving in Alaska by the end of the war. Abie sat in the water at Orchard Beach and drowned. Buster slipped off his roof again and survived a second fall. The Crotona Y moved to the Grand Concourse.

Dumb Jerome, what could I do about Korea? I was thirteen in 1950. Turning sly, I passed the entrance exam for the High School of Music and Art (the school was hungry for boys). Every face I drew had whiskers. I joined the Harlem Y, which happened to be a few blocks from Music and Art. I bench-pressed with George Paine. I saw the dimples in his pecs from six inches away. It was no mean idolatry. We had little room for worshipers at the Harlem Y. We did our curls together. We talked of John Davis, Olympic weightlifting champion, the first human being to raise four hundred pounds over his head in the clean and jerk. Thank God and the catfish that the poundage humped on a barbell wasn't subject to speculation and human whim. Black like George Paine, Davis had become the strong-est man in the world. There was no denying it. But strongmen didn't have the afflictions of a bodybuilder. How do you com-prehend a pair of wiggling biceps? Standards of beauty were corruptible, determined by the fashions of 1950, 1951, and 1952. George Paine would never be Mr. America.

Saddled with trigonometry and the French subjunctive, I stopped working out. It was hard for a boy with the taste of catfish in his mouth to settle into school. I could feel the pull of muddy water. I wore muscle tee shirts at Music and Art until my biceps flattened out. I began fondling girls in the halls. Embittered over Korea and George Paine, and the dismantling of the Crotona Y, I learned the art of soulkissing. "Pecs" on a girl became a revelation to me. It was more pleasant now to unhook a brassiere than to watch myself curling in a mirror. At fourteen I dreamed of marriage, contraceptives with greased tips, gin and tonics with pieces of lime, babies, an apartment on the Grand Concourse, sleek cigars, and other refinements of an ordinary life. I no longer drew faces with whiskers on them. The catfish was dead in me.

TWO

Soldiers' Hotel

I.

I lost out on that "ordinary life." No gin and tonics, no babies, no apartments on the Concourse. All I have is hurly-burly in my head . . . I wish I could say that my father beat me and beat me when I was four and five, that he locked me in closets, devoured my shoes in a mad fit, and made me live under the kitchen sink. Then I could boast of traumas and thirty-year feuds. But he did none of those things. A slap would come from time to time, an angry word, but he was no child-beater, my poor father Sam.

He was a manufacturer of teddy bears and other fur beasts. He had a dream of populating the universe with those crazy animals—a teddy bear in every household—but the only universe they ever populated was our apartment in the East Bronx. They sat on all the shelves, in the closets, turning yellow and beginning to stink.

My father wouldn't give them up. Those rotting bears were his brave new world. He'd been left behind in Europe, a boy of fourteen, when his mother and father got out of Poland in 1925. He couldn't get on the immigrant boat. He had a contagious disease. Pinkeye, or conjunctivitis. He was given a fiddle to keep him company until the pinkeye disappeared. He stayed with relatives in a country town. He scratched on his fiddle for nine months and the pinkeye went away. He arrived in America in 1926 with his toy fiddle. But I don't think he ever recovered from that abandonment of nine months. He existed in some shellshocked space after that. The pinkeye kid.

He was a workhorse at a fur corporation until 1947, a drudge who wet the skins of dead racoons so they could be stretched, cut, and nailed to a board. He picked the middle of a recession to start a business of his own. But how many families near Crotona Park had little cards that advertised CHARYN'S TEDDY BEARS in tooled green print?

Sam lived at the fur market seven days a week. He occupied one corner of a miserable loft, where he made his teddy bears. Little freaks with felt noses and peekaboo glass eyes. They dominated our living room, and they thrived under my bed. You couldn't feel around for a lost penny without grazing the thumbs and toes of a teddy bear. If I twitch now, if I wake periodically with sweat in one eye, it's because of the bears. They weren't inert to me. They were grasping creatures who led us into starvation and ruin.

Things got worse by 1949. My father couldn't pay for his corner of the loft. The cards that spoke of CHARYN'S TEDDY BEARS had to be destroyed. Sam went out of business. It meant more teddy bears at home. I ate their fur in my soup. They looked down at us from my father's credenza with bitterness squeezing out of their glassy eyes.

It was only the Korean War that saved us. Fritzie King, an old girlfriend of my mother's, had opened a small hotel in New Brunswick, at the end of Albany Street. The Indian Hotel sat on its own source of gold; it was a mile from Camp Kilmer, which served as a way station for soldiers coming out of Korea. Stuck at Camp Kilmer until they could be processed and discharged, the soldiers roamed New Brunswick; a portion of them always stopped at Fritzie's on their nights away from camp. These were fat nights for my mother's girlfriend. Because she flourished as a hotel queen, Fritzie could bring us out to New Jersey.

She needed a family of drudges to operate her hotel. There were promises of a partnership, and now it was my mother who had the crazy notion of becoming an entrepreneur. It was a simple move to Albany Street. We packed the teddy bears and left the Bronx. My brother stayed behind. He wanted to become Mr. America. He had to train properly; toiling with hotel mattresses might have compromised the hook in his biceps.

I was learning how to fiddle with oil paint at Music and Art, and I dreaded the idea of transferring to a school in Jersey. The smell of paint had got to me. I wouldn't give up my charcoal sticks and my ox-hair brush. But I had to keep the Board of Education from discovering that the Charyns had slipped into New Brunswick. Pretending to live with Harvey in the Bronx, I commuted from M & A to Albany Street.

My mother had to pay for these commutation tickets. Exiled from the fur market, my father idled with his teddy bears, while my mother slaved for Fritzie King. She was manager, chambermaid, seamstress, laundry girl, and kitchen navvy. She had soap in every groove of her knuckles when she fed my father and me. It was calf's liver (to thicken our blood) and a horde of green peas at the Indian Hotel. No one starved. Most of the fives and tens stuffed in my mother's pockets went to Fritzie, but she didn't begrudge me the money for Music and Art.

I had my cadmium yellows and my cinnabar greens. I was the boy who rode the train to his art school in New York. Who couldn't recognize me with my paint box that reeked of turpentine? I fell into ecstasies on that commuter train, rocking against the straw seats. I was the artist Jerome, lately of New Brunswick, with colors in a box. I wasn't intemperate. I allowed myself a good half year of struggle. Then I would take my mother out of bondage to Fritzie King with the paintings I delivered to Manhattan galleries. How many other fourteen-year-old geniuses could there be who'd inhabited the marshlands of New Jersey and the Bronx?

2.

THOSE teddy bears made me dumb. My father stacked them so high, I couldn't peek over their brains to find out what was going on in the lobby. Fritzie's revealed itself after a few weeks: it was a whorehouse hotel. There were too many soldiers around for Fritzie's to function in any other way. The Army dictated the economics of Albany Street; we had soldiers' bars, soldiers' restaurants, soldiers' hotels.

My father was busy counting the money he'd lost on the bears, so I had to be my mother's night clerk. How should I have known that the women who rented rooms from us weren't soldiers' wives? They cackled at me, they stroked my father's bears, they wore stockings that were paler than my cadmium yellow. They would sit on Fritzie's fire escape sucking dark cigarettes. Could I evict them for that? There was nothing improper about the throw of their legs. They would come downstairs in groups of three with warpaint under their eyes, clutching little jackets in one hand and hobbling on spikes that dented Fritzie's carpet.

This was no uniformed patrol: the whores would separate once they reached the bottom of the stairs, scrabbling to different parts of Albany Street. I never saw them return without some prey, soldier or civilian. The whores had to carry them up the stairs. "My uncle," they would say to me. And I had to nod to the face under a whore's elbow. "Melvin, meet Jerome. He's the night man here. Aint he cute? Gets free art lessons in New York. Jerome, that's my husband Mel."

The men would stumble out in the morning, cursing, spitting, with their belts hanging to the floor. The whores would sleep into the afternoon. They were pleasant girls. I fetched quarts of ice cream for them. I saw the razors they kept in their garter belts. Whatever they took from a soldier, they weren't so grasping as my father's teddy bears. These whores had a very compact world: they swindled the customers who didn't swindle them. Some of the girls had gnarled blue ears. They forced me to imagine horrible fights over money. The cracks in their warpaint and the crooked spaces in their mouths cut under all the vanities of a fourteen-year-old. I couldn't dream of Manhattan galleries with blue ears in my head. I stopped going to school.

Scrubbing twenty hours a day to provide a future for us in New Jersey, my mother would have killed me if I'd told her the news. So I left my morning rituals undisturbed; I packed my paint box, borrowed a necktie from my father, accepted one of my mother's bids for a sandwich—"Fried egg or cucumber and cheese?"—and walked to the train station on upper Albany Street. That's as close to Manhattan and Music and Art as a fugitive can get. I climbed out the back of the train station and headed for the French cemetery, where I could digest my cucumbers in peace. What was there to do after eating lunch at half past eight? I went to Rutgers College.

The old campus sat on a broad hummock above the train station. I would wander in and out of buildings until the groundsmen began to squint. But there wasn't much thieving in 1951, and nobody bothered to investigate a boy with a paint box banging into his knee. I skulked through Kirkpatrick Chapel, touching the cherry wood rails, staring up at the slats in the ceiling that curled around like the hull of a wooden ship and gave the church a mysterious feel that worked harder on me than undulating altars, recessed balconies, and trick pieces of glass. I read off the names of dead trustees and college presidents—Hasbrouck, Clothier, and Doolittle—from the portraits on the walls; names with starched bodies and balding heads could incriminate a stowaway from Albany Street who'd thrown off his schooling. I ran from the church with the rotting perfume of cherry wood in my nose.

There was Old Queens to cross, a venerable building with white shutters and dirty rose-colored bricks. Then the hump of grass to Hamilton Street, and over to Murray Hall and the statue of William the Silent, prince of Orange and founder of the Netherlands. He was perfect outdoor furniture. He wore bloomers, garters, and knee pants, this William, and he was everything a boy could want from his college. But he held no possibilities for me. I was tied to a whorehouse. I grew sad staring at his knee pants, knowing I'd be a truant for the rest of my life.

3.

ONE of the whores took an interest in me. Her name was Sarah, and she was from Baton Rouge. She had a good complexion and handsome teeth, but it was hard to read a whore's face: she could have been anywhere from seventeen to forty. She didn't have the gruff manner of the other girls. They called Sarah a "church whore," and didn't like her very much. She behaved like a "bitch with royal blood." She was up from New Orleans, they said, where she would only put out for priests and college professors. But these girls couldn't get to Sarah. She had a razor in her garter belt, like every other whore at the Indian Hotel.

Sarah wasn't formal around her Jerome. She came to me in peekaboo bra and underpants. She would laugh at my erection, but she wasn't out to tease a fourteen-year-old. She had serious business to discuss. "If a man comes snooping around for Sarah, a tall man, a dark man, with a hair growing on his lip, you tell him Sarah's long gone, and then you run to me."

"Who is this guy with the hair on his lip?"

"My husband," she said. "And he's the worst son of a bitch this side the Mississippi. Whored his own wife, my Mister. Sold me to the merchants of St. Charles Avenue . . . there's a dollar in it for you, Jerome, if you warn me about that man."

So I became the watchdog of the hotel, seeking out faces for that telltale hair on the lip of a tall, dark man. Nothing happened. Soldiers checked in and out. Sarah had her portion of them. I didn't have to guess what went on inside her room. I cursed the life I had: a truant and a watchdog on Albany Street.

A preacherlike man walked in one Saturday night. I wasn't asleep. What was a civilian doing at a soldiers' hotel? He had a starched collar and a churchman's black suit. The hat he wore kept his face in the shadows, but I could dream out who he was: Sarah's husband. He raised the hat high on his forehead and I saw the black hair growing out of a mole on his lip. It wasn't ugly to me. It could have been the single whisker on a catfish. He didn't have a harsh voice.

"You the night man, son?"

I mumbled yes without looking away from him. He showed me the pictures he carried inside the plastic windows of his wallet. "Ever see this woman? She might call herself Effie, Sarah Jane, something like that."

I pretended to scrutinize the plastic windows with all my might. "Sorry. The woman's not familiar to me."

I got rid of Sarah's husband and ran upstairs. Sarah was with a soldier. I knocked on her door. "Sarah, Sarah, the man with the lip."

Her husband had outsmarted Jerome. He waited until I'd gone up to Sarah, and then he followed me. The doors at the Indian didn't have terrific locks. Sarah's husband broke the doorknob off and shoved his way in. The other whores detested Sarah, but they were loyal to her. They came screaming out of their rooms with their soldier boyfriends. It didn't do much good. Sarah's husband punched and kicked at everybody, whores, soldiers, and myself. I caught a bloody mouth from him. Thank God my mother and father were at the movies, or they would have had to struggle with that lunatic. He dressed Sarah, slapped her once, and took her out of the hotel. The whores went back to their rooms. And I was just an ordinary truant again, who stole off to Rutgers College in the mornings and stood in front of that statue in bloomers and knee pants, William the Silent with birdshit on his brain.

4.

IT's Fritzie I have to thank for nudging me out of my sloth. The hotel had shoved her into respectability. She had a mansion in Highland Park, across the Albany Street Bridge, where she lived with her husband, who was always silent in her presence, and a daughter, twelve years old. This girl, named Annabelle, was meant for me. Twenty-seven years ago, in 1951, I had the profile of Gregory Peck. Shrewd as Fritzie was, she couldn't have known about my breakfasts at the cemetery, my procrastinations near the prince of Orange's bloomered legs. She sniffed my potential at M & A: an artist in the family, she must have reckoned. So I became the instrument of my mother's success. Glamor and money would clap hands on Albany Street; Fritzie's daughter and the Gregory Peck of Rutgers College would cement the Charyns and the Kings. My mother could have her partnership, and I could have Annabelle King.

The courtship was slow, very slow. It wasn't innocence that held me down. I understood all the sordid angles of seduction. I was the boy who brought ice cream to whores. They bantered about their customers in front of me. I heard their screams at night, their sex cries to the soldiers they'd hustled from the bars.

I could have borrowed this music for Annabelle. Only it might have turned thin. Annabelle had lived at the hotel before the Charyns came to New Jersey. We had the instincts of rival kittens. We hated one another with a naturalness that was frightening to watch.

Fritzie invited me to take Annabelle to the movies. My mother was the banker of this affair; she put five dollars in my hand. Fritzie had her own part; her gray Cadillac chauffeured us two blocks to the Albany Street art theatre. We went in alone, without the Cadillac. I was gallant with my mother's money (you can smear the walls of a movie house with five dollars in your pocket). I bought popcorn for Annabelle, and muggy root beer for myself. It was three in the afternoon, and we sat among soldiers and their girlfriends, sisters, whores, and wives, and a pair of military policemen, who maintained the law through all the zipping and unzipping of clothes.

No one seemed to care about the bloated movements up on the screen. Most of the tumult happened within the aisles. There were giggles and snores and the shuffling of bodies. What about us? Kittens don't sleep in the dark; Annabelle and I were vicious. She clawed first. After I wet her ankles in root beer. She reached out of the popcorn bag to slice at me with butter under her nails. I chewed her wrist. We came out of the theatre to air our wounds. Fritzie noticed us from the door of her Cadillac. She wasn't blind to our scarred walk and sullen cheeks.

The partnership was dead. Sensing that she'd have to go elsewhere for a son-in-law, Fritzie cracked down on us. She accused my mother of allowing soldiers to stay at the hotel free of charge. It's true. My mother was a rotten businesswoman; she could wash and sew with a terrifying persistency, but she was unpredictable about the idea of rent. She felt sorry for certain soldiers, seeing my brother's face behind their uniforms. She dreamed of Harvey in Korea; when these black thoughts entered her head, she couldn't handle money.

A soldier paid anywhere from seven dollars to fifty cents for a night at Fritzie's, depending on my mother's mood. She was a little more consistent with the whores. She charged them a flat rate, but if a customer robbed them, they didn't have to cry. My mother wouldn't bleed the girls. She didn't run a crude hotel. Soldiers and whores could eat out of her icebox. We had ten or fifteen chairs at our dinner table. The whores went crazy over my mother's rice pudding. The soldiers dug inside her baked apples for a load of cinnamon and honey. Those evil bears in the hall brooded over the loss of so much honey. Their stinking fur could smother the aroma of any apple skin.

My mother didn't scream when Fritzie threw us out. My father grabbed up his animals, and we left without a squabble. The whores grieved for us. They kissed me, their tongues flicking into my cheekbone. "Don't be a stranger, Gregory Peck." The soldiers managed to swipe a military van, and we drove out of New Jersey in great style.

My brother wasn't prepared for us. He'd turned the apartment into a gym. The blunt noses of barbells and dumbbells were everywhere. Pieces of flesh off a rubber mat lay rotting in my father's bedroom. Old honey jars fermented in a corner with a smell more powerful than whiskey. My mother hadn't been Fritzie's chambermaid for nothing. She closed the gym, and invited the five boarders who were staying with my brother to scrounge through the East Bronx for other rooms.

I went back to Music and Art. The paint box trembled in my hand. Would they tear off the fingers of a truant? I prepared stories for my guidance counselors. I had forged documents and notes. I fell into a hole in New Jersey. That's what I would say. No one questioned me. I walked to my easel. It hadn't been touched. There was too much seriousness about the school to bother with one missing boy. My classmates were so absorbed in pecking with their bristles, smearing their yellows and greens, they'd forgotten who I was.

Our return to the Bronx didn't suit the teddy bears; they began to shed day and night. We had fur balls where the honey jars used to be. It became impossible to breathe. My father couldn't salvage the bears. Plagued by my mother, he offered to rip them up and sell their balding coats. He had no buyers. But he did get a job. He became a sweeper in his old fur shop.

One day, while he was at work, my mother, Harvey, and me loaded ourselves up with bears, carried them down to the cellar, and squeezed them into the garbage barrels. It took four barrels to contain the bears. My father wouldn't forgive us. He dawdled over his baked apple for weeks without lifting a spoon. My brother and I stayed far from his elbows. In mourning those dead freaks he might have maimed one of us.

THREE

Lilly

I.

JACK the fiddler was my best friend. He didn't have to worry about food. He would arrive at M & A with a farmer cheese sandwich. I couldn't tell what kind of loaf that sandwich came from, but it had to be a prodigal bread. The sandwich could hardly fit into a paper bag.

It shouldn't have been a big surprise. Jack's father was a grocer. Jack would break off the end of his sandwich, and that got to be my lunch. I was his protector at school. Seniors would poke fun of his violin case, and try to extract tribute from him on the subway: a peach or a dime from little Jack the fiddler. But they skulked off with nothing in their fists. They couldn't get to Jack. My biceps were always in the way.

I was no muscleman by 1952, but I still had authentic "lats" and powerful veins in my arms, and those seniors stayed clear of me. They were also jealous of fiddler Jack. It had nothing to do with farmer cheese. Little Jack had the loveliest girl at Music and Art. She was a harpist by the name of Lilly. We were all infants, doodlers and fiddle-scrapers, around Lillian Feld. She was fifteen, like me and Jack, but Lilly didn't belong in any high school. She had deep throaty bosoms on her chest that could have suckled a hundred boys. She was fecund enough to have been a mother at twelve. And she was supposed to be in love with little Jack.

Nobody knew how many boyfriends Lilly had. They would stand outside the gates at three o'clock, boys in leather jackets, from another school. They waited on Convent Avenue, biting their nails and gritting their teeth like shrewd, lovelorn foxes who expected some share of Lilly. But Lilly went home with Jack.

2.

SHE dropped him before the term was over. Jack's fiddle couldn't hold on to Lilly Feld. Maybe she succumbed to one of those foxes outside the gates. Who knows? Jack had a miserable summer. He couldn't stop talking about his Lilly. Friend that I was, I dreamed of those bosoms while he yapped. His blubbering was a horrible sight. A boy crying in the streets. He was still luckier than any of us. For two whole months he'd had Lilly of the golden boobs.

That summer I joined the Bronx Union YMCA with Jack, swam with him, played ping-pong, took him to the weightlifting room, so he could forget about Lilly and build up his pecs. Rosin bags, grease, and lat machines didn't have much sway over me any more. I suffered through workouts for Jack's sake. He began to cool off. He didn't blubber about Lilly in the weightlifting room. How did I know that he would develop a craziness for benchpressing and dumbbell curls? You couldn't get him away from Bronx Union. The fiddler had become a weightlifting freak.

Jack found other training partners because I wouldn't go to Bronx Union more than once a week. He felt I was abandoning him. In August our friendship broke. I returned to Music and

Art and couldn't look forward to the husks off Jack's farmer cheese. We sat at opposite ends of the lunch room, both of us in muscle tee shirts. Lilly was in my geometry class. She was confused by all the mysterious bodies and shapes a triangle could have. She failed her first three tests. "Will you study with me?" she said. I had old, conflicting loyalties, loyalties to Jack. I mumbled at her, my eyes sneaking over the contours of her sweater like an invisible snake. "Jack's a wiz in geometry. He's the man for triangles."

"I don't want him," she said.

I followed her back on the train to Kingsbridge Road, where she lived with her mother in one of those amazing apartment houses on Sedgwick Avenue, with a deep, deep courtyard and ivy running down from the roofs. Her father was dead. He was once a big hotelman in New York. Mother and daughter lived off his properties. Lilly herself was something of an entrepreneur. Her father had willed her the Mississippi Hotel on West Ninety-third, in Manhattan. My sense of business came from the Monopoly board. That's how innocent I was about money. It was magical to me that a high school girl could own a hotel, even if it was held in trust for Lilly by her mother.

She liked me the moment she saw me, Mrs. Feld. I wasn't a boyfriend come here to stick his thumbs under Lilly's sweater. I was studious Jerome, the geometry professor. The Bronx catfish couldn't have been dead in me. I knew how to perform in front of Lilly and her mother. Boys in leather jackets might show up in the elevator, and disappear by the end of the week. But a tutor who could connect the points of a triangle with a pair of compasses was no temporary thing.

We studied on Lilly's bed. I could *feel* the imprint of her knees on the coverlet. Lilly had a musk that rose out of the skin behind her ears. Our elbows would often knock during a demonstration of geometry. My tongue was always dry. I imagined the soft, luscious constraint of Lilly's brassiere. Oh, I'd seen plenty of whores' tits. Women of twenty-five and thirty. Hadn't I been an errand boy for a covey of soldiers' girls at the Indian Hotel? I knew all the aromas of sex. What about Lilly?

She could make boys howl in the courtyard, but she was incorrigible in matters of geometry. She would blink as I went through a lesson with her. She would laugh and hold on to my finger, or stab herself with the compasses' metal pin. Lilly was blind to the properties of any angle, acute or otherwise. Lines couldn't bend for her. She saw only what was perfect and straight. I still brought her up to a respectable margin. She passed her next quiz by a good point and a half.

I was considered the genius of the house. Mrs. Feld thought I must have been descended from some rabbinical line. She didn't have an inkling of my father's ghostly teddy bears. The Charyns were scholars in her eyes. No, no. It was because of the catfish and the cunning it gave me that her daughter got passing grades in geometry. That was the only edge I had. Little rabbis were scarce in the Polish enclaves of the East Bronx.

It wasn't all a knocking of elbows on Lilly's bed. She was studying to be a virtuoso on the harp, and when talk of the isosceles triangle began to dull in both our heads, Lilly would play for me. The harp could dumbfound a boy bred on the primitive music of the Bronx River. Lilly would have to warm up that crazy thing for half an hour. She would take the harp between her legs, rock it back over her shoulder, then pluck at it with the four main fingers of either hand. The foot pedals clicked, and a buzz came off one string.

I didn't have a fig's knowledge of Beethoven, Bach, or Debussy. It could have been anything that Lilly played on her harp. Then she would do "Ramona," my favorite song. It was about an Indian girl with a rose in her hair, and the idiot who was in love with her. I was the idiot in that song. And Lilly understood how to breathe a shine over me. She would play "Ramona" on her monster harp.

That strange puttering couldn't last. Elbows, triangles, and strings. Something had to happen between the time I studied with Lilly and the doorbell rang, announcing her latest boyfriend, some thug with a pompadour who had picked her up in a bowling alley.

Two months into geometry we had our first kiss. It was a peck on the lips from her tutor, Jerome. Lilly was furious. "What's wrong with you? Don't you know how?" I pecked her again. It was no good. "Didn't your friend Jack ever teach you to kiss?" I was getting uneasy with Lillian Feld. "Dope," she said. "Who kisses with his mouth closed?"

My river gods had failed me. The catfish didn't know shit about kissing girls. It was my tongue that Lilly was after. We rolled on her bed with our tongues in each other's mouth. From then on we had five minutes of geometry and fifteen minutes of kissing in bed. But my progress was slow. It took me another week to plummet from her mouth to her brassiere. Lilly had to grab my hands and throw them under her sweater. That first warmth of nipple was maddening to me. I was holding flesh, cotton, and wool, and I had an erection that nearly split the left side of my pants. How could we undress? Lilly's mother was always in the next room, thinking kind thoughts about the little rabbi who was taking her daughter over the humps of geometry.

Lilly was much bolder than I could ever be. She unhooked her bra without taking her sweater off. I put my head into the wool and sucked those brown nipples for half an hour. Her mother couldn't hear Lilly's gentle moaning or see the hard-on I was carrying around.

The catfish was smarter than I figured. Boyfriends would come and go, but I had month after month of Lilly. If we couldn't undress, we could still probe like crazy with our two hands. "Your older brother," she said. "What's his name again?"

"His name is Harvey."

"Isn't he Mr. America?"

"No, but he could have been Mr. New York City one year if he hadn't pulled his groin."

"Well, you ask Harvey how to sixty-nine."

I didn't have to ask. Sixty-nine, that was where two people pretzeled up and licked each other's parts. But if Mrs. Feld came into the room and caught us that way, with my head and Lilly's hidden in a jungle of legs, she could have had me put in jail. So I played dumb with Lilly.

"I'll ask him, I'll ask Harvey how to sixty-nine. But he won't be able to tell me for a few weeks."

Lilly was curious. "Why not?"

"He's in Alaska right now. Driving big trucks for the Army. I'll write to him. But I don't know what Harvey can say in a letter. I think the Army censors his mail."

I stalled her on the subject of sixty-nine. But Lilly had other schemes. "Dumbbell, do you want to spend the night with me?"

"Here?" I said. "What will we do with your mother?"

Lilly squinted at me with such contempt, it could have broken through all the planes and angles I had constructed for her. "Not here. We'll go to my hotel."

"Your mother would let you do that?"

"Jerome, Jerome, am I ten, or what? I'll tell her I'm staying at the Mississippi with a girlfriend of mine."

3.

I was the one who blushed, talking to my mother. "Ma, I won't be home tonight. You remember Jack who used to be my friend? Well, I made up with him. I'm going to Jack's house."

I didn't need luggage, Lilly said. I was to walk into the lobby like I owned the place. I could smile at the night manager, or

not. It was the same to Lilly. Then I was to look for her
upstairs. Room 1321, that's where Lilly would be. It had been
her father's room, when he would stay overnight in Manhattan.
Her mother used it now, from time to time. It was always kept
spare for Mrs. Feld.

Going downtown I had the creeps. I would be making love
to Lilly with the ghost of her father watching over us. I was an
interloper from the Bronx. What did I have to do with a Manhattan hotel? It had pillars and balconies, stone lions in the
wall, and a winding, green roof that would have been a perfect
hideout for the hunchback of Notre Dame. I didn't see much
business inside the doors. An old woman slept in a chair while
a bellhop picked his teeth. I lit out for the elevators, wily
Jerome.

I had no trouble with 1321. The knob turned for me. Lilly
was in a nightdress. It was the first time I'd seen her without
her school clothes, sweaters and skirts that held flush and
hugged the lines of her body. The nightdress was flimsy and
soft. The brown of her nipples showed through, and the hair at
the fork of her legs. The blood beat over my eyes like a tighten-
ing fist. I kicked off one of my shoes. "Wait a second," Lilly
said. "I'm hungry."

"What?" I hadn't come down to the Mississippi to hear about
hunger pains. I could sniff the mad perfume of those nipples
under the gown. Lilly had arranged for the hotel. She'd
swabbed herself in lilac water. But she wouldn't have her tutor
pounce on her.

"It's only eight o'clock. Let's eat."

I'd had my dinner at home, my mother's chopped steak
clawing at my throat as I dreamt of Lilly in 1321. "What do
you want, Jerome?"

"Nothing."

Lilly ordered up lamb chops, potatoes, and peas, a shrimp

salad, a fruit cup, and a cherry Coke. "With ketchup and plenty of mustard," she barked into the phone. "And don't forget the pickles. It's for Lillian Feld."

I had to hide in the closet when the waiter arrived with Lilly's meal, or the news of our conspiracy might have gotten back to her mother. Lilly wore a blanket over the nightgown until the waiter left. Then she started to devour her food with the slow, cultured nibbling of a Sedgwick Avenue girl who was training to be a concert harpist and would have to eat among refined people for the rest of her life. She made a pinkish mush of ketchup and mustard that she doused on everything. Not even the fruit cup could escape this mixture of Lilly's. It took her an hour to bite her way through the meal, which she accomplished with sips of cherry Coke and touches of the napkin to her mouth. Eating absorbed her. Lilly didn't say a word. She invited me into the bathroom to brush my teeth. I used the toothbrush after Lilly. She was a shameless girl, peeing in front of my eyes. She reached between her legs to wipe herself. She yawned and asked me to flush the toilet for her. "Hey, you over there, how come you're still wearing your clothes?"

She ran into the bedroom, smiled, and pulled the nightgown over her head. Idiot, I thought of geometry, of the points connecting her nipples to her bellybutton and her crotch, and the slight, triangular wiggle of her kneecaps. Lilly rescued her poor tutor. She shucked off my clothes, and with all the signs of a dutiful boy I gave her the condom she'd told me to bring. We had the devil of a time fitting that rubber onto me. Lilly had to roll it with her thumbs. I yelped with pain. It was like having a powerful rubber band attached to your skin.

We kissed and kissed. I had a finger in Lilly, and her nipples in my mouth. Then she signaled for me to stop, and we began to wander all over the mattress. Our skulls disappeared. Lilly had her sixty-nine. What can I say? It was peculiar to be sucked while you had a rubber stocking on your prick. It wasn't Lilly's fault if her lips didn't feel human to me. Lilly could have been a fish, and not a girl.

We must have come untangled in the middle of the night. We woke with our bodies apart, Lilly having most of the bed. She clapped me on the shoulder. It wasn't unkind. She had a proposal to make. "Let's get married in three years."

"You mean after we graduate? It's not so easy to find work with just a high school diploma."

"Who says work? My mother will support us. We'll go to NYU and live here at the Mississippi."

We weren't married yet, so we couldn't leave the Mississippi together. I dressed first and went home. "Ma," I said, "I'll be moving out in a couple of years. I'm getting married."

My mother didn't bother to ask who the girl was. Sophomores with two dollars in their pants don't make such terrific husbands.

"Good luck," she said, and she told me what I could have for lunch.

FOUR

Lilly, Part Two

I.

My engagement to Lilly put me on the spot. I was tutor *and* boyfriend now, and subject to the vicissitudes of her nature. Lilly blew hot and cold. She would make overnight appointments at the Mississippi, and then leave 1321 before I got to the hotel. I had to search the room for some scribble from her. "Jerome, I twisted my ankle and couldn't stay. Lillian." Was she two floors below, with a salesman she'd discovered in the lobby? I wasn't going to knock on every door and beg for her. There were limits to my jealousy.

I could tell the hooks I had in her. She couldn't pass geometry without Jerome. I was at Sedgwick Avenue, next door to her mother, five afternoons a week. I wore holes in Lilly's underpants with the tutoring I gave. She would still talk of marriage from time to time. But the talking was remote, as if she were feeding some bit of fancy in her own head. I did take her home to the East Bronx and introduce her as my fiancée. My brother was there, on a furlough from Alaska. Harvey didn't titter at me. Lillian's bosoms were serious enough for him. We all had ice cream and banana pie.

Harvey hung around for another few weeks. He had news

about my fiancée. "Kid, this Lillian of yours, she's going with Irwin Polatchek. He met her on the E train."

"How do you know it's the same Lilly?"

"He showed me a picture of her. She plays the harp, right? She's at Music and Art. Irwin said something about this hotel she has. He takes her to night clubs and all that crap."

Lilly must have graduated from those boys with the leather jackets. Irwin Polatchek was a certified hood. He was chief of the Polish Barons before the cops destroyed his gang and a judge put him in a home for wicked juveniles. Irwin never had a dumbbell in his hand. He didn't need muscles to slap your face apart. Irwin had a chipped tooth and other battle scars. He was feared in the East Bronx. And he was my brother's friend.

Now Irwin was back on the street. He must have found a new line of work, because the Polish Barons were dead. What did night clubs mean to him? He could piss a hundred dollars away on Lillian Feld.

I confronted her during our next geometry lesson, while my finger was in her pants. "Irwin Polatchek," I screamed. "How do you like his chipped tooth?"

She dug my arm out from under her skirt. "Jerome, have you been spying on me?"

"I wouldn't spy. Irwin knows my brother. Lilly, how much does he get?" Did Irwin touch the golden boobs and diddle between her legs, just like me?

I must have put her in a rage. She destroyed the notebook we used for geometry. Then she slapped me on the ear with her knuckles. It stung like hell.

"Irwin gets nothing from me."

"You mean he doesn't get top . . . or bottom?"

It was part of the secret language we had for describing Lilly's practices with her other boyfriends. "Top" meant Lilly would only undress above the waist, and "bottom" was *everything* below that.

"He gets nothing from me, I said. We drink a lot of champagne. Can you take me into a bar, you dope? Irwin's twenty-two . . . what are you angry about? He's never even kissed me, for God's sake."

"Why not?"

"He's too scared."

"Scared of what? He used to beat people up for a living. Him and his Polish Barons."

"Well, he's scared of me."

I wasn't satisfied with Lilly's tale of Irwin Polatchek. I went to Harvey. I wanted to know how Irwin survived these days. Did he peddle dope to keep Lilly in champagne?

"Kid, he works in a cleaning store. Irwin does deliveries. He makes about thirty a week."

I let out a nervous laugh. "The great Polatchek is a delivery boy? How come?"

"He's sick. He had yellow jaundice when he was in this detention camp. He can't lift heavy things."

I visited the cleaners where he worked. I wasn't dumb. I wore my muscle tee shirt. Harvey was right. Irwin of the chipped tooth was in terrible shape. He was a shrunken, yellow doll of a man with big ears and a bow tie. But the catfish in me whispered how I should be cautious. Wreck as Irwin was, he might have been able to summon the power to strangle a sophomore from Music and Art.

"Irwin, I'm Charyn's brother, Jerome." (Harvey was known as "Charyn" in the East Bronx because of the muscles he had. He was Charyn the weightlifter, and I was Charyn's brother.) "I go to Music and Art with Lillian Feld."

Something happened behind that bow tie. He seemed to scrunch up in all his yellowness, and Irwin began to sweat. Holy catfish, he was in love with Lilly! He could hardly stutter her name. "L-l-l-illian," he said. "Sh-sh-she's great." That champagne was bought with blood. Thirty dollars a week. He spent his whole little wad on Lilly.

2.

MY uncovering of Irwin didn't help me very much. Lilly was straying more and more. Weekends were closed to me. Lilly was booked on Friday, Saturday, and Sunday nights. I was only her tutor-fiancé. Surer of her geometry, she cut me down to one afternoon a week. I had to clutch at her in the halls of Music and Art, if I expected a piece of Lilly. That's how scarce she got. We would meet at a prearranged time, in an isolated corner of the school, and kiss like crazy for three minutes. A gym teacher caught us together. We were marched down to the assistant principal, Mr. Baronet. Lilly was crying. Her mother would kill her, she said. She got so hysterical, she was drinking her own tears. "My fault," I told Mr. Baronet. "Mine." He let Lilly go with a reprimand: she was never to be seen with me again in any hallway of Music and Art. Lilly thanked Mr. Baronet, swore her piety to him, and left. He stared at me soon as we were alone. I wasn't going to blubber for Baronet. I'd just received a letter from him, thanking me for my "good offices" in turning in a wallet I'd found on the stairs.

"Charyn," he announced, with little shakes of his head. "That one, Lilly, you can ruin yourself on her. You're a scholar, I know. Listen to me. You knock her up, and you'll never get to college."

Mr. Baronet had a crooked sense of the biology that was going on between Lilly and me. How can you knock up a girl with condoms and a finger? Anyway, I couldn't get near Lilly after that episode in the hall. She took Baronet's injunction to include Kingsbridge Road and all of the Bronx.

Lilly didn't seem to suffer without a fiancé. She was pulling down nineties and ninety-fives on big geometry tests. I couldn't understand her conversion to the mysteries of the triangle until I saw her walking hand in hand with fiddler Jack. She'd got herself another tutor. There was no point in upbraiding Jack, whose biceps were bigger than mine by now. Lilly had gone from Jack to me, from me to Jack. Was that his fault? She dropped him for a bongo player in the senior class. Lilly could find plenty of Jacks and Jeromes. But I wondered who was tutoring her now.

3.

THE catfish had misled me: I didn't get over Lilly so fast. I was worse than Irwin Polatchek. I had jaundice of the skull. I could feel the leakage in my head. I was bleeding yellow all over the place. Mooning over Lilly, I lost my appetite for triangles. I couldn't concentrate on geometry with that yellow blood pulsing in me. I would sleepwalk through my days at Music and Art.

Homework was out. After school I went down to the Mississippi. I would skulk in front of the hotel, stare up at *our* window on the thirteenth floor, with its balcony that had rusted green in crazy New York. I swear, I could talk to the ghost of Lilly's father as I let that green rust wash over me. He wasn't a bad man, Mr. Feld. The ghost wore eyeglasses. He pitied the lust I had for his daughter. Mr. Feld must have known about the condoms I put on in his old room at the hotel. He'd seen us do sixty-nine. "Jerrrrrome," he said. "You'll never get to college."

I had an amazing recovery after that. The yellow blood must have gone down into my spleen. My head cleared of Lilly. I stopped longing for the golden boobs. I didn't worry about whether her boyfriends were getting "top" and "bottom" from

Lillian Feld. My sense of the triangle had come back to me. I worked my pair of compasses like a vicious, moving claw. I could scratch out a circle and bisect angles faster than any man alive. I was king of geometry at Music and Art.

FIVE

The Polish Barons

I.

I⊤ got lonely being the little scholar, fishing for ninety-nines.

I was elected to the honor society, and received a maroon and blue pin. Arista it was called. Arista. I was among the elite at Music and Art: boys who talked of Williams and Yale; girls who didn't have time for anything but *War and Peace.* I rubbed my Arista pin; I must have been hoping a brown nipple would pop out of the maroon and blue.

The geometry king was coming home one afternoon and saw a different color in the street. It was the black velvet of the Polish Barons. Irwin Polatchek. The hood with yellow jaundice had resurrected his old gang.

I put my Arista pin away and went to the cleaners where Polatchek worked. He was as puny as ever. The jaundice hadn't disappeared. The skin around his eyes had turned catfish gray. But I wasn't going to be fooled by his complexion.

"Irwin, I want to join up."

He touched his bow tie. I didn't hear him mention the gang.

"The kid from Music and Art. L-l-l-illian's friend."

"That's right. Make me a Baron, Irwin. Let me in."

He had to go out on a delivery. I stood behind Irwin and

followed him to Crotona Park. All he did was shake his big ears. "I can't use a genius."

"Who said I was a genius?"

"Lillian."

"I'll grow stupid for the gang . . . you'll see. When do I get my velvet jacket?"

"You have to earn it, kid. Nobody becomes a B-b-baron in one day."

2.

So it was goodbye Arista. I was a novice in Irwin's gang. The king of geometry met with twenty hoods in the cellars surrounding Crotona Park. Irwin couldn't afford a single location. The cops might come down on him. He had to jump from place to place. Irwin was collecting a guerrilla army. He wasn't into thievery this year. Irwin had his scruples. We were to attack anybody who wasn't a Pole. The Barons meant to create a Polish corridor in the Bronx, an alleyway from the Harlem River to Orchard Beach, without blacks, Puerto Ricans, Irish, Germans, or Swedes. It was an insane idea. And I loved Irwin for it. His vision of the Bronx was much grander than mine. To me it was a rotten borough, with a pissy stream in the middle, and fish that leapt out of the mud. But Polatchek had turned the Bronx into a holy war.

We went deep into Pelham to raid an Irish bar. We were lucky to come out alive. The Irishers broke beer bottles on our heads. They destroyed the gang's velvet with their fists and their teeth. But I saw the Irwin that my brother Harvey had told me about, the crusader who'd been beaten up and put in detention homes, and had survived to twenty-two with yellow jaundice. Chandeliers fell from the ceiling. Mirrors cracked where Irwin walked. The Irishers would remember him.

Our ranks thinned after this first raid. Polish mothers wouldn't allow their bruised little boys to run with Irwin and the Barons. We had six stalwarts left. Irwin, me, and four young mules. But soon we swelled to seven. Lillian joined the gang. She hadn't given up her fondness for hoodlums. She was infatuated with Irwin now that he had his Barons again and was carving a Polish duchy in the Bronx. Our stuttering chief brought her with him when he planned our next raid. Cellars were becoming scarce. We met in Crotona Park, under a tree.

It was winter, and we huddled in the snow, while Irwin ranted about noblesse oblige inside his duchy. "B-b-barons don't bend for nobody. Walk a straight line. If you see a guy who aint Polish, chop him on the ear, so he'll understand."

"Irwin," one of the mules asked, "what if it's an old lady?"

"Then you excuse yourself, you say 'Pardon me,' and take her home, because we don't hit on women."

Lilly bloomed under her coat. She had a lord with Bronx manners. She didn't even look at me. I was a vassal to Irwin, one notch over a mule. She wasn't restless around the B-b-barons. She threw out all her other boyfriends. She would only leave Irwin when it was time to study the harp. Lilly wouldn't neglect her music for any man.

But when she held his hand under our meeting tree, her hazel eyes on him, I could feel a slow murder in my heart. I was jealous of the chief. That Lillian, she'd rather lie down with yellow jaundice than smile on Jerome.

I dreamed of forming a rival duchy. What was the use? I didn't have Irwin's capacity to build a gang. Who would follow me?

Brown nipples. I couldn't shake them from my head. I caught her alone in the park, waiting for Polatchek. A meanness crept over me. The hell with my vassalage. I seized Lillian, threw her down into the snow. She snapped at my face, but I gave her the padding in my shoulder to chew, and I dug right into her brassiere. Her tit was prickly and hard as a frozen Milky Way. I drew my arm out from her clothes.

"Drop dead," she screamed.

She was lovely with bits of snow in her brown hair.

"Irwin will bust your face."

But she didn't tell. Irwin might have thrown me off the roof. That would have been the punishment for handling Lillian's tit. She stuck to Irwin under the meeting tree, nuzzled his ear, and I kept thinking to myself, maybe it was better to bump down the fire escape and land on my head in the garbage and die, than to watch Lilly rub up against this lord of mine.

3.

IRWIN had to finance his Polish corridor. He slipped back into thievery. We robbed a delicatessen. Irwin wouldn't expose Lilly to any danger. She was home, plucking at her harp, while we pulled colored handkerchiefs up around our cheeks, like outlaws from the West, and stormed into Greenewald's Berlin Deli a little after midnight. We weren't interested in the salamis on the wall, and the lambs with blood inside their noses. Irwin stopped at the cash register, while the mules and me held six customers at bay. Old man Greenewald wouldn't give up his cash so easy. He argued with Polatchek. "Gangster, go to hell."

The old man reached for a carving knife. Irwin had to act. He socked the old man once in the throat. A rattling sound escaped from under Greenewald's tongue. Blood exploded from one eye. The old man rocked on his feet and did a stuttering dance. Irwin tried to cradle him, keep him from falling. But the old man crashed in back of Polatchek, and brought salamis and two lambs down with him. Irwin didn't open the register. He tugged the beard on his handkerchief mask, and we ran out of the deli.

Who sang on us? The four mules were stolen out of their beds by the police. They wore handcuffs in the paddy wagon. They were kicked and punched into the floor. And Polatchek? He was pushed off a roof. It could have been a rival gang, or the cops themselves. Nobody would say.

I was too scared to attend his funeral. Every gang leader in the Bronx would have skulked around his grave, looking for Barons to eat. So I said a prayer for Irwin and mourned him on my own. *Dear God, be good to Irwin Polatchek. He tried to save the Bronx.*

I expected the bulls to come. But they didn't shake me out of bed. Was it because I was still a novice, and they couldn't tie a velvet jacket to me? I put on my Arista pin and shrank into the halls of Music and Art. It was a perfect disguise. They don't let little crooks into Arista. Every cop knew that.

I figured Lillian to blubber for a week and find a new boyfriend. I was mistaken in her. She grieved for Irwin a long time. Other hoodlums howled at the gates for Lilly. She was deaf to their noisy calls. She had the colored handkerchief Irwin used on his last raid. She blew her nose with it and wiped her eyes.

Without the Barons what was left?

I tried to be serious about school. But once you roamed the Bronx with Irwin, it was hard to settle down. I dreamed of his big ears during important exams, and could only gather in ninety-ones and ninety-twos. I rubbed my hand to see if it was turning yellow. The jaundice Irwin had wouldn't rise up from the grave. My skin was prickly white.

SIX

Midshipman Jerome

I.

IT was 1955, and everybody wanted to be an electrical engineer. Doctors and lawyers were on the way out. That's what our college advisors told us. Lawyers would have to sell apples in the street. "Children," said Mr. Baronet, chief to all the college advisors, "pick the right science, and you can't go wrong." He mocked the paraphernalia of physicians and surgeons. *The scalpel and the stethoscope.* But a slide rule was something else. It would land us in Scarsdale, with a Cadillac and a lovely wife.

I believed in Baronet. I said engineer, engineer, while brushing my teeth. I had wet dreams of the lovely wife. Still, I didn't get any nibbles from Harvard, Yale, or MIT. I sneaked into Columbia, because it had a certain charity towards Crotona Park. It always took in a few children from the Bronx.

Lilly didn't have to worry. She was exempt from Baronet's sermon on engineers. Girls weren't supposed to monkey with science. They could have lots of babies, mourn Irwin Polatchek, or study the harp. They were whimsical creatures for Mr. Baronet.

He was blind when it came to Lillian Feld. She had more ambition than the whole senior class. Lilly took her harp to a

school in Philadelphia. She had to beat out hundreds of appli-
cants: the school accepted one new harpist a year.

And I had the pauper's seat at Columbia College. I was angry
at Baronet. Let him go worship engineers and the split-level
houses they could provide for their wives. I enrolled in the
NROTC.

2.

WE were boys in dark uniforms who were dispised by the rest
of the school. The Defense Department would pay scrubs like
me a small stipend after my second year, enough for books,
clothes, prophylactics, and subway rides. If I kept my hair short
and mouthed wisdoms about the displacement of battleships, I
might even win a full scholarship from the Navy. I could imagine trips from the Bronx River to the China Sea, a junior
lieutenant on destroyer duty, scouring the waters for Commie
submarines.

We were a landlocked Navy, without one canoe, so Columbia
had to give the NROTC a hump of rotten grass to paddle on.
We trained with dummy rifles. Non-cadets sat on the sundial
overlooking South Field and laughed at our oafish maneuvers.

I had to spend most of my afternoons at NROTC headquarters on the ground floor of Hartley Hall, tolerating curses,
advice, and fingers in my chest from the Marine corporal who
was meant to groom us and make us into good naval officers.
All of us had our pictures on the wall inside headquarters. We
were an odd lot, civilian sailors, owned by the Defense Department.

Headquarters had one compensation; it was near the ping-
pong room in Hartley Hall. Since we were welcome nowhere
on campus, we commandeered the ping-pong room. We smuggled in cigarettes and gallons of red wine, we secured buttons

to our tunics with the help of sewing kits, we loosened our black ties, and we drove out the residents of Hartley Hall, who couldn't resist group after group of surly cadets. Some of us played ping-pong.

I wouldn't touch any of the hard-rubber paddles that lay about the room. I brought my own paddle—two sheets of balding sandpaper on a wormy stick that I had swiped from the Crotona Y. The ping-pong-playing cadets weren't prepared for my finesse with sandpaper. I would stroke the ball with an unvarying rhythm that put creases in the foreheads of my fellow midshipmen; they would throw their rubber paddles at the wall in frustration and glower at me.

I didn't have a single friend. Those civilian sailors weren't anxious to be around a "sandpaper" freak. All I had was the prospect of a reunion party of M & Aers on Christmas Eve. The party was at Lilly's house.

My old friend Lillian wasn't interested in a plain cadet. She'd come back to the Bronx with an engagement ring. Lilly had waylaid a mathematics professor from Swarthmore. He had curly red hair and a great bald spot. I brushed against the prof in my midshipman's suit. His biceps were soft and thin.

He had contempt for me and my uniform, this doctor of higher math. Jacob Furyman. His lip turned up at the sight of my Navy collar and the little gold anchors we had to wear.

"How does it feel to be a trained killer, Jerome?"

Had he seen the dummy rifles on South Field? Our maneuvers couldn't have killed the ants under my feet. I was only a picture on a bulletin board. But I didn't know what to say to this prof.

". . . we study famous battleships. We don't fight."

His mouth was quivering. What had I done to Dr. Jake? Lilly whispered in his ear, then she motioned me to a corner of the room.

"I'm sorry, Jerome. You've upset Jacob. It's your uniform. He hates military clothes."

Lilly wasn't nasty about it. She fondled the gold anchors on my shirt the second she got away from the prof. And she threw me out with a kiss. "Write to me, Jerome. I'll see you during my Easter break."

Like a fool I thanked her for inviting me to the party. She could have Furyman's curly red hair. Hold on to your Easter breaks, Lillian Feld. Remember me? I touched your nipple in the snow when you were still in love with Irwin Polatchek.

3.

JACOB Furyman's wrath hung close to my head.

Cadets had to squirm in freshman composition. Our instructor, Mr. Thomas, didn't care much for civilian sailors. He'd lure us into horrible traps. He went through the class list, asking us to declare our favorite author. Dickens I knew, and J. D. Salinger, but I'd never heard of Franz Kafka, that consumptive from Prague, and some crazy Russian called Sholokhov, who wrote about the River Don. Thomas came to me.

"Well, Charyn?"

"Margaret Mitchell," I said.

Thomas smirked. He had his cadet by the tail. *"Gone With the Wind."* He made it sound like the dirt under my chair, something that could be rubbed in my neck. *Gone With the Wind.*

"Is that what they feed you in the Navy, Mr. Charyn?"

"No sir. I read it on my own." When you see a film six times, it's natural to read the book.

"That's not *lit*erature . . . Scarlett O'Hara and all the good little darkies . . . trash, Mr. Charyn, Southern trash. Nonsense and Ashley Wilkes . . . how can you admire a book that defends the Ku Klux Klan?"

"I'm not a Klansman," I said, with the class looking on. I liked Georgia and Peachtree Street and Scarlett, who was as relentless and cunning as the catfish. But I couldn't tell that to Mr. Thomas. He'd have laughed at me. I shrugged and let him go on about *lit*erature and trash.

I sneaked out after the bell rang, in the long black skirts of my midshipman's coat. I walked the city, with skirts that traveled well below the knee. *Scarlett O'Hara.* I could have been a blackbird from the Bronx. The coat was shy of insignias. It was difficult to tell a Navy man's rank from those skirts and unmarked sleeves. I looked like a truncated officer who'd just stepped off a foreign battleship. Soldiers and sailors saluted me. I returned their salutes with a nimble slap of my elbow.

But I got frightened when I saw another blackbird in the street. The son of a bitch was wearing my same skirts. Neither of us would flip an elbow in salute. We sneered, ruffled the collars of our enormous coats, and then we grew smart together.

"Hartley Hall," I said.

"Ping-pong," he answered.

"South Field."

We were both cadets at Columbia College. In our mutual isolation we hadn't bothered to notice one another. He wasn't a Bronx castaway. He was Johnny Broom from the highlands of Tennessee. He got into Columbia as the valedictorian of his senior class.

"We had the biggest graduation ever at Tweedy High. The school can't hold more than thirty-six. The windowsill was my desk. We got so short of pens one year, I had to write with my thumb."

"John, you're full of shit."

We had more things in common than a blackbird coat. John

was a hunter of catfish. He'd delivered gigantic, whiskered "cats" from several tributaries of the Tennessee. He boasted of catfish tall as a grown boy, that could swallow bait and hook and half a man's leg.

"You sure that's not a shark with whiskers?"

John had a "contract" from the Navy. He'd sworn himself to serve five years after he finished school. He had free books and meals and a regular Navy allowance. Still, he was even less of a sailor than Midshipman Jerome.

John wouldn't touch a dummy rifle on South Field. He cut all his naval science classes and drills.

"What if the Old Man finds out?"

The Old Man was Commander Seymour Shirl, head of the NROTC. Shirl could destroy your career in the Navy. He was crotchety and fierce, and we midshipmen slinked around in his presence. Shirl meant nothing to John.

"The Old Man's dumber than a blind pony with a candle up its ass . . . Shirl doesn't have a notion who's in that little Navy college."

"John, they got our pictures on the wall."

"That's what I mean. Skinheads with a black knot on their throat. We could all be Pinocchio or Elvis. It's the same thing. That Old Man won't miss Johnny Broom."

He didn't live in a dormitory like the other "contract" sailors. He had his own apartment on Morningside Drive. How could he support five rooms on NROTC money? I didn't ask.

"Hey buddy, why don't you move in? Grab a room for yourself. I got plenty of space."

"I couldn't afford it, John. I could pay about a dollar a week."

"That'll do," he said.

4.

MY mother couldn't understand why I would want to leave
Crotona Park and "live with a sailor."

"Mom, he's not a sailor. John's a cadet."

"Who'll cook for you?" she asked, suspicious of all cadets.

"We'll cook for ourselves," I told her, the boy who had
trouble boiling an egg.

Dad didn't have much faith in the project. He figured I'd be
home in a week. How could the catfish survive away from his
holy water? A boy could go to school in Manhattan, but it
wasn't a place to sleep.

I hugged mom and dad, brought a carton of things out of the
Bronx, and moved in with John.

He slept morning and afternoon, while I drilled and worked
on my freshman compositions. I wrote about Hamlet, the electric chair, and the Communist menace. John studied my themes
with an interest in every word. "That's a good one, buddy.
Hamlet being an orphan and all."

"What's so special about that?

"Orphans are most likely to talk with ghosts. Why would you
make a ghost of your father if he wasn't dead? My uncle Bob
could use a boy like you. He runs a magazine."

I wouldn't go meet his uncle Bob. I had enough problems
with science, English, and Old Man Shirl. And hopping around
the city with John half the night. Our enormous military coats
allowed us to drink at any bar. No one would squint at us and
say, "Swear to me you're twenty-one." We had the look of
authority and menace in our midshipman's coats.

We avoided the college bars, with stuffed boar heads on the
wall and a hundred varieties of beer and ale. We crept from hole
to hole on Amsterdam Avenue, away from the fraternity
houses. John liked the Wounded Tepee best. The name of that

ratty bar would render him homesick. John's tongue would unfork after a gulp of light beer and he would deliver stories about the gambling boats that still plied the Tennessee. "Buddy, I was known as Blackjack Sid. I'd steal a fool's pants off in front of his wife . . ."

He danced with the divorcées and lonely wives who came to the Wounded Tepee. Johnny would grind and wiggle without ever taking off that long coat. I couldn't dance. I had stovepipes for legs. But some of John's attractiveness must have flicked onto me. I was the friend of Blackjack Sid. And I had a divorced woman for myself. *Beverly.* She wouldn't give me her last name.

I was scared of her thick black eyelashes and the perfume that came up off her armpits like powerful soap. She often arrived at the Tepee with a swollen mouth, or blue marks on her forehead. God knows what other lives Beverly had. I don't think her divorce was so complete.

She stayed with Jerome one or two nights a week. She was never there when I woke in the morning. She must have had a good reason to crawl out of bed in the dark. I didn't intrude. Who knows how many husbands she had to visit at four A.M.?

"Jerome's mistress," John said. "You can find a hundred Beverlys at the Tepee. Why'd you pick on her?"

"I like her, that's why."

John would come home with a new divorcée every other night. They would tear holes in his mattress, have a brawl, and a reconciliation where both of them would weep. He went through women at the Tepee with the push of a Tennessee storm.

"They're cows, all of them. I'm not taking you nowhere if you're going to fall in love with a cow."

"It's my business," I said. He couldn't tell me what to do with Beverly. I was getting fond of those charcoal eyes. Lots of perfume might make her a lioness but never a cow.

Bev was always tired. We would have a Schlitz at the Tepee

and get to sleep. That was fine. I didn't want any virtuoso on the harp. Lillian Feld could have her school in Philadelphia and her balding prof. Beverly gave me peace. I was a midshipman who was trying to lure a "contract" from the Navy so I could have a deal like John's.

Old Man Shirl encouraged me. You had to pass a super-intelligence test, promise your life to the Navy, and have your records scrutinized by a body of admirals, but it was Shirl who held sway over which of the part-time cadets would receive that golden contract. The Old Man could pick you as one of his, or pass you by. The Navy listened to Shirl.

"You're Polish, aren't you, Mister?"

"Yes sir."

Would it have been bad if I were Egyptian or French?

"Your pop's a working man?"

I was reluctant to mention the teddy bears. I didn't want to be sabotaged by "ghosts" with peekaboo eyes. "A working man, sir, all his life."

"I don't like those brats who come from Choate, with la-crosse sticks and handkerchiefs in every pocket. The Navy needs raw blood. Mister, I'll get you your scholarship. But if you disappoint me, I'll run you into that stinking college boy's river"—Shirl was talking about the Hudson, which had been appropriated by the varsity crew as their private sea—"and drown you with my own two hands."

Would I disappoint Commander Shirl when the Navy was about to give their little scholar free books and a commission after four years? Not as a "nigger" in the reserves, but an ensign in the regular Navy. I memorized the great armadas of world history, gave up Scarlett O'Hara and Ashley Wilkes, read *Crime and Punishment* twice to please my humanities instruc-tor, because a "contract" cadet had to be exceptional in every couse he took.

There was a boy in my humanities class who would chortle

to himself over *Crime and Punishment*. He would snigger and say that Dostoyevsky was a bore. His name was Swandowne, and he didn't look like a freshman to me. Swandowne would only wear tweeds to class. He mocked all of us, but he had a special loathing for midshipmen and their woolen uniforms. His father was a curator at some museum, and this Swandowne would have nothing to do with the ordinary rituals of our college. He belonged to an institution known as St. Robert's Hall, which had secret rooms in a secret house. It wouldn't associate with fraternities and a civilian sailors' corps. You probably had to be a curator's boy to get in.

He called Raskolnikov a jellyfish and failed his humanities quiz. "All that bumbling about in Odessa," he said.

"St. Petersburg," I told him. "Swandowne, you didn't read the book."

"Jellyfish."

Was he talking about Raskolnikov or me?

You couldn't be sure with Swandowne. He turned away in his tweed suit and disappeared to St. Robert's Hall.

Swandowne could make you feel miserable and mean. He wasn't angling to become a career man in the Navy. He had St. Robert's Hall. He didn't have to put a check near the right Russian city. Raskolnikov could have come from El Paso, for all Swandowne cared. He was beyond the reach of a humanities quiz.

I caught Beverly loping along Amsterdam Avenue. She must have been heading for the Tepee. It was the first time I'd seen her during college hours. She looked like a wounded animal in daylight. The charcoal was fierce around her eyes. Her mouth seemed to have a rip in it. Something was wrong with Bev. The lioness had rouge on her teeth.

The rouge was little clots of blood. I gave her my midshipman's handkerchief to clean some of the blood off her teeth. The rip in her mouth was only another swipe of blood. Bev fixed herself and returned the handkerchief. Then she grabbed my arm.

"Show me where all the sailor boys meet."

"I can't. You have to be a cadet. They wouldn't let an outsider into headquarters."

She began to cry in the street. "You're ashamed of me, Jerome. You can chew my nipples, but you're a no-good snot. I don't have worms. I wouldn't give your headquarters a disease."

I took Bev into the ping-pong room at Hartley Hall, which was far enough from headquarters to save me from Shirl. My sandpaper paddle was home at Morningside Drive, so I had to pull a bat with rubber pimples out of the cupboard. Bev watched me play. I was awkward with rubber pimples in my hand. I needed the scratch of sandpaper to liven my game. But the boys in the room were more interested in Beverly than any action on the ping-pong tables. They sniffed at her perfume and adored the black stuff on her eyes.

I had a new status among these cadets. I was the Polish kid who gave them a lollapalooza to look at. They put down their pimple bats. They couldn't concentrate on a spinning ball. They had Beverly the lioness in their stable. They howled like moon-driven boys.

I plucked Bev on the sleeve of her squirrel's-hair coat, thinking it was about time for us to vanish from Hartley Hall. But that howling drew other people. Our drillmaster rushed in with his two seaman aides. Corporal Barnett Rosen of the United States Marines had the idea that he was policing a battleship. His name for Hartley Hall was "the tub." He glared at Beverly in the ping-pong room, quieted the howling cadets, and shoved me to the side. "Mr. Charyn, get that bimbo off this tub. The Old Man is down the hall. Do you want to lose your scholarship?"

Shirl had sent my papers in to Washington. Who knows

when my "contract" would arrive in the mail? But I had that perverse edge to me, the defiance of Crotona Park. Truth is, Swandowne had poisoned my love for the Navy. Damn his tweed suit! He made me feel ridiculous in Navy wool.

"Corporal Rosen," I said. "I don't see a bimbo in this room . . . that young lady is my sister."

Rosen couldn't take the chance and insult a midshipman's sister, even if her eyelashes were as thick as her nose. He had to withdraw from the ping-pong room. I plucked at Beverly again, abandoned tables and cadets, peeked through the hallway of Rosen's tub to avoid Commander Shirl, motioned to my "sister," and got the hell out of there.

SEVEN

Portrait of the Artist as an Old Civilian Sailor

I.

ROSEN caught on to Johnny Broom's negligence towards the NROTC. He broke into our flat with his seaman aides and collected Johnny's books and the different articles of his uniform. Johnny couldn't run to the college deans for help. The Navy had put him in Columbia. And the Navy, under Shirl's signature, was throwing him out.

Rosen tried to implicate me. He said to the Old Man that I had shielded Johnny Broom. Shirl wouldn't listen. I was still in good standing with the Defense Department. My scholarship should arrive any week.

But you can starve waiting for the mail. I went to see John's uncle Bob, the magazine man.

His office was in the Flatiron Building, that great slice of stone pie on Twenty-third Street. He had a cubicle overlooking Madison Square. How could any magazine be published in a closet? I didn't trust this uncle Bob. He was a Tennessean with long, fleshy ears.

"The nephew says you can write."

"I've only done a few compositions, uncle Bob."

"So what? You're some kind of sailor. Give me a story about pirates by tomorrow night and you'll get fifty bucks."

"Which pirates did you have in mind?"

"Here," he said, handing me a big fat book. "Pick the ones you like."

The *Cromwell Encyclopedia of Historical Personages, Places, and Things* must have been fifty years old. The binding had begun to unravel, and left a porridge of string. It caused the *Cromwell Encyclopedia* to ride between its covers like an old cargo ship. A page would drop out and fall into your lap. I decided to take *Cromwell's* home with me before the section on pirates disappeared.

It was a dangerous encyclopedia, full of distortions and broken facts. If you believed *Cromwell's*, the War Between the States had continued into the twentieth century. It was a struggle unto death. The South had adopted a "scorched earth" policy, destroying farms and crops to wage a guerrilla war with the rest of the country. The guerrillas couldn't be identified, of course. I wondered if *Cromwell's* was a bible for the Ku Klux Klan.

There was precious little about pirates in the book. All I could make out was that Jean Lafitte, the pirate hero of New Orleans, had a brother named Pierre. Oh, I could have gone to the library and secured any number of pedigrees for the two pirate brothers. But I didn't. Uncle Bob must have had a reason to burden me with an encyclopedia that was so stingy with its facts.

I thought of the Bronx River and wrote about the Lafittes. I had them hide in pirate coves, and come out to strike at British merchantmen. They owned the Gulf of Mexico, together as brothers and pirates. They were in love with the same girl, a French marechoness, who appears in the New Country after her husband, the marechal, dies. This love was uncontrollable, and created a horrible split between the brothers. They disbanded to form two rival pirate companies. In the end, Jean murders Pierre over the marechoness. She betrays Jean to whatever authorities were in power. I wasn't sure about that. *Cromwell's* was very thin on the subject of civil and military control in the days of Jean Lafitte.

I put a guillotine into my story and had Jean repent on the way to having his head chopped off. "La pauvre Pierre," he says. My French was weak, but I didn't trouble myself over it. I had a pirate story for uncle Bob, about wickedness in the New World.

He paid me on the spot, in old five-dollar bills. And he didn't sit on the story. "Pirate Brothers" was in the next issue of *Triton,* Bob's adventure magazine. But you couldn't find Jerome Charyn. Somebody named Roger Bissenwick had usurped my story.

I went to the Flatiron Building and confronted Bob. I stayed with him in his closet. Why had my name been lopped off?

"That's the breaks," Bob said. "We always have a 'Roger Bissenwick' in *Triton.* Who would read a 'Jerome Charyn'? Newcomers are hard to sell."

Once I was told the realities of publishing, what could I do? I became Roger Bissenwick for uncle Bob. *Triton* was a monthly, and I couldn't hope to pay our rent with one Bissenwick per issue. So I was also Clarence Minor, Walter Tuck, and Garse Wood. I was Wilfred Glass, the fencing master, Eddie Heath, who hunted oysters with chicken necks on a pole, and Byron France, card shark and confidence man. Half the issue came out of my hide, with a few twisted borrowings from Bob's encyclopedia of the wounded South. I shouldn't complain. I had over three hundred a month from *Triton* magazine.

But I joined Swandowne and got a zero on my next humanities quiz. I forgot the names of Anna Karenina's husband, boyfriend, dog, horse, and son. It didn't bring me closer to

Swandowne. We weren't compatriots in idiocy and sloth. My zeros weren't so pure as his. I was a cadet, and he was St. Robert's Hall.

I hurt in all my other courses. My compositions began to smell. I couldn't afford to drop too far down in naval science, or my "contract" would never come. So I cheated on a quiz, copying answers from the dolt in front of me. Rosen was there, and now he had his revenge. He reported me to the Old Man. Shirl went sad around the eyes. Jerome, the working man's boy, wouldn't bring him the raw blood he needed. I was given a court-martial and severed from the ranks.

The college found out. Columbia had its own rule book. The deans wanted to erase me from the freshman class. But who can understand the Navy? Commander Shirl went in to scold the deans. He brought me with him, so Columbia could have a look at the human article it was going to cast aside.

The deans were in terror of Shirl. They voted to keep me around. I wasn't a midshipman any more. But at least I had a college.

2.

SCRIBBLING, sleeping late, poking about in *Cromwell's* for a fact or two, I got to respect that encyclopedia. I warmed to its sense of guerrillas in the South. It gave my stories and articles a passionate bent. Cowboys, pirates, and fishermen would brood over their "lost country" and a very dead past.

A phone call from Beverly jolted me out of an "Eddie Heath" on oystermen feuding over a barrel of chicken necks. I couldn't understand her blubbering at first.

"Your mother died?"

No, Bev had been jailed somewhere in the heart of New York City.

"Jesus, did they put you in the Tombs?"

Cromwell's could take me through work farms in the Alabama of 1905, but it was negligent on the penal colonies of New York. Girls didn't go to the Tombs. They had their own detention house, the Jefferson Market jail. Bev wasn't there. She was inside the holding pen of a cheap department store on Third Avenue. My girlfriend was a shoplifter, and she'd been caught with some swag under her coat. Now I know why Bev was so tired during the day. She traveled from store to store, lifting things.

Twenty dollars and my signature on a card got her out of the wooden cage she was in. The store detective boasted that he had her in his files for a year. "I didn't want to prosecute the bitch," he said to me in private. "She's a pathetic case."

"How do you mean? She's big, strong. What's so pathetic about her?"

"Jerome," he said. "She works for a guy named Jim Slats. He's got a gang of women, and all of them are crooks. Jim stays out of whoring. He doesn't want his bitches pulled off the street. His fortune is in shoplifting. The percentages are on Jim's side. A bitch makes four-five hundred passes, and she gets bitten maybe once. Your girlfriend was unlucky today."

Beverly wouldn't talk about this entrepreneur named Jim.

"Nice guy, leaves you in a cage."

"You'll get your twenty dollars," she said. I couldn't find her Jim in the phone book, but there was a Slats Pawn and Coin Shop near Canal. Johnny Broom told me to mind my own business and let Beverly the cow stay a shoplifter, but when he realized I was going down to Slats', he agreed to come along. In the fury over my court-martial and disgrace before the deans, Corporal Rosen forgot to collect my uniform. I decided to wear it to Slats'.

We got on the subway to Canal Street. John wouldn't stop coaching me. "Pawnbrokers like to keep a gun in their place.

So don't put your head over the man's counter. You'll lose it."

"Are you guessing Slats' style?"

"I don't have to guess. They got pawnbrokers in Tennessee."

We went into the pawnshop. It must have been a low time of year for Slats. The windows were barren, and he only had a few cracked fiddles on the wall. He didn't look that much older than John or me. He had tiny scars, or bite marks, under one ear.

"Jim Slats?" I said.

He wouldn't answer me. He stared at my uniform for a while. "I can give you fifty cents for the hat and the military pants. If your socks are wool, I'll buy them too. But your coat is worthless to me. They attract moths in the summer, and you can't beat the dust out of a big Navy coat."

"I didn't come here to bargain with you, Mr. Slats. The pants aren't for sale. I'm interested in one of your girl thieves."

The bite marks seemed to bloom on the side of his face. "What girl thief?" he finally muttered.

"Tall Beverly."

He invited us into the back of his shop. We walked through a curtain and entered a large room that was filled to the ceiling with women's lingerie. You had to breathe in stacks of panties, girdles, pajamas, and bras. This Slats must have supplied every lingerie shop east of the Mississippi.

"Did she send you over to squeeze me a little?"

"Bev doesn't know I'm here. I don't like the way you do business, Mr. Slats. Letting your employees sweat it out in a wooden box."

Slats hit me on the nose. I couldn't duck under the path of his elbow. That swing was much too sudden. I landed in a pile of brassieres, with squirts of blood on my uniform. Those brassieres deadened my fall. It was like floating into a soft, soft place. I picked myself up. The pawnbroker smacked me again. I had blood on both cheeks.

John wrestled Slats to the ground. But we couldn't keep him there. He scratched John on the head and bit my hand. If he had a gun among the lingerie, he couldn't have gotten to it. We made sure of that.

Slats developed a harsh, whistling cough. We tied his ankles together with all the girdle straps we could find. We left him with his contraband nighties and bras, and barreled through the curtain with our scars of war. John had a scratch that nicked his eyebrow and ended at his lip. And I had a bloody nose and the prints of Slats' teeth on my hand.

I saw Bev at the Wounded Tepee. She snarled at us. Bev wouldn't have anything to do with me and John. "Clowns and sailor boys," she said. It turned out that lots of women at the Tepee belonged to Jim Slats. It was a shoplifters' bar. We weren't so welcome any more. John and I bought our last Schlitz and got out of the Tepee.

3.

JOHN watched me scribble night after night, and he began to question me about my slavery to uncle Bob.

"How much does the uncle give you for a piece?"

"Fifty bucks."

John's scratch hadn't healed, and it writhed with the movement of his lip. "That robber, ask him for six hundred next time."

"If I excite your uncle, we'll have to carry our furniture into the street."

"Six hundred," John insisted. "Not a penny less."

I quoted Bob my new price for Roger Bissenwick.

"You're fired, Jerome. You'll never work for the pulps again. I'll see to it."

I was halfway out the closet before he clutched my arm and

pulled me back inside. He slid a chair in front of the door to narrow my steps. He was a shrewd editor, uncle Bob. Imprison the boy, and then bargain him down.

"I'll pay you a hundred clams for every story you deliver. That's my final price."

"Six hundred, Bob, or you'll have to bury Roger Bissenwick. You can't find another drudge. We're inseparable, me and Bissenwick. We have our own style."

4.

AT six hundred a story my voice began to change. Words wouldn't cuddle on the page. I could barely meet the deadline of a Bissenwick per month, and also give Bob an occasional Byron France, or Garse Wood. The uncle found other drudges to fill the back of the issue. And I walked around with hundred-dollar bills.

Swandowne was like a mad smoke in my head. I bought tweed trousers and a tweed vest at Barney's menswear. Swandowne stared through me and my clothes. I could have undressed in front of his eyes, gone naked through the class, chortling over Dostoyevsky, Tolstoy, and Thomas Mann, and I still would have been a midshipman from the Bronx. I didn't have a rat's chance of making St. Robert's Hall.

I threw my tweeds into the trash can and returned to Barney's, grabbing at whatever pleased my eye. I had one herringbone, one sharkskin, one corduroy suit, each with a matching vest. I bought cuff links, tie clasps, zebra-striped shirts.

I mailed packets of money to my mom and dad. It only confused them. A freshman with hard cash. They saw Sing Sing in my future. Their son had moved out of the house to become a thief. It was pointless to show them samples of my work. I couldn't explain Roger Bissenwick. They would have thought

I was mocking the Charyns, to write with another man's name. I could hear my mother speak. "Jerome, you can go to jail for things like that." Hadn't my father put CHARYN on his teddy bears? It was all the history he had. To a Pole from Crotona Park it was criminal to monkey with a name.

They wouldn't take money from me. They weren't unkind about it. The packets had made them hysterical. My father said you couldn't trust the post office to keep delivering hundred-dollar bills. "You should open a bank account," my mother said.

I was cursed with that new abundance of mine. It didn't get me closer to John. He had urged me to jack up my price, but he wouldn't go near our treasury. He talked of holding cards in a downtown gambling den. "I can make all the money I want."

"This isn't riverboat pinochle," I said. "They're mean downtown. They don't like strangers to walk in."

"How would you know?"

What could I say? My sense of gambling had come from Warner Brothers. I couldn't imagine George Raft letting a riverboat prodigy into one of his card games. But it was dumb to put Hollywood in the way of my friendship with John. "I'll back you," I said. "It'll give you a start."

John's eyebrows made a narrow curl. "No charity. We have to write up a contract if you decide to be my money man. It means I work for you. You get seventy-five percent of the profits."

"What about a fifty-fifty split?"

"I'm writing the contract, not you." I didn't argue. If Bissenwick could provide for me and John, I'd feel better about the money. It was like having a racing horse for a friend, being John's money man. And I figured, the more "Bissenwicks," the more John can run.

5.

IT wasn't so easy. I could do the stories, but John couldn't win. He had feeble connections in New York. Nobody seemed to care about "Blackjack Sid." He'd make the rounds of "suicide poker," games where you go on and on until players drop out and one man comes home with the money. John didn't have a chance, even with all his riverboat tricks. He was up against a bastard's army of cousins and brothers. They could always nick an outsider who got lucky on them. If John beat them in poker, they would cut his pockets off, slap his face, and warn him not to come back.

The loss of revenue didn't hurt. I was a lot more bountiful than any gambler. I had my old "fifty-dollar" rhythm. I could make a "Bissenwick" faster than a single round of suicide poker. But I couldn't help John.

A lunatic grin had settled onto his face from those hours of concentration. He wore a dark gray muzzle most of the time. "We'll win, we'll win. We'll make a killing, and then you can tell Bob to stuff *Triton* in his ear. No more Roger Bissenwick."

I was a sophomore now. On probation. The deans would have a legitimate excuse to get rid of me. I wouldn't sit for my exams. I had zeros everywhere. But Bissenwick had taught me about the elastic properties of a name. I hired a kid from City College to become "Jerome Charyn." He was a filthy thug, a pre-medical student who was desperate for pocket money. I paid him by the hour to sit for me. He forged my signature on examination booklets. I read those booklets myself. The thug had impeccable grammar and a sophomore's authentic whine.

The deans had to take me off probation. Charyn the cheat, that midshipman who discredited Columbia and the Defense Department, the only boy at school who'd ever been court-martialed, was earning A's and B's.

It was in one of those twilight years at Columbia College that I ran into Lillian Feld. She was vacationing from her harp. "I'm on a shopping spree, Jerome."

Gimbel's wasn't uptown. What was Lilly of the harp doing on 114th Street? "Where's Dr. Jake?"

"Who?"

"The guy you were going to marry. He couldn't stomach my uniform. Professor Furyman."

"Jacob?" she said. "I returned his ring. That was months and months ago. I'm going with an opera singer. Mario."

While she mumbled this, Lilly stared at my corduroy vest and the cuff link at the bottom of my sleeve.

"You look different," she said. "Your hair is longer . . . and you don't have that old man's coat."

"I dropped the Navy," I told her.

She couldn't have been so thick with Mario the opera singer, because she invited herself up to my rooms. Lilly took delight in undressing me. She put her cheek to the corduroy. Then she poked through my closets. "Jerome, I love your shirts."

The author wasn't stingy. I gave her a zebra-striped shirt.

She was startled at the smooth way I nibbled her body, my tongue in all the hollows I could find.

"Jerome, you've been with older women . . . I can tell."

Yea, a shoplifter with a pound of muck on her eyes. That was my expertise. But the thought of "older women" excited Lillian, and she plucked at her Jerome. I wasn't her monster harp. I was a boy with feelings. I didn't have a gilded chassis, with pedals and strings, something she could rock between her thighs. Poor Jacob Furyman. He must have been Lilly's Pinocchio. She winked at Jake, touched him with her strong fingers, and discarded the clever wooden boy. Didn't you know? Harpists are powerful girls.

Lilly sat around in my corduroy vest. It was tight on her. I liked the constraint of her chest cavity under corduroy skin. I opened the closet door.

"Here, take another shirt."

Then a bitterness grabbed hold of me. I was back in Crotona Park. It was in the days of Irwin Polatchek. I had to wrestle with Lilly in the snow to get near her brown nipples again. She was a Baron, one of us, and Irwin's lady.

"Did you forget Polatchek?"

Her boobs thumped against the corduroy.

"Forget? I still have his handkerchief . . . I loved those big ears."

"Then why are you fooling with an opera star?"

Lilly unbuttoned the vest, rolled it into a ball, and slapped me on the head with it.

"Big talker. Should I marry a dead man? Would that make you happy?"

She socked me in the ribs and started to cry. "I would have eloped with Irwin. I really would. He didn't give shirts and vests away . . . you lousy Jerome."

6.

I didn't have time to worry over Lil. I was up the creek again at Columbia College. That thug who sat for all my exams decided to disappear. Maybe he'd gone to medical school in Switzerland or China. He didn't give me any notice. I had five exams to take. The fifth was a murderous one. A literature course. I had to report on the whole of Marcel Proust. Millions of characters and a magic sponge cake. Swann and his girlfriend Odette. Albert and Albertine. Barons and little boys. Deaths and disappearing acts. *À la Recherche du Temps Perdu*. How could I read the son of a bitch?

For once my own dumb past was on my side. You see, I'd

read that mother of a book, ages ago. I was thirteen and ambitious, and I discovered Proust on the shelves of the Boston Road Public Library. It was my luck that I started Proust from the back. The library only had the last volume of *À la Recherche* (in English, of course). So I dipped into *Le Temps Retrouvé*. It was about a baron who liked to get whipped. And it had ideas on history and time that were wonderful for a thirteen-year-old. "Pain is the force that girdles the globe." Things like that.

Other volumes appeared on the shelves. And finally I worked my way to the beginning of Proust. It was a marvelous gift, to watch history come crashing down, to go from Albertine dead to Albertine alive, from disintegration and disease to holidays in a country village. That's what I wrote about on my exam: the effects of reading Proust in reverse. I scored an A-minus. "Interesting and original," the instructor scratched on my booklet, "but a bit on the simple side, don't you think?"

Who was I to argue with a college instructor? He had his Proust, and I had mine. It was the A-minus that mattered in the end.

A letter arrived from the deans with blue print on the envelope and a small "king's crown," the official mark of our college. Would I please send them nine dollars to cover the cost of engraving a little gold key? I'd sneaked into Phi Beta Kappa on the strength of Marcel Proust and my thug from City College.

I wore sharkskin to the ceremonies. The deans shook my hand. That mishap over the Navy embarrassed them now. I'd given them the mark of Zorro. The prodigal son had come home to slash their faces with a Phi Beta Kappa key. I left the ceremonies after a speech about "moral worth and the good scholar."

There was another senior near me in College Walk. I could smell that spotty material on him. Swandowne and his tweeds. He must have woken up from a four-year nap at the secret house of St. Robert's Hall. I wanted that bastard to look at my gold key.

"Swandowne, I just came from Phi Beta Kappa."

He blinked.

"Do I know you?" he said.

"I'm Charyn from your freshman humanities class . . . you used to say how Dostoyevsky was a bore."

Swandowne didn't remember the good scholar Jerome. "Sorry," he said, grazing my shoulder and continuing down College Walk.

I arrived at the sundial with a blizzard in my head. The boy with the gold key. I'd given myself the mark of Zorro.

I noticed shiny black shoes at my feet. Then a pair of military cuffs. Corporal Barnett Rosen was standing over me.

"Come on. I'll treat you to a beer."

I followed Rosen to a bar that was stuffed with military people: drillmasters and their aides from the various ROTC's.

"The Old Man had his hopes in you, Charyn. He said you'd make a terrific officer."

"Well, don't grieve over it. I've done all right."

I showed him the Phi Beta Kappa key.

We had our beers. We pissed in the men's room. The corporal sobered up with a drillmaster's trick. He took some baking powder out of his pocket and gargled his throat. I went to my rooms on Morningside Drive, while Rosen returned to Hartley Hall with the yeasty breath of the Marines on him.

EIGHT

The Immortal Paul

I.

JOHN walked out on me. He couldn't make a go in New York. His gambling had turned to shreds. He'd come home beaten up after a wild card game, the pockets torn out of his pants. You could see his skinny thighs. He'd rush about the city looking for new players. At first I begged him to take more money from me. "No one can destroy Blackjack Sid." I thought it was better for him to have *some* occupation. But those beatings changed my mind.

John left without opening a drawer. Were his old things, underpants and athletic shirts, booty for his friend? I wouldn't wear out John's clothes. I brought them to uncle Bob.

"These are John's. He forgot to take them. Why won't you tell me where he is?"

"Because he knows you'll send him money in the mail. When he's ready, he'll get in touch."

The author went back to work. *Triton* had become a little giant among the adventure magazines. You couldn't find many copies around Morningside Heights. Bob would mumble something about distribution problems: his men couldn't bring *Triton* into the Upper West Side. Were they being mugged on the

Triborough Bridge? Truth was, people didn't look at us in Manhattan. Bob's genius lay in other parts of the country. *Triton* was beginning to flood the South and the Southwest. Bissenwick was read in Savannah, Ft. Worth, and all the territories on the "chicken neck" rim, between Pensacola and Corpus Christi. Oystermen loved us. Dirt farmers. Guys who liked to skin snakes.

"I want an article on Paul Morphy."

"Who's Paul Morphy, and where can I find him?"

Bob looked at me with all the contempt he could summon from a closet on Twenty-third Street. "The greatest chess player in the world. Humans couldn't play with Paul. He was too much for them. The first and the best, that's Paul Morphy. A Southern boy. Raised in New Orleans. He was sitting in his bathtub when he died . . . around eighty years ago."

Bob chanted this portrait like some evensong. He stole it out of *Cromwell's,* I imagine. The uncle had a gravedigger's mind. He was always robbing that encyclopedia.

Bob was being shrewd. A Southern hero from an earlier century could help him along the "chicken neck" rim, where *Triton* was already big. I went to *Cromwell's* to sniff out Paul. The article on him covered seven pages in the encyclopedia. It was stingy with its facts. Paul's entry was a rambling, hysterical record of people and places that maligned him and caused him to suffer. It had a word or two about his Spanish-Irish ancestry; his father had been a judge. Where did Paul go to school? He could have been a pirate or a merman, and nobody would have known the difference. The encyclopedia declared him champion of the world at the age of twelve, without mentioning who his opponents were. He went to New York, *Cromwell's* said, where a man named Paulsen irritated him by sitting at the table for ten hours and never moving a piece. It was a plan to drive the young Morphy insane. The encyclopedia breaks into speech. It has Morphy announce: "Louis Paulsen will not win a game from me while I have the power to breathe."

In spite of the traps set for him, Morphy destroys the best players of New York City. He goes to London to meet Staunton, the English master. Staunton dodges him for a year. Morphy goes to France. Players hide from the wonderboy. They shiver in his presence and will not play. He returns to America, and the encyclopedia has Morphy sing again. "I will give odds of Knight and move to any player here." The Americans also run, and Morphy retires from chess. It brings him no peace. He's stuck in New Orleans during the Yankee occupation of that city. The occupying army makes fun of him, calling him "little chess master." The encyclopedia lists nineteen soldiers who harangued Paul, from commanding general down to a sergeant in the supply corps who marched a load of donkeys through the streets. Where could *Cromwell's* have found such a list?

Morphy's troubles don't cease with the end of military occupation. Small-minded men, jealous of him, try to steal his clothes. He has to disappear into his dead father's house. He lives in isolation, walking the verandahs of his Royal Street home. He dies of apoplexy while taking a bath. *Cromwell's* has Morphy sing from the grave that his championship was "but a hobby" to him. "I despise the professional. He seeks lucre from the game of chess. We should not have these plunderers around. The only reward is the cool, bittersweet love of checkmate!"

2.

I consulted other encyclopedias and books on the major strategies of chess. *Cromwell's* hadn't been quite so rabid as I thought. Most authorities considered him the greatest master of all time. We even had something in common. He was born in 1837, exactly one hundred years before I came along.

I shoved across the campus in my old midshipman's coat, thinking, thinking of Paul. I had pages of notes in my pockets. It must have been during a storm. The visibility was rotten. Figures lurched in front of me. I avoided them with sudden swipes of my shoulder. You could navigate in a midshipman's coat. You could skirt around people and run.

A man came out of the storm. His coat seemed darker than mine. I couldn't get around him. It was Commander Shirl. The sleet pounded on his back. He had ice in the rims of his commander's hat.

It was instinct and a fear of storms that made me salute Commander Shirl.

"Stop that," he said. The Old Man didn't punish me for wearing a coat that belonged to the United States. He was Shirl of the Marines, not a sheriff of stolen property.

"Charyn, how do you survive?"

I had to move close to hear the Old Man, with that sleet falling down on us.

"I'm an author, sir."

"An author? I don't see your name in print."

"Well, sir, I'm much more popular in the Southwest . . . I'm writing a piece on Paul Morphy at the moment."

"The chess player?" he said. You couldn't fool the Old Man. He knew as much of Morphy as I did.

"Wasn't he from New Orleans?"

"Yes sir."

"Then what are you doing in Manhattan?"

How could I answer Old Man Shirl?

"I'm leaving, sir . . . tomorrow . . . for Royal Street."

3.

THE uncle didn't like it. He ranted at me from his closet. "We don't transport writers from place to place. They pick up their own carrying charges."

"You want me to write on Paul? Well, I have to go to Morphy country."

"Why? He's dead. What will you learn in a dead man's town?"

"I don't know. But I can't do him from here."

Bob broke his policy and gave Bissenwick seven days in New Orleans.

"A week, you hear? Then you're on your own."

I took the plane to that country of mine. The hotel was on Royal Street, two blocks from Paul's house, which had been turned into a restaurant. The tables in the courtyard couldn't spoil my view. I could see the balconies and the circular windows near the top, and shake any restaurant out of my head. I dreamt of Paul while people hurried in and out. I wasn't curious. I wouldn't eat a meal at Paul's house.

I had a trove of books and charts with me, and uncle Bob's encyclopedia. I began to piece a sensible history for Paul. But dates and genealogies couldn't get me to write. I walked Morphy's streets. I had po' boys at tiny restaurants. The thought of fried catfish disgusted me. Yes, we'd roast a two-pounder over a barrel in the Bronx and pick at the rough gray-white flesh. But that was a boy getting even with his river god, a god who would leer at you and kick yellow mud in your face. I had no quarrel with the Mississippi catfish.

I saw them in the stalls of the French Market, puny gutted things, discolored and dead. There's nothing so distasteful as a catfish without whiskers. A catfish alive is another story. It has a wonderful gray slime on it, the slime of mud and water. That slippery grayness can disguise the catfish from an enemy and help it "ride" along the riverbank. Who can worship a catfish with its slime washed off?

I had to move out of the hotel. My week was up, and I wasn't getting closer to an article on Paul. I dipped into my own pocket to stay in New Orleans. I lived in a rooming house at the "shabbier" end of the Quarter, on Barracks Street, by the Esplanade. I had a pickpocket, a grounded river pilot, and a half-breed cowboy beggar on my floor. But you couldn't find them about the place. Jackson Square was "sofa" and "living room" for them.

The river pilot happened to be a chess maniac. He carried gleanings from Morphy's better games inside his shirt. This fellow Amos understood the arcane patter of openings and end play. He could talk of Philidor's Defence until my eyes went dull and I had to sleep. Drunkenness had cost him his license on the river. Amos wouldn't tell you how many barges he'd managed to cripple. If he couldn't have catfish and Mississippi mud, he'd have Paul Morphy in his shirt.

We'd go on pilgrimages together. We'd eat our po' boys out of a sack in the old French graveyards and visit Morphy's tomb. Amos would throw a penny under the little gate and sing a prayer for the dead Paul. Then we'd stand in front of the house on Royal Street, lamenting that if Paul had a ghost, the ghost would have to "live" in a restaurant. Customers complained. They didn't want to look at two gaunt creatures while they sampled their gumbo and "dirty" rice. The cops put a scare in us. We'd be hauled in as vagrants, they said, if we blocked the windows again.

Amos was prepared to squat on Royal Street out of devotion to Paul's games. I dragged him to the corner. "He's dead, you clod. He doesn't know we're fighting for him."

"Cities are never kind to their own heroes," Amos said. That muttering was too familiar. I'd swear he had something to do with the article in *Cromwell's* on Paul. But Amos wasn't old enough. He hadn't been on the river in 1905.

He was a violent man. We would argue over the details of Morphy's existence. Like any river pilot, he rejoiced in all kinds of smut. "Morphy was a transvestite. He strutted around New Orleans in his sister's clothes."

"You can't prove that."

"I know ten sailors who'd testify that their grandfathers had Paul Morphy in the back yards of Pirate's Alley."

"Your sailors are a lot of shit."

He pulled a knife on me.

I ran to a different rooming house with all my clothes and Morphy papers.

4.

NOTHING helped. Catfish. Mud. Notes on Paul. I couldn't scribble his story. I zigzagged through certain streets, avoiding Amos, my brains deep in Morphy country. I had the facts, the various colorings, but not the written word. Hell with *Triton* and the "chicken neck" rim.

I was Charyn the street singer in New Orleans. Here, I'll tell you my song. Somebody's grandfather flees Ireland for Spain. Did he strangle his British landlord? Or spit on the king's image and have to run? No matter. Michael Murphy becomes Miguel. He takes a bride. Is she Spanish? Nobody knows. But the metamorphosis is complete. Michael is now Don Miguel Morphy of Málaga, Spain. His son Diego is a restless kid who leaves Málaga for the New World. He marries a certain Miss Creagh, but the good lady dies on him. So Don Diego has himself a second wife, Louisa Peire, a daughter of the Huguenots. He has eight children from these two wives. Diego's a prosperous man. Merchant, philanthropist, and Spanish consul to the port of

New Orleans, he speculates in cotton, land, and convict labor. The Morphys are now established in New Orleans.

Having grown rich, Diego dies in his consul's chair in 1814. His son Alonzo marries Louise Telcide Le Carpentier, a French Creole girl of consummate skill. She's a harpist and composer of melodies. I think of Louise and her harp, and my mind falls on Lillian Feld. Lilly of the golden knees. She ran through Jerome and little Jack, stealing whatever geometry she could, wept for Irwin and went on to professors, opera singers, and whatnot. Forgive me, Louise, wife of Alonzo and mother of Paul, that the harp between your legs should invoke my days of sixty-nine with Lilly at Manhattan's Mississippi Hotel.

—Hey brother, you off your wig?

It's the halfbreed from my old rooming house on Barracks Street, the begging cowboy. He has a proposition to make. He'll pass me off as the bard of New Orleans. I'm supposed to babble histories for a nickel. The singing lunatic who can find your family tree.

Shit. I haven't gotten to Paul's birth yet, and the cowboy is bothering me.

"Cowboy, I don't sing for strangers. Scram, will you? Take your money dish to Jackson Square and do your own singing."

He'd like to splatter my brains against some stucco wall, but the cops are on the street, so the cowboy says, "See you, Jerome."

5.

SHUSH, there's Louise in the music room. Her arms have grown a little fat. She's had four children by now. Edward, the oldest son, Paul, the middle boy, and two girls, Malvina and Helena. Judge Alonzo Morphy has come home from Louisiana's high court. He doesn't disturb his wife. We can hear her plucking at the harp. The girls are in the sewing room. Their crocheting needles move like doddering snakes across their doily boards. The judge has sherry in the parlor. He's not alone. His brother Ernest, the chess king of Louisiana, is in the house. He's come with another enthusiast, Eugène Rousseau. Alonzo has called young Edward down from his room. The boy arrives with his pieces in a velvet sack. He's already the strongest player in Alonzo's house.

The parlor has been turned into a chess emporium. The three men and the boy go to their tables. Edward is something of a prodigy. He can trounce any man or woman in New Orleans except for uncle Ernest.

A different boy comes into the room. Ernest smiles at "leetle Paul." He'll be ten in a month. No one has bothered to teach him the moves. But "leetle Paul" stands with his mouth above the tables and watches uncle, father, brother, and Eugène Rousseau.

A revelation will hit at them around the time of Paul's birthday. They've been dunces for over a year. The "leetle" one can play. In a house full of chess he's taught himself the moves. He mates his father, the weakest of the four. He isolates Eugène's rooks, hobbles his bishops, and Rousseau has to resign. Paul goes up the ladder. He's at the third rung of players in the house. He has to sit with his own brother Edward, who's merciless at twelve and a half. This same Edward has caused seasoned men to shiver. Forget the ordinary *potzers* and fleas! Alonzo wouldn't let scum into his house. The most accomplished gentlemen players fear the sight of Edward's board and velvet sack.

Madame Louise senses that hurricane in the parlor. She abandons her instrument and rushes out of the music room. A rotten melody has entered her head. She gasps when she finds Paul and Edward at the table, brother against brother. She pleads with her husband. "Why do you encourage them to play?" Her heart is pounding like a bishop's stick under her music shirt.

Alonzo doesn't listen to her. He could be in a trance. His eyeballs seem part of the chess table. Edward the merciless is sitting scrunched in his chair. His back has gone crooked. There is no emotion in "leetle Paul's" face as he reduces his brother, piece by piece.

Edward vows to himself that he will never play in company again. He's learned the moves from his father, become a prodigy at his uncle's knee, read Staunton's handbook of chess principles, frightened New Orleans with his bishops and his rooks, and now this baby has unclothed him, left him with a rubble of pawns around an imbecile king.

The Morphy household wonders over Paul. Did his talent creep from the wainscoting like a splinter of ghoulish, brilliant chess? The little one will study no books. He mocks Howard Staunton's principles and rules. But he's a polite little bugger around the house. He won't hurry his uncle Ernest into a game. Months go by. Paul turns eleven. The chess king of all Louisiana laughs to himself. "Come, leetle Paul, show your uncle how you steal an army off the table."

The chess king advances his men and grabs a rook from the boy. Ernest feels ashamed that *he* should have to humble little Paul. But you can't be maudlin at the table. The leopard has to strike. A bishop falls. The "leetle" one has a strange, scattered army on the board. King Ernest can't discover any design to it. He grabs his second rook. Little Paul doesn't smile or frown as the uncle shaves his army. The king begins to feel a certain dread. "Leetle Paul" is a mesmerist. He soothes you with dark, sleepy angel's eyes. Ernest had been tricked. The "leetle" one mates him with a knight and two pawns on the twenty-seventh move.

Alonzo claps. What else can he do? Should he console his brother? Ernest is a gracious uncle, but he won't be unkinged

so fast. The board is set for another game. Ernest shakes off his
drowsiness. The leopard is prepared. "Leetle Paul" can't charm
him to sleep. Again pieces drop to the side. Ernest's lines are
snug, but he smells nothing but defeat. The boy has crept into
Ernest's army and ruined his play. The devil's own gift he has.
He gives you the center of the board and lets you bite, bite, bite.
Then he sneaks around your men and clobbers you with a
rocking horse.

The king is dead. Long live "leetle Paul!" Ernest hugs his
nephew. Peace is restored in the house. If he's taken Louisiana,
where will they find experts for him to play? But the little one
recoils from chess. He sticks close to the family. He won't play
outside of their Royal Street address. The Hungarian master,
Johann Jacob Löwenthal, comes to New Orleans. The Morphys
invite him to Royal Street. Paul seems listless. He doesn't like
strangers in the house. But with his father and his uncle
prompting him, he readies himself. He's a runt of a boy, and
he has to sit on a pillow and two books to see above the table.
Löwenthal isn't deceived by dark eyes on a boy. He's cautious
at the table. The "leetle" one is a wretch in his chair. Paul and
the Hungarian blunder through thirteen hours of play. Dizzy
and weak, and unable to press his advantage, Löwenthal agrees
to a draw.

He returns the following afternoon. The Hungarian notices
a new party. Edward stands behind his brother. He's come
down from his room to watch the "leetle" one play. He hands
Paul his velvet sack of chessmen. Löwenthal is alert to the
difference in Paul. Those black eyes are severe. He's like a
marvelous cat with a pillow and two books under him. You can
feel music come out of the boy. A harp with whiskers meowing
at you. That's Paul. Löwenthal loses the game.

How can I sing of other victories? Paul goes off to school in
Alabama. The "leetle" one's at a Jesuit college, St. Joseph's of
Spring Hill. I grub through my notes. Where are the records of

his Alabama games? Paul didn't bring his chessmen to school. The champion of Louisiana, who defeated his uncle and meister Löwenthal, sinks into obscurity. The wonderboy is now a college mongrel. He writes home to his mother for warm socks and packets of tea to tide him through the Alabama winter. Such is the dissolution of Paul.

6.

MANHATTAN Island. October, 1857. A touch of frost has come and gone. It's Indian summer in the streets, and the New York Chess Club is holding the first American Congress of its kind: a tournament where only the very best will be invited to play. No round robins, it will be "knockout" style. The winner will have to slug his way through a heavy field.

The club, after a bit of controversy, decides to invite a Louisianian who has just earned his law degree. It's twenty-year-old Paul, that forgotten wonderboy who went into Alabama and hasn't woken up since. His father's been dead for a year. Alonzo was struck in the eye with a Panama hat. It's an evil accident when a swollen eye can kill a man. Alonzo contracted congestion of the brain, and his family had to bury him.

The boy's in a sullen mood at the tournament. He doesn't mingle well. He drinks a glass of sherry before games and chews on a biscuit. He's a shrimp and a mama's baby, a boy without a beard. He gives the impression of a dull, chinless creature. No one will take him seriously. But he wins. He "knocks out" player after player. The tournament officials are puzzled by the shrimp. He has women's hands with veins all over. He doesn't smoke cigars. He murders you in a quiet, mannerly way.

The American Congress has invited a monster to New York. This Louisiana schoolboy with his law degree is eating men alive at the tables. He sits down with the Congress' own star,

Louis Paulsen, a giant out of Germany who's been living here for a while. Louis is just twenty-three, but he looks like a great bear next to Paul. He mutters, taps his fingers, smokes. The chessboard trembles with each exertion of the giant. They sit and sit and sit. The giant ponders every move. He yawns, and a horse drops from the table. One of the referees has to pick it up. This rumbling bear, who disturbs the order of things with the slightest impulse of his body, had begun to irritate Paul. Morphy whispers into his cuff: "Paulsen shall never win a game of me . . ."

He returns to New Orleans, champion of the United States. The schoolboy who slumbered so long in Alabama is celebrated and adored. He's voted president of New Orleans Chess amidst all the hullabaloo. But the cheering isn't so loud on Royal Street. His brother Edward is lately in the cotton business and has little time for chess. And his widowed mother is disturbed by the attention that has come to Paul. She knows how frail he is. She would like him to forget this wickedness and use his law degree.

But the Americans are fired up. The European masters have treated them as cowboys and idiots in matters of chess. The idiots are scorned in England and France. Chess clubs throughout the country beg Paul to cross the Atlantic and end this disgrace. Money begins to pour in. The American Congress has taken up a subscription to defray Paul's costs. The message is a simple one: *the Louisiana cowboy must go*. Paul sits on Royal Street with his mother. He can't ignore his countrymen. But he returns the subscription money. He won't allow any Congress to finance him. "I am not a beggar, dear sirs. My father has provided for me."

He sails for Europe with a tiny bundle burrowed from his patrimony. He arrives in Liverpool the day before he's twenty-one. He heads for London without the thought of birthday parties in his head. The sea voyage has weakened him. But he won't dally at his hotel on Cockspur Street. He challenges and defeats the best London players. He gives a blindfold exhibition at the Philidor Club on Rathbone Place, destroying six Philidorians with his back to the chess tables. London is astonished. A boy who's never shaved in his life has beaten the entire Philidor Club without so much as looking at a pawn.

One man eludes him. That fellow who wrote the handbook of chess. Howard Staunton, champion of the British Isles. Staunton is close to fifty. He can only make himself look ridiculous sitting down with "leetle Paul." If he wins, they'll say that Staunton takes advantage of cowboys from America. And if he loses, then he loses to a boy.

Staunton is a literary critic, devoted to Milton, Shakespeare, and Swift. His publishers are hounding him, he says, for new pieces on *Hamlet* and *Lear*. He can't get out of Birmingham for a "job" of chess at the Philidor Club.

But he holds the boy on a string, promising to play him in a month, when his work on Shakespeare eases up. One month grows into four. The boy turns gloomy on Cockspur Street. He runs to Paris, showing up at the Café de la Régence, where all the French players meet. Quiet Paul numbs the café, going through one "champion" after the other until the Régence becomes a sad little mortuary chapel.

—*Hey, Jerrome.*

It's the halfbreed. He's on my tail again. I can't sing a word. I look at him and get sores on my tongue. He still has this silly idea of making his inheritance out of me.

"You singing anyway, bro'. I get my guitar. We go down to the river. You put your knees in mud. Because the tourists, they like singers with muddy pants. We give them George Washington, Mamie and Ike, anything they ask. You got them stories locked up. Sing for a living, man. Sing for bread."

I can't.

I won't sing for anybody's supper. The cowboy's, or mine. He turns his head to slap palms with a fellow halfbreed. I run into the alley at the side of the big church. It's too late. The half-breed's botched my rhythm. I'm short of breath. I have to leave Morphy in Paris, at the Hotel de Breteuil.

NINE

The Immortal Paul, Part Two

I.

THE world had a new champion. "Leetle Paul." Europe is his charnel house. You can find a "dead" master wherever he goes. Staunton is the only one who's escaped Paul. Why should it matter? Staunton isn't the best. Adolph Anderssen is much, much better, and Morphy beat him, seven games to two. But it nags at Paul that he couldn't have Staunton at the Philidor Club.

He comes home after fifteen months, haggard and puny in his coat. Those Atlantic crossings aren't for him. The "leetle" one is a rotten sailor. New York goes crazy for Paul. He has to give a speech:

> "Chess is the most moral of amusements. Unlike other games in which lucre is the end and aim, its mimic battles are fought for no prize. It is eminently and emphatically the philosopher's game. Let the chess board supersede the card table and a great improvement will be visible in the morals of the community."

The tumult continues in New Orleans. Paul seems oddly removed from chess. His mother is mortified how feeble he's grown. The skin hangs from his neck. His dark eyes have a burnt-out look. He makes a pact with his mother. He will give up his championship and go into the legal profession. He will not play "a public game or a game in a public place," as the chess critic Sergeant tells us in *The Unknown Morphy,* nor will he "encourage or countenance any publication of any sort in connection with his name."

It's a pact Morphy doesn't break. He becomes the "missing man" of chess. He has cards printed up with the following legend:

PAUL MORPHY, ATTORNEY-AT-LAW,
12, EXCHANGE PLACE,
UP STAIRS, NEW ORLEANS

His lawyering doesn't work. Morphy has an absence of clients. Men don't come to a chess wizard for their legal problems. He has to give up his office on Exchange Place after two months.

He's anxious and withdrawn. He can't even extend his family line. We have no Morphy sons or daughters on Royal Street. What girl of breeding would go about New Orleans society with a gamester, a boy-husband who carries the ghost of chess on his back?

Morphy leaves for Paris, disgusted with himself. There is no record of what he did on the Continent. He couldn't have gone to the Café de la Régence without sullying the agreement he had with his mother. Did he sit in a public garden? Or play skittles on the sly? He's the "unknown Morphy" now. A year is twisted out of his life.

The failed lawyer comes home. He's still without a bride. He lives on Royal Street with his mother and Helena, his baby sister. Louisiana secedes from the Union, but Morphy doesn't go to the front. He has little to do with the War Between the States. Mostly he walks about the city, or remains inside the house.

The Union Army captures New Orleans, throws its mayor out of office, and establishes military rule. That doesn't stop Paul from having his walks. The noted publisher, Dr. George H. Putnam, who arrived with the Yankee invaders, remembers Morphy at this time:

> "One saw in the street only old men, women, and coloured folks. In enquiring in regard to one handsome young fellow who was passing, I was told that it was Paul Morphy, lawyer and heretofore chessplayer. He had not gone to the front with the men of his own age and social standing. On the other hand, he had no intention of taking up arms against his State. He remained, therefore, between the two great war parties, sympathising with neither and exposed to the loneliness that must always come to the 'in-between' man. He ought under the circumstances to have carried himself off to Paris or elsewhere. Remaining in his own city, he was exposed to the criticisms and gibes of the older men whose sons had gone to the front, and of the girls of society, who had no patience with a Louisianian who would not fight for the pelican flag."—*Memoirs of a Publisher,* pp. 30–31

2.

ROYAL Street, 1879. The Yankee invaders have long been gone from the city. Paul is forty-two. He has a certain fleshiness, but he isn't stout. Except for that bewildering look in his eye, he could still be a boy of twenty. He's become a near recluse. He walks up and down the galleries of his mother's house. He has a pet saying that he repeats over and over again: "Il plantera la bannière de Castille sur les murs de Madrid au cri de Ville gagnée, et le petit Roi s'en ira tout penaud." (He will put the flag of Castille on the walls of Madrid with the cry, *the city is ours,* and the little king will go away with mud on his face.)

Let the scholars ponder over this. Does it help to pick at every word? None of them has unraveled Morphy's hidden song. It's a cry of pain, you ask me. In that boiling head of his, Morphy is declaring his own impossible state. The conquerer of Madrid becomes the king who has to run away. Morphy *cannot* win. His body is seized with chess, but chess is only a bagatelle. If he reveals his ambition, to win and win and win, it undermines the "seriousness" of the Morphy men, bankers, brokers, judges, and diplomats. The Irish Morphys come out of Spain to plant their flags in America and "seize" the ground. Paul is ashamed of his madness for chess. He can't earn his manhood with pieces on a board. But by giving it up, by "sacrificing" chess, he remains stuck in the shadows, a boy all his life.

3.

HE'S proud of his linen. He won't wear a soiled shirt. On Sunday afternoons he walks to his brother's house on Rampart Street. Edward is now master of the New Orleans cotton market. He has a son and a daughter in *his* house. Paul plays with Regina, his little niece. Edward has lost that old grudge against his brother for supplanting him in chess. He has a love for Paul. But the "leetle" one is going mad. He's suing half the male population of New Orleans. He claims a league of gentlemen is trying to steal his inheritance and his clothes. The league will poison him the first chance it gets. The "leetle" one locks his best shirts away and will only accept food from the hands of his mother, his baby sister, and his little niece.

How can Edward console Paul, assure him that no such league exists? The "leetle" one will say that the league is made up of all those men who despise him as a chess player and want to destroy his life. Edward sits on the verandah with his brother, drinking lime juice that little Regina has prepared for them. A fellow from the cotton market arrives, Edward's dear friend. Paul jumps out of his seat. He cannot abide the smell of strangers.

He returns to Royal Street.

The editors of a book on "notable Louisianians" have inquired if they can include a biography of him as "the most celebrated chess player in the world." Paul scribbles out an indignant note to these editors. *He has nothing to do with biography. Paul Morphy does not play chess. His brother is with the Cotton Exchange and his father was a judge. Paul has no profession. His father left him $146,162.54 at his death. And the rogues of New Orleans would like to have these thousands for themselves.*

He sends a servant out to deliver his note to the biography people. Then he bolts his door from the inside and we watch him undress. He puts on his sister's petticoats and wears them in his closet. Let my old friend Amos sing about Morphy the transvestite. It's a river pilot's lie. Morphy doesn't color his lips and go out looking for sailors. He sits in the closet, all alone. He takes no delight in the feel of his sister's linen. It's a ruse, a clever man's trick. He's hiding from his enemies. How will the league of gentlemen recognize Paul in his sister's petticoats?

4.

JULY 10th, 1884. Morphy is dead. He took a cold bath on a hot day and died in his tub of brain fever, like his father before him.

Silly people talk of suicide, that Murphy bled himself with a razor. There is no proof of this. It was "the shock of cold water" that killed him (*The Unknown Morphy,* p. 33).

Why isn't a mass sung for Paul at the old cathedral? He's buried without any fuss. His "enemies" visit the grave site. It's not for crazy Paul, the dead man who pestered them with absurd litigations over the past fifteen years. Why would they want to rob the little chess player of his clothes? They bring flowers for Paul to show Edward that Louisianians don't abuse the living or the dead. Their monies are tied to Edward. He's master of the cotton market. They can ill afford to insult the man.

He doesn't notice their flowers or their drunken faces. Edward grieves for Paul. He blames himself. His nose was in the cotton market while "leetle Paul" was smothering to death. The climate of New Orleans was not good for his brother. Paul festered in this city of old, old wounds. He'd retired from the world at twenty-one, an "amateur" in his father's house. Damn the cotton business. Edward should have taken Paul somewhere. They could have picked oysters out of the riverbed. Sailed the Niger to Timbuktu. Edward would have found an occupation for his brother. They would have built canals together. Edward and Paul. Chess had come between them. That stinking, madman's game. Edward shut his eyes in the cemetery and wished to God there were no such instruments as horses, rooks, and queens.

TEN

The Little King

1.

TRITON's come to town. Uncle Bob's discovered me at my latest hovel on Barracks Street. "Goddamn, Jerome. Goddamn."

He catches me in my pajamas.

"Three months," he says, clapping his hairy fists. "Where's my Roger Bissenwick?"

"Le petit Roi . . . tout penaud."

"What?"

"The little king is dead."

"Jerome, you get back on that hot wire of yours and gimme my goddamn story."

The bastard goes through every pocket in my wardrobe. I'm too sleepy to resist. He has all my notes and Morphy gleanings now.

"Where's Johnny Broom?"

"Bubba had himself an accident. He fell off the Natchez bridge. He's a drownded Johnny."

My arms have shriveled in New Orleans, but I grabbed Bob by his collars and gave them a twist.

"I'm joking, boy. Bubba's alive."

The uncle didn't even stop for a drink of "chicory" at the French Market. He got out of New Orleans with my notes. I had to sing without any proof in my pockets. I mixed up birthdays with deathdays. I couldn't remember each chess master in Morphy's life. Löwenthal, Anderssen, and what? I got down and rubbed my hands in Mississippi mud. Those Morphy gleanings didn't come back. I couldn't bellow a full, continuous song any more. I had to rant in snatches and isolated bits.

I blame uncle Bob. He's a scoundrel, a graverobber, and a thief. He distributes unholy stories from his closet in the Flatiron Building. *Triton* hit the stands in New Orleans three weeks after Bob had come and gone. Its cover story was "The Little King" by Roger Bissenwick. I can't say what Bob took from my notes. But "The Little King" was a piece of smut.

It had a river pilot's disregard for history. The Paul Morphy of *Triton* magazine was a lunatic, a lecher, and a sodomite who paraded in women's skirts. The Yankees had eaten his mind. He was a good, regular boy before he'd gone up to New York City. He caught distemper and everything else in the swinish brothels that posed as chess clubs. He didn't recover from his mad fit and had to retire from chess. Then, during the occupation of New Orleans, the Yankee soldiers corrupted him. "Le petit Roi" lost his reason entirely. The villains turned him into a male bawd. They took his body and broke his heart. He became the lunatic of the city, wandering in its streets, and died of a swollen brain.

Triton's circulation doubled because of "The Little King." Bissenwick was the hero of the "chicken neck" rim. Bad Bob had Roger's fan mail forwarded to my Barracks Street address. The letters arrived in bundles that were wedged into the bottom of my mailbox. I had to pick them out with a knife.

Some of those bundles were scarred and ripped, but I read all of Bissenwick's mail. There wasn't a hate letter among them. *Triton*'s readers adored "The Little King." Their devotion to that faked Morphy saddened me, and then I grew sick. Bob had hit upon a crazy pulse. There it was. The rape of the South. In Roger Bissenwick's voice. Paul, the virgin prince, sullied and sodomized by Yankee invaders and pigs. I believed it myself.

I wrote to unc' Bob. "Thanks for the Bissenwick letters. Please stop sending them. I'm going blind looking at the mail. Sincerely, Jerome."

The bundles disappeared from my mailbox within a week. But something arrived in their place. Small checks from *Triton* magazine. Thirty or forty dollars at a time. Were they Bob's notion of royalties? Who cares? "The Little King" was keeping me alive.

I couldn't eat forever off one lying story. Uncle Bob stopped his flow of checks. I dug into my mailbox for the unc's familiar envelope with that old sea god in the corner, Triton, half-man, half-fish, with the conch that he loved to blow. There wasn't a sea god to be found.

And I didn't have a magic conch with a fundament of music in it for the tourists of New Orleans. Triton wouldn't blow for my meals. What could I do? I had a dead bank account and no Morphy gleanings to spur my songs. I had to join the cowboy or begin to starve. We had our own beggar's station in Jackson Square. He took out his guitar picks, pieces of bone that he lashed to his fingers and gave him a skeleton's fist, and I delivered songs on any subject that the tourists desired. Bayous, bullfrogs, corn palaces, Mayan gold and blood. We could do forty dollars on a sunny day. We had our eats, black cigars, and money to "sell" to those beggars who didn't know how to sing. The cowboy had a banker's mind. He wanted two dollars for every dollar he gave. But loansharking isn't a business for beggarmen like us. Two gorillas arrived out of nowhere and cut off the cowboy's left ear.

The same two lads had come for me. They knocked on my window at Barracks Street. They wore hats in the summer and striped shirts that I remembered from my Bissenwick years.

"What's your name, kid?"

"Paul," I said, because I didn't feel like saying Roger or Jerome.

"Are you the spieler?"

I shrugged.

They asked me again. "Are you the boy who sings?"

Figuring they were out-of-towners, I gave them Morphy's little tune. "Il plantera la bannière de Castille sur les murs de Madrid . . ."

"Sonny, you like the Esplanade? You happy here?"

"Sure," I said, "mais ce n'est pas Paris!"

The first gorilla touched the second gorilla on the shoulder. "Can't you tell, Jacob? He's a loon."

"Pardon us," they said. "Go on singing, sonny boy. But don't sell your dollars, for God's sake."

I lost my partner over the gorillas who knocked on my window.

The cowboy blamed me for the bandage he wore on the side of his head. He looked at my two good ears and was furious. By every right I should have been mutilated together with him. Then we could have gone on with our act. He would murder me with a rock if I went near his beggar's station now. So I had to sing without the support of those fabulous bone picks the cowboy had for his guitar. Tourists wouldn't come to me. I lived on potato chips. That's what my singing brought in.

2.

My landlord and his five sons threw me out of Barracks Street. They didn't need all that muscle power. One son would have been enough. It was less of an inconvenience than the landlord could have known. What did I have? Shirts, socks, a midshipman's coat, herringbone and sharkskin that were a hindrance in the Louisiana sun. I moved in with all the other beggars of Jackson Square.

We weren't an unhappy lot. Any fool can get along without a mailbox. We caught on to the habits of the police. We had our own "pigeons" along Pirates Alley and at each end of the square. The "pigeons" would warn us when the cops were about. We would scatter to different cafés with whatever goods we had, or hump down on the rocks near the riverbank. I preferred rocks and mud in times of crisis. It was easier to camouflage yourself. The cops would seldom cross the railroad tracks to steal a beggar from his Mississippi roost.

Why the hell was I crouching on a rock? I could have gotten out of New Orleans. It wasn't only my paupered state that held me there. I was involved with the little king. I trudged Morphy's streets in the worst blazes of July, hugging the midshipman's coat that really belonged to the cadets of Columbia College. It was bedroll and blanket and tented house for me.

I went into a mom and pop grocery store away from the tourist routes and pulled a Dr. Pepper out of the icebox. I hadn't come to beg. I paid for my Dr. Pepper with the few pennies I had. This mom and pop didn't like "Jackson Square trash" to drift into their store. Mom snaked hard glances at me. Only a man without scruples would wear a winter coat in July.

I was about to take my Dr. Pepper into the street when I heard the regulars at mom and pop's make fun of Marlon Brando. It wasn't Morphy that got me into trouble. It was my old hero from the Bronx. They were talking of Brando's Western, *One-Eyed Jacks,* which tells of a bankrobber named Rio and the friend who betrays him, Dad Longworth. Brando is more like the Count of Monte Cristo than any stinking bandit. He goes through the picture wearing a long cape. Mom's regulars thought it was a silly thing. "Did you see Marlon's fat ass?" they said.

No catfish could preserve me. It whispered in my head, *Get out, Jerome, get out.* But I had to mix in.

Did I level some critique at mom and pop? Spit out lines from *One-Eyed Jacks?* I don't remember. I was wrestling all the grocery people. Jars of honey dropped from the shelves. Mom beat me around the shoulders with a broom. Pop took out his spray gun and shot mosquito repellent into my eyes while angry customers chewed off the ends of my coat.

I kept praying for the cops to show and get me out of this hellhouse. I'd been kicked, thumped, blinded, and chewed in a mom and pop grocery store. I heard police sirens and said, "Thank God."

I didn't go with the cops.

Some wise guys bound my arms with enormous leather straps and threw me into an ambulance. They were just as crazy as the grocery people. They banged my shins with a pipe when I asked for a drink of water. I learned to shut up inside this ambulance.

3.

IT was some kind of hospital the thugs had taken me to. The hospital had its own little police station and criminal court. I was carried into court without my proper clothes. The thugs wouldn't give me underpants to wear. I felt humiliated to go before a judge with my balls swaying under a long green hospital shirt. The judge had a red face. All the grocery people were there. They howled at the judge and two civilians. I'm not Pinocchio, your brainless wooden boy. The two civilians didn't work for me. They were the court's own psychiatrists.

I started to laugh.

Don't ask me why. The judge looked just like a chicken. His black robes fell around his body like useless wings. A wattled neck rose out of his laundered collar, shivered once, and went back inside. His nose was big and very sharp for a judge. He screamed at me from his high bench.

"Who the devil are you, young man?"

"Le petit Roi," I said.

The judge appealed to his henchmen.

"What does he mean? What is he blabbering about?"

"Do you know my father, sir?"

The judge seemed afraid to answer me. That chicken neck sank into black silk. "Who is your father?"

"Judge Alonzo Morphy of the Louisiana Supreme Court."

He was more confident now. "Never heard of him. Morphy? There's no judge like that."

He'd gotten his footing again, this hospital judge, who ran a lunatics' court, and he shouted the law at me. "The injured party, Mr. and Mrs. Donald Snow, say that you entered their store on Clio Street sometime in the afternoon of July the twenty-first and willfully destroyed two hundred dollars' worth of goods."

"They are slanderers and thieves, sir. They ought to be whipped."

The grocery people yammered from their gallery of seats, but the judge quieted them. He didn't expect such eloquence from a Jackson Square bum.

"Why should *they* be whipped, and not you?"

"Ask them yourself, sir, if they didn't bring up the subject of Marlon Brando's fat ass."

"Speak sense," the judge warned me, "and don't you dare use foul words in my court."

The two psychiatrists approached the bench. They whispered "paraphrenia" and "dementia praecox." These civilians wanted to choke me off. But I wouldn't stop.

"Do they sneer at Paul Newman and Monty Cliff? I know Monty had an accident, and the surgeons had to rebuild his face. But Brando has to take shit from everybody. You didn't grow up in the Bronx, Your Honor. You didn't train at the Crotona Y. He was the first real lifter Hollywood ever had. A bodybuilder, one of us. Mitchum had the arms. Lancaster had his lats. But they didn't smell of the weightlifting room. Not like Marlon Brando. I could imagine him with the special curling bar that the Weider brothers invented to get at the double peak in your biceps. An ordinary bar won't do. You need one that bends in and out. The snake is what we called it. You think I didn't notice when Brando lost his definition in *Viva Zapata!* But he was still beautiful, Your Honor, with a hook missing here and there. So when people cry, *fat ass,* it enrages me. What do they know? How can he work out and do so many films? When he was on location with *One-Eyed Jacks,* could he bring his training partner along? Tell them to be a little kinder and not to say fat ass!"

The thugs who stole my underpants were summoned into court. The judge had ruled against me. No more speeches for the little king. The thugs bound me up with their straps, and while the grocery people jabbed their fingers into my hospital shirt and the psychiatrists said, "Bad boy, bad boy," I was trundled out of that lunatics' court.

4.

IT's a funny hospital I was in. The matrons carried .44's. They didn't have to act surly with us. They could blow our faces off any time they choose. But it was still an odd proposition to have women guarding you when all the patients were men.

I couldn't figure out the hospital's idea of a ward. Was it saving money for itself by banding us together? Or did it assume bedlam was one universal thing? We had geldings, convicts, and beggars like me in the ward. The beggars I had known from

Jackson Square decided to be my enemy at the hospital. They bowed and said, "What's the weather like, Your Majesty?"

They told the convicts how I was the little king of Royal Street. The convicts would also bow and push me to the floor when the matrons weren't looking. They needed someone to despise in this madhouse.

They would follow me into the latrine and go directly to my seat on that long wooden potty we had. "Look, the king shits."

I had to fight them off to preserve my sanity and stay alive. The matrons saw my gnarled ears and gave the little king jam sandwiches out of pity. But they couldn't stand watch every minute and hold bedlam's army off my back.

The convicts took on kitchen work so they could drop Louisiana roaches into my soup. I ate less at the hospital. I babbled to myself to ease the hunger pains. Then I started to weep.

"His Majesty's crying," the beggars reported to their convict friends. The geldings sat near me. The convicts pushed them away. They wanted to observe their victory. The ward had made the little king cry.

The fuckers hadn't won a thing. I was crying over Paul. In the deadhole of this hospital I'd begun to think and think about his life, the waste of it after he was twenty-one, the mad business of his suing people, hiding in closets, wearing his sister's clothes, when he should have had his chessboard and whatever else a genius needs.

The beggars surrounded me like the jackals that they were. "It must be worth a dollar, each royal tear. Majesty, cry a little stronger, will you? So we can bottle the stuff."

The beggars did come up with a plastic baby bottle. God knows where they could have found one in this ward. But they began to whoop in alarm. I watched their bottle being crushed in somebody's paw. It was Sid Cummings who'd decided to step in. My crying had made him curious. He was the dreaded "Ripper" from Lake Charles. He'd cut the throats of sixteen men and women. The plea of insanity had saved him from the gallows, the oven, an acid bath, or whatever it was Louisiana did to its murderers in the primitive days of 1963. He'd been sentenced to remain in this hospital for a fixed period of 511 years. There was to be no reprieve for Sid. No pardons, no parole. If science could preserve us, keep us alive for a century or two, it wouldn't help Sid. He'd have to go the distance in this ward.

"Watcha all whimpering about? I can't sleep in that noise."

I told Sid Cummings. Morphy's birth, life, and miserable death. He whimpered together with me. The ward was struck with instant paralysis. It had never seen the "Ripper" cry. No one would say "Majesty" to me. *Little king* disappeared from the ward's list of vital words. I was Charyn the Bronx imbecile who had a long, mad cry with their own Sid.

My diet picked up. The convicts went into the kitchen to strain my soup. I ate with Sid Cummings. We had wine at our table. That's the luck of a celebrated murderer. People were willing to smuggle things into the ward for Sid. The matrons flirted with him. I swear, they would have taken off their gun belts and crept under the table if Sid had wanted it. But he wouldn't lie down with correction officers. He'd rather go without women, like the rest of us.

Queens weren't tolerated in our ward.

"Aint natural," Sid said. "I wouldn't bait a fairy, Jerome. But that ass fucking is against the Lawd."

Whatever was or wasn't "natural" to Sid, he would weep every time I mentioned the story of how "le petit Roi" had to hide from the scoundrels of New Orleans in his sister's clothes.

"Bullhaids," Sid muttered, wiping his eyes. "Ever' one. Tauntin' that boy. Aint no tragedy to live without hair poppin' around on your cheeks like yesterday's lambchops. He must have been the sweetest-lookin' king in the city."

Then Sid started to swallow and groan and wag his head. The

matrons had to come with a mess of rope and tie him to his bunk, or he would have done damage to himself. The beggars confided in me now that I was Sid's lunch and dinner companion. "The Ripper's having one of his fits, Jerome."

"What's he 'fitting' about?"

He was remembering that "long night," eleven years ago, when he tore up sixteen of God's creatures with a razor from his uncle's barber shop. The sixteen had been a family of hunters and their wives who'd come to Lake Charles for the ducks. Sid was a retarded man-boy of twenty-seven or so. He heard the guns pop along the lake. Then God spoke into his left ear. "Sid Cummings, you save the ducks." He wasn't going to turn from the very God who hollered at Abraham and Moses, and wrestled with Jacob in the dust, and delivered Jesus from that boneyard called Golgotha. He went with his uncle's shaving tool to the cabins around the lake, where the hunters were sleeping with their wives. He made sixteen swipes. His plunging arm was so quick, he could dispatch a husband and wife in three seconds, if they were lying close. He was bloody and wild when he returned from the lake. Sid buried the razor and hid out in the woods.

He wasn't looking to be famous. He'd done God's work. But the papers got after him. Dumb little Sid who swallowed garbage and floated his own turds in a wet ditch had become *the Ripper of Lake Charles.* It was the ugliest mass murder in the Bayou State. "Where Will the Ripper Strike Next?" asked the *Times-Picayune.* People locked their doors. Sheriffs' posses and vigilante groups scratched the state. Sid was half a mile from home. His uncle found him. He was chasing bullfrogs and catfish in the Calcasieu River.

Sid recollected all sixteen throats. The whitish pulse of the ladies, and the hairy Adam's apples of the men that would bump up and down in the middle of a dream before the razor cut a perfect arc: you don't have to go very deep to gut a man's throat. When the memory hit too near, Sid would scream. Tie him to his bed for a day, and the Ripper'd be all right.

5.

WE had wine for dinner, and the matrons were beginning to think I was cute. They'd never heard of a lunatic with a Phi Beta Kappa key. I was something of a gentleman to these hard-bitten girls. They would stammer in a shy way and talk philosophy and ethics with me.

"Jerome, is it the pull of gravity what makes some people insane?"

"Miss Edna, I swear I don't know."

And I'd run to Sid with a wet rag. It eased his boiling forehead when a fit was upon him. I'd tell him about Paul while his arms were tied to the bed.

"Sid, when he retired from chess he'd go to the opera with a monocle in his eye."

"Which eye?" Sid would ask, in between his moans.

"His right one, I guess. I think that's your monocle eye."

Goddamn, I had food, I had friends, and I didn't have to play Roger Bissenwick, or sing to tourists in Jackson Square. So why did the judge's henchmen have to come for me?

"We're taking you out of this ward, Jerome. You're a lucky boy. You're going to Shuttleford Grange."

"Keep your Shuttlefords," I said. "Sid Cummings will vouch for me. I'm staying here."

I wanted to scare the pants off them with the mention of Sid. I'd turned sly in captivity. I was hoping they wouldn't disturb the Ripper's best friend.

I'd miscalculated. The Ripper wouldn't back me up. "Don't you be spoiled, Jerome. You have a chance to get out of this rotten corner, you take it now."

"I'll go if you go."

He rapped me on the ear with a knuckle of his. It wasn't the whistling that got to me. My pride was shot. He'd slapped me like he would a silly dog.

"I aint got no locomotion," he said. "I'm gonna die in this dirt. But you get out."

"You'll be sorry," I said. "Who'll be here to tell you stories about the little king?"

"I don't forget a story once it's told."

He squeezed up the whole side of his face.

"What's that?" I said.

The Ripper had me now. "That? That's the monocle in Mr. Morphy's eye."

ELEVEN

At Shuttleford Grange

I.

MY hospital shirt was snatched away and I had to get into my street clothes or take a beating from the thugs who'd stolen my underwear in the first place. That's how the hospital was run. I couldn't say goodbye to the matrons, the convicts, the geldings, the beggars, or Sid. I was in transit, you see. Between one asylum and the next. I could have been a whiff of gas to the thugs. I had no rights.

But I didn't have to sit in an ambulance this time, all belted up. They drove me to Shuttleford Grange in a nice orange van. I could twiddle my fingers, scratch my ass. It was the same to them. Send the dummy to the next asylum. That's what was on their work sheet.

It took seven hours to find the place. And it was the silliest asylum you ever saw. Shuttleford Grange didn't have shotguns or fences or a big shackled house and mad barking dogs. It was a nest of cottages on a hill.

"I want to go home to the Ripper and all my pals."

The thugs hurled me out of the van and deposited me in front of a cottage. They didn't wait around for a receipt. Those mothers drove off and left me on the grass. I began to scream.

"Hey, hallo, I'm the new boy here."

A man came out of the cottage, saying "Sorry, old chap," and welcomed me to the Grange. He carried my coat and encyclopedia indoors. There were to be five of us living in Bartleby House.

We had a female person among us, Mrs. Gartens, a housewife who was in a deep malaise. Then there was Tolkerson, the mathematics wizard who could have been Morphy himself. He was made a professor at nineteen until he fell into a wondrous decline. Tolkerson was thirty now. But he had the startled, hairless face of a perpetual junior high school boy.

The other two were Fairbanks and Philpott. Fairbanks had been the president of a textile company before he "lost his grip." It was Fairbanks who had welcomed me to the Grange. "I have to find my grip, old man."

Philpott was our group leader. He was a graduate student in psychology out of Tulane. Philpott was writing his thesis on us, and we were his charges, his thesis material, and his children.

Our cottage was considered the "neurasthenics wing" of Shuttleford Grange. We were known as the Bartlebys.

A doctor would come down from the head cottage and ask, "How are the Bartlebys this morning?"

The five of us—Philpott was a Bartleby too—would shake our heads and say, "Doing real well, Dr. Smith."

I wagged and smiled with the others, but I was feeling murderous about Shuttleford and my cottage mates. They'd have Jerome the Ripper if they didn't watch out. A madhouse was one thing. Geldings I could take. But I didn't belong with neurasthenics. That was the zombies' disease, where you followed the leader and walked around with a dull, witless stare.

I had enough energy in me to lay Shuttleford to the ground. I warned Philpott. "Get me a transfer. Put me in a cottage where they play tough. The Lake Charles Ripper, you know him? I told him stories for seven months. You see the nicks in my ear? Convicts and crazy people bit into that. Philpott, I'll disappear on you . . . I'll get you into lots of trouble."

He didn't chain me to the cottage. I had free run of Bartleby House. But he wouldn't respond to my threats. So I took my belongings and shuffled down the hill. It irked me, it troubled my head, that a hospital didn't think enough of its patients to go after them.

I went back up the hill.

I ate with the Bartlebys, I slept with them, but I was only a guest in their cottage. I put on my rumpled herringbones and decided to look for girls.

There was a canteen on the premises. The catfish boy went for a visit. I was no gelding. I didn't have to moo at the sight of a girl. I had balls in my pants and a cock that could sing and snake around for its supper. But the girls at the canteen disregarded my Bronx looks. They danced among themselves and I couldn't cut in.

2.

ONE step, two step, follow the leader. That's how you do the zombie walk. The catfish boy had crashed. I fell into line. "Philpott, what's wrong? I functioned perfectly in that other institution. I had geldings to play with. I had Sid. The matrons packed .44's, but they were beginning to make eyes at me. You put me in this cottage, away from all the wild men, and my head hurts. Philpott, I can't breathe."

"It's your past, Jerome, it's chewing at your insides. You've been cannibalizing yourself year after year, and it's finally caught up with you."

"What's all that chewing about?"

"I wish I knew. A blockage somewhere? A fantasy that's

spilled into a new hole? Some dread coming back . . . that your father might kill you, let's say."

"My father didn't have time to kill me. He was the teddy bear man. He made fur animals that nobody wanted to buy."

"It could be a thousand things. Those teddy bears. Your mother's breast."

What did the leader want from my mother's breast? "Cure me, Philpott."

"I'm not a magician. You'll have to cure yourself."

Why couldn't God speak to me like he spoke to the Ripper? Then I'd twist this Tulane wonderboy around his textbook truths. *Cure myself.* Was that the way out of Bartleby House? Then let them shut the door and give me the Ripper's sentence of 511 years.

I listened to the other Bartlebys. They might have clues for me in their own sad stories. Mrs. Gartens had simply gone amok. Left her hubby and five adorable kids, got on a bus, and yoyoed up and down the state. The police discovered her by accident in Baton Rouge. She'd locked herself in the toilet of the bus station, and the cops had to pry her out. Mrs. Gartens was sitting in her own filth. She'd never bathed or washed or wiped herself after leaving home. Her husband was a man of quiet authority. He didn't talk of loony bins. A rest for the missus at Shuttleford Grange.

"Don't you miss your kids?"

"Five girls, and they can have their father," she said, with a bitterness that shocked a Polish boy like me. I heard of drunken, philandering dads, but the wives of Crotona Park never ran away.

"Mrs. Gartens, what's the name of your girls?"

"Suzie, Alice, and the others," she said. "Father's little dears."

I ran to our leader.

"Philpott, you're making a big mistake. Mrs. Gartens is getting worse. She has five daughters, and she's already lost three of their names."

The leader didn't chide me for interfering with his work. Mrs. Gartens hadn't forgotten, he said. She was too guilty to pronounce the names of all five girls.

I moved over to Fairbanks, the textile man, who had a seizure of uncontrollable crying in his office one afternoon. This crying baffled his employees and his family. It continued for twenty days. You could have watered pecan trees with Fairbanks' crying. He packed a suitcase, kissed his wife, drove here to the Grange.

"I have to find my grip, old man."

And then there was the mathematics wizard, Tokerson himself. That Morphylike creature. Nineteen and he's a full prof. A bomb landed in his brain. Tolkerson becomes a "catastrophist." He can predict future events—landslides, locust swarms, rat and dog bites—on a three-dimensional graph. If you can pinpoint the bumps along a smooth, cylindrical surface, you can tell where the next catastrophe will fall. His predictions were viable for a week, and then the cylinders turned against him. Land that should have rippled and cracked refused to budge for Tolkerson. The rat bites he predicted occurred at the wrong end of town. The locusts never came. And the Bartlebys got the "catastrophist" for themselves.

He had a big head. No, it's not true. Tolkerson had a body that seemed to dwindle on him, and it made his head look enormous. He was the only genius at the cottage, yet it was murder to pull a sentence out of the "catastrophist." My regard for him was fierce. I considered him a baby brother.

"Tolkerson, should we go to the canteen? Watch the girls dance?"

I wasn't the leader here. He wouldn't follow Jerome. Were little bombs going off? Explosions that didn't register on his face? Had he withdrawn his "deep mathematics" from the cylinders to the insides of his head? Tolkerson didn't need any of us. He could lock out plants, rats, houses, and trees, and play "catastrophe" with himself.

I envied him that. My baby brother. Tolkerson the wiz.

Without a "catastrophe" to comfort me and contain my zombie's mind, I developed Fairbanks' old symptoms. I began to cry and cry.

"Help me, Philpott."

"Nonsense. It's part of the cure."

I wailed. But no one seemed alarmed. The Bartlebys moved about the cottage.

"I want my brother Harvey," I said. How could Harvey come? He was a patrolman in New York. He'd graduated from the Police Academy before I left for New Orleans to write about Paul. I'd gone to Harvey's graduation. The commissioner shook his hand. Harvey won a sharpshooter's medal. He was the second best student in his class.

I heard a light, kissing noise. It was the slap of a ping-pong ball. We had a table at the cottage. Philpott was playing with Mrs. Gartens. He held out his rubber paddle to me.

"I'm sandpaper," I said. "I don't play with pimples."

But our leader had the resources of a whole Grange behind him. He reached into a manila envelope and produced my wormy sandpaper bat from the Crotona Y. I didn't take the bat with me to New Orleans: Morphy and ping-pong wouldn't mix. So how did it get from Morningside Drive to the Louisiana uplands of Shuttleford Grange? The leader wouldn't tell. It was the Grange's personal business, the secret of Bartleby House.

The hell with the Bartlebys. I took my sandpaper bat. Mrs. Gartens gave me her place, and I fed the leader a few of my sandpaper strokes. Funny that the pock of sandpaper could relieve me of my crying fit. A slice of the catfish had come back. I walloped the leader.

TWELVE

Harvey

I.

SNOW. Doctors, nurses, and group leaders rush out of their cottages in canvas shoes. They bite at the flakes like little children. And we, the Bartlebys, have lost that urge to play. Snow is snow. Even on a Louisiana hill.

Tolkerson speaks. "Dimwits," he says. It's his first word in a month. He points to the seam on a cracked ping-pong ball. The seam is cluttered with markings from Tolkerson's pen. He's turned that ball into a three-dimensional graph. And he's scribbled a message under the seam: *Small flurry. December 6. Not more than an inch.*

"Mrs. Gartens," he says, as if he's questioning an infant. "When did it snow last at the Grange?"

"Two years ago."

Tolkerson corrects her. "Two years and seventeen days."

The genius is on target again. He's predicted the "catastrophe" of a twenty-minute snow fall. He squashes the ping-pong ball in his fist and sidles away from us with a body that's diminishing all the time.

"Why are we inside?" I ask. "It's Tolkerson's snow. Can't we touch it?"

Tolkerson's snow. The logic penetrates, and the Bartlebys mobilize themselves. We join the doctors on the hill. We punch the snow flakes. We open our mouths and let the flakes sit on our warm tongues.

Charyn breaks up the party. I slump back into Bartleby House. The snow has made me cry. Watching it, I thought of our enclave in the Bronx, and the winters when we would be snowed in for months. I can't tell you what went on in Manhattan. But the snow plows didn't come to Crotona Park. The schools would declare a holiday for Polish kids. It didn't matter. We were too dumb to learn.

Long winter? Who cared? I would hide behind my mother's sofa half the day and pretend I was Alan Ladd out on the China Sea (it was 1944). I wrote to him in Hollywood. *Dear Alan, Is it warm in China today?* I got back the first letter in my life. *From Alan Ladd.* He didn't have any news. Just a glossy photograph of himself. He was blond, he smiled, and he wore a shirt open at the neck.

But if I didn't have Alan of the China Sea, I did have Harvey Charyn. He was dark like my mother, with thick black hair and eyes that made him look Japanese. No one called him Jap in catfish country. He was Marco Polo on the Bronx River, exploring that muddy bayou of ours for dead turtles and junk off some forgotten boat. He couldn't sit still long enough to eat. He had the mischief and the energy of a boy who didn't have to crouch behind sofas and be Alan Ladd.

A Sea Scout, he marched in parades that took him across the Bronx. He had white spats and a magic ring that could whistle for you when you sucked on it with a deep breath. But I didn't have the power in my lungs. The ring never whistled for me.

2.

I'M here at Bartleby House, in a small flurry of snow, dreaming of Harvey's white spats. I was a Sea Scout once, a midshipman at Columbia College until I was hurled out of the civilian Navy. I wonder what my friend the Ripper is doing now? Sid and his 511 years. We have plenty of "Rippers" in the Bronx. Dutch Schultz was one of us. Legs Diamond. Twelve-year-olds who are "hit men" for Latino mobsters. The Bronx breeds murderers like a series of twisted plants, one more grotesque than the other. It's a landscape without a center point, or a locus that you can cling to. Its parks are anonymous. Its streets are pocked with gigantic holes. All it has are catfish and a hill across from a dried-up swamp: Riverdale, where Toscanini used to live. But Riverdale was an exotic hump of land with rich fathers and beautiful young girls from Music and Art (Lilly wasn't my only girlfriend). You went up that hill, you visited there, to steal those girls from the rich fathers. But it was only an excursion. The girls went home and slept in their beds without you. And you trekked to Southern Boulevard, or whatever dusty bin you happened to crawl out of.

But I did have Harvey. My history comes from him. Memories interfere with one another, like roots cracking through the bottom of a flower pot. Harvey at seventeen, having an argument with my father. He was preparing for the Mr. New York City contest, and he had no time for family chores. Sam went into a rage and shot a broom at Harvey. The end of the broom struck my brother in the eye. His face began to swell. I was sure he would rip my father's head off. The instinct was there. I could feel that crazy electricity pass into me. But he didn't touch my father. His cheek was black for a month, the eye discolored and raw.

Then it's Harvey at eight, and me, the baby, at five. We're

in the mountains, picking huckleberries in a field. We've filled a monster pot that my mother had given us, to help make a huckleberry pie. My fingers, my shirt, my head are all a powdery blue. We had a pot to carry. We weren't looking at the sky. A goddamn storm had begun to drop down on us. We couldn't race across the field and hold that pot of berries. Harvey had to navigate. He led us into a clump of bushes, the rain whipping at my sleeves. It's like a tunnel inside. We've come upon a hidden cache of berries. The pot is already full. But the new berries are fat as grapes. Harvey couldn't leave them alone. He pulls off both our shirts, knots them at the edges and turns them into a second pot. And we pick like maniacs in the storm, Harvey warning me not to throw the berries hard into the shirt-pot, or they'll bleed all over us. So I fondle a berry at a time. No harm can come to me. Harvey can always find the secret bush that will cover your head and keep you in huckleberries . . .

Harvey at thirteen, working on a chicken farm. Ten hours of breathing and living in a coop for most of the summer, near beaks and filthy wings. Harvey can't have dinner with us. He comes home too late. But that's not the reason. We eat in a community dining room, in one of those country cooking lanes reserved for makers of teddy bears and members of the furriers' and ragpickers' union; the stink of feathers and shit on Harvey would disgrace us and drive all the other furriers and ragpickers away, prove how my father has fallen into poverty and has to rent out his oldest son to the chicken farmers. But the feathers couldn't bother me. I'd wolf my dinner and wait for Harvey on the road. It's eight, eight-thirty, and you can see Harvey with the sun shrinking behind him. The feathers have a glow, a soft burn to them. The Polish furriers can sit, eat, and laugh. That's not my stinky brother. The feathers on him spit tongues of fire as he walks up the road.

3.

IT'S gone. Tolkerson's twenty-minute snow has disappeared from the earth. The stubble outside our cottage isn't even wet. The doctors have all gotten back to work. Mrs. Gartens is knitting five separate scarfs. One for every girl she has. Our leader is right. She hasn't forgotten her daughters. The needles click with a compelling rhythm and then stop, as she goes to the next scarf. Mrs. Gartens is no less a mother for being at Bartleby House. She couldn't even say what possessed her to get on that bus. What's so crazy about the urge to run?

We're pulling for Fairbanks. The textile man has found his grip. He's been groomed for recovery in the quiet, mysterious way of the Bartlebys. "You'll visit me, won't you, Mr. Charyn? I might have a job for you at the mill. An assistant to the president. Something like that."

We have a round of hugging and goodbyes. Philpott has ordered a cake from the head cottage. We eat and clap our hands and mumble cheerio with shortbread in our mouths.

The Grange's own limousine comes to pick up Fairbanks. It's a long blue wagon that could seat a dozen Bartlebys. But Fairbanks is the only passenger. He wears a tie and a crisp white shirt. He waves to us from the window.

I nudge the wiz. "Tolkerson, wave to Fairbanks, will you?"

Tolkerson's scribbled on another ping-pong ball. Will it snow again? What's this new "catastrophe"? He twirls the ball. I understand what Tolkerson means. *Fairbanks won't make it.* The textile man will be back.

4.

HE comes to us with a filthy collar. The points are crumpled, and reach over like two scarred wings. It's the same shirt he wore on his way out. His tie is knotted twice. Slow strangulation? The wish to weigh your head down with an extra loop of material?

Fairbanks was only gone a week. He's in Louisiana shellshock. He doesn't say "old boy" to me, or "old chap." Son of a bitch, what happened to him once he got outside the Grange?

"Charyn," he says, "I'd like to hear about your brother. Harvey, isn't it?"

I tell Fairbanks about the chicken feathers, waiting for Harvey on the road.

"Your father sentenced him to a chicken farm?"

"Hard times," I protest. "We were in debt over my father's teddy bears."

"What about you? Why didn't you have to work in all the feathers and chicken crap?"

"Mr. Fairbanks, I was only ten . . ."

It's a poor excuse. A ten-year-old can hop along with any chicken.

"Maybe the farmer only needed one boy," I said. "Wouldn't it make sense to pick the stronger brother?"

"But he might have gotten you at a cheaper price."

Never mind the dirty collar. Fairbanks hasn't lost his business head. He drums on our coffee table with his thick fingers. "I worked in a chickencoop," he said. "Long before I was ten. But I have no right to mix into your father's affairs."

"Maybe my mother put him in the coop," I said. "Harvey himself could have asked for the job."

The possibilities I toss at him seem to satisfy the textile man. Fairbanks touches my shoulder and goes upstairs to his room with that double knot around his neck. And I think to myself, *Yes, yes, I should have been sentenced to the chickencoop with Harvey Charyn.*

THIRTEEN

The Unmentionable One

I.

WHATEVER "parish" the Grange is in, whatever wilderness, we're allowed guests. Mr. Gartens comes. You'd think he was an ogre who tossed his wife to the Bartlebys. He's not. There are no cruel lines on his face. He treads through the cottage like a sorrowful bear. He's brought gifts for Mrs. Gartens and the house. Curtains for her room. A container of ping-pong balls. A sunhat for the leader.

He holds hands with his wife.

"The girls sure miss you, mom."

"How are the girls?" she asks.

"Fine, fine, Marie."

It's like some strange luxury, an exotic twist, that "Marie." She's always been Mrs. Gartens in the house. But the mention of her girls excites her.

"They're afraid to see their mama, aren't they?"

"No, no. It's midterm week. And Cissy has the flu."

"It's a lie! You told the girls I'd run after them with a butcher knife."

"Marie, I wouldn't tell them that . . ."

She starts to punch, to tear at his clothes, and Mr. Gartens has to flee. We say nothing about the man. If we defended Gartens, she'd scratch her own eyes.

"They're daddy's little dears," she says, and we nod to her. The turmoil in her head can't be soothed by curtains and ping-pong balls. She goes back to knitting scarves for her brood of girls.

Other guests arrive. A woman for Fairbanks. She pretends to be his niece. Are the niceties for us, or the people at the head cottage? Would they chuck her out if she wrote "mistress" on the Grange's little green card? She's Flora, and she's lots of fun. She wears two gold rings and she likes to be bounced on Fairbanks' knee. So what if he writes out a check for Flora at the end of her visit? He can write all the checks he wants. He's still the president of his company.

Me and Tolkerson don't have guests. The wiz won't see any of the old colleagues who condemned his theories. Why should he sit with his tormentors, those "noncatastrophists"? He'd rather scribble on a ping-pong ball.

"Charyn," Fairbanks says. "I'd love to meet your brother."

"Ah," I lie. "Harvey can't come. Cops are on the street. They don't get passes to Louisiana."

I haven't told my brother where I am. My mom and dad would cry if they knew I was at Bartleby House. They'd blame themselves. The Charyns had turned their son into a lunatic. Fannie would run to Louisiana with her failing eyes and rent a cottage at the bottom of the hill. She'd send Sam over with some cookies, so her son won't starve, and harangue the doctors for my release.

I write them once a month, without giving a return address. "Mom, did you ever hear of the Louisiana Purchase? I'm doing research on it for this encyclopedia called *Cromwell's*. I have to stick around the upper provinces of the state. Love, Jerome."

Sly is what I am. Catfish sly. Writing letters from a monkey-house.

2.

"CHARYN, your brother is here."

Philpott woke me out of a crazy sleep. I'd dreamt of a huckle-berry bush. Growing inside the cottage. The berries weren't topnotch. They were bitter, more gray than blue. They looked like the tits on the underbelly of a dog.

I put on my Bartleby pants, the dungarees I like to wear on this Louisiana hill. "Harvey?"

I hop downstairs.

It's a false alarm. The leader only wanted to get me out of bed. There's some rascal in our main hall. He doesn't have Harvey's pecs. My brother was nearly Mr. New York. Philpott brought an impostor to the house. He has a moustache and the beginnings of a bald spot.

"Jeromey," he says. "We were worried about you."

"Hey kid, fly a kite, will you? Go away . . . Philpott, you fucker, did you give him my name?"

The other Bartlebys have come into the hall. They smell this pretended brother of mine. I plead with Fairbanks. He's heard of Harvey. He knows.

"Chicken feathers," I scream. "That's not him."

I roll around on the floor. "Get him out of here . . ."

Our leader whispers to the kid. And then the impostor goes. I crawl out of the cottage, dumb and vicious, like a four-legged beast. "Marvin, wait for me . . ."

He's halfway down the hill. Still crawling, I catch up with him. "How did you find out I was here?"

"A man came. He told mom."

"Does he have a lot of flesh on his ears?"

"I don't think so. He says you work for him and you got sick."

"That's uncle Bob. Look, tell mom I'm okay. They're good

to me on this hill . . . hey Marvin, are you lifting weights?"

"No, I'm a senior at New York Polytech."

I get up off the ground. "You finished junior high?"

He looks at me, pitying the warp of time in my head. "That was seven years ago."

"Marvin, do you need some money?" I search my pockets for a crumpled dollar bill. The pockets hang out like the tongues of dead calves.

He helps me get my pockets back inside my pants. I'm afraid to hug him, this brother Marvin that I lost somewhere.

I return to the Bartlebys.

They can read my panic. We're all brothers and sisters up here. Mrs. Gartens puts her needles away. The leader gets rid of his new sunhat. Fairbanks catches me as I begin to fall. I've got a fever. I'm burning up. They bring me a jug of lemonade. The sugar's supposed to normalize my temperature and get rid of vertigo. "Two brothers," I say. "I have two."

They tell me *shush,* be quiet, but I babble out my song of twenty-two years ago. I'm eight, you see, and Harvey's eleven. There's no fucking idyll between us. We're the Charyns, and we're tough. We fight, and Harvey lets me win. He teases me, and I throw a seltzer bottle at him, chase him up a city tree.

Then something happens. My mother has a swollen belly: Marvin comes riding out. He has such tiny fingers, and he's red all over, bloody red. My mother sends me and Harvey to summer camp so we won't interfere with her red baby. Harvey's among new friends. He doesn't want to suffer much of me. I watch him while he's rowing on the lake. There were girls with Harvey. He wore a strange shirt that showed his biceps off, and he had oil on his hair. I want my brother back. I pick a fight with him. He doesn't run away. I've provoked him in front of his friends. He socks me twice in the face. It wasn't any swollen lip that tore shrieks through my head. Harvey could have murdered me if it had been done with that usual play of brother to brother. He was declaring something with those two blows: I should expect no comfort from him.

He became a benefactor to that little red baby, and I lost all my rights. I couldn't hurl seltzer bottles, or chase Harvey up a tree. If I have amnesia, so what? Why shouldn't I want to be the baby in the house?

"Charyn, you're burning up . . . drink more lemonade."

The fever dies. My face begins to cool. "I had a guest," I say. "My brother Marvin. He took a Greyhound from the Bronx."

Mrs. Gartens picks up her knitting needles. The leader puts on his sunhat. But Fairbanks is still interested in the Charyns.

"When will your brother Harvey come to see us, old boy?"

"Fairbanks, don't you ever listen? Harvey's a cop. The city wouldn't let him on a Greyhound bus. They need him in the street."

He wipes my forehead with a kitchen towel and waits with me while I drink another glass of lemonade.

FOURTEEN

The Bartleby Cure

I.

Two brothers now. Did I have three? How many more lay on the side? Bundles and bundles of red babies screaming to be let loose. Jeromey, the ugly older brother, the witch of Shuttleford Grange. I would hide them as fast as my mother and father could procreate. Put a spell on these brothers, so they're short of calves and thighs. Keep them as six-year-olds. Then I could be the giant of the house.

Mrs. Gartens walks naked in her room. She has the scars of many births on her belly: they look like pieces of silver, silver dents in her skin. I admire the dents, stare at her lovely bottom. But it doesn't lead to love bites. Mrs. Gartens and I don't know how to call upon the passion that would take me into her room and have me shut the door. I try.

"Marie," I say. It's no good. She can rave at her husband, but she can't put her arms around me. I love the path of silver on her skin. Away from this cottage, I'd be licking every stop along those silver lines.

I'm wanted up at the head cottage. It's not a joke. The cottage asked for me. *The Charyn boy.* My first interview at the Grange. A progress report. Maybe they're checking up on the leader, who knows?

I wear my herringbone vest, the last remnant of my big money days.

All the doctors are Navy men. You can't fool an old cadet. I can tell a captain from a lieutenant commander. The hill is crawling with them. A hundred lieutenant commanders in the wilderness. And I didn't see one uniform until today.

The chief interviewer offers me tobacco and a hickory pipe. I grab the pipe. I smoke with them. The tobacco tastes like fish.

They have me in their manila folders, from my days in the Bronx, through Columbia College, and my seven months in the madhouse with the Ripper of Lake Charles.

I don't like their warm-up question.

"Who's the president of the United States?"

Are they fiddling with me? I'll fiddle back.

"You mean that fella with the big ears? The tall guy. Lyndon Baines Johnson."

They scribble in their folders.

"Who's the governor of Louisiana, Mr. Charyn?"

I haven't had time for governors, studying Paul Morphy and getting locked up. I throw them bits of knowledge out of Bob's encyclopedia. "Louisiana's full of bayous, sirs. They're streams that don't go anywhere. They just stop dead. The state flag has a mama pelican in it that feeds her three young pelicans, Harvey, Marvin, and Jerome."

"Mr. Charyn, what the hell is the matter with you?"

My bones begin to shake. You think it's so easy? Sitting in a room with lieutenant commanders, sucking on a stinky pipe?

"Who's the person you most admire?"

"Ashley Wilkes."

The officers shrug. Did they expect me to say John Paul Jones or Admiral Nimitz? *Ashley Wilkes.* He was one of us, a Bartleby. He fell into a long, long freeze after the South collapsed.

The chief interviewer stares at me. "An effeminate character in a woman's novel? . . . why Ashley Wilkes?"

Because he belonged in Crotona Park, I wanted to tell them. Because he loved Scarlett and couldn't have her. Because he lost out to Rhett Butler's moustache. What did these commanders know? They had their uniforms, but did they ever walk on yellow mud?

They drop Ashley Wilkes.

"Tell us about your father, Mr. Charyn. He made fur animals for a living."

Bastards, how did they learn about the teddy bears?

"Well, he tried . . . you see, the bears turned yellow. But my father couldn't abandon them. They were like America to him."

"How's that?"

"He was left behind . . . in Poland, sirs. He couldn't get on the immigrant boat with his mom and dad . . . gave him a fiddle. The pinkeye kid. He played and played until the pinkeye went to bed . . ."

Am I dreaming? There *was* a fiddle in my father's past. Only the story didn't come from him. It was my mother who told me about his eye disease. But where's the fiddle? I never saw it.

"Why are you whimpering, son? We won't harm you."

The doctors let me up from the table. I can keep the hickory pipe. I walk down from the cottage, showing them the slump of my back.

The Bartlebys hold my arms when I try to stuff the pipe into our leader's mouth. I've made a brilliant recovery from my crying fit in front of the lieutenant commanders. I'm fierce as those water gods of mine slapping in yellow mud.

"Philpott, we have things to discuss. Outside."

The leader isn't afraid. He walks out with me.

"Tell me what's going on, or I'll jump into the next cottage and murder everybody. Why are we plagued with officers all of a sudden? This is no country asylum. Who are you, Philpott, and what is this place?"

"It's a satellite," he said. "A substation of Bayou L'Outre Naval Hospital."

"And we're your guinea pigs."

"No, the Grange has more independence than that."

"Then why did they take me out of bedlam and bring me here?"

"You got lucky, that's all. Charyn, what are you bitching about? Has anybody whipped you, boy? You get food and fresh air. And you're not chained to the cottage wall."

"Who are you, Philpott?"

"I'm a medic at Bayou L'Outre, assigned to the Grange."

"Why's your hospital so interested in us?"

"Nam," Philpott said. "The war in Nam."

"We're not soldiers and sailors."

"You're just as good . . . the Marines are zombieing out in the jungles."

"Yeah," I said. "We're a little study farm for the Navy. A pilot project. Well, I'm getting out."

I didn't like Philpott's smile. "You got legs. Carry yourself. You can run over to Arkansas. It's only seventeen miles. Just follow the bayou. But you be quick. You're on loan from bedlam, Charyn. A ward of the state. Louisiana owns your hide. It might chase after you. People don't like crazy boys hopping around. You could get a pitchfork in your behind."

I go indoors to rally the Bartlebys against Philpott and the Grange. "This isn't a monkeyhouse in the woods, it's a combat zone. They're experimenting with us, fucking with our heads . . . Tolkerson, you're the scientist. You know their gimmickry. Fairbanks, Mrs. Gartens, listen . . ."

I can't sway my little brothers and my little sister Marie. They won't be disloyal to the leader.

"Come on, get dressed, we have to scram."

Not the Bartlebys. They'll sit tight until the Marines move

into our cottage and practice jungle tricks on us. I pack my gear: sandpaper racket, vest, and hickory pipe. I'll take my luck out on the bayou. Arkansas, here comes your favorite son. Only what's that scratchy music? Scrape, scrape, scrape. Louder than Lillian's monster harp. Like fingernails on a window screen. What have those lieutenant commanders done to me? I'm listening to my father play, and I never saw his fiddle in my life. That toy bow cuts across the fiddle strings. My father scrapes and scrapes.

The Bartlebys catch me on the stairs. "Look, his face is frozen." They summon that rat bastard, Philpott himself. But the leader doesn't hurt me. He wraps me in blankets and sends me hiking through the cottage.

"My father's trying to kill me," I shout. "Philpott, he's scratching this terrible music in my ear."

"Shush," the leader says. "It's nothing. You're having an anxiety attack."

2.

THE leader gives me a coloring book and a pack of crayons. I draw whiskers on the cartoon figures in the book.

"Philpott, what happened? I told a story about my father for the doctors. And the story started to scratch."

"Shush," he says. *"Draw."*

I do Morphy's knights and rooks in the margin. The crayons snap on me, and I have to mend my "green" and "blue" with Band-Aids from the medicine chest. I draw my friend Sid. What the hell? I give him an eye disease. Let the Ripper have conjunctivitis in my coloring book.

My fingers are smeared with crayon wax. I'm the Crayola boy of Bayou L'Outre. The big baby from the Bronx. The lieutenant commanders have gone down off the hill. It's safe to leave the cottage. I shuffle over to the canteen with crayons in my pocket.

"Hello. How are you? I'm Mrs. Brindle. Fannie Brindle."

Fannie's my mother's name. I look up. This Fannie is one of the volunteers who operate the canteen. They arrive with bags of quarters and dimes, say hello, and sell us things: apples, lollipops, and dental floss. But Mrs. Brindle isn't like the other rich matrons who come here, bored, hysterical wives with a bit of the Bartleby in them. Fannie is trim and beautiful, younger than this graying thirty-one-year-old with gaunt cheeks and wax on his fingers.

I don't know how to speak to her. She's from the "outlands," where people ride in cars, shop, go to dinner, and make love, and I'm from the half-dead.

"Fannie's a good name," I sputter.

She laughs. "You're kind to say that. My husband keeps wanting me to change it. He swears that no one under a hundred is called Fannie any more."

"That might be true in Louisiana, Mrs. Brindle, but Fannies are popular in the Bronx. My mother's a 'Fannie,' and I have three girl cousins that are 'Fannies' too."

"That's nice," she said. "What's your name?"

"I'm Jerome . . ."

"My husband's Maynard," she said. "He buys and sells houses, but he has a passion for ducks."

A duck hunter? Maynard shoots at ducks? I'm glad the Ripper wasn't around, or he might have had another of his "hard nights," gutting duck hunters along the bayou, after hearing the voice of God.

I bought apples from Fannie. I hate apples, but it was an excuse to hang around the canteen. I had the urge to undress the good Mrs. Brindle in front of those other volunteers. The catfish put a swelling on me. I was a Bartleby with a new crayon in his pocket.

Mrs. Brindle offered to take Jerome on a ride around the Grange in her '67 Dodge. I didn't protest. It was an ordinary practice. The head cottage approved of these "small picnics" with a volunteer.

We picnicked in and out of Mrs. Brindle's car. "Why are you shivering?" she asked.

Shiver? It was the beating of a wild heart. It had nothing to do with the months and months I'd been without a woman. The biting we did in the car and on the brown bayou grass was personal to Fannie and me. It eclipsed Maynard and his ducks, and my desire to disappear from that odd prison on the hill. You think I couldn't have gotten Fannie to drive me into Arkansas? But how would we have maintained our picnics after that?

"You're like a gypsy," she said. "Your eyebrows are so dark."

"But my sideburns went gray on that hill up there."

"They'll let you out, Jerome. You'll see."

"How? I'm a prisoner of war."

"Don't talk silly," she said.

Fannie began to volunteer herself six and seven days a week. I was always at the apple bin, or close to her Dodge, when she could escape from her chores of selling lollipops and counting up the silver. I'd abandoned my coloring book, and it irritated the leader.

"I told you to draw!"

"It's over, Philpott. I haven't heard my father's violin in weeks."

"Listen, Charyn, that kind of music can always come back. You've been neglecting us for the lady with the Dodge."

"Philpott, shut your mouth."

"You won't say that the next time I have to cover you with blankets and march you around. Mrs. Brindle has a husband out there. Watch your step. And you could take your meals with us once in a while. I hope Fannie's apples give you the shits."

Why should the leader care who I ate with? The hell with him and his spying tongue. I had my canteen wife. We picnicked whenever we could. We would roll on that brown grass, at the edge of the bayou, with the sun throwing patterns on our bodies through the leaves. I was Jerome the tattooed warrior, and Fannie was my sunburnt squaw. She had a daughter at home, a girl of three. Jessica Brindle.

"Fannie, why don't you bring her? I'd love to see your little girl."

"Maynard doesn't like Jessie to visit the canteen."

"Tough on Maynard."

So Fannie brought the little toddler, cute as pie, with blonde curls and chubby hands. Baby Jess. She babbled in her Louisiana tongue. Called me "unca Romey," because she couldn't pronounce the J at the head of Jerome.

We were in the woods, and I posed as an Indian chief for baby Jess, knotting my shirt into a papoose, and carrying her inside the knots. The warrior with the little girl on his back. Her fingers clutched my hair, and I could smell the lovely creases in her arms and legs.

"God," Fannie said, "she'll grow up and want to marry you."

"What's wrong with that?"

"I'll drown the both of you." Fannie laughed at her own idea.

I almost had a fainting spell. It wasn't the dread of Sam's violin that got to me (I'd have withstood my father's music). It was the pleasure I had with those two women. Blonde and sweet to the eye. Crazy how things grope at you. I wished I had a child. I was jealous of Maynard. I began to plot like a bandit inside my skull. Ah, when I completed the Bartleby cure, I'd grab his wife and baby Jess. I'd compensate Maynard, of course, get him a few toy ducks. He'd have pets to keep him company. I wouldn't want to leave Maynard alone in the house.

I'll make myself a family. Blonde creatures to go with the gray in my hair.

We strolled through the woods, Fannie, Jerome, and the papoose child. I wept, hiding the tears with a handkerchief and pretending the big daddy whale had to blow his nose. What more could a Bronx imbecile ask from this crazy world?

"Fannie, can you and Jess spend the night . . . at Bartleby House? Come on, tell Maynard you had to go fishing . . ."

"He'll fish for my head."

She had to take the child home. Jess tried to hold on to her papoose. "Unca Romey, unca Romey."

"Jessica," Fannie muttered, "you be good now. Give uncle Romey back his shirt."

I squeezed my fist into a ball. It was tough to part with a family you'd just acquired.

We left the woods and Fannie drove me to the bottom of the hill. Jessica peeked out of the Dodge. "Bye-bye, unca Romey."

I waved to that little girl. They disappeared, and I went up towards the cottage. Funny how you can sniff strangers in the grass. A bunch of guys were standing right under the chimney. They didn't belong to the Grange. They had hunters' hats, and the cutest shotguns you ever saw, with a silver design on the barrel that must have been made special for the ducks. *Maynard Brindle and his men.* I got on my belly and slithered into the bushes behind Bartleby House. Nam, our leader said. I'd give them plenty of Nam. A catfish can breathe in the jungle and wait out all the Maynards in the world. They must have been eager to land their Jerome. The hunters stalked the cottage for an hour. Then they shook their duck guns and went down the hill.

I climbed into the cottage through a window at the back. The Bartlebys were pale as Jesus. I'd neglected them, it's true, but they hadn't grown bitter towards me. "Jerome," the leader said. "Those duck guys would like to kill you. One of 'em spotted you in the woods. Didn't I tell you not to go around rogering other people's wives? They scared Mrs. Gartens half to death, and shoved poor Fairbanks into the wall. We didn't say a word about you and Fannie Brindle."

"I'm sorry . . . I am. I thought we're a Navy satellite. Does the head cottage allow hunters on its lawn?"

The leader gave me a look that only a Bartleby could understand: I was a lost creature who should have stuck to his crayons.

"This is Louisiana. You get between a man and his wife, and that's the beginning of a shotgun party. The Navy can't interfere."

The Bartlebys had all my belongings bundled up. Mrs. Gartens was sniffling. Tolkerson had a twitch in his right eye.

"I have to warn Fannie," I said. It was futile. I didn't know where Fannie lived.

Philpott seized me by my pants. "Forget that Fannie," he said. "And stay off the roads. You follow the bayou, and you keep your head down."

"Yeah," I said, "it's only seventeen miles to Arkansas."

"Seventeen miles is better than duckshot in your liver."

The Bartlebys gave up whatever cash they had on hand, and Fairbanks wrote me a personal check for two hundred dollars. Where can you cash a check on the bayou?

They hugged me, my little brothers and my sister Marie, with the silver dents in her skin that I would never touch.

I started to bawl. "Philpott, I should have listened to you. Where's my coloring book?"

"Get out," the leader said, and he was crying, just like me. Violin? Teddy bears? Marvin's moustache? The Bartlebys were as much of a family as I'd ever have . . . if I couldn't have baby Jess. Oh, the hunters didn't worry me. I'd been walking streams all my life. Maynard Brindle wouldn't catch this boy. The frogs would sound my way to Arkansas. I lurched into the woods with *Cromwell's* under my arm.

FIFTEEN

The Opera Singer's Wife

I.

SEVENTEEN miles.

It was a push, an infant's hike, for a kid that grew up on the Bronx River and was washed in yellow mud. I kept to the bayou's north wall. Were there serpents and green-nosed alligators about? I'd laugh at them from the edge of the bayou. Or read to them out of uncle Bob's encyclopedia, describe the fall of the Confederacy, the ruin of "that Grand Old Army in Gray," until the serpents and alligators wept.

But I stumbled into a goddamn duck blind. I was bush-whacked by Maynard and his men. They wore whistles at their throats, and they climbed on top of me. I had a shotgun in every ear. I could taste the silver on the barrels.

"Don't you move, sonny boy."

A tall man came out of the scrub. He didn't wear boots like the others. He'd searched the bayou in plain old moccasins. He could have been a young Gary Cooper if it wasn't for his mean grin. The hunters climbed on me some more and hopped around that mean man.

"Maynard, we caught the dum-dum!"

Maynard Brindle hunkered down in his moccasins. I still had

shotguns in my ears. "I could blow your head into the water. They wouldn't miss you, lover boy. How did it feel, lyin' in the bushes with mah wife?"

Could I explain to Maynard that I was a prisoner of war, and Fannie gave me sustenance.

"You have a mouth," Maynard said. "Tell me, how did it feel?"

I wanted to tell Maynard about the sun on our bodies, the tattoos it put on me, but then that scratching started up. I had a duck gun on both sides of my face, and a fiddle in my head. The scratching was worse than any death Maynard could propose. I cried for him to shoot my head off. I shuddered in the bayou grass.

"Maynard, the dum-dum's having a fit."

The hunters cringed at the sight of me. But Maynard didn't back off. A part of his meanness went away. "What's wrong with you?"

"My father," I said. "He's trying to kill me again . . . I'm all right for a while, and then he plays this fiddle in my ear. It goes scratch, scratch, and I'd like to die . . ."

Maynard pushed those shotguns off my face and picked me out of the grass. He didn't send me back to the Grange. He wanted me as far as I could get from Fannie and her apple bin. He drove me around with the hunters in his car, put me on a bus, and paid my fare to New York.

"Thank you, Maynard."

"Don't thank me, you son of a bitch. I hope that fiddle drops you into hell."

2.

I didn't stay put on Manhattan Island. I went from rooming house to rooming house. I was like some animal who'd been thrown off the bayou, and was restless and crazed, and unwilling to live in one spot. I chewed crackers and took my coffee on the sly, huddled in the darkest region of a downtown luncheonette. I'd think of Fannie and baby Jess. I wrote to Bartleby House. But I had to be careful and disguise my voice. Louisiana could grab me right off the street. *Dear Bartleby House. This is an old friend, the fiddler's boy. Remember him? How is the young married lady from the canteen?* (I didn't dare mention Fannie by name.)

Philpott never bothered to answer his "old friend." But I did get a note from Mrs. Gartens. Was it a forgery? Who can tell? "Mr. Charyn, people in military suits have been looking for the fiddler's boy. The leader says it would be smart for the fiddler to stay out of touch. I can't forward your inquiry to Mrs. Brindle. Mrs. Brindle isn't here. She gave up her canteen duties the day after you left."

The news was easy to follow. I was a nonperson in the eyes of the Grange, a missing convict.

I walked at a faster clip. I changed rooming houses again, switched from coffee to tea. No one could recognize my habits now. A wirehaired terrier bit through my stocking on East Eleventh Street. "Little bastard, I'll feed you to the crocodiles."

A woman with a round, pretty face tugged at the dog's leash. I stared at the hole in my stocking. "I'm awfully sorry," she said. She had a fur coat with a high collar. The outline of that coat on her chest didn't fool me. "Lillian?" I could smell the golden boobs.

Lillian blinked. Had the bayou coarsened my features that much? She failed to recognize her old geometry tutor.

"Music and Art, Lilly . . . it's Jerome."

"You're so gray," she said. "And gaunt. What happened to your biceps?"

"I lost them in the woods."

The terrier was at my stocking again.

"Alyosha, get away from there . . . Jerome, why didn't you keep in touch?"

"Hard times, Lilly. I had a fight in a grocery store, and the judge gave me murderers and a few geldings to play with."

"You were in jail?"

"Sort of. You can call it that."

Lilly liked the idea. It was the second time she'd had a convict for a friend. Me and Irwin Polatchek. I started to brag.

"I'm on the wanted list. Louisiana is looking for me . . ."

"Louisiana?" she said, aroused by the mystery of it. Her eyes were getting bigger and bigger.

"I escaped from a prison camp, swear to God. Lilly, what about you?"

She'd married her opera singer, Mario, and given up the harp. She wouldn't compete with her husband's career. Mario was the "gifted" one, she said. She taught music at a private high school. Her husband was on the road, touring with a Canadian company. Lillian invited me upstairs for a drink. She lived on University Place.

We locked Alyosha in the bathroom, and I couldn't help it, how can you be loyal to a canteen wife? We kissed like crazy on Lillian's couch. Alyosha whimpered and scratched on the door.

"Should I flush him down the toilet?"

"Murderer," she whispered, biting me under my neck.

We didn't spoil Lillian's sheets. I undressed her with my convict's paws and we made love inside the fur coat. Lilly had gone a little fat, but her nipples were as brown as ever. A goddamn Viking ship stood in the corner of the room. The ship had ears, pedals, and feet. It was Lilly's monster harp.

"Will you play 'Ramona' for me?"

She stepped out of that fur blanket with dimples in her back, took the monster between her legs, and plucked out "Ramona" for me without warming up. And I cried for those days of sanity, when I was catfish strong, and could bisect any angle with the needle on a pair of compasses.

"What happened to the Mississippi Hotel?"

Lilly frowned. "Prostitutes took over the place. We had to sell . . ."

Her mother was in Florida, and the "dowry" that the hotel brought in paid for Lilly's apartment and her husband's opera lessons. Lilly had to rush. She fed me a glass of white wine and put me out into the street.

"Jerome, I'll be free around midnight. Ring the bell."

So I rang her bell and stayed with Lilly. Alyosha crawled into bed with us. He snuggled between Lilly's tits and my hard shoulder.

When was the opera singer coming back? It wasn't like Lilly to abandon her harp for any husband who was eating oats in a Canadian opera company. And where was this high school she taught at? She didn't get out of bed to feed Alyosha until one in the afternoon.

Alyosha was her only pupil, I'm afraid. "Lil, don't you have to go somewhere to teach?"

"I'm on vacation," she said.

"For how long?"

"Long as I like."

Some job she had. It seemed closer to a furlough. What had happened to the boys and girls of Music and Art? I was AWOL from Louisiana, and Lilly was drifting with Alyosha on University Place.

Slowly, slowly, the news leaked out. A whisper at breakfast, a mumbled word while she bathed Alyosha and gave him a shampoo. That tough girl who rode on top of geometry and went to Philadelphia to become a virtuoso on the harp botched her first recital. She couldn't play in front of crowds. She would sit on stage with her harp, warm up, rock the monster until it purred, but her fingers would go dead soon as the concert was to begin. All those eyes on her, like predators stripping off her clothes, fondling a naked Lil. It didn't matter if she wrapped herself in scarfs. Everything would whirl away from her body. How could she perform Debussy with her underpants floating over her head? Her brassiere kissed the ceiling. Her scarfs bumped like clouds. Hysteria, her mother called it. Mama had her hypnotized. It didn't help. The scarfs bumped twice as fast.

I moved in with Lil. One night I came over with my encyclo-pedia and left it there. Then my sandpaper racket. My entire wardrobe was at Lil's. I kept worrying about Mario. Would the opera singer catch us in bed? But if Lilly didn't shiver, why should I? And don't forget Alyosha. Alyosha was Lilly's dog. Alyosha would save us from harm.

But I could still smell doom in the pockets of my Navy coat. And that doom arrived. I heard a lock jiggle while Lilly and me were snacking under the covers. It wasn't the grocery boy. It was somebody with a key to Lilly's front door. Who else but Mario?

The door opened, and a woman came in, clutching an enor-mous suitcase. It was Lillian's mother, Mrs. Feld. Ah, I could finish my sandwich. Lilly began to get into her blouse. Her fingers couldn't make the buttons hold. I watched her, with pita bread in my lap.

Mrs. Feld motioned to her daughter. "Who is he . . . a customer off the street?"

I spoke up for myself. "Customer? . . . I'm from Music and Art. You remember, the little rabbi, Jerome."

The lady took an umbrella out of her suitcase. "I'll give you a Jerome," she said, and she aimed the point of the umbrella at my eyes. Was she going to blind me for eating pita with Lilly in bed?

I ducked under the umbrella. "Lilly, please, get your mama away from me."

But Lilly was frozen into some posture I didn't understand.

Her jaw was agape. And her hands were over her chest, where the buttons had failed. Did she have to hide her own nipples from mama Feld?

I couldn't toy with the logic of buttons and breasts while an umbrella was scratching my cheek. She'd have both my eyes in a minute. "Hey," I said, slapping at the umbrella. "I'm innocent, I swear."

I had to gather up my clothes and other stuff, and still dodge that crazy woman. It wasn't an easy trick. I couldn't dress and hold my encyclopedia, without the umbrella flying into me. She jabbed me under the heart. The thrust of it raised me off the ground, and it looked like the umbrella would bore right through me and split my shoulder in half. But she pulled back on her sword, hoping to jab me again, in a better place.

"Bum," she said. "I know you. You call yourself Jerome, or Clark Gable . . . you ruin a girl's marriage, and you go on to your next victim. Just like a spider. Well, we don't allow spiders in here . . ."

What could I do? Alyosha sided with the umbrella lady. He tore into my cuffs, and I had two attackers on my tail. "Alyosha, Alyosha, who fed you and combed your hair?"

Smart dog, that Alyosha, he recognized where the power lay. It wasn't with Lilly or me. He worked in tandem with Mrs. Feld. He barked and chewed, and she turned the umbrella into a bludgeon. She whacked and whacked. "Ladykiller, huh? You think it's fun to break up a man and his wife? Spider, you killed my Lilly's career . . ."

She whacked me through the door, pulled Alyosha inside, and cut me out of Lillian's life. It was a lesson for me. Catfish boys can't go home again. Lillian was the Bronx. She was "Ramona" and geometry. She was Irwin Polatchek. She was Music and Art.

I moved into the Mississippi Hotel. Why not? Lilly had sold out. It wasn't in her mother's hands any more. It had a different clientele. Widowers and winos, whores and out-patients from Bellevue. Did the whores scream and throw their garbage out the windows? They were friendly to me. I wondered if any of them had worked on Albany Street, in New Brunswick, where the Charyns had drudged for Fritzie King. But that was in the old days of the Korean War. These whores were a gentler lot. They didn't have razors in their garter belts, and there weren't many soldiers around that they could lure into their rooms. So they laughed and screamed, and in their idleness the whores played chess. Morphy's game had come to the Mississippi Hotel.

SIXTEEN

Little Paul

I.

THE first rule I learned at the Mississippi was that whores will cheat at chess. They pocketed rooks and kings in their skirts with utter indifference to the affairs of a game. They wouldn't open lines of attack, or protect a vulnerable piece. They just liked to steal. I couldn't play with them. I would think of Morphy, and get heartsick over the peculiar patterns that the whores had arranged. The little king would have had nightmares looking for a combination against these girls. Paul was the Southern aristocrat, and the girls were something else. Like the armies of the North, they stole whatever was in sight.

I turned to ping-pong.

The Riverside Table Tennis Club took me in. The club was under the street, in the windowless basement of a movie house near the Mississippi Hotel. You walked down a flight of stairs, passed through a green door with scars in the wood, and entered a long, dirty room. There was a corridor on the left side, a gallery with camp chairs, protected by a rail, for ping-pong lunatics, housewives, and hoboes coming out of the rain.

The club was partial to strangers. You couldn't fall down and die under one of the tables without being noticed. Ping-pong lunatics had a curious camaraderie: no one felt stranded inside the club's green door.

Its owner, Marty Reisman, was once the best ping-pong player in the world. Reisman had a hard-rubber bat. Seeing him chop at the ball, I was embarrassed to use sandpaper from the Bronx. So I taught myself to play with rubber pimples. I chopped, I smashed with my elbow held high, I developed terrific sidespin, and began to haunt the club. From two in the afternoon, when Reisman's opened, until midnight, I was under Broadway, listening to the bounce of ping-pong balls.

I played Hungarians who were prominent in the ping-pong circles of Eastern Europe up to the Second World War, and I beat them all, old men in undershirts, with medallions on their chests. I destroyed housewives from West End Avenue, who brought their children and their dogs into Reisman's basement, and abandoned them for endless games of ping-pong. But I got unlucky in my third week at the club. I lost to a ten-year-old boy. His bat was much thicker than mine, and multi-layered, like a fat sandwich that could suck in the ball and fling it back at you. My slams meant nothing; my sidespin was feeble against the soft flesh of the sandwich bat.

I growled at the boy. "What the hell is that?"

"Sponge," he said.

"Where can you buy it?"

"Paragon's." Then he looked at me. "Ask for a Butterfly." I ran down to Paragon Sporting Goods on Eighteenth Street, and got my Butterfly bat, paying sixteen dollars to the clerk. Sixteen dollars for two pieces of sponge on a wooden board, and a handle painted black.

It took weeks to educate my hand and eye to the properties of sponge. I couldn't control the Butterfly; the ball sank in, then spun off the table. The Butterfly had its own pull. It was a weapon with idiosyncratic ways; either you adjusted to them, or you returned to rubber pimples.

I fell in with a gang of "serious" players: a history professor who grunted at you from his end of the table; a shirt manufacturer who arrived at Ninety-sixth Street in a Lincoln Continental and put on his sweat pants among the dead beetles in Reisman's changing room; a junkie who had an iron grip at Reisman's tables and shivered soon as he walked out of the club; and a black postman who had to wear a truss whenever he played.

We allowed nothing to intrude upon our lives at Reisman's. The junkie might have broken into half the newspaper shacks on upper Broadway scrounging for dollars, but he wouldn't have borrowed a dime from any of us. We didn't care if the shirt king was Paul Newman's own haberdasher, or if he had lunch with Norman Mailer. We never bandied stories about occupations, habits, and interests away from Ninety-sixth Street. We talked ping-pong. Did the Butterfly handle rattle too much? Where could we get the best price on a gross of Nittaku balls?

We would have shrugged our shoulders at regular tennis. It was much too slow for us. Our eyes couldn't have tolerated the oafish dimensions of a tennis court. We needed a nine by five table, a tight green net, and a pale ball that could squash under our heels, at Marty Reisman's.

2.

I ran out of money, and I had to ask the scalawags at my hotel, those winos and graduates of Bellevue, how to fish for a job. *Diane & Co.,* they said. It was a kosher catering service.

Many of Diane's mules, dishwashers, and general drudges came from single-room hotels on the West Side. I joined the other sixteen or seventeen mules at the Mississippi who worked for Diane & Co. We were called the "rubber chicken boys," because we carried a thousand chicken wings and slabs of roast beef from one kosher affair to the next.

But my ping-pong suffered. Working for Diane, I couldn't keep regular hours at Reisman's tables. I missed practice sessions. I was a mongrel to the gang of "serious" players. It didn't matter to them that I would have starved without Diane & Co. I was a rotten character who allowed external affairs to get in the way of ping-pong. They "hit" among themselves, barring me from their tournaments. "Have to eat," I piped to the shirt king. "Can't be helped . . ."

The shirt king was disgusted with this mention of my private life. He wiped his bat with a paper towel. "Charyn, did you hear me cry about the death of button-down collars? I lost a whole line of shirts. You're not my accountant, so why should I sob to you? Do us a favor. Disappear."

3.

I was ashamed to go home to my mom and dad, or show myself to my natural brothers, Marvin and Harvey. I was a single-room-occupant who went from his job with Diane, throwing rubber chickens around, to a cellar on Ninety-sixth Street, where I was ignored most of the time.

Only Reisman and a few of the runts would "hit" with me. But Reisman was out of town. I had to play with that ten-year-old boy who first told me about the Butterfly bat.

"Spot you seven points," I said. How could he win? His head barely came up over the table. You saw his dark eyes through the spaces in the net. He had no reach. He'd have to wiggle his elbow and lunge at the ball to get anywhere with me. I smiled with all the heartlessness of a ping-pong player who smells his advantage over you.

The runt *butterflied* me to death. His spinning balls shot past my cheek. He had a crazy cannonpower in his strokes. He hopped like a chicken to cover the territory on his side of the net. But the hopping paid off. He turned my edge of the table into a little neurasthenics ward. I was the mummy of Ninety-sixth Street.

"I'm Charyn. What's *your* name?"

"Paul."

The mummy shivered. I was back in New Orleans, I swear. Paul. Dark eyes and angelface.

"Does your mother play the harp?"

"No," he said. "Charyn, is there something wrong with you?"

"Did you ever have a judge in the family?"

Those eyes came up off the table like two burning cand-lewicks. "Mister, you have a mouse in your head."

No mouse. I was fine. You can't fool the catfish. *Leetle Paul.* This runt was the Paul Morphy of ping-pong. He'd come through Reisman's green door a year ago, all alone, sat in the gallery, and watched. He didn't skip a day. Those dark eyes sucking in the bouncy-bounce at seven different tables. He was much shorter then. He had to stand on a box to play. He had a beginner's bat, with a bald piece of sponge. He whipped it back and forth. No one bothered to teach him the strokes. A runt like that. He taught himself to chop. And now he had a murderer's field of vision. He would angle the ball with his Butterfly, a gift from Marty Reisman, and sock you into the ground.

He took a liking to Charyn, defending me from the scorn of the "serious" players. Reisman's was having a doubles tourna-ment, and my enemy, the shirt king, was made captain of it. He approached little Paul.

"Who's your partner, kiddo?"

"Charyn."

The shirt king hollered at him. "He's unreliable, and his backhand sucks. He cries about money all the time."

"Charyn's my partner," little Paul said.

The shirt king had to take me into the tournament, or lose little Paul. Nobody expected us to win. I would hamper the runt's game. I was slow of foot, they said. I'd block Paul's view, and keep bumping into him. Bullshit. We rode through that tournament like a pair of merciless sweethearts. The best teams in the house couldn't steal more than twelve or thirteen points from us.

Little Paul was shrewd. He didn't need an "ace" on his side. He was looking for a partner who could steady him, give him confidence, and not compete with his game. A catfish like me, a mudcrawler, who could sneak in front of a table and then sneak away.

My legs had grown strong from hours and hours of catering for Diane & Co. I wore a ribbon to work. Ribbons don't tell lies: it announced in blue and gray that the bearer of this stretch of silk was entitled to half a ping-pong championship. The ribbon gave me clout with fellow busboys and other lowlifes from Diane's. Ping-pong was a royal game to them. They'd all played ping-pong and chess.

But the ribbon didn't endear me to our manager, Harry Snell. Harry was the one who hired us. We were part of his "team." The largest banquets always went to Harry. He had us dancing like midshipmen, or Marines. Some of the kitchens we worked were bigger than a fort. We would slap down a ton of food—enough cole slaw and green peas to choke a family of giants—and then remove each trace of ourselves from the banquet hall. Harry could solve the logistics of any catered affair.

My ribbon made him see blood.

"Charyn, take it off. The customers will think you're a snot-nose with a ribbon like that. They have to digest their carrots and peas. They don't want to look at a busboy who's a ping-pong champ."

"I won that ribbon," I said. "It's mine."

"Charyn, stick it up your ass."

I could have walked out on Harry and gone to a different manager. Diane's didn't care if you hopped from one kitchen gang to the next. But who could say the other managers were better than Harry? I cursed him under my breath, *fatso, fucker, bum,* and took the ribbon off.

4.

I had my bat. I had my ping-pong shoes. Harry couldn't touch me and Paul. We were getting famous. Guys were coming from everywhere to challenge the West Side champs. They couldn't believe our game. "A kid," they said, "and a jerk-off with a lot of gray around his ears."

We let them have their fun. They giggled before they served. They touched shoulders and whispered strategies in each other's ear. Then we tore out their guts. I didn't have to coo at little Paul, tell him where to hit. He was master of the table. I leapt around his body, a fluttering ghost who lobbed the ball back at you, so the runt would have that extra moment to dig in on a pair of rockinghorse ankles and shove his elbow into your mouth.

Those guys couldn't win. The runt was too powerful, too adept. He had Morphy's genius in him, that rare ability to sunder you, split you in half, without putting a crease in his own dark eyes. He was an innocent. Murderers usually are. But what about his forebears? Not one Creole uncle in the ancestor bin? And where were his mom and dad? Nobody claimed him after our victories. He wiped his bat, zipped it into a plastic case, and walked out of Reisman's cellar.

Did he go to school? The runt wouldn't tell. He didn't have pets or preoccupations. He went down into Reisman's and played. Where were the marks of his boyhood? Old gray ears

was more of a child than the "leetle" one. Yet I worried about
the ambiguity of Paul, the lack of any guardians surrounding
him.

"Here, lemme buy you some candy or a Coke?"

"I'm not hungry," he said. "But don't starve yourself, Charyn. *You* eat the candy."

"I see food day and night . . . chicken wings. I like to fast
when I come to Marty's place."

"Well, I'm fasting too."

I stopped trying to pin a father onto Paul. Maybe he had no
use for moms and dads. But the "leetle" one wasn't so tough
as I thought. Two brothers showed up at Reisman's, and the
sight of them bit under Paul's heart. You couldn't mistake their
curly black hair and the brown ping-pong satchels of the Harvard-Cambridge club. Ephraim and Lewis, the Dunstan boys.
Ephraim was the American singles champ, and Lewis, his baby
brother, was number three in the country. They wore sweat-
bands around their wrists and tight yellow headbands. The
news of "Reisman's deadly doubles" must have got to Harvard
Square. The Dunstans had come down from Boston to play
Paul and me.

Ephraim and Lewis unzipped their red bats. Ours were
green. Paul stood far back in the cellar and mumbled to himself,
a pale little man with his Butterfly. He was all shriveled up. "I
can't hit Ephraim's loops. Nobody can."

"We'll piss on his loops," I said. "We'll make him swallow
the ball."

"Yeah, I do all the work. You move your ass, and that's it."

"Insult your partner, come on . . . I'll play the Dunstan boys
myself."

My war cry must have tugged at the kid. He went to the table
and put his dark eyes near the net. Green bat or red, we'd win,
Ephraim or not. The Dunstan boys couldn't keep up with Paul.
The runt took care of Ephraim's loops and other tricky shots,

and I did my usual lobs. They were the ones who banged and bumped, unable to hold down the rockinghorse. Catfish, bedlam, and a little boy beat the two brothers and their marvelous red bats. Some champions. They didn't even shake our hands. Disgruntled, with bitter teeth, they packed their gear, ignoring us. The great Dunstans from the Harvard-Cambridge club. Couldn't they have said to little Paul, at least, that his topspin wasn't bad for a ten-year-old? What would it have cost this Ephraim and his baby brother Lew? It wasn't a tournament match, it was a few lousy games in Reisman's cellar, among roaches, beetles, and black ants.

The Dunstans left, and I said to Paul, "Should I take you home?"

"What for?"

"It's dark outside."

"Charyn, I know where I live."

I wasn't being nosy. I wanted to celebrate with the runt, have a knish, or a glass of milk, something to hold that fever of the games inside of us. But he took his bat and disappeared.

Then, two days after we slugged Ephraim and Lewis, I was coming back to my hotel from a catering gig in Brooklyn Heights, and I saw the little one in a supermarket. Paul's head. It was stranded in a particular aisle. He wasn't alone. A big fat woman with red stuff on her face was with my ping-pong partner. He was holding her hand, pulling her across the aisle, as if she were a dray horse. Her cheeks wobbled, and the red paint she wore seemed to split apart and close again, like wounds on the side of her face. *Charyn, don't mix in.* I should have gone away from the window, left Paul with that painted witch, whoever she was. Only I couldn't.

I let them come out with their bag of groceries, the woman hugging the bag that was beginning to tear, while Paul led her over the street. I followed them.

I heard a strange squeal. It was Paul coaxing the witch to

move. *Sarah, Sarah.* The bag split, and the ketchup bottles exploded on the ground. Paul salvaged whatever he could, apples, cottage cheese, a bruised can, but the witch would have stayed there, scooping ketchup up with slivers of glass. *Sarah, Sarah.*

He brought her home. They lived in the cellar of a half-vacant brownstone on Ninety-first. Upstairs, by the roof, the windows were black holes in a dead house. You could still find curtains on the middle floors. But who knows what a curtain means? The rooms behind them might have been abandoned for years. Not the cellar though.

The stinks coming out of there were recent stinks. Mustard, ketchup, and sour milk. Paul's home. I ran to Ninety-sixth Street and cornered Marty Reisman. Marty was reluctant to gossip about any of his patrons, reveal their lives away from ping-pong. He was a good friend to us all.

"That runt's my partner. I have a right to know. Who's fat Sarah? A lost grandma, a crazy aunt, what?"

My bullying didn't get to Reisman. I could have ranted for another hour. He must have seen that desperate spittle in my mouth.

"She's his mother," he said.

"His mother? Marty, how's that? She looks over fifty."

"She is."

Paul was the child of her old age. Hadn't I gone to college? I knew my holy book. Sarah, the loyal wife of Abraham, barren for ninety years, and then she carries Isaac in her when she's a hundred and five. God, what those birth pangs must have been like! But it was *this* Sarah that I was worried about. She was a Portuguese seamstress who'd lived with her mother on Amsterdam Avenue. The seamstress fell in love at the age of forty-one. Some gigolo? Marty said no. He was a West Side optometrist, a widower, it seems. He ran away from Manhattan while Sarah was in her fifth month. The Portuguese mother looked at that belly on her forty-one-year-old girl and grew irate. She kicked Sarah out of the house. Sarah had the child and moved into that cellar on Ninety-first Street. So you see, Paul had a father somewhere, but he was like any posthumous child, born without a dad. Sarah raised him in that cellar. She was still in love. She couldn't concentrate on her sewing needles. The boy grew up in the dark with a mother who babbled about a missing optometrist. Paul became a thief. He would raid the supermarkets and the Latin grocery stores. Nobody could keep him in school. His grandmother tried to kidnap him from the cellar and bring him to Amsterdam Avenue, where he could grow up in the sunlight, without wicked Sarah, but the little one cackled in his grandmother's face. "I have a mama. I don't need you."

Then he discovered Reisman's. He was drifting through the neighborhood, with yams under his shirt, stolen from a nearby market, and he wobbled downstairs to Reisman's door, yams dropping out of his shirt. He thrived in Marty's cellar. It was just like home to him, the spidery feel of being underground. He learned to play with a bat he lifted from a hobby shop. He watched with those dark eyes and picked up every stroke, forehand, backhand, drives and chops. Then Reisman gave him the Butterfly. He was devoted to it, like any of the ping-pong lunatics in Reisman's cellar. But the runt had an edge over us. He replaced the dad who ran away from Sarah with a sandwich bat. He became his own father on Reisman's seven tables. He wasn't a ten-year-old with a toy in his hand. He was Paul the murderer, who chopped at you with his Butterfly. It's no wonder Ephraim and Lewis fled from us. They'd never encountered such furious grit.

5.

"PAUL, should we go to the zoo on Sunday . . . feed the pelicans and the alligators?"

"What zoo? Marty doesn't close on Sunday. The tables are here. Who wants to look at pelican shit? Charyn, we have to practice."

"Practice, he says! We wiped out the Dunstan boys. We turned Ephraim into a crybaby. He'll never leave Boston again."

"He doesn't have to. That's where the Nationals are. I wrote to Boston. I told Boston to watch out. We're competing in the men's doubles this year."

"I can't. Let the doubles come down to New York."

Those dark eyes took me in. "A tournament doesn't travel."

"Then screw the Nationals. Anybody who wants to play us can knock on Reisman's door."

"Knock on your head, Charyn. I'm going to Boston."

How could I go with the kid? It would finish me at Diane's. Busboys were on call seven days a week. None of the managers would tolerate a busboy who took overnight trips. But it was more than that. I could have quit Diane's and catered for somebody else. I still couldn't go to Boston. I was a runaway from Bartleby House. You think I wanted my picture in all the newspapers after we won the Nationals and stepped on Boston's face? I'd be a sucker to advertise myself, and give Louisiana a chance to grab at me. *Jerome Charyn and Kindergarten Dropout Take Men's Doubles from Harvard-Cambridge's Best.*

Paul went up with Meyerwitz, the shirt king. But Meyerwitz didn't have the temperament to play around Paul. He was bearish at the table. He wouldn't lob for the runt. He hacked at the enemy with his Butterfly. The "leetle" one had to come out from behind the shirt king's body to have a peek at the ball.

Boston ate them up. Paul never got to see the Dunstans' red
bats. Ephraim destroyed the singles competition and then entered the doubles with Lew. He waited for the runt to get past
the preliminaries. But the runt didn't make it. Paul and the shirt
king died in the second round, losing to a pair of grocery clerks.

Reisman's came down on Catfish Jerome. I'd betrayed the
club by not accompanying little Paul. Reisman himself didn't
utter a word against me. But how could I "hit" with him when
there was a mood of blackness on every face? Paul couldn't
stand the smell of me.

"What's a tournament? We can still cream the Dunstans if
they come to us . . . let's play."

"Play with your dingdong," Paul said. He turned his back on
the monster and took his warm-ups with Meyerwitz the king.

SEVENTEEN

Diane & Co.

I.

AH, the kosher catering service. We had to have a rabbi at every affair to bless the food and kosherize the place. The rabbis who worked for Diane's had their own union and employment agency. The Rabbis' Local it was called. A rabbi couldn't get on the "rubber chicken circuit" without paying his dues. The Local would send this guy Fish to our gang. Martin Fish was Harry's man. Fish belonged to us.

He wasn't a rabbi who looked the other way. You couldn't smear him with a hundred dollars to avoid the bother of inspecting knives, forks, and spoons at the Algonquin and the Essex, or wherever our kosher party happened to be. Fish was a vast bulldog of a man. He would march into the kitchen of the best hotel with a blowtorch and a barrel of rain water and push everyone aside. The blowtorch was to get rid of grease.

He'd put on his goggles and shoot flames across a hotel kitchen until Fish decided it was clean. Then he'd wash the silverware in his barrel of water. The host and hostess at a party would consider him a pain in the ass. They always tried to get him drunk. He drank their schnapps and stuck to his barrel and his salting of the kitchen shelves. He could slow a party down by three-quarters of a hour. But Harry insisted on Fish. "I don't want some gink of a rabbi who'll take his shekels and go home. Fish won't cheapen your affair."

He was like another boss. "Charyn, you took those knives from the unkosher drawer. Put them back."

He'd split my head if I argued with him, or shoot fire in my face. I learned to tread softly around this Fish. "Yes, rabbi . . . no, rabbi. These spoons came out of the barrel, I swear to God."

He would cuff me on the ear for that. "Don't lie with the Lord's name on your tongue."

I wished his rain barrel would fall on him and crack him in half. But nothing could hurt Rabbi Fish. He was all the muscle Harry needed to hold us in line. We were slaves to Diane & Co.

My particular friend among the slaves was Robinson. We consoled one another. "I'll use that blowtorch on Fish, you'll see. And I'll wash Harry's ears in the same barrel with the spoons." Robinson was sixty. He'd been in and out of Bellevue half his life. But he read the classics in the rear ward. He knew Dante and Virgil and Leo Tolstoy.

Harry hated Robinson almost as much as he hated me.

"Robinson, you crippled goose, why don't you retire?"

"Listen," Robinson said, "I'll retire when my father retires."

Robinson, Sr., worked the same shift with us. He was eighty-nine. That skeletal old man was the best busboy in the place. He danced out the kitchen door on a pair of velvet slippers and delivered rubber chickens to a table with more aplomb that we would ever have.

"I like your father," Harry screamed. "Your father stays. Robinson, why should he retire on account of you? Poor man, to have a son with a twisted head. Robinson, you and Charyn are the crappers on my list. I'll fix you both."

He wasn't going to fire us. We knew that. But his taunts would dig into Robinson. The old man had to pause on those velvet slippers and put an arm around his son. "Harry doesn't mean it. He loves to persecute his men."

I didn't care. We had a war going on. Harry could shove his rabbi with the blowtorch. He shouldn't have messed with Robinson and me. It woke the catfish in my blood. And I began to scheme. I'll steal Harry's job away, I promise you. But we didn't even know who we were working for. None of us had ever met Diane, except Robinson, Sr.

"Diane used to hang around with the kitchen gangs when she was a girl. Her uncle named the company after her. Charyn, she had the cutest eyes."

Good, good. Because if I could get to Diane, I'd send Harry spinning on his ass.

"Mr. Robinson, how long ago was that?"

"Forty years."

I groaned. "Then she's seventy, this Diane."

"Don't be foolish," the old man said. "She's forty-five. Diane lives in St. Louis. She has Missouri blood."

"She owns us, for God's sake. Doesn't she come to New York . . . to inspect the kitchen crews?"

"Sure she comes, but Diane doesn't mingle much with busboys any more."

She'll mingle. "Just you point her out."

It must have been the wrong end of the year. No Missourians came into our kitchen. Harry had us by the balls. "Charyn and Robinson," he would say. "Robinson and Charyn."

But we carried our load. We didn't fail the crew. You couldn't find a rubber chicken under the table when Harry's gang was on the job. It was during a tiny affair for the Little Hebrew Sisters of Jackson Heights that Robinson, Sr., touched me with his incredible blue-veined hand. "There she is."

I saw a schoolmarm, a sweet lady in glasses with mother-goose frames. Her mouth was puckered and her hair had gone gray in the middle, but her body wasn't ruined at all. The schoolmarm had been around before, posing as Harry's book-keeper. It angered me that mothergoose couldn't reveal herself as Diane. Were we too dusty for her? We fed the Little Hebrew Sisters, we washed our hands.

"Mr. Robinson, you know her forty years. Couldn't Diane say hi to you?"

"She will. She'll wink before she goes."

Well, Diane could save her winks. I wasn't a skeleton in dancing slippers. I was a boy of thirty-four. Sunken in the cheek, I admit, blasted from my days in the monkeyhouse, but I was going to make my pitch. I waltzed close to mothergoose with ten rubber chicken wings on my shoulder. I wanted her to catch me in profile. Hadn't the girls in my mother's whore-house called me Gregory Peck? Suppose it was during the Korean War? Gregory was getting older too.

Harry must have sensed my scam. "Hey Charyn," he howled over the Little Sisters' heads. "Get away from the bookkeeper."

I didn't disappear so fast with my rubber chickens. But it's hard to talk and balance a loaded tray. My cheek bumped against Diane's gold-wire glasses. "I'm Charyn," I sputtered. "Pardon me." She didn't shriek, or move, or anything.

"I read Dostoyevsky. I'm no bum. Diane, I have a Phi Beta Kappa key."

Harry came running, and I had to float with the tray. He trapped me in the kitchen after I'd dumped the chicken wings.

"Pisser, I'm wise to you." He screamed at the whole kitchen. "Any of you clowns bang into my bookkeeper again, I'll have you arrested for assault."

"Assault," I said. "You have a funny idea of assault."

But it was dumb to make war on Harry in the kitchen. Rabbi Fish was behind him, and Diane had gone from Jackson Heights. She left us with all the Little Sisters and a kingdom of carrots and peas.

2.

Phi Beta Kappa.

Diane must have figured I was a raving boy. She knew Harry hired misfits, freaks like Robinson, who was in and out of Bellevue. And I'd lost my ping-pong home at Marty Reisman's. I had a dead bat in my bureau. It was like living in some slow, equatorial wind.

I heard a knock on my door. It couldn't be the hotel agent. I'd just given him the rent.

A voice came through the crack in the door. "Jerome Charyn?"

It sounded like a bullfrog off the bayou.

"He's not at home," I said. "Charyn's in Santa Fe."

"When he gets back, tell him Diane would like to see him."

Was it a bayou trick? "Wait." I opened the door. A man let himself in, not a sheriff or a naval officer, only a man. He had hair on his knuckles, and puffy scars around one eye. He could have belonged to Jean Lafitte.

"I'm Teddy. I work for Diane, and Diane's downstairs."

He didn't shove me out of the room, but he gave me short notice. I had to put on my jacket and follow him. Diane was in the rear of a simple Oldsmobile. I got into the car with her. Mothergoose wasn't voracious. She didn't pat my knees.

"Where is it?" she said.

"What?"

"The Phi Beta Kappa key."

I couldn't produce for Diane. I'd misplaced the damn thing, dropped it in the mud while I had Morphy on my mind. The catfish took over and started to babble its own lying song.

". . . inside the mattress. A key like that. Someone might walk in and steal it off the dresser."

She was going to send Teddy upstairs to poke around for the key.

"Tell him not to bother," I said. "I lost it. You can't hold on to one little key for half your life. It eats a hole in your pants. Or the pickpockets get at it, and they give it to their girlfriends."

"Jerome Charyn, you never had a key."

"I did. And I was a midshipman until the Navy threw me out."

"How do you spell Dostoyevsky?" she asked.

I wasn't going to play the idiot for her. But I didn't leave the car.

"Dostoyevsky had a twin, you know. Pavel, or Paul. Paul wrote the books. But he was crippled at birth. He had purple splotches down his back, and a withered arm. He was too ugly to go in public. So he decided to give Feodor credit for *The Brothers Karamazov*. But when Pavel died, Feodor couldn't scribble a line. He hired an actor to play his corpse, and then he dropped dead."

Diane started to laugh. "Harry said you were a troublemaker. What do you want?"

"My own kitchen gang."

"What should I do with Harry?"

"Drown the bastard. Him and Rabbi Fish."

I got out of the Oldsmobile and the man with the scars drove Diane away.

Harry cursed me at our next gig.

"You made Diane, didn't you, pretty boy?"

"How?" I said. "I saw her seven minutes. She gave me a quiz. Inside her Oldsmobile."

"Seven minutes, huh?"

Harry could talk. He wasn't bumping through the kitchen with a load of spoons from Fish's barrel.

"Charyn, get the monkeys to clean up."

"Why? I'm not finished with the spoons."

"Give them to Robinson, you dope. You're the new manager. I have to work the Siberian route, Buffalo and Rochester. I hope the mice eat up all your carrots. You won't survive. The crazies will rebel on you. You'll fall apart."

Fish went with Harry to Buffalo. The Rabbis' Local sent me a lazybones who arrived without a blowtorch and wouldn't bless a spoon. He was a bribable son of a bitch. The hostesses got to him in a hurry. He would go on a "sightseeing trip" through the Essex, while we slid around in all the grease. But the hell with this rabbi. The gang put out for me. We were the sharks of Diane & Co. The hairiest gigs went to us. Three thousand Jewish firemen. Kosher gravediggers from twenty-five cities. What did it matter to the crew?

3.

I met the "leetle" one on Broadway with his mother. They'd gone marketing again. Sarah held the shopping bag. Paul steered her through the traffic on the street. He wasn't a ping-pong artist right this minute. He was a boy with a lovelorn ma. His eyes darted until they grabbed onto me. A howl went through his body. He would have liked to disclaim Sarah, shove her in some doorway. He didn't want his old partner to connect him with a fat, dull-eyed witch. But he never let go of her hand.

Paul hated me. I'd put an angry groove in his chin. Did I remind him of the father who ran away? That silly optometrist.

"Paul?" I said.

He dragged his mother around me, as if I were another obstacle on the street, and they fled, little Paul and the hippo lady with red cheeks.

What's a ping-pong bat? What's little Paul? I missed that

pocking sound on a green table. But I had the crash of silver-ware to console me.

And Harry Snell. Harry wasn't a success in Buffalo. He didn't have enough Robinsons and Charyns to wield a powerful crew. His busboys would disappear on him before dessert. Not even Rabbi Fish could help. Rain barrels weren't popular on the Siberian route.

Diane didn't need another manager. So he asked to join my crew. I took him in. Why not? He brought Rabbi Fish along. And we didn't have to step in grease. It was good to have a rabbi with a blowtorch.

When I saw Harry puff and cough out his heart, I sat him down until his head turned a color that wasn't so gray.

"I was wrong," he muttered. "I should have let you wear your ping-pong ribbon."

I took something out of my pocket. The silk was frayed along the edges and curled in the middle. "I gave up ping-pong, Harry. You can wear it for me."

That balding silk revived old Harry. He pinned it to his breast. And I had to figure, it's a crazy life, when managers and busboys slide up and down, and what I was worth today might not even get me to tomorrow.

EIGHTEEN

Diane & Co., Part Two

I.

WHAT did a mule from Crotona Park know about the Sabbath? I had to learn. We'd have the devil's work to do if a gig began on Friday, after sundown. It was a whore of a time for my crew. We'd park our truck in front of the Pierre and unload the chickens and all. The truck couldn't return to the commissary. It had to sit still during the Sabbath. Fish would bless the truck and tie it like a cow to the white awning of the Pierre. The rabbi used a long rope. The cops couldn't intrude upon Rabbi Fish. This cow truck was part of Hebrew law.

"Fish, where does the law come from?"

"Don't be nosy," the rabbi said, grabbing his rain barrel. "The law is the law."

What the hell did they teach him at the Rabbis' Local? To turn trucks into cows and catch rain water in a barrel? The Pierre screamed at us.

"Charyn, you're blocking the entrance. Get rid of the rope and that jalopy of yours."

"Sorry. The rope stays. Rabbi's orders."

I came back to the Mississippi after one of those Friday night gigs and found my room picked clean. A man stood in the shadows near the door. His face emerged, and the puffy scars around his eye grew more and more distinct. It was that chauffeur who belonged to Diane. Teddy boy.

He brought me to a townhouse on Gramercy Park West. I was frightened, because the house had iron railings and a side porch. It was Morphy country again. The middle of Royal Street. You weren't supposed to have verandahs in New York. I went up the stairs with Teddy. Diane was on the top floor. She lived in the roof. Teddy didn't stick around. He delivered old gray ears and that was it.

My underpants lay stacked in one large drawer of a chiffonier. My encyclopedia was on a writing table. My coat was in the closet.

Mothergoose was shy.

"I couldn't visit you in that dumb hotel . . . if you don't like it here, Teddy can always take you uptown."

"No," I said. "It's perfect."

She would come out of Missouri once or twice a month and share that roof with the catfish for a couple of days. It wasn't sordid. It wasn't low. She was gentle with her squaw. I would ask her how she got into kosher catering. Diane wasn't Jewish. She belonged to the Methodists. "It's New York," she said. "My uncle understood the business. You had to be kosher if you wanted to break in."

Diane's was now the second largest caterer in the world. Roosevelt had used her knives and forks. Rockefeller. Richard Burton. Mae West. New England millionaires. Different churches came to Diane, kosher or not. She catered fundraising parties for them. But she didn't have a manager's grasp of things. She was ignorant of blowtorches and the value of rain water.

Whatever she had in St. Louis, mansions and a hubby, children, deer in her back yard, she never bragged about it on Gramercy Park West. There was some red wine in the house.

Portugal's best. Eight dollars a litre from a shop on Irving Place. The cork was blue. The wine bubbled out like purple mud. We drank the whole litre. Our mouths thickened with that blueness of the cork. I licked her back and it went blue. Diane was happy. Deer in St. Louis. Rubber chickens in New York. And a squaw that could paint her shoulders blue.

I wasn't alone when Diane left for Missouri. I had Ted to watch over me. "He'll keep you out of trouble . . . and drive you where you have to go."

Hell with mothergoose! I didn't need a babysitter.

"Teddy, push off."

He went with me on my catering gigs. He would stand at the edge of a banquet and watch our customers chew.

He gave Robinson a fright.

"Robinson, that's only Ted. He babysits for me."

My gang would get the shivers every time one of them had to walk around scarface to load up with carrots and peas.

"Teddy, sit in the crapper, will you? You're scaring my busboys."

So he moved into the crapper during my gigs. I prayed that too many customers didn't have to pee. But then I figured, if Ted was my shadow, I'd make some use of it.

I ordered him to take me into the Bronx.

The scars were jiggling now. "There is no Bronx. It's Apache land. Charyn, you'll get us killed."

"Never mind. I want to see my mom and dad."

Ted drove me through the Indian territories: those parts of the Bronx that were fields of rubble and dust. Buildings had been sliced in half, or bulldozed into the ground. You could find an occasional roof near the elevated tracks that went out to Pelham. The Poles still had five blocks near the Bronx River. The catfish had provided for them. As long as you had fish in that water, mothers and fathers were safe.

Teddy waited downstairs like a frontier sheriff, and I dropped in on Fannie and Sam. I wasn't a boy in rags. I was a manager at Diane & Co., with a crew of hundreds under me. I couldn't impress my folks with a fat wallet.

They were fiercer than Jerome. My father chewed on a potato. He didn't have any gray around *his* ears. My mother asked me why I hadn't phoned my two brothers.

". . . busy, mom. I'm on my feet most of the day."

They saw how thin I was and sallow, and they began to cry over me. I should move back in with them, they said. It was unhealthy to be a bachelor all the time. My father broke his potato, and offered me the bigger half.

I kissed my mother and father with potato meat on my lips and ran to the frontier sheriff.

"Teddy, get out of the car."

"Apaches," he said. "If they hurt the wagon, Diane will scream."

I took him down to the Bronx River. He stepped in yellow mud with me. The riverbank was swollen with junk. There were more bottles and cans than I could remember.

"It's the Apaches," scarface said, suddenly an expert on river politics. The bottles and cans were playmates for those mud-crawling friends of mine. He trembled when he saw a catfish come out of its perch in the mud to slap a bottle with its fins; the bottle shot across the mud and landed in the water.

"Joe DiMaggio," Teddy muttered, and we went up off the riverbank.

2.

IT was like having an homunculus stuck to your ribs. That's how hard it was to shake this Ted. I'd have to surrender pieces of my own gut to lose him for an hour. I'd be his homunculus if I didn't watch out. Turning the corner to escape from Ted,

I ran into Lillian's mother in the street. She had the same old umbrella.

"Jesus, I haven't touched Lillian, I swear. I'm in the kosher catering business. Ask my friend with the scars on his face. He'll be here in a minute."

Mrs. Feld was more subdued. She didn't go for my eyes with the umbrella tip, and call me the spider who broke up marriages. "Rabbi Jerome," she said, "the geometry professor who pulled my Lillian through Music and Art." She hugged me and began to cry.

"Where's Lilly?"

"On the loose. My daughter's a bum."

"What about the opera singer . . . Mario?"

"He left her a year ago. Lillian's with a motorcycle gang. They stole her from the house. They took Alyosha and moved them to Avenue B."

"Stole her and the dog? Mrs. Feld, this is New York City. Why didn't you get the police?"

"What can they do? My heartless daughter won't give up her motorcycle gang."

Lillian always preferred men with colors on their backs. Was she looking for Irwin Polatchek among the motorcycle gang? But Rabbi Jerome promised to rescue her and Alyosha for Mrs. Feld.

I waited until Teddy arrived. "Hurry up." And we went down to Avenue B. Mrs. Feld had been wrong about the motorcyclists. It was a Ukrainian social club that held her Lil. The Ukrainians made good money, it seems. They were plumbers and house painters who kept their wives and daughters at home in Brooklyn while they guzzled vodka and carried on at their social club. Ted and I walked through the door. I couldn't tease out Lillian's status with the club. She had all her clothes on, but she and the dog were drunk. Lillian was a puffy yellow-white. She must have been cooped up here for a month. The dog had a rash. His wire hairs didn't bristle any more. Alyosha was going bald on Avenue B.

The Ukrainians slapped dumbbells and barbells around. They grunted at us without their shirts. Lilly smiled. She had a cup of vodka in her hand.

"Jerome, Jerome, the good little boy with gray hair."

"Lilly, your mama's worried about you. She doesn't think you should live in a men's club. And look at poor Alyosha. His teeth are falling out."

Lillian splattered vodka on the wall. "My mother can go to hell . . . and 'Yosha likes it where he is."

"Lillian, have a heart . . . we went to high school. We kissed. How can I leave you with dumbbells and vodka bottles on the floor? You might trip. Who'd watch over Alyosha if you had to go to the emergency ward?"

"You're crazy," she said. And the plumbers began to move close to us.

"Beat it."

They shouldn't have growled at Ted. The scars near his eye jumped like frogs under the skin. One side of his face grew dark. He had the look of a man who could eat up Ukrainians, swallow them whole, like a crocodile. The plumbers hid from Ted. I grabbed up Alyosha, and brought Lilly out into the street. The sunlight was murder on their eyes. They had to squint and squint, they were so used to the gray interiors of the club.

"Lilly, that's no life . . ." Was she better off with her mother, or the plumbers on Avenue B? I wasn't so sure.

I returned Lilly to Mrs. Feld, and I went to my roof on Gramercy Park West with that homunculus of mine. It was a monkey's world. Friends died or disappeared on you. And enemies became your godmother.

NINETEEN

The Maoists Amongst Us

I.

WE called them skulls. They would hover around Diane's central office, waiting to be grabbed up by this gang or that. They wore tuxedos without pockets, undershirts and Salvation Army sweaters with the sleeves ripped away. Most of them had the prickly scalps of mental institutions, with bumps behind each ear, bald patches, and a groove where the clippers had eaten into their necks. They were the skulls that we hired.

The stronger, meaner skulls went first. They provided the horsepower of a crew. They would charge into the kitchen, knocking lesser skulls aside. They didn't tire out. They could carry your banquet on their backs. But they were trouble. They would spit and fight and pound on the tables, and bring chaos to the banquet halls. I wouldn't let such "horses" into my crew.

On hiring day I recognized a skull with a little ratty crop of hair on his head. It was Johnny Broom. We hugged and clapped hands, a pair of old sailors from Columbia College.

"Johnny, what are you now? A gambler, or a fisherman?"

"Buddy, I do odd jobs and read Chairman Mao."

"Keep still," I said. They didn't admire Maoists in the central office. "Come on." And I put him in my crew.

He kept a little brown book in his pocket. He studied the book during lulls in the kitchen. He had a funny reading style. Johnny would whisper out the words to himself. It was filthy Chinese propaganda. All that gummy stuff about the holiness of labor, when we were kitchen mules. I didn't mind the whispering until I saw Robinson and his dad with their own brown books. Robinson, Sr., stopped wearing slippers. He had ordinary waiters' shoes.

"Charyn, we may go out on strike."

I appealed to Robinson.

"Watch your dad, for Christ's sake. Where the hell are his slippers? He's not so wonderful in black shoes."

"My dad's as swift as he ever was. He's on a slowdown."

We didn't have a union at Diane's. Except for the Rabbis' Local, we hired skulls and scalawags. I can't say why. The company didn't reveal its policies to us. And now Johnny was trying to organize my men. He'd converted the Robinsons. How many more had gone over to him? The skulls were lining up.

It might never have happened if Teddy'd been there. The homunculus had gone out to Missouri on a mission for Diane. Rabbi Fish could have hurled his rain barrel at the Maoists and flooded their brown books. But Fish was strangely passive. "I make kosher," he said. "I don't mix in politics."

The Maoists struck our next catering gig. It was a party for blouse manufacturers. They had their young models at the tables, girls with incredible bodies and brittle mouths. You could imagine them parading in customers' showrooms with rouge on their nipples, and a luster coming off their perfect breasts. The manufacturers pawed these girls the minute the party began. The girls kicked off their shoes. Hands crept under the tablecloths. It was a saturnalia without spoons and forks. My busboys were under the spell of Johnny's brown book. They wouldn't cart silverware or ladle the soup.

It was up to Harry, me, and Fish, and the few loyalists I had. We couldn't provide for six hundred manufacturers and their models. The soup came at awkward intervals. There were no napkins out. Harry went from table to table with a bunch of celery stalks.

"Robinson," I said, "don't desert me now."

My old friend was sitting in the kitchen with his dad.

"I'll work if my father works, but why should we have to feed those swine?"

The Maoists would glint through the kitchen door when one of the loyal busboys shoved himself into the banquet hall with a tray on his shoulder.

"Good men should not serve fools," Robinson, Sr., read from the brown book.

"Mr. Robinson, this is a kosher catering service. It's not a busboy's paradise."

He shouted other passages at me.

"Defy your masters. They're like alligators without teeth. You can drown their heads in the mud and let the turtles ride on their backs."

The rhetoric was becoming familiar to me. It had a Tennessean's voice. It was the Chairman according to Johnny Broom.

"Mr. Robinson, alligators don't need many teeth. They can bite you with their gums."

I left him there and tried to cater that goddamn manufacturer's party. There was lots of kissing around the tables. Buttons disappeared from the models' clothes. We were two hours into the gig and we hadn't gotten soup to everybody. The models smiled and let busboys peek into their blouses, but the men became harsh without food in their bellies. They turned on Harry and me.

"You shitters, we paid nineteen dollars a head. You bring one cauliflower, and you call that a meal."

The blouse manufacturers hurled down the tablecloths in

their fury, spilling soup bowls onto the floor, and making a tiny sea. The models would have stayed with us, but the manufacturers took them by the sockets of their arms and herded them out of the building. The models left buttons and shoes behind.

I walked into the kitchen and yelled at Johnny's people. "Smart, huh? A sitdown strike. You read from your brown books, and customers go unfed. Goddamn skulls, you let a gig run out the door. Will you hold your principles for half an hour and help us clean up?"

"We can't," Mr. Robinson said. "If we touch a broom, it means the strike is over."

So the loyalists had to get down on their knees and gather buttons and shoes, and then mop up that little sea in the banquet hall. It was maddening labor.

We were like pygmies, sloshing around in spilt soup. Our shirts began to darken and rot with our own sweat. Our cuffs were leaky.

I had anger in my gray hair. We mopped and mopped while the strikers parleyed in the kitchen and did their political dance.

Strange men hugged the sides of the banquet hall. They winked at us, said "Shhh." They were carrying lengths of rubber hose. I heard a scream from the kitchen.

Teddy had arrived with a dozen goons. They were bashing Robinson and the others with their rubber hose. They couldn't touch the old man. He dodged their wicked slaps with his waiter's shoes. He was also trying to help his son. But the goons put burly arms and burly necks between Robinson and the old man. I shouted to Ted.

"Lay off."

Teddy only laughed. "Go play with yourself. Schmuck, this isn't your fight."

I wasn't so worried about Johnny Broom. He'd huddle in the corner somewhere and survive the hose attack. And Mr. Robinson? That ninety-year-old man could shuffle for hours against

Diane's goons and never miss a step. But he was shuffling with
tears in his eyes. He couldn't get close to Robinson. That son
of his was wailing. Robinson's screams rose above every noise.
He was frightened of the rubber sticks. He must have thought
the kitchen had disappeared, and he was in Bellevue now,
wrestling with his keepers.

Help came from Rabbi Fish. He was a catering rabbi who
earned his livelihood in the kitchen, kosherizing spoons and
drawers, but that didn't make him any less of a holy man. He
preserved the Maoists by aiming his blowtorch at the goons.
"You miserable bandits, I can fry your ears, believe me." We
heard the whoosh of his flame, as the rabbi burnt a scar in the
wall where Teddy stood.

The slap-slap of the rubber stopped. The goons went out of
the kitchen.

2.

TEDDY was there when I got to Gramercy Park West. He'd
come without his rubber hose.

"Charyn, you know how much you cost Diane today? This
isn't the Riviera. It's dog eat dog. We're shutting down your
crew. But I don't want those bastards slipping into another
gang. So you give me their names."

Diane's couldn't put a tag on every skull it hired. We had a
rotating army. Busboys might faint after a single gig, return to
Bellevue, or sit in their hotel rooms for a year. The payroll
would arrive in a huge sack, and it was my job to distribute it.
I had the only records of my crew. And I wasn't going to sing
for Ted.

"Charyn, start remembering some names."

The bedroom door opened, and Diane came out. She should
have been in Missouri. It wasn't the right week for Gramercy

Park West. She was wearing a soft red robe that seemed perfect against the gray in her hair. It was no hurried thing that Diane had put on, no small flourish after arriving from the airport, a simple dressing up for the old squaw. Diane hadn't just stepped off the plane, I'll bet. She was around during the strike in the kitchen. It wasn't Ted who ordered the attack on my men. It was Diane.

She sent Ted away from our roof.

I thought we'd cuddle now. She slapped me on the face. Rough backhanded slaps they were, with the force of milady's knuckles. Blood ran down my ear.

"Whore, I buy you thirty-dollar socks, and you betray me."

"I've been faithful," I bawled.

"Sure, faithful to your gang of busboys . . . I want those chickenshits flogged. Every one of them."

"Diane, Mr. Robinson's nearly a hundred. He's worked for you half his life."

"Tough," she said.

Her robe slid apart during that forage of slaps. I burrowed in, taking the punishment, slap, slap, slap, and sucked on her nipple with all my strength. I'd overpowered Diane. The knuckles ceased to chop. They were caressing my bloody ear. Her robe fell off like a pair of dusty wings.

"Jerome, who made you such a bitch?"

3.

I got up when I heard her snore. I walked out with uncle Bob's encyclopedia and whatever else I could carry in the pockets of my midshipman's coat.

I went uptown to warn the Robinsons.

"Pack," I said, "quick . . . the company's going to come down hard on you."

Robinson shuddered, but the old man looked me in the eye. "We'll take our chances."

"Mr. Robinson, you don't have any chances to take. Diane's sending out her dogs. Pack, I'm telling you."

The old man saw me for what I was: a catfish with a tail that could flick in any direction. That tail went from good to evil with the slightest turn. Still, Mr. Robinson wouldn't let me go without a little touch. He put his blue-veined hand on my shoulder for old time's sake.

"Charyn, you hang out with the worst element. That's why you're always tumbling into some dark hole."

"I can't help it, Mr. Robinson. I grew up on a narrow river."

I left the Robinsons and looked for Johnny Broom. I tried the Flatiron Building. Uncle Bob occupied the same closet on Twenty-third Street. He wouldn't tell me where Johnny was.

"Johnny? He's like the wind. You can't nail John . . . Jerome, you're a dirty quitter. You walked out on me."

"Yeah, I went from Royal Street to bedlam. And then the Navy picked me up and tossed me in a prison camp. Bob, how come my sandpaper racket showed up at the Grange?"

"Why ask me?"

"Because you shipped it there."

The uncle turned shrewd. "The sandpaper cured you. Remember that."

"Bob, how did I get to Bayou L'Outre? Who worked the switch?"

"That commander of yours from the NROTC. I got him on the phone. We didn't want you to sweat it out in some back ward, with murderers and idiots. So the commander got you into that farm in the woods. He saved your life . . . you'd still be on the ward if it wasn't for him."

Goddammit, you couldn't tell what was what in these bloody times. The wolves lick your feet, and the lambs hiss and tear out your eyes.

4.

WHAT had happened to that civilian Navy of mine? The ping-pong room was gone. Hartley Hall lay half asleep. A few cadets skulked through the building with rabbity eyes. That was the NROTC. Vietnam had depleted Shirl's fund of cadets. It was 1971, and you could be lynched for wearing a midshipman's uniform around College Walk. The Navy couldn't hold maneuvers on the grass without provoking a riot. It stuck to its corner of Hartley Hall.

I couldn't get to Shirl. Corporal (now Sergeant) Rosen blocked my way.

"Can't I thank the Old Man for a favor he did?"

"Charyn, the Old Man doesn't have a minute."

I understood. Shirl was protecting me and him. He'd have to notify Bayou L'Outre if he talked to the runaway kid. So I stepped out of Hartley Hall.

"Mister."

That was Rosen calling. I shuffled to the edge of the campus with him.

"The Old Man told me to give you this."

He handed me a crumpled letter from Fannie Brindle. The letter was four years old.

"How did it come to Shirl?"

"Never mind. Just keep it and get out of here."

The letter had been written on a Greyhound bus. In stabs of red ink. *Darling, I love you,* she said. She was running to Houston with her little girl. *Come for me.* She'd hide under the name of Fannie Smith. I cursed whoever it was had kept the letter out of my hands. I might have been with Fannie, instead of bouncing rubber chickens at the Pierre. Poor Shirl. I'd gone through Morphy, bedlam, ping-pong, and Diane's, and he was still a lieutenant commander at Columbia College.

Didn't the Old Man ever get to graduate?

He'd die in Hartley Hall. Not me. I couldn't stay in Manhattan. Teddy would break my bones. Here comes the catfish boy. Four years late. I'll find Fannie Smith.

TWENTY

Boomtown

I.

THERE were nine Fannie Smiths in the Houston telephone book. I dialed them all from the air terminal and found six at home.

"Pardon me, but are you the Fannie who sold apples on top of the hill and took me for rides in your '67 Dodge? . . . ma'am, don't call the police. It isn't necessary. I'm hanging up . . ."

I wasn't discouraged. I copied down the addresses of the last three Fannies and rode out of the terminal in a taxi cab.

"Twenty-nine Braesbayou Yard."

That was the seventh Fannie on my list.

A boy answered the doorbell. "Grandma Fannie went to church," he said.

My Fannie couldn't have become a grandma in four years. I thanked the boy and got back into the cab.

"Driver, Little John Woods."

"Take you as far as Beechnut. Then you're on your own. Little John Woods is in Gurney. And Gurney impounds anything that moves. Got themselves one hell of a mayor. He's a pirate, that Lamar Jones."

"What is this Gurney, and why does it have its own mayor?"

"Ask Lamar."

He dropped me at Beechnut and I crossed over into a grassy area that was the beginning of Little John Woods. There was a sign stuck in the grass:

WELCOME TO GURNEY TOWNSHIP, USA

No Peddlers, No Paupers, No Rats,
and No Bare Feet Beyond This Point

It was like a small country of its own in the middle of Houston.

I saw Chryslers in the driveways. The houses were made of brick or wood that came from some extraordinary forest: it seemed as fierce as stone to the eye.

A cow walked in front of me with a bell on its throat.

It was a lovely, landlocked place, this Gurney, with Chryslers, cows, and no bare feet. I followed the road, thinking of Fannie Smith.

A brick-red car rattled alongside of me. I said hello. The men in the car didn't smile or touch their cowboy hats. It was the Gurney police. They scrambled out of the car, four men in brick-red shirts and rolled-up dungarees. They looked like divinity students.

"We don't allow paupers. Didn't you read the sign?"

"Who's a pauper?"

They plucked me into the car and drove me straight to city hall, which was a low building in the heart of Little John Woods, with a firehouse tacked onto it, a police barracks, a library, and a jail. I wasn't fingerprinted or anything. I was trundled over to the mayor, who was also the chief magistrate. I noticed the swelling of a pistol under his magistrate's shirt. Another divinity student, only Lamar Jones wore a moustache, like my brother Marvin.

"State your business."

"I'm in Houston to track down a friend."

"He's lying, Lamar," one of the deputies said. "I'll bet he's with the Scotch Tape Gang . . . he walked into the woods on a scouting mission."

The mayor frowned. "Scotch Tape Gang? Does he look like a Meskin to you? Meskins don't have gray hair. But it's peculiar . . . people never take walks in Little John Woods. Show me your driver's license."

"I don't have one. Your Honor, when I was nine and a half my father bought a car. A Plymouth. It had that emblem of a sailing ship on its hood. I sat in the back while a cousin tried to teach my father how to drive . . . it was like being on a river. My father never learned to steer."

"You should have parked in the next township. You come waltzing in on foot, blaming your father, blabbing about this and that. That's why we have vagrancy laws. To protect us from drifters like you. The Court will please rise . . . Jerome, I sentence you to six months in the city jail . . . boys, get me a sandwich before I starve to death . . . Court's adjourned."

Six months for stepping over the Gurney line?

I was thrown into a closet with a skinny Meskin by the name of Marcos. The dumb jail didn't even have a lock on the door. Marcos could wander through city hall and then return to his mattress in the closet. No wonder the deputies latched on to me. The jail wouldn't have been complete without its two convicts. The township would have to send all other vagabonds away.

Marcos was a ward of Little John Woods. He lived at the jail most of the time, as an incorrigible boy. He wasn't born in Gurney. The township had no Meskin district. He was from one of the barrios north of Little John Woods.

Convicts had to earn their keep. We were carpenters, plumbers, grocery boys, among other things. Now I understood my talk with the "judge." A driver's license wouldn't have saved my skin. Lamar would have found some excuse to hold me. He'd have made it illegal to wear yellow socks or have gray in my head. I couldn't have won against his penal code. Gurney depended on convict labor. Me and Marcos were the township's sanitation force.

Lamar didn't want to house and feed a gang of drudges that might become eyesores in Little John Woods, and destroy the rhythm of city hall. He must have figured that two slaves could run the show.

We fixed the pipes in Lamar's private tub at city hall, collected trash, painted the town's fences, mowed lawns, but our main concern was the gulley that ran through Little John Woods. Blackheart Bayou it was called, because of the bitter taste its water had. It would overflow the gulley walls during a hard rain, and the two of us would have to get down and sweep water and mud back into the bayou with enormous brooms.

The Meskin liked to call me Jeronimo, because it sounded better in his ear than Jerome. He was thirty-six, like me. He'd had a few months at Jeff Davis High, but his vocabulary was bigger than a boy from the Bronx who had catfish on his mind.

Marcos pitied me when I told him I'd never been married. He had wives in El Paso, Juarez, and Houston's Fifth Ward.

"How do you support them on a convict's pay?"

"That's easy. I have shares in nineteen oil wells."

"How much money have your wells brought in?"

The Meskin shrugged.

"Then your wives must support themselves."

"Hombre, I contribute whatever I can . . ."

"What's this Scotch Tape Gang that Lamar's deputies tried to lay on me?"

"Bandits," Marcos said. "They murder gas station attendants and leave Scotch Tape on their mouths."

"Why Scotch Tape? Something to silence the dead?"

"Who knows? It could be a high school trick."

I didn't care for such high schools. And I was too depressed to hunt for Fannie in my convict suit, overalls with the words PROPERTY OF LITTLE JOHN WOODS stenciled into the seat.

Stepping out of jail one morning, I looked up, and there was Fannie Brindle Smith. We'd been a few yards from each other during that first week of my labor for Lamar Jones. She hadn't noticed the hairy convict who trekked in and out of the closet, and I didn't stop to think that Fannie might be a clerk in the mayor's office.

"Fannie . . ."

Four years on the "rubber chicken circuit" must have diminished me somehow. Or was it my convict's overalls? Fannie didn't recognize the boy who'd robbed her apple barrel. But she looked again, and she laughed. She ran out from behind the mayor's counter at city hall to hug a convict with LITTLE JOHN WOODS on his ass.

We had sandwiches at the city's expense. Lamar didn't say a word. Fannie went in to have a talk with the mayor. Marcos kept winking at me.

"Hombre, he's going to give us the sewer detail for a month . . . that's the mayor's girlfriend you been kissing. It'll be cozy, you and Lamar sharing the same toothbrush."

"Marcos, shut up."

But the Meskin was right. Fannie didn't come out of the office. She stayed in there with Lamar. And we drove to Blackheart Bayou with our instructions for the day. We were scheduled to clear muck and dead frogs out of the gully. The town lent Marcos its only pickup truck for our work in Little John Woods. Marcos had free use of the truck. He would ride out of Gurney and bring back an enchilada lunch.

My eyebrows were on fire. They'd burn around to the side of my head and scorch both my ears if I didn't get away from this damn township. I saw blood. I wasn't going to shovel dead frogs. "Marcos, help me escape . . . I'll finance one of your oil wells, I swear. I have a bankbook under my pillow. It's yours."

The Meskin took black mud from the bayou and held it against my ears. My face began to cool.

"Lamar would love you to run. He'd throw a bounty on your head."

"Who's afraid of bounty hunters? Louisiana's looking for me. That's not all. There's a thug named Teddy in New York who'd chop off my nose for a nickel . . . and I'm on the Navy's wanted list."

"Then why should you run, hombre, when you got a perfect hiding place in Little John Woods?"

"I'm not going to stick around while Lamar paws Fannie Smith."

2.

HER eyes would lower the minute we marched into city hall. We'd come off the bayou with bags of dead frogs. I don't know what Lamar did with the frogs. The Meskin swore he had a deal with some company that turned the frogs into pocketbooks and stuffed toys.

I was out of Fannie's life. She was with that frog collector, Mayor Jones. Why should I embarrass her with the sight of my convict's overalls? I used the jail's back door. The master wanted frogs? I dredged the bayou for those swollen-bellied creatures.

"Hombre, don't work so fast. One bag, two bags, but thirteen bags a day?"

It was the stench in my own black heart that got me to live around dead frogs. My face would disappear below the walls of Blackheart Bayou, and Marcos would have to call down into the hole.

"Eat an enchilada. It's good for you."

But I wouldn't climb out of that stinking hole. I took the enchilada and ate it with muddy fists.

"Marcos, I'm leaving Houston when my sentence is up."

"You crazy? This is boomtown. Everybody's coming here . . . and once Lamar has you, he doesn't let go. He'll give you another six months."

3.

CURLED up, a mattress away from Marcos, I had a dream after mucking through the bayou all afternoon. The frogs I'd bagged had come alive. They burst out of the sacks with a great push of their heads. It was raining frogs, like the bitter storms of old Egypt. Blood leaked from their bellies. And the frogs could talk.

"Jerome, come with me."

I got up off the mattress and followed that frog voice out of jail. The frog looked more and more like Fannie Smith. We crossed the woods and went into a cottage at the southern tip of Gurney.

"Sorry, Jerome. Lamar took an awful long time to pack. I couldn't invite you over with him in the house. He gets crazy when he's drunk."

We kissed like two lost children meeting in the woods. I shucked off the Gurney overalls. Then I heard a scream.

"The frogs," I said, clutching Fannie.

"It's Jessica. She's having a nightmare. She'll be all right."

I'd forgotten. Baby Jess. She stumbled out of the next room in girl's pajamas. A woman-child of eight. She didn't have chubby fingers any more. She had crust in her eyes, and goddammit, she was hugging a teddy bear. I told myself I wasn't going to twitch over Jessica's bear. It hadn't come from my father's stock. Not all the teddy bears in the world were evil. Some of them had to be good.

"Where's unca Lamar?" she said, measuring me with her brown eyes. Who was this old gray ears standing in his underpants in mama's living room?

"Lamar's moved out, honey. But you can see him tomorrow . . . this is your uncle Romey. He carried you on his back a long time ago."

Uncle Romey? She didn't remember the lunatic from the Louisiana woods. Ignoring me, she took some macaroni salad from the fridge, fed herself and the teddy bear, and returned to bed. The bear had a strip of macaroni on its woolly mouth. It was nothing to smirk at. The messy face grew panther eyes in the dark.

Fannie shut the bedroom door, and we had the living room to ourselves. I sniffed the back of her neck like a prairie wolf. I'd come out of that grave in Blackheart Bayou to spend the night with Fannie. Would Lamar run a bed check at the jail? Who cares? They could come for me in the morning, bend me over the counter at city hall and break my arms and feet, as a lesson to future convicts that they were not to sully the women of Little John Woods. Let them break as many of my feet as they could find. My overalls were on Fannie's chair. My socks were in a corner of the room. I was sleeping at the cottage tonight.

TWENTY-ONE

El Coco

I.

FUNNY guys in boots and pointy hats were skulking near the cottage window. You could see their shadows bump across the wall. Spotlights played on our ceiling. It was the sheriff of Harris County and his men. "What the hell are they looking for? The Russians and the Red Chinese?"

"El Coco," Fannie said.

The sheriff had mounted an invasion party at the edge of our woods for one stinking man? Who could be worth that much? Coco is wetback talk, an affectionate term for phantoms and spooks. El Coco was the leader of the Scotch Tape Gang. The sheriff's men thought the Phantom was hiding in our woods. Lamar didn't hinder their search.

Our mayor needed a friend. He'd rather walk with the sheriff than be on his own when the Houston police decided to squat at our borders in their baby-blue shirts. Stubborn bastards, they could wait six months for El Coco to come out of the woods. And we'd have a ring of cops around us.

But it didn't matter to El Coco. Baby-blue shirts or the sheriff's men. Nobody could find him. The sheriff had blood-hounds and criminologists from Austin who understood every

Chicano trick. The dogs screamed as they stepped in Blackheart Bayou. It was an unholy place for bloodhounds and men.

2.

THE dogs are gone, and the Meskin and me have the bayou to
ourselves. We know how to skate along the surface. You have
to chop with your ankles and glide with your hips, to crawl on
mud. And that's when I figured the Phantom's no jerk. He's a
mudcrawler too.

Marcos went off to get our enchilada lunch. And the logic of
it smacked me behind the ears. There wasn't another mudcrawler in the neighborhood. Marcos was the Phantom. He had
to be. While the sheriff poked with his spotlights and his dogs
sank into the mud, El Coco lay on a mattress in city hall. It was
a perfect cover. The Meskin could walk in and out of jail
whenever he had the urge. He was Marcos the convict who did
odd jobs for everybody in town.

I scrutinized El Coco after he returned. We got into our
guacamole, and I said, "Does it take very long to find the right
taqueria? You were in that goddamn pickup truck two hours."

The Meskin didn't answer me. He looked across the road. A
tank was cruising in our woods, an old Ford with a cowcatcher
in front that could have knocked a cottage down. We saw eight
"roughriders" in the Ford, redneck high school students from
inside the Octopus somewhere (Octopus was the name we had
for Houston in Little John Woods). They drove behind us,
tossing beer cans at our heads. We ducked, and the cans fell into
the bayou. They were on the prowl for wetbacks, convicts, and
queers.

They charged out of their tank, grabbed us by the collar and
whipped us against a tree. They took off their belts and smoked
our backsides with the buckles. It was great fun. I'd have welts

on my ass that Fannie could smooth with vanishing cream.

The roughriders made us undress. They started to judge our pricks, mocking us for the pubic hair we had, and the jiggle of our balls. I was waiting for El Coco. When the Phantom barked and jumped, I would go for their eyeballs. The odds would shift from them to us. They had the tank with the cowcatcher, and we had the bayou. They'd be drinking black mud until their bellies burst. We would skate out of their reach while they floundered in Blackheart Bayou.

The Phantom got down on his knees. He prayed in Meskin for his deliverance. The roughriders laughed. That's when Lamar walked into the woods.

It wasn't the pistol he carried that frightened those boys. It was Lamar himself. They scuttled for their tank. "Dewey Jones," the mayor called.

A shiver went down the roughriders' backs. The mayor stopped them with a shout.

"Dewey Jones, come over here. That's public property you've been scarring up. Where's your sense of justice? Convicts aren't candy poles. Apologize. And quick. That gray boy is Jerome. And Marcos is the Mex."

"Sorry, uncle Lamar," the tallest of them blubbered.

"Not to me, you dumb bird. Apologize to them."

The roughriders shook our hands. "Sorry, Marcos. Sorry, Jerome."

They weren't rednecks at all. They were from Little John Woods. They probably belonged to Arista, or some other honor society for youngsters from the Southwest. They loved to chase convicts, and bang into stray cows. Who was I to be so righteous about them? The Polish Baron from Music and Art. I was a hoodlum with an Arista pin for two and a half months.

Ah, I was mistaken in that Mex. El Coco wouldn't have gone down on his knees to high school boys. Marcos was a jailbird who took long lunches, and that was it.

Maybe the Phantom was an Anglo: Lamar Jones, the mayor who robbed gas stations on the side. Goddammit, El Coco could be anybody. One of the sheriff's bloodhounds. Fannie. Or Jerome Charyn.

3.

JESSICA was almost nine. She couldn't get used to my presence in the cottage. She didn't say uncle, or daddy to me. I was the man who lived with her mama. The guy who belonged to Mayor Jones, her *unca Lamar.* I was patient with her. She probably missed her true dad. Maynard the duck hunter. There were too many of her mama's boyfriends around the cottage. First unca Lamar. Now the convict with mud on his pants. The forgotten one. Unca Romey.

I decided to treat her to lunch.

"I have school today," she said.

"Come on . . . we'll go into the Mexican district. We'll have some green sauce."

She didn't argue. But she wouldn't hold my hand. We were both playing hooky. I should have been out on the bayou, hunting dead frogs. The hell with it. This was Little John Woods, where a convict could declare his own holiday.

We went into the barrio north of the woods. Never been to these parts. All the houses were on stilts. Some of them had refrigerators on the front porch. The roads were patches of dirt. Children played in the shells of rusted automobiles that rocked like squeaky carriages. No one waylaid us.

We wandered into a taqueria that existed on a sidewalk made of wood. The taqueria was a dry goods store as well as a restaurant. It sold shirts and live parrots and a newspaper called *El Norte.* You passed through a turnstile to get to the tables. We weren't snubbed as gringos from Little John Woods. The waitresses smiled at Jessica. And here, in this taqueria with a wooden sidewalk, I could be her dad.

A fiddler played at lunch, a castaway from some ancient mariachi band. He was feeble, and his elbow shook as he scraped out his tune. He could have been a hundred or more. The fiddler had a shiny skull. He serenaded Jessica, accompanying his fiddle with a warble he produced deep in his skinny throat. It sounded like a rooster in agony. But Jessica enjoyed it. He wouldn't accept a dollar from me. It was the old man's pleasure to sing for such a pretty girl.

We had tortillas that tasted like Mexican hot dogs. Jessica drank a glass of milk. Beer arrived in a pitcher that was dark as the mud in our bayou. I swallowed it down with a lick of salt, the blackest beer in the world.

A man came into the restaurant. He had a cape around his shoulders that obscured most of his body. His head was scrunched into the middle of the cape, and you saw eyebrows and two ears. Those eyebrows must have revealed something. The restaurant hushed. Men and women at the tables showed their infants to him. He creased up his eyebrows, and the men kissed the edges of his cape. El Coco. I didn't have to stare at that turtlelike trundling of his head. Or his eyebrows. And his ears. I noticed what was under the cape. He had convict's pants.

Marcos.

That kneeling to the high school boys was a sham. El Coco wasn't going to give up his roost in the township to slap eight yokels who meant nothing to him. He could have cut their gizzards out, buried them under the cowcatcher. Then where would he have to hide? So he trembled and prayed in Meskin to high school boys. And he sucked me in with that act of his.

The Phantom sat down at one side of the taqueria. Idiot, I should have paid the bill and run out with Fannie's daughter. El Coco hadn't spotted us yet. But I swallowed my beer. The cape dropped under his nose. His eyes fell on me. He was a killer, all right. The handyman-convict had gone out of him. The bones bristled above his jawline. He never even smiled.

Jessica wanted a beef taco. I told her shush and dragged her through the turnstile, with the parrots near the window squinting at us. We tramped down the wooden sidewalk and stepped onto the road.

"Hold your horses," she said.

Could I hint that a murderer was on our tail, that I'd unmasked the Phantom on his home grounds, and who could tell what he might do? So I clutched her arm and pulled.

It wasn't my own craziness that compelled me out of the taqueria, because a gang started to collect on the sidewalk. The gang followed us. Muchachos with old, wrinkled faces. I'd swear they were under twelve. Did they get those wrinkles at some lost junior high? I kept pulling Jessica. "Run, run." All I could think of was the damned Scotch Tape that went over your mouth when you died. The streets were confusing. I couldn't find the road that would take us back to our woods. That little Meskin district swelled into row after row of houses that looked the same. Refrigerators on the porches. Stilts.

Jessica slapped at my fingers. "Let go of me."

Finally I had to carry her. The infants grew into an army. They blocked the end of every street. I had nowhere to run with Jessica.

Then that cape stood in front of us. El Coco. Jessica was tired. She began to whimper out of crossness with me.

"Be still," I said. ". . . please."

And I addressed the cape.

"Señor, she's a little girl . . . eight years old. She doesn't know a thing."

El Coco held the pockets of my shirt and shook them hard. "Pig, why did you come here?"

"Green sauce," I said. "Enchiladas . . . we wanted Mexican food."

"You should have rolled a tortilla in your back yard."

They tossed us into a beat-up station wagon. One of the infants drove. The tires bumped along the dirt, and soon we were out of the barrio. They let Jessica off a few yards from Fannie's cottage.

"Baby, go inside."

The Phantom punched me on the ear. "Shut your filthy mouth." The ear erupted into small explosions. I could feel the tremors in the roots of my nose. The tremors wouldn't stop. They were so violent, I was sure my ear and nose would break off and leave me with empty hinges on my face. The muchachos made fun of me. The tremors softened, and the wounded ear went to sleep.

The brat behind the wheel was a pro. The wagon swerved away from these woods and the independent village of Gurney, and brought us into the Octopus. We were on Bissonett. The infants shrank into their seats; this way the cops couldn't discover so many Meskins in one station wagon, and scream, "Scotch Tape Gang."

El Coco avoided Meyerland, where the Octopus could get at him from the sky with its helicopter patrols: Meyerland was where the gang had "hit" most often.

Marcos wouldn't talk to me. He was snug in that cape of his. The brat cruised round and round. Then El Coco touched his lip. He'd decided on a gas station near Houston Baptist College. I saw that attendant at the pumps. He was a boy. Blond and sweet. God, I wanted to yell. *Leave your money box and get the fuck out of there.* The Phantom shoved my face against the window.

"Look," he growled. "It's like the movies, you stupid prick." He didn't get out of the car.

The blond boy came over to the wagon. Sixteen. A sophomore somewhere. With a smile. The Phantom never had to open his door. A muchacho shoved a gun out the window. It was like a cap pistol, I swear. I heard two, three pops. Blood spilled from the side of the boy's face and splattered my window. His legs danced out from under him. That's when the Phantom reached over me and held the dying boy by his ears, while a muchacho ran a sliver of Scotch Tape across his mouth and grabbed the money box. The Phantom let go, and the boy dropped softly to the ground. And we disappeared.

I was in some dumb fog, and then a fury ripped up out of me as we crossed the Buffalo Speedway. "Motherfuckers, tape my mouth too . . . go on."

"Hombre, it's not necessary," the Phantom said with a twisting smile. "You're one of us . . . our gringo accomplice."

"Why are you so sure I won't yell to the police?"

"Yell all you want . . . that nice little girl and her mama from city hall . . . hombre, do I have to show you what your yells will do?"

"Die," I said. "You and your childrens' army."

He laughed and put me out of his station wagon at the edge of Little John Woods.

TWENTY-TWO

On the Bayou, with Two Black Hearts

I.

I didn't have to dream of that blond boy. The image of Marcos holding him by the ears, that's what stuck to me. I thought of killing the Phantom, beating him over the head with a shovel while we were out on the bayou, getting the mayor his frogs. I could plan it and all, feel the delicious moment of his skull cracking, his brains turning to putty in front of my eyes, but I'd never lift that shovel. El Coco knew his man.

It was the catfish's fault. The catfish could teach me to lie and invent fabulous tales. But it didn't have murder in its blood. It would rather eat a tin can than avenge itself on another creature. I shut up about the blond boy, sheltering Fannie and Jessica with my silence. And I worked with the Mex.

He wasn't El Coco in Little John Woods. The bristles went out of his face. His shoulders slackened. He was the handyman again. But my lips would curl with hatred whenever I had to look at him. I wasn't going to acquiesce to his miserable disguise.

"Butcher . . . it takes a pair of balls to shoot blond boys in the head."

We crouched with shovels in our fists.

"Let them close the gas stations. Then they won't lose their boys."

"Coco, your reasoning sucks."

He whipped up that shovel near my face. It brought a wind to my cheek.

"Good," I said. "I'd like a duel in the mud. Because I'll zap you once, twice, Coco, before you murder me. And you'll walk away with half a mouth. You'll remember your convict friend."

But the bitch wouldn't duel with me.

"It's lovely how you train those muchachos of yours. If they rob and kill by the time they're eleven, they'll cry with boredom when they hit fifteen."

"They won't have to cry. They'll be dead. But it's better than watching their brothers being dragged off by the cops, punched for some crime they didn't do, and dropped into Buffalo Bayou if they can't confess fast enough . . . did you ever see a Meskin deputy around here?"

"That doesn't give you the right to pick off gas station clerks . . . take your bandidos and knock heads with the sheriff, have a shootout with the police."

"Sure, we'd last two minutes. Then they could walk into the barrios and do whatever they like. Hombre, our mortality rate has gone down since my gang arrived. Meskins don't come floating up off the bayou. Just mention Scotch Tape, and the cops shit their pants."

"Coco, you have slime in your heart . . . kill, kill, kill."

"Prick," he muttered. "Are you dead or alive?"

We slapped our shovels into the muck, kicking at the blades with our heels, eying one another in anger and distrust, and I thought, he'll lose his charity and send a muchacho to tape my mouth. It's only a matter of time. And even if he doesn't, hell comes to me in the shape of blood on a car window and a boy falling to the ground. The boy would fall and fall and fall with each bite of the shovel. My head began to clutter with memories of snow. The Bronx mingled with Texas. Coco became Irwin Polatchek. And I was a member of the Scotch Tape Gang, clamoring for a borough of Poles in the Lone Star State. The mind hits at you if you don't watch out. Irwin Polatchek. The dead chew in your ear and the living go pasty and begin to stink.

2.

SOMETHING annoyed me about Lamar. If I could guess the Phantom's lair, how come this mayor who could preserve our independence from the Octopus was so dumb? A killer skulks in convict's clothes, maintains his own closet in city hall, and all of Gurney is blind to him. Maybe the blinders were a bitter joke.

I got into the mayor's rooms. No one bothered to stop a convict who was as familiar as a wart.

Lamar winked at me. "How's the little woman?"

"Fannie's my business now," I told Lamar. But I couldn't get him to explore the subject of who Marcos really was.

"Funny how the sheriff keeps tracking Coco to these woods. His dogs run on the bayou and sink in the mud. I'd say Coco's using Blackheart Bayou as some kind of shield. Think on it, Lamar. How many Meskins are that acquainted with the bayou?"

"Only one."

I'd have this whore of a mayor in another minute. "Who's that?"

"Marcos, the man with three wives."

"Then why don't you have the sheriff question him?"

"And make myself look dumb? . . . who'd believe that skinny-

ass Mex was El Coco? Tell you what, Jerome. You dial the
sheriff. Give him your Coco story, and see how hard he laughs."

I went home to Fannie and the child. I hugged them with
such alacrity, they grew alarmed. Why was I squeezing the
wind out of them in the middle of the day?

"Monster man," Jessica wailed. "Let go of me."

Monster? If I squeezed long enough, I figured that blond boy
might disappear. He wouldn't lie still. He'd get up and fall, get
up and fall, a boy with a money box ripped from his chest.

Fannie coughed into my ear. "Hon, you'll strangle us . . .
you're not holding clay."

I let go.

Jessica held out her tongue. "Mama, he's such a creep."

Fannie made me a tuna fish salad to quiet my nerves. But I
couldn't swallow that falling boy with the tuna fish. I couldn't
fiddle him out of my head.

TWENTY-THREE

The Author of Little John Woods

I.

It was to break the fall of a dead boy that I started writing again. Not Bissenwicks. Jerome Charyns. Simple tales about pirates and scalawags. I didn't rely on uncle Bob's encyclopedia. My pirates were dredged up from a different source. I had them sail their flagships among the bayous. They were villains, but they always had a peculiar angle to their greed. They were closer to Irwin Polatchek than Blackbeard, or Jean Lafitte. They would cut a man's throat out of some twisted purpose. Revenge? Suspicions of jealousy? A slight to their honor? I called uncle Bob.

"Pirates?" he said. "Kid, that was ten years ago. War stories are big this year."

"Then I'll try *Mademoiselle.*"

"Don't be such a snot . . . lemme have a look."

I sent him one of the stories.

It took weeks for the uncle to call me back. He mocked me on the telephone, chuckling from his closet in New York.

"Your money days are over, kid. Three hundred, or goodbye and good luck."

"I'll take it, but there's a catch, uncle Bob . . . I won't be your Roger Bissenwick."

"Bissenwick? Why should I wake a mummy like that? I'll publish you as Jerome."

"The Pirates of Blackheart" appeared in the April issue of Bob's magazine. Perhaps it was dumb to bandy my name when I was still a fugitive. But who cares? Louisiana could wrestle with Lamar over my body. No one interfered with the convict. I went on writing and scratching for frogs. But the clerks and firemen at city hall read my story. I had to autograph their copies of the magazine. Even Jessica was nicer to me. I heard her chatting on the phone. "He lives with us, I swear to God . . . he's my mama's boyfriend."

I had status, respect from every corner of Little John Woods, but a blond boy can eat through "respect" like a crocodile. While I scribbled I was fine. The pirates eased my guilt. I could laugh over them, grovel in their nastiness, celebrate their plunder and all. But how could I scribble day and night, day and night?

And there was that murderer out on the bayou to remind me of things. I shoveled with him, the rancor building up. He had a copy of *Triton* rolled in his back pocket. I expected him to sneer at my pirate story, to call it a piece of filth. The bitch stopped shoveling and shook my hand.

"Jeronimo, you're a motherfucker when it comes to pirates . . . hey, is that pirate with the moustache and the missing ear supposed to look like me?"

"Don't flatter yourself. Dig. Lamar needs his frogs."

2.

THE Wellesley Club of Houston asked me to give a talk at their annual luncheon in May. I agreed. I wanted to shame Lamar, show him that a convict of his town, a man *he* had sentenced to hard labor on the bayou, could address refined women who'd gone to college in the East.

I talked about my father's violin . . . Harvey, the teddy bears, Fritzie King, and Linda Darnell. I had to work Hollywood in somewhere. I wasn't rude. I didn't mention tits or anything, that Darnell was built like Lillian Feld, with the same broad shoulders, round face, and bosoms that would have been the envy of Orchard Beach. She had died in a hotel fire, Linda Darnell. All my heroes were going. Alan Ladd, Tyrone Power, Irwin Polatchek, Darnell. Only Brando was left.

We had a polite question and answer period. The women were interested in teddy bears, pinkeye, and my father's violin. I'd misled them. They thought he was a virtuoso of some kind. Would I bring him to Houston if the Wellesley Club paid for his trip? "Retired . . . Sam doesn't use his violin. He has a case of fiddler's elbow."

It's a pity, the women said. They would have loved to hear him play. They wanted to know about the author who secluded himself in Little John Woods. Did I have a family?

Yes, I lied. "W-w-wife . . . and a daughter of n-n-nine."

Soon as I got off the platform, the stuttering went away. But the tongue that betrayed me up there was telling me something. I returned to the woods and pleaded with Fannie. Her mouth opened wide to take a swallow of air when I said the word *marriage.*

"Honey, are you out of your mind? I have a husband. Maynard, remember him?"

"I don't care. Lamar can marry us. He's a judge."

"And they'll steal Jessica from me when I become a bigamist."

"Who'll ever know? Gurney has its own laws. Lamar's like a king. He can write a few lines in the town's books and annul your first marriage."

"Just like that," she said. But she was softening to the idea. She began to sniffle. "You really want to marry me? . . . a swamp girl from Lake Charles. I only had a year of college."

And what were my four years? Anna Karenina's horse and a gold key that I got because of Marcel Proust. Lamar married us at city hall. He grinned at the irregularity of our wedding knot. A convict takes a married woman for a bride in a town that had the Octopus on its borders. Who knows when Houston will swallow Little John Woods? But we'd still have our names in the marriage book. We had wine at the ceremony. Fannie wept. Jessica had her friends from grammar school. Marcos came out of his closet to wish us luck. He danced with my new wife.

Fannie was flushed with wine and other men's kisses when I brought her home. I took a bride at thirty-seven. Suppose it wasn't orthodox. Maynard and the sheriff of Harris County can come knocking at our door. They'd have to pump me with holes to get their bride back. Fannie belonged to me.

I drank in the smell of her hair. I popped every button on her wedding shirt. I took her nipples into my mouth while Jessica remained at city hall with unca Lamar. I ate the creases in her back. I nuzzled between her legs, and she held on to my scalp, her body slapping like a beautiful fish. Jerome and his mermaid wife.

3.

LAMAR had a wedding gift for us. "How long have you been convicting, Jerome?"

"Nine months."

"Hell, I can't keep track of everything, boy. Why didn't you tell the jailer your six months was up?"

"Because you'd have given me another year for opening my mouth."

"That's true. But we can't allow a married man to shovel dirt for free. I'm putting you on the payroll . . . sixty dollars a week."

I wondered why Lamar wouldn't release me altogether. He could have grabbed another bum who strayed into the woods. He wanted me out on the bayou.

The whore had a good reason.

Mayor Jones was romancing my wife.

I stumbled into the cottage a little too early one afternoon. It was horror and a crazy wildness that landed in my chest. I was like a bullfrog frozen in the mud. I couldn't take my eyes off Fannie. Her head was back on the pillows. A vein seemed to crawl up her brow. Her chin rose higher and higher. Lamar's buttocks were red. I bit my knuckles and got out of there.

I tramped through the woods with a hollering in my ears that was like the hiss of rats in a Bronx sewer. I might have hurled myself into Blackheart Bayou and drowned in mud if a hand hadn't pinched the seat of my overalls and pulled me away from the bayou wall.

It was Coco's hand. He turned me around and saw my puckered face. He didn't have to ask where the dents had come from. The Phantom knew. Did Lamar pay him to have me do busywork for the town, collect those stinking frogs, to clear his own way to the cottage?

"Hombre, come with me . . ."

We rode the pickup truck into Little Mexico. He parked outside the taqueria with the wooden sidewalk. Marcos slicked down his hair, combed his moustache, sprinkled drops of perfume under his armpits, put on the blanket cape that went above his nose, and the serf of Little John Woods became the Phantom of the barrios.

Coco and his friend stomped onto the wooden sidewalk, went

around the parrots in the window who bowed their heads and muttered, "Señor, Señor," while the whole restaurant stared at us, because the Phantom had never come with a gringo. But when his eyes fluttered softly over the neck of his cape, the restaurant began to stir. Men and women touched his cape as he passed, and we sat down near the left wall, where Coco had a view of the windows and the fire exit. The ancient musician who had warbled to Jessica on our last visit materialized suddenly out of a dark corner and started to cluck with his throat. He clapped, fiddled, sang, and danced for El Coco with the persistence of a lovesick cavalier, and he was a hundred years old. The Phantam took this musician by the ears, scooped him into the folds of his cape, hugged him, and let him go.

The musician returned to his dark corner.

The Phantom's army of boys assembled around the table. He introduced his army to me. Hector, Chapito, Billy, Red, Chi Chi, Hernando . . . Hernando was the boy who drove the station wagon. He was the Phantom's twelve-year-old lieutenant. They had Pepsi-Cola with a piece of lime drowned in the bottle, and we had pitcher after pitcher of Mexican beer. They didn't plan their robberies at the table. And with beer in me I could forget that I had killers on both sides of my lap.

Later the Phantom led me out of the restaurant. I remembered saying adios. He stuffed his cape under the floor of the pickup truck, messed his hair, let his eyes go dull, and he was a convict again.

"Will you help me get rid of the mayor?"

"Don't be foolish," Marcos said.

"Three hundred dollars, three hundred, to tape his mouth."

He smacked me across the face. "You shut up. I'm not your little hit man from down the corner." And he tossed me out of the truck.

"Hombre, be careful with that gringo in city hall . . . you'd be smart to lend him your wife."

The smack didn't hurt. My head was swollen with beer. "Coco, shove your advice . . . I'll lend him a fist."

I banged his hood and wobbled a half mile to the house. Fannie and Jessica were in their pajamas, gawking at me. "Husband, it's nearly midnight."

I waited until Jessica was off to bed. Then beer and fury took hold, and I ripped the sleeves of Fannie's pajamas. I shook her until the bones rattled under her eyes. "Bigamist, huh? Lamar should have let me become the judge. I could have married you and him, and found myself a crocodile to fall in love with . . ."

I couldn't shake her forever. She wouldn't fight back.

"Lamar never did move out. He just changed his routine. He comes courting when I'm in the muck."

I felt a jab in my hip: a bronco had charged me from behind. The bronco was Jessica Brindle Smith. She would have butted me out of the cottage and into the hairy night woods if her mama hadn't said, "Baby, it's nothing. Men and women shout all the time."

"Mama, why'd he tear your pajamas?"

"Those old things?" Fannie said, wagging her shredded sleeves. "They decided to fall apart."

Jessica believed her. She kissed Fannie, poked me in the ribs to say she was sorry, and went to her room.

Fannie looked at the wall. "I wanted to live with you, and I didn't know how else to do it."

"So you struck a bargain with the son of a bitch. You gave him his afternoons . . ."

She whipped her hair around, this wife of mine. "Yes, he could send you to Pineapple Junction, keep you holed up for the next twenty years."

"Pineapple what?"

"The sheriff's prison farm . . . all the vagabonds Gurney doesn't need go there. I process them from city hall."

"Lovely business. You're the Pineapple clerk."

"Go to hell . . . you . . . you show up after four years in a prison suit . . . I was doing fine. How do you bargain with a mayor? I'm a runaway wife . . . you miserable skunk."

I could have packed and gone to the jailhouse.

I undressed the bride, helped her out of her torn pajamas. We kissed standing on our feet. I knelt and chewed the blades of her hips. Then I brought her down to the living room rug. Who can explain the perversity of husbands and wives? Knowing that Lamar had touched her, had been inside my Fannie that afternoon, puffed me with rage and an unholy desire. I ravaged the wife, with my own black heart at work, thinking of her head on the pillows, and Lamar's buttocks rising like a sinister snail.

TWENTY-FOUR

Jean Lafitte and the Emperor Jones

I.

I was an author of pirate stories stuck in the woods with his new family and unca Lamar. If I didn't watch out, the Emperor Jones could put me on a chain gang called Pineapple Junction. He had a pistol, his judge's robes, his firemen and his four deputies, but I was going to win. I would lie in the mud, wait, nod at him from my closet, and then I'd pounce and tear the neck off Lamar. A headless mayor would look just right at city hall.

I didn't stalk him outside the cottage. I let him have his afternoons. I slaved in the creek with Coco, turning grim around three o'clock.

The Meskin wasn't a dope.

"Hombre, think about the frogs . . . or another señorita. Those alcaldes, they got their special privileges. They walk in and out of your home. Do you have an old girlfriend?"

"Sure. Her name was Lillian. I know her twenty years."

"A high school sweetheart?"

"Ah, I was third on her list. She loved this guy Irwin Polatchek."

"Who cares? What part of her body did you like best?"

"Nipples," I said without a moment's hesitation. "She had beautiful brown nipples."

"Then close your eyes, hombre. Remember Lillian's nipples . . . and Lamar will go away."

So I had an afternoon of brown nipples. The nipples took me to her harp. And the song "Ramona" she would play. I didn't capture many frogs. But the Meskin was right. I passed through that three o'clock dread.

"Marcos, you made a deal with the Emperor Jones, didn't you?"

"The same deal as yours, Jeronimo. We're peons . . . indentured servants."

"That's not what I mean. He's letting you hide in the woods. He wants you to throw terror into Houston, scare that big Octopus, so it won't have the energy to swallow his village. He has the Phantom on his side."

"Hombre, he doesn't have shit. He's the emperor of a dumb forest and a fire truck."

"Could be." And I went back to digging in the creek. His lieutenant, Hernando, came out of the barrio with a pitcher of beer for us. I licked that wonderful beer while Coco sent the boy away.

"Stupid, would you like the sheriff to catch us holding hands?"

But his anger wasn't real. The Phantom took delight in Hernando's pluck. The boy rode into our woods in the gang's station wagon to relieve two convicts of their thirst. Next thing he'll be offering the sheriff some beer. The gang roamed wherever it pleased.

I got to the cottage around seven and washed off the mud. ". . . chicken feathers."

Fannie was at the stove. "Will you stop mumbling."

"Chicken feathers! The mud in the creek is like the chicken feathers my brother Harvey used to wear. I figured if I was alive long enough I'd end up in some kind of crap."

"Eat your soup," Fannie said. I heard a braying outside the cottage. It was the sheriff's bloodhounds. Their braying was a bit too joyful for me. It didn't sound as if the dogs were in trouble.

"Goddammit, Jerome, do you have to leave the table? Where are you going now!"

We had that tension of Lamar between us. That mayor who had turned my marriage into a circus act. But I didn't discuss the Emperor Jones.

"Fannie, those dogs wouldn't be smirking unless they found something good. I've got to see what the hell it is."

I went out the door and into a blitz of light. The sheriff had wired the whole fucking woods. His lamps hung from trees, or crouched like ironbacked turtles on special trucks. The road was hogged with deputies in brown shirts and pointy hats. They didn't have the smell of failure on them. They were grinning under their hats.

They must have gotten shrewd in the last couple of weeks. Their other marches into our village always ended with grime in their mouths. They would step in mud and go home without the Phantom. I'd come off the bayou with Marcos just an hour ago. Was he inside city hall, eating frozen tacos out of the mayor's icebox? Grins on the sheriff's men made me think the Phantom might not be in his closet. And dogs don't bray like that when they're sinking into mud.

I followed the deputies across the woods. The braying got louder and louder. It was like barking out of hell. Did you ever hear a pack of dogs howl bloody murder? They had Coco up a tree. Those animals surrounded the trunk and leapt up into the branches to snap at Marcos' legs. His pants were missing above the knee. The hounds had chewed away all that material. They would have shredded the Phantom up to his shoulders, that's how high they could leap.

But it puzzled me.

Even if they had sniffed him by some marvelous accident, Coco should have been able to get onto the bayou and lose the dogs. Unless he was bushwhacked right out of city hall.

It had to be Lamar. Our mayor was standing with the sheriff a few yards from Coco's tree. The sheriff spoke into a bullhorn.

"Hey Mex, come on down from there . . . that Scotch Tape stuff is over. I'll count to seven. Then I'll whistle to the dogs. They're playing with you, boy. They can rip the eggs out from inside your pants. I trained them myself."

Coco spit blood at the sheriff from his tree. One gob of it landed on the sheriff's hat. I could tell. Blood on his hat disturbed the sheriff. He hooked two fingers into his mouth and gave a whistle. The dogs began to tighten around their collars. They brayed harder now. They stopped chewing Coco's knees and went for his crotch. The Phantom crawled deeper into the limb of his tree and kicked a bloodhound in the eye.

I wanted to get near Lamar, but the sheriff's men shoved me away. The Octopus must have been breathing heavily on Lamar. The Phantom had lost his usefulness. Killing blond boys wasn't enough. The Scotch Tape Gang couldn't slow Houston's drive to gobble up the village, and turn our woods into one more of the Octopus' hairy legs. The Emperor had to act. He fed Marcos to the sheriff's dogs and made himself a vassal of the county. Who knows? Was it a treaty under the table? Tit for tat? Lamar delivers Coco, and the sheriff promises to support the integrity of Little John Woods.

But the sheriff was a man with blood on his hat. He needed vengeance right now: a Phantom with a pair of severed balls. The hounds jumped into that tree with a whirl of their spines; each one was like a bullet with hair on its face. The sheriff didn't have to count to seven. His dogs were only an inch from Marcos' crotch. They leapt from both sides of the tree. How long could he kick at them?

He shook his branch to distract the dogs and then dropped to the ground. He tumbled over once, twice, on his bloody knees and rose up from the grass. The sheriff clutched his bullhorn. It made an electric whine.

"Freeze, you monkey man . . ."

Coco was running for the bayou. The dogs bit his heels. He spilled onto the grass and got up again.

"Freeze, I said."

Coco shouted and ran. *Tu madre, tu padre. You motherfuckers.*

The sheriff raised an arm, and his sharpshooters unloaded their pump guns into the Phantom. Raw splotches of blood appeared on his overalls. His body spun with every hit. But he ran. Little red wells bubbled out of his back. His knees jerked. He plummeted into the grass, his jaw striking the ground. He died six or seven feet from the bayou wall.

The dogs gathered round and pulled on his shirt. But his death wasn't over with. I heard this crazy scream. His muchachos ran out of the bushes. Nine boys with popguns. They stood over Marcos and shot the dogs in the head.

The sheriff waved off his men. He wasn't going to murder young boys. The muchachos didn't continue the fight. They allowed the deputies to capture them. My eyes went from boy to boy. Coco's lieutenant wasn't with them. Hernando hadn't come into the woods to shoot at dogs.

The sheriff wouldn't handcuff the boys. He was much more primitive than that. He bound them together with an enormous rope and paraded them on a truck. Ambulances arrived with surgeons and stretchers and gunny sacks for the dogs. That patch of earth near the bayou, with blood and guts and trampled grass, was like any battlefield. Would the village put a marker on that spot to celebrate Coco's last stand? Ask the Emperor Jones. Lamar was liable to have a eulogy for his own dead convict.

2.

No eulogies in Little John Woods.

But the barrios went into mourning. They seemed to shut tight, to throw a blanket around themselves, as men and women snaked through the streets with candles in their fists. Straw likenesses of Coco were built in ghetto parks. Children stayed out of school. The barrios had a new day to remember: Doce de Junio, when Coco was shot down in our woods.

The mourning lasted a month. The effigies disappeared from the parks. Old women carried off an arm or a leg to worship in secret. They had their holy legs of straw.

Cops raced through the barrios with their sirens on.

A Meskin boy was found at the bottom of Whiteoak Bayou.

Gas station clerks began to arm themselves against future gangs.

I took the Phantom's cape out of its hiding place in the floor of the pickup truck, rolled it up, and stuck it behind a brick in Fannie's cottage.

I gave notice to city hall: Lamar could scratch himself. I wouldn't go out on frog patrols. I wasn't his convict any longer.

If his deputies came for me, I'd hit them with a shovel. Fannie disapproved. "They'll throw you in Pineapple Junction."

"I'd rather peel potatoes for the county than get the Emperor his frogs."

"Peel potatoes? Your hands will peel. It's not a prison hotel. You can't check out at six. You'll sleep with murderers and bums."

"I've slept with murderers before."

She began to cry. "Go to Lamar and tell him you're sorry . . . it's your only chance."

"I'll go when I can dust him with the shovel . . ."

But I didn't have to go anywhere. Lamar came to our street. He was riding a goddamn pony. He wore a cowboy's bandanna, and he had a guitar sitting on the hind bow of his saddle. He wasn't playing judge or Emperor Jones. I could have wiggled my ass and Lamar wouldn't have looked. He wasn't interested in me. He was there to court my wife.

He plucked that damn guitar from the vantage of his pony, crying out a love song that was like the belch of a frog. I ran after him with the shovel. He didn't stop his singing, or bother to squirm in the saddle.

I felt a boot crack me on the skull.

I couldn't remember falling down. Lamar squatted next to me. He was grinding his pistol into the hollows of my cheek.

"A lunatic jumps you with a shovel . . . you blow his face off. That's justifiable homicide . . . or self-defense. I'm the mayor here."

I saw Fannie behind his shoulder. She tugged at his wrist. "Lamar, please . . ."

"Honey, you ask that boy to invite me inside."

"He doesn't have to invite you," she said. "It's my house."

"No, I want him to do the inviting."

My tongue was fat, and I couldn't blow air around it fast enough to talk. But I could think a sentence or two. *Piss in the creek, Lamar. That's all the invite you'll get.* It was dumb thinking. I'd have a better chance to attack him inside the cottage, once I was on my feet again. I shaped the word *inside* with my lips.

"Thank you, Jerome."

The mayor scooped me off the ground with his arms and carried me into the cottage. I could have been a gunny sack for all he cared. Then he shackled the pony to Fannie's little porch and returned to us with his guitar. The pony scratched her head against the side of the cottage. The roof shook, and Lamar yelled from the window, "Bernice, will you cut that out?"

The pony was quiet.

Lamar smiled. "I'll have some tea and biscuits, honey."

So my wife had to feed the son of a bitch, while I sat in the corner like an invalid from that sock he gave me with his boot. Hearing him chomp on his biscuits and suck hot tea, I had a longing to rush at him and take bites out of his forehead. But I was dizzy and weak.

The door opened and Jessica marched in with a satchel of books. Her eyes crinkled at the sight of the mayor and his guitar. She hugged him and climbed up on his lap. Not a word for Jerome.

"Unca Lamar, unca Lamar!"

"Now, now," he said, stroking her hair. "You calm down, baby girl, and your mama will fix you a snack."

She drank from Lamar's teacup and shared his biscuits, chomping the way he did. I wasn't deaf and dumb to their carryings-on. It was old reunion time at the cottage, and I was odd man out.

"Have some tea, Jerome."

"Worms," I said.

"What's he talking about? *Worms* . . . why are you scaring the little girl?"

"Worms," I said. "Worms is where Marcos lives . . . under the ground."

"That's no subject for ladies. So shut your mouth."

"Worms, worms, worms."

He grabbed me by the collar and shoved me onto the porch. I looked into the pony's eye. She had ribbons in her forelocks, this Bernice. And her eye had a universe of colors in it, flecks of orange, red, and green. You could have lost yourself forever in that pony's eye.

"Do I have to give you a pistol-whipping?" Lamar said on the porch.

"Whipping won't change the truth. You put Marcos with the worms."

He picked me up by the elbows and knocked my head against the porch roof. Bernice showed her gums and her big yellow teeth.

"Listen, don't you take advantage, just because we're kin."

"Kin?" I asked.

"Being Fannie's husband . . . that's the same as kin."

"Frogs are my only kin . . . frogs and catfish."

He pushed my face into a spider web and then lowered me down. He laughed at the mess on me. I had a spider's silk in my mouth. It tasted like the blue skin on a hundred-year-old egg.

"Jerome, you're a famous man in these parts. We don't get to see many authors in Little John Woods."

I growled at him.

"Why'd you sell Coco to the sheriff?"

"I didn't collect a penny for that Mex. And there was a price on his head. He was getting sloppy, that's all. I mean, if a bird like you could discover who he was, the whole of Texas might find out. How would it look? A mayor harboring murderers and thieves. They wouldn't appreciate it at the governor's mansion. I'd lose my friends. The statehouse could go blind to Gurney. Politics is mean. I'd have to give up the village . . . for one lousy Mex. If you say Coco again in front of the ladies, I'll twist you in half."

The pony was kissing me. Her nostrils were pink and ticklish and soft as felt.

"That Bernice," Lamar said. "She falls in love with every fool." And he shoved me back inside the cottage.

I had to boogy for the mayor. He rapped on the box of his guitar with two knuckles, while I sashayed Jessica around the room. I wasn't a good partner for her. Knees and elbows got in the way.

"Unca Lamar," she said, "it's like dancing with a horse."

Fannie stood near the mayor with a hand over her mouth. She couldn't hide her giggling. Lamar touched her knee.

I went right on boogying with Jessica. The pony scratched the outside wall. These were hard times. You had to fish around for a friend. I'll take Bernice.

"Worms," I said.

The mayor dug his guitar into my ribs.

That's all right. I had a surprise for him. A little resurrection party, with the Phantom's cape as the guest of honor. You'll see.

"Mama, why does he have to step on my shoes?"

The pony must have heard us. She whinnied from the porch.

3.

I couldn't put on that cape until I did a special pirate story, something for the Mex. Fifteen years ago I'd started with Jean Lafitte. So I did another "Jean," in memory of El Coco, the murderer who was my friend. This Lafitte had nothing to do with the War of 1812. He wasn't Andy Jackson's helpmate and the hero of New Orleans. He was a stinking brigand and a dealer in human flesh. He smuggled "black diamonds" (Negroes) into the United States. He had no brother Pierre in this story. He was a cutthroat who loved to ruin other men. He took over Galveston Island and built a fortress and a town, "Tres Palacious," in a grove marked with three tall trees. But Jean didn't have the island to himself. It was filled with Karankawas, a cannibal tribe. The Karankawas ate a dozen of his men, boiling them in a big laundry pot they stole from town.

The pirate was outraged that these Indians should think so little of Jean Lafitte. He drove them from the island in a war that lasted seven days. He fired his cannons at the Karankawas and chased them along the sand. His men stood slightly behind their leader. They weren't so anxious to fight with cannibals. Lafitte jeered and returned with the skull of the Karankawa chief. He kicked his own men and beat them bloody for being cowards in the Indian war.

He was in such a rage, he would have welcomed the Karankawas back onto the island. But the Karankawas wouldn't live around such a bitter pirate. They held to the mainland, where they continued their cannibal ways.

Lafitte set fire to "Tres Palacious." He couldn't forgive the cowards. He sailed off in his flagship, the *Pride,* with a few of his most loyal men. "Tres Palacious" burned to the ground. You couldn't discover a human face on that island for another ten years. Not even the Indians walked on Lafitte's sand. They were convinced the pirate left a ghost among the ruins that would come at them with a rusty sword. The Karankawas named him Ki-Ro-Na, "The Man Who Bites at Heads."

It was this story that I wrote for Marcos. I never mailed it to uncle Bob. I didn't want "The Man Who Bites at Heads" to appear in the uncle's bloody magazine.

TWENTY-FIVE

Inside the Octopus

I.

AUGUST 15th. The Octopus breathes in front of your eyes. The air is like clay. You can mold it with your fingers, watch it turn from its ordinary yellow to blue-green. You walk from one burning cloud into the next. The heat can fry your tongue. It's Houston.

I don't mind swimming in a fog of clay. I'm from the Bronx, where the catfish develop blisters during August, as they slap themselves in the boiling mud. I've swallowed yellow air before. I've touched fire escapes that took off pieces of your skin. I've stepped on tar roofs that mummified your ankles for an hour, until the sun began to cool.

The barrio was in the same yellow fog when I hiked over the borderline of Little John Woods. My hair was like a nest of sticks on fire. My eyes were summer coals. My nose was itchy under the blanket I wore. The sidewalk of Coco's taqueria had gotten tricky with the weather. I had to climb over humps in the wood. I passed through the turnstile, gathering the hem of my cape. People shivered at the thought of me. But they couldn't bring themselves to mutter *Coco* to a devil in a cape they had once adored. Their jowls swelled in confusion. The waitresses clutched their bosoms and the plaster figures of El Coco that had already begun to crowd the barrios. You could find hordes of them at any bazaar. Their scalps and eyes were painted black. Every cape had furls scratched into it by hand. Some family of artisans must have devoted themselves to the making of these statues: a cottage industry producing black eyes and hair. But I was going to put these artisans out of work.

Por Dios, the waitresses said. "Who is this guy?"

I took Coco's table near the left wall. A waitress brought me a pitcher of black beer. She looked into my eyes, and then, after a moment of doubt, she stooped to nuzzle the cape. She ran into the kitchen to tell her girlfriends and the cooks about the man with *cabos negros,* black hair, eyes, and brows, and a little gray around the ears.

The dregs of Coco's army began to arrive, one by one. Six underfed boys, with Hernando as their spokesman. They had their popguns under the table. Hernando didn't smile. The guns were aimed at my belly. I would leave the taqueria with my bowels on the floor if I couldn't satisfy the boys.

"Some joke," Hernando said. "You can pull shit on kitchen helpers. They're superstitious, man. They believe in monkey-shines at the graveyard. But I don't think the dead have a second chance, do you?"

"That depends," I told him. "Dead's a funny word."

"What's so funny about it?"

"You blow on a dead man and you can't tell what will happen."

The guns twisted deeper into the belly part of my cape.

"Hey man, you do riddles for a living, huh? . . . Chi Chi, should I shoot him in the prick? Then he'll learn not to come around in a cape that don't belong to him."

I let the cape fall under my nose.

"I'm Jeronimo," I said. "The ex-con. I worked with Marcos . . . in the woods. Hernando, I want to revive the gang."

They laughed with a bitterness crawling through their teeth.

"You crazy . . . Marcos grew up in the jungle . . . I watched him bite the fingers off a cop."

"Marcos isn't here. All you've got is me . . ."

"Prove to us you ain't sucking the sheriff's armpits. It would be nice to trap us in one car . . . you get the reward money and we get the whip."

"Try me out . . . but I'm the boss. What I say has to go."

"You hear?" he told the muchachos. "Bushy mouth is the boss . . . hey, what if we shoot you in the prick?"

"Shoot," I said, praying to the catfish and Marcos' corpse.

The guns disappeared from my belly. "Jeronimo, why you so slow?"

We scrambled out of the restaurant, six fleecy warriors and the Batman of Little John Woods. But Hernando wouldn't play Robin. He had the popguns and the expertise behind the wheel. I was a former convict, and a ghost, up from the bayou to lay havoc inside the Octopus. The gang's station wagon was in a shed behind the taqueria. Its fenders were dusty, and the windshield was spotted with live bugs. The wagon hadn't been used since Coco dropped from his tree and was mangled by sharpshooters and the sheriff's dogs. We had to scrub the wagon down with lots of soap and water. My cape got wet. The muchachos giggled at their new boss.

Me and my lieutenant had the front to ourselves, and the other five muchachos sat shoulder to shoulder in the rear, like a gallery of roosters. Hernando was considering how many gas stations we could knock off in one long, devastating ride.

"Gas stations are out," I warned him.

"Who invited this nut?" Hernando asked his friends. "Marcos always said to specialize . . . that's how you get to be famous. We do gas stations, man. That's our number."

"No more . . . and no killings either."

We barreled out of the shed.

Hernando stopped the car in the middle of a block that was full of rubble and had ditches on both sides of the road. "Chico, you'd better go home . . . because I think you're into baby stuff."

"'Nando, you need me . . . six kids in a station wagon could be any gang . . . Coco is what makes them shit. We're changing our tactics, and our style . . . let's hit an ice skating rink. That'll surprise the bastards. Take me where they have some summer snow."

"Cinderella city," Hernando said. "All the little rich girls skate and go shopping . . . at the Galleria."

What did I know of the Octopus? Shoveling dirt for months and months, I'd never been to the Astrodome, or the other air-conditioned wonders that the Octopus loved to crow about, underground streets and shopping malls, buildings that looked like caterpillars made of glass.

"We hit the Galleria, man, we won't get out alive. The mothers will seal it off so tight, it'll be like walking into a birdcage."

"Let me worry . . . leave it to the boss."

I had Irwin Polatchek in mind, and his conquest of Crotona Park. We weren't going to build a Polish corridor around here. But I'd romp through this Galleria like Irwin would have done, and give the Octopus a taste of the Bronx.

We parked under a super highway and combed our hair. I folded the cape, stuffed it into a plastic bag that I could carry inside my shirt without an obvious bulge. We followed the highway until we entered an underground fortress; the fortress turned into a huge, air-conditioned mall that was like the top three decks of an ocean liner that never moved. The Octopus had a right to crow. You couldn't find such a place in the territories I had come out of. The Crotona Y would have been a pygmy hut inside the Galleria.

I wasn't there to marvel at the works. I crouched behind the muchachos and put on my cape. Then we fanned out. Our target was a little restaurant near the Galleria's ice skating rink.

The gang struck from five directions at once. We were heartless and swift. A tornado had seized the lower deck. Men and women were horrified. *The cape, the cape.* El Coco ought to be dead.

We emptied the cash register while young girls in tutus gawked at us from the rink. Hernando flirted with them and pushed a few busboys in the face. The manager of the restaurant must have gone berserk. He started to slap at the muchachos. I saw the gun come out of Hernando's pocket. He held it against the manager's skull. That dreamy look in his eye smelled of murder. The manager rocked and moaned with a popgun at his brains. I slid my hand under the manager's hairline and stuck a finger in the barrel of Hernando's gun.

Hernando gritted at me. "I shoot, boss, and your finger will go up to the roof."

"'Nando, put that thing away."

The gun went into his pocket, and then he taped the manager's mouth. We had to run for the exits because cops in baby-blue shirts were arriving from the opposite end of the Galleria. I let the cape roll off my body. I had it inside my shirt with four swipes of the wrist. The boys were startled to see Batman become old gray ears in under a minute.

Hernando dug his fist into my back. "Chico, run. The baby blues are behind us, man."

So we lit out of there, rode the back streets and deposited the station wagon in its shed. The muchachos divided the loot among themselves. Chi Chi, the youngest, received the lion's share: two hundred and eighteen dollars and sixty-one cents. Hernando took a hundred. The gang saved thirty dollars for me.

"I don't want it . . . buy a few flashlights with the money. We'll need them if we go prowling after dark."

I returned to Little John Woods. Mother and daughter were at home. They didn't mention Lamar's pony, or treat me like an extra dad. Did I have furrows somewhere, grit around the eyes? Could they feel I'd been out on a raid, this author of pirate stories they lived with, the village fool . . .

Fannie trembled when she got close to me that night.

"You're different," she said. "I don't know."

We made love under the blanket, with Fannie clawing at my neck. It was mean and cruel and delicious. Suddenly she was frightened of Jerome. And I thought, you need a bit of strangeness to satisfy the wife. Terror always wins.

"Honey, I won't let Lamar in the house . . . I promise."

"I piss on Lamar. He can ride his pony through the door. See if I care."

She began to whimper. I wasn't going to tell her she was beautiful when she cried, that I liked Bernice the pony and hated Lamar, that I was a general who got thirty dollars from the gang and wouldn't accept the prize.

"Jerome, what happened to all the gray? . . . your hair is getting black."

"Ah, it's gray enough."

And I started to eat her own blonde hair.

2.

THE newspapers were full of us. The radio and the television blasted out our story. The Scotch Tape Gang was back. Another Phantom had arisen. With a change in sensibility. He didn't attack gas stations on the edge of town. He didn't murder boys. He stabbed the Octopus in the heart. He went into the Galleria to steal, punch, kick, wink at girls in tutus, and tape a manager's mouth. The new Phantom was much more invidious than the old. You couldn't be sure where he'd strike. Every sort of police was on his track. Blue shirts and brown shirts. The sheriff had replaced his murdered bloodhounds with a fresh stock of dogs. The manhunt was just beginning now.

Let them holler and beat their chests. They didn't plunge into the barrios while this Phantom was alive. The thought of Coco was enough to cool them off.

Meskin boys didn't end up in Buffalo or Whiteoak Bayou. The barrios had their bazaars and street fairs without disturbance from the cops. Hernando invited me to dinner at his mama and papa's house. They lived in one of those cottages with a refrigerator on the porch. Hernando's porch was like a tiny marketplace. Old men played dominoes; chickens flew on top of the rails. We ate indoors.

You froze inside that cottage. My lieutenant had bought an air conditioner for his mama and papa. It hung out the window like a dinosaur's tooth. The windowsill rattled with every grunt of the motor. You had to hold the dishes down. But the family seemed to take pride in the shivering of the cottage. Would the porch break away and jump into the next yard? The old men wouldn't have noticed; they'd have kept up with their dominoes during the catastrophe.

What were sliding dishes and a runaway porch? Hernando was determined that his mama and papa wouldn't suffer from the heat. I figured him to be twelve, but he was older than that. Fourteen. He'd finished school at eleven to join Coco's army. Truant officers didn't come chasing after him. He was one more forgotten boy. But he had a superb education in the Scotch Tape Gang. He drove like a wiz and learned the English language by listening to the Phantom, who could jabber with mayors, judges, and college graduates.

I was an infant at fourteen, raised near a shallow creek; my mentor was the catfish. I drew whiskers at Music and Art. I pumped my biceps and drank a quart of milk. I had fur animals under my bed. CHARYN'S BEARS. I was in the heart of the heart of some distant country called the Bronx. I couldn't buy an air conditioner for my mom and dad. I didn't have forty cents in my pocket. And Hernando? He was a lieutenant without biceps and quarts of milk.

His father hadn't worked in years. Old Hector was a chairmaker with a withered arm. Even in a boomtown a crippled Mex wasn't worth very much. You can't sew the bottoms of too many chairs with an arm slapping against your side. Hernando's mama was a *criada* at a hotel on Prairie Street. The boy was angry that his mother should have to pick the hair out of tubs and sinks. But he couldn't support the family on a bandit's pay. The gang had been wily and daring under Marcos. Still, the muchachos were lucky to break even on their raids. They sank their profits into the station wagon, which succored them and was a marvelous getaway car: the upkeep was incredible. They had to worry about batteries and brake shoes, tires and transmission gears, and an engine that got into the habit of causing fires and floods. How often did Hernando drive with flames under the hood, and fluids leaking from the bottom like precious brown blood? The muchachos wouldn't consider changing cars. The wagon was a live creature to them, a member of the gang.

Sitting in that cottage on my frozen ass, tasting soups and meats and blue corn tortillas with Hernando's mama and papa, I thought of my own mom and dad, and how I'd neglected them. I was over the hump at thirty-eight. A pilgrim in his middle years, severed from Crotona Park. I was a Texan now, married to Marcos' corpse and Little John Woods. And to see a fourteen-year-old boy devoted to his family made me bitter about myself. I'd left my mom and dad in a borough that was slowly burning to the ground. Teenage arsonists commanded the roofs of the East Bronx. How long could the catfish protect Fannie and Sam? There wasn't enough water in the Bronx River to spare that Polish enclave from smoke and ruin.

I whispered to my lieutenant at the table. "'Nando, get some sleep. Tomorrow we drive your buggy into the Bronx."

"Soak your head," he growled back. "You drive, man. I'm staying here."

What could I do? I closed my eyes to images of fire and stuck a blue corn tortilla into my face.

TWENTY-SIX

Fiddles and Things

I.

DIDN'T have to go to the Bronx. The Bronx came to us.

The firebugs had a feast in the summer of 1974. They put Crotona Park to the torch. Trees and grass burned with a cruel appetite. The fire didn't stop at the edge of the park. It crossed the street. A third of the borough disappeared. The Bronx River was sucked dry in the fire storm. Turtles, frogs, and the catfish were scorched to death. The mud turned gray. Not one catfish survived.

Fire was something the Poles understood. Wars among the Rastafarians hadn't been able to drive them out. Teenage gangs could piss on their roofs. But smoke curling out of the windows got them to pack their bundles and flee. Fannie and Sam went to live with my brother Harvey on Long Island. They roasted ducklings in Harvey's back yard. Then they visited my brother Marvin. Marvin was in New Jersey.

It took a month for that fire to burn itself out. You could taste the smoke a hundred miles around. Pieces of ash from the Bronx drifted over to New Jersey. My father held the ash in his hand. He began to cry. He felt completely orphaned without his turf near the river.

I shouted at him on the phone. "Come to Texas . . . we have plenty of rivers here . . . and mud."

I had to get the town's permission to add a wing onto Fannie's cottage for my mother and father. That's how tight the building codes were in Little John Woods. You couldn't sneak on an extra roof without Lamar's okay. "Sure," the mayor said. "Bring your folks out here . . . but you tell your carpenters not to screw with the front of the cottage. You start defacing property, and the value of the street goes down."

I went to Hernando's dad and put him in charge. The crippled chairmaker, Hector, arrived with two of his friends and a bottle of mescal. He showed me the worm in the bottle. You couldn't have mescal without a worm in it. The worm guarded the bottle and kept the mescal pure. I was a fool to hire three drunken carpenters and their guardian worm. But old Hector could hammer in nails with his one good arm faster than a team of Polish draymen. He and his friends were artists with a bevel and a saw. They tacked on a room to the side of the house in one long session of continuous labor. They finished their mescal and offered me the privilege of swallowing the worm. It was supposed to cleanse your insides and suck the poison out of you. I declined. So Hector himself swallowed the goddamn thing, begging the worm's pardon and shouting *salud*.

My mom and dad journeyed to Houston in a Greyhound bus. We had *two* Fannies in the cottage. They got along fine. The two Fannies talked about my profile. "Gregory Peck," mom told my wife. "They used to call him Gregory Peck on Albany Street."

"Who's Gregory Peck?" Jessica wondered out loud.

"The handsomest movie star in the world, you little idiot," my wife told her daughter.

"Don't believe them," I said. "Tyrone Power was better looking . . . and Marlon Brando, before he got fat."

"Who's Marlon Brando?"

Jessica started to laugh. "Just teasing," she said. "Unca Jerome, you belong in the Stone Age."

They took my mother shopping with them. I didn't worry so much about her. She'd make a good pioneer. Hadn't she gone out to Jersey and run a hotel for Fritzie King? She'd thrive in Little John Woods. But my dad? I couldn't bring him along on a raid, like a teddy bear in the car. Suppose we were captured. How would it look if my own dad ended up in Pineapple Junction? My mother would have to come with sandwiches for both of us. It would be a terrible thing.

He sat in his room while I wrote pirate stories (I was finished with Jean Lafitte). Having your dad around can be dangerous to your work. I couldn't think up adventures for the pirates. They stopped injuring people. They turned sluggish aboard their pirate ships, and yacked among themselves. Their heads were stuffed with drivel. They wouldn't slit throats any longer. They talked, talked, talked.

Uncle Bob took the stories, but he complained about the pirates' slow drift. "Christ, have them pull a sword once in a while. It might create a little breeze. Jerome, when do the fuckers start sailing again?"

I couldn't get them to sail, with my father in the cottage. The wind wouldn't blow. It was dead on the bayou.

I heard a scratching sound from my father's room. It gave me the chills, because it was like a spook coming into the house. My father did have a violin. And he was playing it in the other room. It had to be the fiddle my mother had warned me about, the toy he got when he couldn't come to America with his mom and dad . . . on account of conjunctivitis. Some aunt had hoped to bribe his grief away with a fiddle. The pinkeye kid.

I approached his room. He must have heard my footsteps. The fiddling stopped. I wasn't going to spy on my dad. Let him have his phantom violin. I went back to my pirates, and their dead wind.

2.

MOM became a Southwesterner while my father fiddled in secret. She went to the Houston fat stock show with my wife. She
ate tamales and stroked an enormous cow with the silken body
of a whale. And I couldn't get my father out of the cottage.

His scratching helped my stories along. A wind blew down
on the pirate ships that was so fierce, it shut the pirates' mouths.
They returned to the business of slitting men's throats.

There was a face in my window. Child, or old man, it flitted
about much too quick. A pirate? Or some lost brother of my
dad's, with his own violin? I stepped outside. Hernando stood
near the window with his shoulders humped up like a cat at
war, ready to hiss and spring at an enemy.

"Are you waiting for the sheriff? It's not a prison farm, for
Christ's sake."

He darted into the house. Hernando wouldn't take coffee. I
had to give him a cup of Jessica's pink lemonade. His gun fell
to the floor, a pathetic lump of tin. I could have squashed it
under my heel. He shoved the gun into his pants and swilled
the lemonade.

"Hey boss, how come you disappeared on us?"

"Who says I disappeared? The Bronx burned down . . . you
know that. Your father built a wing for my mom and dad. My
dad is touchy. I don't like to leave him alone in the house."

"Save some time for us. The gang's starving . . . and we're
out of gas."

His eyes swelled and his forehead rippled, as the scratching
started up behind the wall. His mouth couldn't hold the lemonade. He gagged and spit into the sink. "A chicken's dying in the
other room."

"No, it's my father . . . he's playing the violin."

"Don't fuck around. A violin can't scream."

"Ah," I said. "He hasn't practiced in forty years."

"Lemme see this violin."

"Shhh . . . you'll frighten my dad."

Hernando couldn't live near those "chicken screams." I grabbed my cape, rolled it up, and followed him out the door. The gang was parked under a tree. I gave the boys money for gasoline.

Hernando shook his head. "No more skating rinks. We pop a few gas stations, we can coast for a month."

"Why go back to the old ways? . . . that's dumb. We have to build on our reputation. I want to hit the fat stock show."

"We're warriors, man. We don't frig cows and bulls."

"Nobody's asking you to frig a cow."

We went into that monstrous lot in front of the Astrodome: field after field of cars. It made you dizzy just to look, because your eye couldn't take in the ends of the lot. You could have sailed to the Indies and back in those fields. And the 'Dome? It was a covered metal dish, puny somehow, like a shell that was about to crack open and reveal the pale, blind ribs of a vast, pink-bellied insect.

We tramped across the parking lot, the boys grumbling at their leader; how would we ever find the wagon again in that maze of cars?

When a guard turned his back to whistle at some cowgirls, we crept under a barrier and into the Astrohall, home of the fat stock show. It was a concrete tent, fit for circuses and rodeos, the running of small businesses, and the parading of cows. It had a recruiting station inside the doors, a miniature smoke-house, a booth that hawked encyclopedias, burrito stands, stalls where you could have your Stetson steamed and blocked, trac-tor salesmen, and cotton candy machines. Stomachs were growling, and I had to feed the boys. They gobbled cotton candy, with that awful pink web stuck in their mouths. And this was the Scotch Tape Gang. A refugee from Crotona Park and six boys unwinding paper stalks until they had nothing to lick but their thumbs.

We marched into an enormous holding pen where cows from different herds sat in trenches with their ancestry and dates of birth written on a card above their heads:

> Miss Delila 75
> SIRE: Beau Geste
> DAME: Perfect Lady
> Calved—Feb. 6, 1972

Then there were the "sheiks" of the herd: the bulls on display, in their own separate quarters. The sheiks had spotted noses and bands of muscle on their necks that reminded me of weightlifting in the Bronx.

They moaned softly when the cowgirls arrived with pails of food. Cows and bulls. It was mysterious, a church of animal flesh, all with pedigrees. And I couldn't get in. I stood there wishing I had been born into a world of cows.

Ah, I'd forgotten the boys. We had mischief to do. I couldn't lull them with cotton candy, and dreams of Delila 75. I put on my blanket cape in a dark corner of the pen, and the gang exploded, grabbing the purses of three cotton candy vendors. The sheiks snorted at my cape. The cowgirls dropped their pails. Tourists blinked, and we were gone, the cape tucked in my shirt.

We roamed the goddamn lot, going in dizzy circles until we stumbled upon the wagon. And then we crept away from the 'Dome.

Hernando divvied up the take. It was less than a hundred dollars. The wagon got sixty for plugs, oil, and other medication; the rest was put in Chi Chi's pocket. His father had hanged himself in jail, and twelve-year-old Chi Chi was beholden to support his mama and two baby sisters. The gang practiced a radical socialism among its own members. I wondered if the muchachos had read Johnny Broom's little brown book.

The boys dropped me off at Little John Woods. I was shivering. I couldn't count on my river gods. The catfish had been roasted in a fire storm. The Bronx River was a dry gray hole. Nothing could live in gray mud. All the beautiful yellow was burnt out of it. So I put on my cape in the woods, hoping it would relieve the shivers. And it did. I was Batman again, swathed in Coco's blanket. But Lamar's deputies were combing the woods for vagabonds. They jumped at the sight of me. "Coco," they yelled. "The Phantom." They were about to scatter, but something must have entered their minds. Four deputies with guns in their belts, and only one blanket man: me. They drew their guns and chased the blanket man in their brick-red shirts. The guns went off with a terrible racket. The ground rocked under my feet. Branches shattered in my face. The idiots were shooting up Little John Woods. I wasn't going to spill my blood to these red shirts. I'd lure them into Blackheart Bayou.

I slid down the bayou wall, and they followed me. Their knees sank in. They were like a band of infants that couldn't skate on black mud. They sloshed about, hollering and praying to Jesus. They held on to the shrubbery that grew along the bank, and I skated up the bayou, towards home.

3.

BERNICE the pony was on our porch. She dipped her head in hello as I went into the house. Lamar was drinking tea with the whole tribe: the two Fannies, Sam, and Jess. He sat with his boots off, the Emperor Jones. My dad put schnapps in the mayor's tea. Lamar banged on the table.

"Goddamn, Jerome, this is one hell of a family . . . wish my daddy was alive."

The bitch actually started to weep. My mother offered him a cookie. Lamar put on his boots. "Jerome, got a favor to ask . . ."

He led me out of the cottage with a knuckle in my back. The pony followed us down from the porch. Lamar shoved me into the trees.

"Don't you ever bring your act into my village . . . Herman called. My number-one deputy. He was swimming with his teeth in the bayou. You nearly drowned the slob. You're a nuisance, Jerome. I'll gonna have to take down your pants in front of city hall and whip your ass. That's what we do to little boys that go around in a bandit's cape."

He pushed me deeper into the woods, while Bernice nuzzled my shoulder with a special kind of love. Some team they were, the mayor and his pony. One licked you, and the other bruised you up.

Lamar slid his hand into the neck of my shirt and popped every button along the line. He brushed his fingers against the cape. "Carry your own disguise, huh? Did you rob the Phantom's grave? You skinny prick, you've got all your people in the cottage sittin' there. I could burn them out whenever I like."

"You drank tea with my father, you son of a bitch."

"So what? Why do you think I let you build on a room for mom and dad? Now your clan is under one roof. I'll skunk them with fire if I have to. You behave, sonny chil'."

I leapt into his shoulder. But he swiveled around, seized my belt, and hurled me into the grass.

He walked over me with his boots, stepping on my knuckles, up my arm, and onto my ribs. I howled from the pinch of his heels. Then I saw an arm whirl out, lovely in the elbow and at the wrist. The arm belonged to my wife.

"Get off of him, Lamar."

"I was only foolin', honey."

"Get off."

He climbed down from my ribs. I could feel the dents that whore Lamar had put in me.

He was nervous around the wife.

"How come you won't visit with me, Fan?"

"Shut up."

"We had swell parties before Jerome came to Texas. You ask Jessie girl. Ask her which uncle she admires. Lamar, or the creep?"

"Go on. Take your pony to city hall."

He climbed onto the pony's back and rode into the woods, his face lost in Bernice's neck.

"Thanks," I mumbled, searching for my buttons in the grass.

"I told you not to mess with him. He's got a crazy streak."

She swabbed me in peroxide when we got to the house.

"Was he born in Texas, honey?"

"Stop honeying me. You're just like that jackass. Lamar's from Albuquerque. He got into trouble with his father, and he ran down here."

"Didn't he say his daddy was dead?"

"Oh, he's always lying. You can't believe Lamar. He studied to be a dentist. But they threw him out of college. So he sweet-talked the village and bowed and shined people's boots. They had to give him the mayor's job to get him out of everybody's hair."

"Who told you this?"

"The honchos in the village. Only they can't elect him out of the job. He's dug his claws in. He'll be mayor for life."

And there it was. The emperor's story. A boy of twenty-one appointed mayor of a little "bedroom" village that didn't even have a fire pump. It was a joke. He was given a desk at city hall and an allowance to play with. But he wasn't in the mood to play. He began collecting revenues, and writing a code of laws.

Lamar hired deputies with the money he pulled in. He bought a fire truck. He expanded a broom closet at city hall and declared it a jail. It wasn't grim, or medieval. The jail had an open door. The village began to enjoy the fruits of convict labor. They'd garden and whitewash your walls, and attend to the bayou.

Blackheart had turned into a rotten sink. The Octopus would empty its garbage into our creek. Folks didn't have much respect for a body of mud that crawled through our woods like a sluggish, watery worm. Convicts could shovel the filth out of the creek, including dead frogs. But there are no convicts now. Marcos got killed and I became the Phantom's little brother.

Lamar had his pony, his gun, and his guitar, and I had a blanket that was shedding green hair. He was resourceful, ruthless, the man from Albuquerque. I'd seen the whore with his nose in Fannie's tits. He'd hooked my stepdaughter with his pony and his guitar. He'd made friends with my mom and dad. I was a pilgrim without his river gods. But I'd win.

TWENTY-SEVEN

Scotch Tape

I.

LAMAR was right to be jealous of my family. He had a cot at city hall and frozen enchiladas. Why shouldn't he come over for my mother's pancakes and my father's schnapps? The bitch was pushing me out of the cottage. He would stand next to my mother while she grated carrots and onions and give her a kiss. "Good to see you, mom."

He looked like my brother Harvey with his thick head of hair and Japanese eyes. Harvey was a detective in Brooklyn. But if he decided to leave homicide, who knows? He might become the sheriff of Harris County, or the boss of our woods. Texas had the newest wave of pioneers. Whole avenues of South Vietnamese. Wetbacks who lived underneath the stilts of certain cottages in the barrio. What about a street for Poles?

And the whore Lamar? Now he had two Fannies to fuss over him. Mom's pancakes and my wife's behind. I wondered if he was getting ass from his pony too? One day I'll capture Bernice and ride her to San Antone, and the whore will scream for his missing nag.

I went out on a raid with the gang. I had mischief in me, a black, black heart. I didn't care how many mouths we taped.

249

We passed a string of nudie bars and go-go shacks on Kirby Drive, when I heard a familiar pluck. "Stop the car."

"Jeronimo, there's a lot of baby blues in this traffic. Let's pick a deserted street."

Once a girl plays the harp for you, you don't forget. We trooped into a go-go shack called the Naked Edge. There were no adornments on the outside. It could have been a panhandlers' barn, some beggars' station on the road. But it was blue inside, a nightmare blue that streaked your face as you entered. I wasn't wrong about the harp. Lillian sat on a platform, bathed in cheap blue light, and plucked out a song. A topless and bottomless go-go musician, she'd had her dream of performing without her clothes. But it wasn't Debussy. It was shitkicker music in a redneck bar. Men made grabs at her ankles. They howled at her blue nipples and her blue rump in the chair. Her eyes were fixed on the ceiling. She had the slow, stuttering moves of a wind-up toy.

I jumped onto the platform and pulled down Lillian and her harp. The boys were amazed at the cheek I had. They helped me carry that monster, with its foot pedals and golden prow. The rednecks were still clutching Lillian's ankles.

"Hey, cowboy, where you goin' with our merchandise?"

The muchachos took out their popguns, which had a silvery glow in the blue light. The rednecks slunk into the corners, and we kidnapped Lillian from the go-go shack, laying her harp in the bed of the wagon.

Had the shitkickers forced her to swallow a lousy pill? Lillian was in some dark reverie. Her face was swollen and yellow. She didn't blink once.

"Lillian, it's the catfish man . . . Jerome . . . your favorite tutor."

We drove her to Fannie's cottage. I looked for the mayor and his nag. The coast was clear. I threw my cape around Lilly's shoulders, and the boys lugged the harp onto the porch. It rocked for a moment, and the porch shivered with the monster's weight. The boys said goodbye to Lilly. What a gang I have. We save drugged girls from living in horrible shacks.

I brought Lilly into the cottage. "Mom, you remember Lillian Feld from Music and Art . . . she was my fiancé for a month . . ."

No one seemed suspicious of the blanket and the harp. My wife welcomed this old girlfriend of mine. She must have noticed the hysteria in Lillian's eyes. Thank God the blanket hid the rouge she had to wear on her nipples and her kneecaps to satisfy the shitkickers of Kirby Drive.

Jessie adopted Lillian Feld. They became sisters and companions, sleeping in the same bed. Lilly was much healthier in the morning. The yellowness was gone. Whatever drug she'd eaten had worn off. Polish tea flushed the poison out of her head. She talked of her trip from Irving Place to the go-go alleys of Houston. "I had a rotten manager, Jerome. He said there was a big demand for harpists in the Southwest. Some demand . . . I can't go back to Irving Place. My mother will kill me if she finds out."

"Ah, you can stay with us. We have plenty of room . . . Lilly, where's your dog, that Alyosha?"

"'Yosha died,'' she said. "My baby was hit by a truck."

I liked that mutt with his wire hairs. Poor little bastard. It's not so easy to replace a dog. Where could you get another Alyosha?

While Fannie was at city hall and Jess was at school and my mother was out shopping, Lilly would practice in her room. She liked to pluck with no pajamas. I could smell her nakedness. I knocked on the door. *Come in.*

She played "Ramona," and I stared at her brown nipples. We made love in Jessica's bed with the abandon of Music and Arters, while my dad scratched on his fiddle behind the wall.

Lilly had her tongue in my ear. "I should leave," she told me.

I heard crackling noises inside my head. That's how far a tongue can go. "Jerome, your wife . . . she'll see us together. And don't forget Jess . . . it isn't fair."

"Lil, remember that time we wrestled in the snow? . . . when you belonged to Polatchek?

"I remember. You raped me, you skunk."

"Rape? I couldn't unbutton my pants. All I got for my trouble was an ice-cold tit."

"Well, that's rape in my book . . ."

Lillian had a point. But that didn't keep me from knocking on her door. I would watch Fan and Jess for any signs that they were on to me and Lil. Jess was happy with her new sister, and Fan had the same enigmatic smile, with or without the harp. A blonde angel she was, who fed me apples on a Louisiana hill, ran to Houston with her little girl, and took me into her house after a gap of four years. She kept Lamar as her lover, and became a bigamist to "marry" me. When I held Lil, I could feel the glue of her nipples and the beating of her heart, but I couldn't get under Fannie's skin. Why had she chosen me from that barrel of lunatics at Shuttleford Grange? Her love was like getting pricked by some exquisite needle. Fannie stabbed you, and the pain was delicious, but you didn't know why. You couldn't explain the wife.

2.

IT was brown nipples and my father's violin. Pirate stories and my gang. Our raids took on the languid music of a dream. How long can you be a boogeyman? The Octopus had learned to tolerate the wounds we inflicted in its rubbery heart. The boys were becoming penniless around me. The station wagon continued to lose blood. The springs collapsed inside the upholstery. You sat with prongs in your ass.

"Hernando, I always wondered . . . why did Marcos start using Scotch Tape in his gang?"

Hernando shrugged, but Chi Chi said, "I know . . . he was too poor. The other kids at school had their rolls of tape. He had to borrow from the teacher. It bugged him all those years. So he took his revenge . . . he taped and taped and taped."

"Bullshit," Hernando said. "Chi Chi made it up. Marcos would have told me . . . I was his lieutenant, man."

"Yeah, then you didn't listen."

They dug into their pockets, ready to have a duel in the car. I had to grab the wheel from Hernando, before we bumped off the road and onto somebody's lawn.

"Who cares about Scotch Tape?" I said, and the guns shrank into their pockets again. We robbed a fish stand on Navigation Boulevard, leaving the proprietor ten dollars to buy gas and get home. Chi Chi wanted to tape the fins of a dead catfish, as a reminder of who we were, but I said no. "It's bad luck."

"Boss, you gotta give me somethin' . . ."

So I let him tape a flounder—or was it some other hump-nosed fish, with its head slapped to one side?—and we high-tailed out of there.

We took the back roads, driving against traffic, and got the wagon halfway into the shed, when the trees began to light up and sway with electrical energy. The sheriff had his own little act prepared. The barrio snapped with a hellish glow from arc lamps hidden in the trees around the shed. The sheriff had his bullhorn. "Come on out, chil'ren . . . you too, spider man."

The boys weren't going to surrender. You could tell in the grit of their teeth how much Marcos had taught them. But I wrestled with the boys until the guns dropped into the upholstery, and we struggled out of the wagon with our hands in the air.

The lights were a bitch. All I could see were shadows with boots on. Those shadows were ablaze. But somewhere, among the boots, I could tease out the contours of a pony.

"Lamar, did you send Bernice to finger us?"

"Shut your mouth," a voice crackled from within that buzzing song of the lights.

Hands tried to shove me away from the boys.

"You cunts," I screamed. "I'm with Hernando."

I was socked on the cheek with a horse's bit, hanging from a knotted shoelace. My legs were shackled, and three of the sheriff's posse lifted me into a truck.

"Take me with the gang."

I started to bite the posse's pants. They threw a canvas jacket onto me with long, long arms that could be tied around my chest. I foamed and spit and cackled at the bastards. Then I sobbed with a fierceness in my gut I couldn't remember having before. What would they do to the boys? I'd wheedled Marcos out of the grave and given the muchachos nothing but idle plans and pauperhood. We were robbers who couldn't make a dime. And I'd led them into the sheriff's lights.

They drove me downtown in their terrible truck, to the idiots' ward at the county jail. I had assistant district attorneys drinking hot soup with me. I was chained to the bed. I called everybody a whore and spilled my soup on the district attorney's men. They flopped me over, like a naughty whale, and the medics stuck a needle in my ass.

I woke with a face near my bed.

"Go on, stab me with your needles. I won't sign a confession until you give me back the boys. We're a gang. We belong together."

The face had a chicken neck: it sat on a bumpy stalk. The guy was too old to be a medic. Medics don't wear diamond rings. He had a silk handkerchief and dyed red hair.

"We can plead insanity," he muttered, "or get hit with murder one."

"Who the hell are you?"

"Billy Sunshine."

Sunshine was the most feared criminal lawyer in the Southwest. Prosecutors shivered at the thought of Billy Sunshine. He defended society wives who shot their husbands, bandidos in the oil business, dentists with one mistress too many that they had to push out of the way.

"I can't afford you, Sunshine. The gang's worth shit. And I only get three hundred dollars for the stories I scratch. Even my pirates are down and out."

"That's all right, son. I'm fond of you. I'll take the case."

"What about the boys."

"I never mess with juvenile court. But don't you worry. The state can't hang a thing on them. It's you they'll want. The spider man."

"What spider man? . . . Sunshine, who hired you, anyway?"

"Your mama did."

Ah, she was always getting me out of jams. Here she hires Sunshine, the very best, and when I was a goddamn truant, stuck to Irwin Polatchek and his Barons, my mother went to Music and Art and talked to the principal himself. She got on the IRT, broke her heel in the middle of Harlem, hobbled into the principal's office, and had him strike my name off the truancy lists. Fire storms and the state of Texas couldn't defeat Fannie Charyn.

"We go the insanity route," Sunshine said. "If that won't wash, we'll agree to a morals rap. One thing, we've got to wave a jury trial. It'll be a fuzzy street we're traveling on. We go to trial, and the district attorney will swear the other Coco was a fake. He'll have that jury pointin' a finger at you. Killer Jerome. The spider man."

"The boys will speak out for me . . ."

"Don't count on it. The DA will keep them off the stand. It's easier for a cowbird to shit his weight in gold than gettin' youngsters to testify. The court'll protect them from a monster like you . . . so we'll try crazy first. And you'll have to sit in this ward, because they don't let crazies out on bail."

"Fine. I've been a lunatic before. I had geldings for company, and a mathematics wiz."

"Remember, Jerome, play the fool, but no visitors. I can't have you weepin' and huggin' your mama. The guards are tattletales."

I was crafty with my jailers. I sang pirate stories to them, I drew whiskers on a piece of slate, but it got lonely scratching with yellow chalk, while I was chained to the bed. *Murder one.* I'd been a convict half my life, it seems, shifting from one jailhouse to the next.

Sunshine came to cheer me up.

"You can drop the idiot routine. It won't go down with the DA. He wouldn't bite. We'll take the morals rap. Corrupting infants. Puttin' them on the road to crime. It's not a felony. You'll only have to eat half the pod."

"Sunshine, talk English, will you? Half the pod? What's that?"

"Six to nine months at Pineapple Junction."

Pineapple Junction.

I had the creeps.

The sheriff's own prison farm; he fed his hound dogs on convicts' hands and feet.

I rattled my chains at this super lawyer.

"Sunshine, I like it here. I think I'll stay an idiot a little while longer."

Sunshine wagged his chicken neck. "No chance. You're not listenin' . . . it won't wash with the DA's office."

"Who cares what will wash? You defend hatchet ladies, for Christ's sake. No one's ever beaten you in court."

"I told you . . . we can't take this one to a jury. They'll convict . . . the DA will destroy your *two* Phantom theory. This is

Texas, son. You mention a masquerade and the jury will howl for blood . . . yours and mine."

Sunshine took me upstairs to the judge. He told me to nod and keep my mouth shut. He'd do the talkin' for us. It was Billy Sunshine vs. the People of Texas. The bailiff unshackled me so I could stand up straight and nod a little better. The district attorney's men whispered to the judge. The sheriff peeked in, smiled, and disappeared. It was a curious game, because the DA's men would wink at Sunshine and then squabble with him. The judge had to quiet them down. He asked if I was Mexican, but Sunshine wouldn't let me speak.

"He's Polish, Your Honor. A good Polish boy. His mama and his daddy have moved to Texas."

"Then what's he doing with a Mexican gang?"

"He stumbled into piracy, Your Honor. You know about these authors. They have a sick imagination. They like to act out all their fantasies."

"Well, it's a sloppy bit of acting, in my opinion. And he'll have to pay for it. But I've read his stories. He can whittle a sentence when he's not too lazy."

The district attorney's men agreed.

What kind of a hearing was this? Were they going to punish me for my pirate stories? The DA's men accused me of "moral turpitude." The word *Phantom* was never discussed. I was a Polish import from the Bronx who piped evil songs to the boys until they went astray. But you should have heard this Sunshine. He got the bailiff to look into my eyes with pity and regret. I was a misguided rascal, Sunshine said. A poor renegade. The piper of Little John Woods.

I had to promise the judge I wouldn't go near the boys. If I was caught in their company, with just the tiniest whisper, or the raising of an eyebrow, he'd have me *and* Billy Sunshine thrown into the state pen. Sunshine had risked his standing in court that I wouldn't prey on Meskin boys and blow my "filthy pipe" at them. I didn't understand Texas law. Could that chicken neck be shackled to his own client and share my fate? The judge hollered and let the spit fly. He'd explode any deal between Sunshine and the DA's office if I turned foul.

Meantime, the judge gave me "half the pod" to eat. I was sentenced to nine months of labor at the county farm. The bailiff tied me to six other prisoners, and we were led off to a bus.

The lawyer pumped my hand.

"You chew that pod, Jerome, and you'll be all right."

I got to thinking, that deal the bastards made, it smelled of fish. It's a wild country, this America, where you're an idiot in the morning and a demonic mastermind by the end of the afternoon.

The chains scratched into my legs. The prisoners pulled on the chains. I tripped twice, shuffling onto the bus. They laughed and sang wetback songs. I was the gringo author. No one said a word to me.

TWENTY-EIGHT

Pineapple Junction

I.

IT was more like a factory than a prison farm. It didn't have many free acres, with horses, chickens, and championship bulls. The prison manufactured soap and feed for cows and pigs. It also had a cannery. The sweet gluey smell of pineapples engulfed the prison in a thick brown fog that got into your hair and your clothes. You breathed pineapples. You felt their stickiness in your cuffs and under the band of your wristwatch. After a week, the leather on the band would turn from black to brown. That was Pineapple Junction.

The prison had its own railroad terminal, with a good mile of tracks. These tracks crept right up to the cannery door. The pineapples would arrive in smallish crates, and the whole prison had to get out of bed. The pineapples meant a flurry of work. The convicts would eat breakfast in the dark, divide into special unloading teams, and attack the crates. No one could tell where the pineapples had come from, because the crates were unmarked. The Yucatan was our guess. Were they grown on a Mexican prison farm? Why not? Our sheriff had contacts with jailers everywhere.

The cannery was his great pride. It supported Pineapple Junction, and fattened the county's treasure chest. The sheriff wouldn't tolerate slackers. Only the sickest convicts and the very, very lame were exempt from the chore of unloading pineapples. He vowed that no prison under him would ever operate at a loss.

We climbed up into those stinking railroad cars, the floors crusted with ancient pineapple juice. It was like trying to walk on a thin coat of jelly. You slipped and nearly broke your ass, but you lugged the crates down off the cars and through the cannery door. The wooden ribs of a crate would often rot in your hands. A pineapple might come tumbling out, turn into a soggy bomb, and explode, with dead beetles swimming from the bomb. You'd want to scream, but you might choke on your saliva that was like pulp in your mouth. So you shut up and let the beetles swim in the little rivers of juice.

I was among the lucky souls at Pineapple Junction. Yes, I unloaded the crates, but I never worked inside that miserable plant. The sheriff remembered that he had an author around. I was put in the library. I didn't have to catalogue books. I taught Dostoyevsky to Meskin convicts.

The sheriff examined my syllabus and warned me about "inflammatory remarks." He fingered my prison shirt and said, "You start revolutionizing with them books of yours, bub, and I'll build a gallows for you. It'll be the first and last hanging of my career."

The sheriff growled and all, but he sat in on my class and did the reading I required. Here, in Pineapple Junction, I cursed my own spotty education. Marcel Proust and the Boston Road Public Library. I had to catch up on Shakespeare, Melville, Dostoyevsky, and Bernard Malamud. My mind swelled with memories and notes from different books. I lectured on Paul Morphy, Hamlet, and my dad. I had to tell the class who Morphy was. They couldn't look him up.

He wasn't in the *Encyclopaedia Britannica.* That's how much he'd fallen in a hundred years. The *Britannica* went from "Morphology" to "Gouverneur Morris." Fie on all your books that leave out the greatest chess player in the world!

The class liked the way I wove in Morphy and my father's violin. ". . . the gift of chess turned Paul into a very special child. When he tried to throw it away and become an adult who didn't have to push wooden pieces on a board, he fell into isolation and madness. His chess was like my father's fiddle, only Morphy was a genius at it. Chess was vulnerability and magic, a source of incredible weakness and strength. It gave him power over other men, but his fiddling shattered the little king, split him into the boy who couldn't become a man. He became a ghost instead.

"Look at the other fiddler . . . Hamlet he's called. A sadfaced prince who conjures up his own dead father, destroys his sweetheart, kills his uncle, and chides his mama for going to bed with a king. Dying, he asks his friend Horatio to stick around and tell the prince's story to the world.

"And what is the prince's story? That he can jump into a grave like any wild boy? Hamlet is the disease that defines us all: the need to shape the bones of our existence into some imperishable history. Who are we? Where do we come from? Why will we cease to exist?"

The sheriff stopped me after class. "Hell, Jerome, you don't need Billy Sunshine. You can outtalk that blabbermouth. I'll hire you in a minute if some goddamn judge ever gets down on my case . . ."

2.

HAMLET and Paul Morphy began to pay off. The sheriff removed me from his "pineapple list." I didn't have to suck coffee in the dark and unload smelly crates. I could dream of new lectures as I lay curled on my back.

I had visitors from home. Mom and dad. One of Lamar's deputies drove them up to the Junction in a brick-red car. I didn't have to stare at Fannie and Sam through any chicken wire. The sheriff practiced minimum security at his prison farm. You could stroll on the grounds with your mom and dad, introduce them to the chaplain, the cannery bosses, and the sheriff. I was privileged on this farm, a magic man, the prison lecturer. My classes on Raskolnikov and the fiddler's art were akin to voodoo. Convicts would moan and punch the floor in the middle of a lecture. I was the Phantom's gringo brother who had a burr on his tongue that was the mark of a story-teller.

The convicts were appreciative of my dad. He was the *violinista* who appeared in his son's prison lectures. They wondered if he was hiding the fiddle under his coat.

We had tea and bonbons in the sheriff's private dining room. My mother brought me two dozen sandwiches in a shopping bag. The bag hadn't been tampered with. The gatekeepers wouldn't search Charyn's mother. "Mom, they don't starve us in prison . . ." How could I refuse sandwiches that took her a day to prepare? I gobbled cold chicken and liverwurst.

"Mom, dad, where's my wife . . . and baby Jess."

Dad looked at his shoes. Mom said, "Jerome, they're busy . . . Fan is working day and night. Poor girl. She never sleeps. And Jessica has school and her riding lessons. Lamar takes her out on the pony . . ."

I was in a black mood when they left. The wife wouldn't come. Was she ashamed to have a husband at the county farm? It didn't make sense. I was a convict and the village slave when I first bumped into Fannie at city hall. And Jess? She had her pony rides. She didn't need a yardbird for a dad.

The telephone rang in the prison library.

"Charyn, it's for you . . . an outside call."

I picked up the phone. "Fan?" My knees were shaking. I can't help it. Any convict wants to hear from his wife.

It was that leech from the Flatiron Building in New York. Uncle Bob.

"Jerome, give us a pirate story. What a bio line we can run! *Written at the state penitentiary by Jerome Charyn, Triton's regular man.* Hey, it's like O. Henry. Didn't he go to jail?"

"I'm not O. Henry, Bob . . . and this is only a farm. I lecture now. On Dostoyevsky."

He laughed. "This isn't Moscow, old boy. Stories on epileptics don't sell. And I wouldn't pay a nickel for the Karamazovs, Alyosha and his crazy brothers."

I hung up on the prick.

Bob must have provoked me, because I started to scratch lines on a page. It wasn't a pirate story. I wrote about Sam. I tried to figure what it was like for him to be a boy in Poland, walking around with a fiddle, and no mom and dad. The pinkeye kid again.

I drudged up all the facts my mom had told me. Something about a pogrom. A massacre my dad had witnessed. Only the massacre was on the other side. Tough Polish Jews with rifles and sabers had hurled back an army of peasants. It wasn't my dad's village that was under attack. He'd decided to run away from the aunt who was minding him. To hell with America! He was going to Peking. He grew weary after six miles and fell asleep in some Jewish farmer's domain, a field of tall grass.

The rumbling of the ground woke my poor dad. The field was like an ocean. That rumbling arrived in waves that would advance and recede into the ground. He worried about his fiddle, that it might snap off at the neck and he would have nothing to take with him to Peking. He was a boy of fourteen with a clear vision of the world, pinkeye or no pinkeye. He meant to earn his living in China as a street musician. He was shrewd in this. How many Polish fiddler boys could Peking have? But if the rumbling didn't stop, he'd have to go to China and learn to fiddle with toothpicks in his hands.

Was it a giant causing shivers in the earth with the crush of his boots? A golem set free by the magical rabbis of Prague to restore righteousness into a universe gone mad? Would the golem destroy everything in sight? Flowers, trees, the continent of China, and my dad?

Sam peeked out of the tall grass. This golem was made up of many, many people. An army, in fact. Peasants with their children and wives. Such armies had come to Sam's village. My father would hide in the cellar until the crazy people murdered chickens and cows and broke enough Jewish skulls to tire themselves. Then the army would trickle off, and there would be feathers, blood, and wine outside the cellar window.

But these peasants were marching on another village. Sam noticed their drunken red eyes from his hiding place in the grass. Women and children were up front with the men. They carried sticks with sharpened nails at the head. Perfect to brain a chicken or scratch the eyeball of a cow . . . and for the human chickens, what could be better than your own fist?

Along with the groan of the earth, you heard chopping noises in the grass, as the peasant army shoved itself across the field. The peasants could eat a house, Sam figured. Bite off a roof.

Chew up a street with their jaws. Only the pogrom never got to the village.

Marksmen rose up from the grass. Jewish volunteers with rifles and swords from an earlier century. Long, tinny things that clattered in the sun. But the rifles could shoot, and the swords could cut deep into the shoulder. The explosions weren't loud: little pops, with feathers of smoke that swam around and died in the trees.

The peasants hadn't expected Jews with rifles. They were startled, unprepared. They stood clutching their sticks, and dropped with a terrible scream into the grass. Necks were blown off. Arms were shattered. Women had to plug the holes in their guts with two hands. It was unthinkable! Polish Jews interfering with a pogrom.

Then the army recovered itself, and found that instinct to flee. It abandoned the wounded and the dead, climbing over the backs of fallen comrades to get out of a rifle's way. If you couldn't crawl, you were left behind. And my father felt as if twenty golems had seized him and were pressing down on his head. Should he laugh or cry? Or just disappear, like a boy of clay? Jews had scattered the pogrom, but men, women, and children were writhing on the ground. Boys his own age had strings of blood that settled into the clefts of their chins, making a spider's design. What could my father do? He wanted to help the wounded boys. But those hawk-eyes with the rifles spotted him from their end of the field. How could they tell he was a musician on the road to Peking? The fiddle he was carrying could have been a gun. They aimed at him and fired. Bullets ripped the ground near his legs. My father hopped across the grass, dodging bullets, and sneaked home to his aunt. He gave up the idea of walking to China. Let another boy become the fiddler of Peking!

3.

I sent "The Pinkeye Kid" to uncle Bob. He said *Triton* wasn't the place for pogroms, but he didn't turn the story down. He ran it in the next issue, and two months later it won an O. Henry award as the second best story of the year.

"Didn't I tell you?" he gloated on the phone. "You and O. Henry . . . darling convicts. They're always good for a prize."

I was worried about mom and dad. I'd kept "The Pinkeye Kid" out of their hands, but it was reprinted in the Houston *Post* after the O. Henry awards. They arrived at Pineapple Junction with the same shopping bag of sandwiches. Mom chatted about the other Fannie. "She sends you kisses, Jerome . . . she'll show up next week."

It was always next week with the wife. She hadn't come to see me once. I kept looking at my dad. I searched his face for signs of anger, or *any* attitude towards "The Pinkeye Kid." I'd gone altogether gray in prison, but Sam had a tartar's black hair. He could have been my son. I mean it. I was the crumbling old lecturer who had to serve "half the pod" in this pineapple village. And he was the fiddler boy.

"Dad, did you like the story?"

"What story?"

Ah, mom must have hid the newspaper from him. No. "The pogrom?" he said. "Liar, I wasn't going to Peking . . . I was minding a neighbor's cow. And I didn't run home to my village. I bandaged two of the pogromniks with my shirt. Then I ran . . ."

"Dad, it's just a story."

"So? Stories can say the truth. It doesn't cost more than a lie."

He didn't mention his fiddle, thank God. My mother pulled on his arm and said it was time to go. We've been conspirators all these years, me and my mom. Where would I have gotten my stories without her? My fuel was Fannie Charyn.

I had another visitor an hour after they left. It wasn't the wife. Lillie had hitched a ride to the sheriff's farm.

"Jesus, are you still in Little John Woods?"

"Why not?" she said. "Your mother's nice to me. And somebody has to take care of Jess."

"She's no orphan. Where's her mom?"

"Fan's moved into city hall . . . with Lamar. Jess sleeps at the cottage."

"He's a fast worker, Lamar . . . fingers me and the gang and steals my wife."

"She's not your wife. The mayor granted her a divorce."

"Some justice of the peace. He marries, divorces, squeals on you . . ."

"I'm sorry, Jerome."

"Hell," I said, shivering in my guts. "Wives come and go . . . you can't be happy until you've had one divorce. I wish Lamar had sent me the papers. Husbands are always the last to know."

Never marry again, you'll see. You go to Pineapple Junction, and the wife crawls into Lamar's nest. At least Lil was here. My custodians in the library winked and turned their heads away. They knew what fierce blood a convict can have when a woman's on the premises. Lil was thirty-nine, like the old yardbird himself, and even if her musical instrument had crazed her a little, she was still a foxy girl with big brown eyes and plenty of cleavage.

We had a reading room to ourselves.

We took our pleasure under the table. That table danced for us; it seemed to twist around as much as we did. "Jerome, Jerome," she said, with the creak of wood in my ears. "I shouldn't have broken our engagement . . . you could have been my husband at Music and Art."

Wouldn't have worked. The studious little rabbi and his Lil, with their own suite at the Mississippi Hotel. And mama Feld in the adjoining room. Face it. Catfish don't make good husbands. They're devious and fickle, and can wound you with the drive of a tail. Lilly was better off with the dream of her harp. One day they'll accept her in the concert hall without her clothes. Why can't a woman be naked and pluck Debussy? Until then she can practice in our cottage, with my dad behind the wall.

"Jerome, would you like to walk out of here? I could arrange it . . . I think the sheriff is in love with me."

"Where did you meet the sheriff?"

"On the way to the library . . . I might get him to open the gate for you."

No, no, no. Wouldn't let Lil distribute her favors, just like that. She's practically a Charyn, her living in a cottage with my mom and dad. Three more months, and my half of the pod would be over. I'd do the "three."

Must have hurt Lil by slighting her offer. Her shoulders stooped as she wiggled into her underpants.

"Ah," I said. "Even if he loves you, the sheriff can't deliver. What would he tell that judge in Houston . . . that Charyn escaped from the library? It would throw a black mark on his prison."

We climbed out from under the table, kissed, and Lil seemed in a happier mood. The custodians themselves brought her to the front gate.

4.

I reached my fortieth year at Pineapple Junction. The sheriff sent a cake with forty candles into the library. I cut through the chocolate with a plastic knife. We had a tiny feast, Jerome and all his students. They were versed in the sad fate of geniuses like Melville, Hamlet, and Paul Morphy. And they'd read "The Pinkeye Kid." My father was a hero to them.

"Hey, *professor,* write another story . . . about your dad."

But I couldn't write. Forty years old, and a yardbird. I sucked on a candle. The wax went down with the chocolate. I'd have had those forty candles, eaten every year, if the sheriff wasn't with us. He'd say that chewing candles didn't mix with Dostoyevsky. And I'd be out of a job.

TWENTY-NINE

The Geek

I.

WE had movies every night. Old favorites that a convict could adore. *Sands of Iwo Jima, Rhapsody in Blue,* and *Nightmare Alley,* the one we liked best. It was a carny film I'd seen thirty years ago at the RKO Chester, when movies cost eighteen cents. We loved Tyrone Power as Stan the bum who breaks into the big time as a "spiritualist," and then falls back to the carny and becomes a geek. It was this geek that connected up the gray convict and the ten-year-old boy of Crotona Park. It was the *thing* I remembered about *Nightmare Alley:* that character who swallows live chickens. He stands in a pit that you never see, and the carny master tosses him a chicken whose head he's supposed to devour. The chicken's a blurry mess of feathers on the screen. White feathers. It squawks as its body whirls into the pit. The crowd screams and shivers with horror and disgust. And the carny master has to hide his greatest attraction, because you could be arrested for having a geek in your show. The geek is billed as half man, half monster, a guy who feeds on snakes, chickens, and rats. The crowd can scream its head off. As a Polish boy growing up on a river, with the catfish as companion and muddy god, I felt a kinship with the geek.

Thirty years later, at Pineapple Junction, I knew what that kinship was. The carnies were gone, unable to compete with television, Disney World, and the fat stock show, but I had become that biter of chicken necks, the geek. I'd chew birthday candles, pages of Dostoyevsky, my mother's sandwiches, Lillian's nipples, my father's violin.

And the geek was going home.

The sheriff had to give up his lecturer. I'd finished my half of the pod, chewed it to death, and there'd be no more talk of fiddlers at Pineapple Junction.

"Muchachos, that fucking *Britannica* can put Morphy in the grave, it can rip him out of its twenty-three volumes, but I'm telling you, Morphy's alive!"

2.

I had the Little John Woods limousine service. A deputy arrived in the village's brick-red car. The sheriff started hugging me.

"You be good now . . . we don't take repeaters in here. They'll send you up to Huntsville. You won't lecture and you won't be in the pineapple business. They'll write 'Dostoyevsky' on your hide, and that's the closest you'll get to a book."

I wasn't stupid. The Phantom was ancient history, a retired myth. Geeks never wore a cape. I rode out of Pineapple Junction in that brick-red car. My students waved their prison handkerchiefs from the library window.

"Adios, *professor* . . . we don't forget. Hamlet, man. Lots of ghosts . . . and the little king."

"Mais oui," I muttered. "The little king stepped in mud and went down the river with all the other ghosts."

The deputy figured I was high on pineapple juice, and he ignored me on the trip to Little John Woods. He dropped me

at the cottage, but I didn't go inside. I hiked to city hall. Bernice
was in her tiny stable behind the firehouse. I felt her warm, wet
nose. She snuffed the hair on my hand with her powerful nostrils and banged the stable floor with one of her hoofs. Lamar
didn't deserve such a gentle pony. I went in to look for that
whore and my wife.

They were eating a salmon steak in the courtroom, which
was their Sunday kitchen. Lamar had a napkin at his throat.
His pistol lay on the judge's bench. "Howdy, Jerome."

"Keep your howdies, Lamar. I want my wife."

"That's a shame. The little woman got herself a divorce."

"A divorce from you doesn't mean very much. You never
performed a legal act in your life."

"I married you, boy. Don't forget. And I can shoot your chin
off for going near my bench."

Fan's mouth began to twitch. "Shut up," she said. "Both of
you."

So I appealed to the wife. She was lovely with all that anger
unsettling her blonde hair. I heard a whimper in my throat.

"Why are you with that skunk, Fan? He ratted on me. He
gave me over to the sheriff."

"It wasn't Lamar," she said. "I told him to do it . . . I wanted
to see your ass get burned."

She was the squealer then. But why?

"Jerome, you took that dumb bitch into my daughter's bed.
Jessica asked me about your lousy love stains. You can have
your Lilly with the harp between her legs. But not on my
daughter's mattress. Dribble with her in your mother's room."

"A couple of pokes," I said, "and I get put in chains for
that?"

I moved over to slap my wife. Lamar went for his gun. It was
a wasted effort. Fan walloped me on the forehead with her fist.
Geeks can swallow chickens. They can't fight.

My jaw landed in the salmon steak. But I still had my wits.

"It's okay when you fiddle with Lamar, but I rescue an old friend, sleep with her once, twice, and I have to go to jail . . ."

"You can suck her tits until the moon starts to bleed, but not on my daughter's bed."

The mayor didn't have to throw me out of his rotten court. I left on my own two feet, with lumps of salmon hanging from my chin. I fed the salmon to Bernice.

3.

I was king of a household that was moving into debt. Lil and my mom offered to become salesclerks at Sakowitz, or Esther Wolf's. I said no. I sat down to do a story for uncle Bob. It was about my mother, not her life in Texas or the Bronx—"The Salesgirl of Sakowitz"—but her childhood in central Europe, where she was orphaned at the age of three, when her mama, Sarah the Wise, the one Jewish landowner in a town of Poles, died of typhoid fever. Fannie didn't have a father to begin with. Gossipers claimed that Sarah had slept with a Polish colonel, and out of this "union," my mother was born. Or that she'd taken the village idiot as a lover, just for spite. Whatever, there was no husband around to inherit Sarah's many holdings: a slaughterhouse, a candle factory, two flour mills.

The merchants of the village were ready to pounce on Sarah's holdings. But you see, my mother was a very shrewd and articulate little girl. Already she could bark and spell like Sarah the Wise. So the draymen of the two flour mills had to take orders from a three-year-old girl. Fannie had her benefactors, a merchant here and there, a police sergeant who might have been in love with Sarah: my mother's mother only slept with gentiles, it seems. How could Sarah the Wise have protected her holdings by sleeping with poor Jews? She'd never have crawled under the barriers that said Jews and Jewesses couldn't own land.

The little queen of the village would go from property to property with her mama's accounting books and a fierce-looking gentile who carried Fannie's silver in his pockets. This gentile was the police sergeant, of course. And Fannie was the wonder child, the orphan who conducted business while she grieved for her mother.

The merchants grumbled over this obscenity, that they should be ruled by a three-year-old. But soon my mother was five and six, and she had a firmer grasp of things. She taught herself to flirt. She would whisper into the ear of a prominent baker. She wouldn't be six forever, you know. Wait, wait. She might be marriageable in another seven years. So the merchants paid out silver and dreamt of the holdings they might acquire if little Fannie could ever become their bride. The idiots began to compete for her favor. Imagine, sending gifts of produce to a girl who wasn't seven. It increased my mother's holdings, made her less and less dependent on these men.

But misfortune fell on her. The police sergeant dropped dead. The merchants pondered this act of God. Why should they court a seven-year-old girl when they could chew up her holdings among themselves?

So the little queen had to run from the village with as much silver as she could carry in her scarf.

4.

"THE Landowner's Daughter" won another O. Henry prize. Some readers complained. They said that elements were too phantasmagoric. *Mr. Charyn, a girl should know who her father is . . . I can't believe a three-year-old would boss a town the way*

Fannie did . . . Mr. Charyn, you nearly made your mother into a courtesan . . . But overall, the response was good. A certain producer wanted it for the movies. It got the Texas Writers Award. And the Houston *Post* reprinted it, with a few cuts, where the language was too strong.

Dad saw the *Post,* but he didn't mention Sarah the Wise and mom's career as an infant entrepreneur. He looked at my gray scalp and returned to his room, as if his son were the family spy, revealing our heritage to strangers. Lil grabbed the newspaper and said, "Your mom's an amazing character . . . getting around grown men before she was six."

Jessica marched my mother into her class. Mom played the little queen. "An orphan has to be tough," she told Jess' school chums.

"But how did you learn accounting when you were so little, Mrs. Charyn?" the teacher asked.

"The trick was being without a father," mom said. "I was always at my mother's knee. I watched her put checks and crosses in her books. I heard her shout at butchers who had a payment due. I won't lie. My mother lent out money at a very stiff price."

"Your mama was a shylock?" the genius of the class blurted out.

"Don't frown . . . it was a common practice. Money claps hands with money. That's a Polish proverb."

The class loved her. How many mothers had climbed out of their cribs to run a slaughterhouse?

I was edgy about the whole affair. I'd taken my mother's stories and spun them into myths. Was she really a bombshell at five, six, and seven? "Jerome, when are you going to write part two and tell people how I starved for ten years, came to America, and married your dad?"

"Mom, I'm not a talking horse . . . material has to sit with me a while."

5.

IT was the rainy season. A wind would come down from the north, the temperature would drop madly in a few minutes, and a shivering rain would fall. An hour of it and you'd have a flood. There wasn't a sewer in Little John Woods. The trees would bend, Blackheart would overflow, and you could bathe in your living room.

I'd suffered all this when I was out on the bayou with Marcos, before the sheriff's men chopped him down. We knew how to wrestle with Blackheart, sweep water from its swollen sides, as if we were bailing a drowned battleship. Or we'd jump into that mad, swirling creek, and follow the flood for a bit. Blackheart couldn't destroy the Mex. I'd hold on to him and we'd race with the water, while it swallowed frogs, trees, and somebody's front porch. We rescued cats, and once we pulled out an old lady and her frightened dog. You could never tell what Blackheart had it in its mind to eat.

But I didn't work for Little John Woods any more. The bayou wasn't my business. Lamar's deputies could come with their hip boots and battle the creek. I had to slap water out of our cottage and a find a snug, dry place for my family to sleep.

That north wind blew over the tops of our trees and took a trolley ride down to Galveston, where it whistled along Postoffice Street, shook the Strand, shattered stones in the city graveyard, nibbled at the seawall, and fell into the Gulf.

Signs were posted in the novelty shops of Little John Woods: CLOSED DUE TO HIGH WATER. The water began to recede. The shops opened again and had their usual flood sales. Blackheart disgorged itself, and the waterline dropped and dropped. Dead frogs lay on the twisted banks. But I didn't trust that creek. It had a miser's heart when it came to swallowing water and holding it in.

Jessica wanted to go riding on that wet ground. She started to beg her old dad. "Can't I, please, please, unca Jerome?"

Lamar sat on his pony, scorning me.

"Mr. gray-headed man, would I go out with Jess if I didn't think it was safe?"

"I don't like the way the air smells, Lamar."

"That's because your nose is stuffed."

He reached down, laughed, and scooped Jessica up, up and onto the pony. My daughter touched the ribbons on the pony's neck. Bernice snorted twice, and delivered her two riders into the woods.

But the geek was right. The sky went purple in half an hour, wind sucked at the cottage, and the storm came in harsh and sudden wisps. Damn the mayor and his pony rides! He shouldn't have gone out with Jess. The rain pounded like a thick blue wall in front of your eyes. The porch flooded, but I couldn't stick around to preserve the cottage from ruin. Jess was in that storm, with a cowboy and his pony.

The water froze to my shirt, and I had to travel into that blue wall of rain. It blinded you and knocked you about. How the hell could you steer?

It was dumb instinct that carried me to the bayou's lip. I saw a girl in a tree. Lamar had tied my daughter to a limb with his own torn shirt. I shouted up into the tree.

"Jess, where's the whore and Bernice?"

But that shout couldn't get through the rain. The wind snarled it up. So I had to slosh in the mud and fight a storm that could hurl you into Blackheart and wash you away. I hit at the rain with my back. I ate wind like chicken heads. Geeks are indestructible.

A nickering came up from the bayou. No one but a pony could talk in a storm. The wind must have thrown Bernice into the bayou along with Lamar, while he was lashing Jessica to the tree. I could catch two heads riding on the water. Horse and man, they were moving in and out of a rough circle. Their heads would disappear and then rise in another spot.

I jumped into the creek. I shoved and shoved at Lamar, until I got his ass above the water and out of that spinning circle. But we couldn't save Bernice. I pulled on her ribbons, and hugged her around the belly, trying to buoy her up. The ribbons fell off in my hand, with clumps of braided hair.

We got Jessica out of the tree. She wouldn't go to unca Jerome. She climbed onto Lamar's back. He was sobbing like an infant, over his lost pony. His mouth was an inch away and I could hear his muttering song. "Best little gal I ever had . . ."

I held him by the shoulder, and the three of us bit water and barreled through the rain.

THIRTY

The Catfish Man

I.

LAMAR had a shotgun funeral. He made the whole village come out for Bernice. He had his deputies herd men and women through the windows and the doors of soaking cottages and chalets. The funeral was held outside city hall. Lamar kidnapped a preacher from Meyerland, and the preacher delivered a sermon on a horse he'd never met. He yakked and yakked about the vicissitudes of Bernice's soul. I couldn't follow his line. Was the preacher saying that God would or wouldn't provide a heaven for Bernice?

The village elders stared at this lunatic preacher and the man they'd put into office. Lamar Jones. They had tolerated his eccentricities: a pony, convicts in a closet, a mistress at city hall. But to be marched out of their homes to celebrate the drowning of a goddamn horse, when they had a flood to deal with . . . They met in secret that afternoon, ripped up Lamar's "constitution" and his code of laws, declared themselves the governing board of Little John Woods, and locked the mayor out of city hall.

Lamar had to come live with us. He was still mumbling about his pony. He seemed to have a rainstorm inside his head. My wife was devoted to him. She put up a hammock in the living room with a pair of fisherman's hooks. When the two of them lay in the hammock, the cottage would rock. You couldn't think. You couldn't sleep.

I had to write with that infernal rocking in the house. What better than a love story? The courtship of my mom and dad. Could I make it out of silk? No. I had to weave some bitterness into the romance. Mom was an orphan working in a dress shop. She lived with an old couple on Attorney Street, near the Williamsburg Bridge. She attended night school, carrying a cloth-bound notebook to class. It was the second grade, you see. She was learning penmanship and the rudiments of American history. Dad wasn't in her class. He was an elephant in a fur shop who happened to have a room right under the bridge. He worked sixteen hours a day.

Coming home from his shop, he spied her walking to night school. Dad fell in love. An orphan with dark eyes. A girl who led merchants by the nose when she was six. She was poor now, with a single cloth coat. But she had lots of boyfriends. They would follow her to night school. One even enrolled in her class. What chance did my father have? Should he join the line of suitors? These were men who could talk poetry to her. Radicals, they read the New York *Times*.

He didn't have the energy to compete with them. He stood in the damp corridor of the night school and thrust a few miserable dying flowers in her palm as she came out of class. My mother thought the man was crazy. Who throws dead flowers at a girl without leaving his name? Mom found out who he was. An elephant in a fur shop.

The couple she lived with nagged at her to see him. "A furrier is like a doctor," they said. What did she need with an elephant? She had boys who recited Pushkin to her, songs about gunpowder and the moon. But there he was, outside her class, with a candy box in the shape of a heart. The box was red, with bowties in the middle. Candy is candy, but it's not a poem. She wanted to give it back. She looked into the elephant's eyes. Did she *see* the fiddler, an orphan just like herself? She took the candy and married him in two months.

2.

"THE Red Candy Box" sold half a million copies for uncle Bob. I missed out on the O. Henry awards, but so what? Texas gave me a special prize: a scroll from the Southwest Institute of the Arts, putting me on the permanent fellows' list.

"Dummy," my mother said. "It was a *blue* candy box." But she cried over the details of the story. "The poems I used to hear . . . I had Mr. Pushkin under my pillow every night."

My father wouldn't talk. He went to his violin when the house was quiet and the hammock didn't rock.

Lamar picked his teeth. Our village was going over to the Octopus. The selectmen who had dumped Lamar figured it was time for Houston to adopt Little John Woods. "Sombitches," Lamar said. "They're letting Houston eat our rump. Soon you won't have a tree. They'll turn Blackheart into a canal for kiddies. That's right. You'll have kiddy rides up and down the creek."

But he continued to sit on his ass. That cottage was like a bus station, with hammocks and beds, and people going in and out. You know what? I missed having Bernice. The warm nostrils of a pony was no small thing. And the wife? She was an enemy who lived across the way, in a hammock with Lamar. I could feel a rage boil up. What's going on? Geeks never get angry.

I was the man with a scroll from Texas, a geek without an appetite. I couldn't have swallowed a chicken, dead or alive. I wasn't a goddamn story book. The well was dry. How many red candy boxes could I write about? Then I saw an ad in the *Post:*

the world champion of table tennis would be at the Houston Coliseum tomorrow. My own little Paul. Seventeen he was, the destroyer of Hungarians, Poles, and Chinese at the Internationals in Hong Kong. He offered to spot any Houston player fifteen points. I took out my old sandpaper racket. The hell with sponge! I'd come out of the Bronx with sandpaper, I'd gone through bedlam with it, and I'd hold on to its wormy power.

I walked six miles to the Coliseum that next afternoon. You couldn't knock on the door and play the champ. You had to pass a qualifying test, "hit" for one minute with Marty Reisman. Marty was Paul's manager.

"Charyn," he said, hugging me. "Where'd you run? You haven't been down to the cellar in five years?"

"Marty, it's more like six."

We couldn't gab too much. Customers were waiting to qualify. So I volleyed with Marty, lunging at his serves with sandpaper in my fist. Marty frowned a little. "Have you been hitting with freaks?"

Could I tell him that ping-pong wasn't so popular among Texas inmates? "I'm rusty, that's all."

Reisman took pity on his old friend. He let the geek into the house. I "qualified" to play little Paul.

Marty picked ten of us, ping-pong yokels. I could have trounced those other nine when I was a regular in Reisman's dungeon, with my Butterfly bat. Now I had a balding piece of wood, a dead stick to go up against the champ.

I drank a glass of milk. Then I joined the yokels in a tiny corral on the Coliseum floor. The promoters were shrewd. They couldn't have brought a dozen frogs out of the bayou for table tennis. Houston wasn't a ping-pong city. So they combined little Paul with a boxing olympiad, and half the barrio turned out. Ping-pong was the novelty act, to be sandwiched around "Termite" Watkins, the local star, and middleweights from Tampa, Corpus Christi, and East L.A.

In that corral, waiting for ping-pong and little Paul, we were only a few yards from the ring. The management wanted to display us, show the geeks to the crowd. So we sat near the red, white, and blue ropes, with cuspidors at each end of the ring, for the fighters to spit blood and rinse their mouths in Gatorade. You could hear the fighters breathe, see their red faces, when a glove would hit. The "Termite" punched his man silly. This was his "warm-up" for Madison Square Garden. The kid from Tampa got dropped in the third round. Corpus Christi won on a TKO. Cowgirls came through the ropes with cards that declared the number of each new round. They wore the tightest jeans in America. Ah, you had "Termite" Watkins, lost mouthpieces, blood in a cuspidor, and girls with thighs that scissored out and could easily have snapped your head off.

Then the fights were over.

Workmen hovered around the ring until it collapsed like a cardboard ship that was shoved into a corner of the arena. They ran to set up the ping-pong table before everybody disappeared. The announcer couldn't hold more than a hundred guests. If you were lucky, you discovered a face in every third row.

We stood in our corral, while Paul entered the arena. He wasn't that dark-eyed boy with a crazy mama, a shrimp who could barely get his nose to the edge of the table. He was taller than this guy Jerome. He had a headband and colored ping-pong shorts, and the muscles along his thighs looked like a small city of worms and swollen lines. He didn't use a green bat any more. He had a red son of a bitch, with a handle that could have come off an axe. He stared at the ten of us. Then his eyes landed on me. He hadn't forgotten the partner who had "betrayed" him and wouldn't go to Boston to beat the Dunstan brothers. The old contempt was there. His smile was like a noose. A slight shiver traveled across his underlip and was gone.

He whispered to Marty Reisman. I knew what it was about.

He wanted to save me for the end.

He took on the yokels, one after the other. He would dart back to retrieve an impossible shot, switch hands, and play lefty for a while. He would stretch his body in murderous ways, his thighs rippling under the shorts. A curious thing happened. The muchachos who'd come for "Termite" Watkins and were outside sipping beer and ogling the cowgirls, began to peek into the arena. The Coliseum was filling again. They liked this boy who could jump thirty feet and find a little white ball.

The promoters were stunned. They should have booked the ping-pong artist for their next olympiad. *Mamacita!* Let him put on a pair of gloves with the "Termite," and they could charge thirty dollars a head.

The nine yokels fell to Paul.

Now he had me.

He smirked at my sandpaper racket, but with a net between us he wouldn't acknowledge who I was. The tenth yokel of the Houston Coliseum. The hombres whistled down at the champ. "Paulito, give this one something to eat. He's old and gray."

They could laugh. But you see, I didn't intend to lose. Even if my brothers the catfish had been burned alive in the great Bronx fire, and that miserable creek of mine was a hollow of dead clay, I still had the catfish in my blood.

I wasn't Paul's hobbyhorse, a toy he could twist to his own delight, and amuse the crowd. I had to relearn the game in two minutes, while I had that fifteen point spot.

I'd get my rhythm back, or chew the table, like the geek of geeks. Paul spun around and delivered looping shots off his hip that made a dull, sickly noise against my bald racket. He played out a macabre dance, hopping, gritting his teeth, as if he was ready to commit murder on the table. He was going to sacrifice me to his ping-pong demons, boil me in a "pot" with his marvelous strokes. But I was the wrong duck. That sickly noise improved. I was getting wood off Paul. The sandpaper was biting at his sandwich bat. Suddenly I was the kid who danced. I didn't have those springy thighs. Forty and gray, I gasped between shots. But he couldn't keep up with my catfish music. He'd tired in his tenth game.

Reisman was a clever manager. He read that mad grit in my eye. He began his stalling tactics. He toweled the champ's shoulders, had him change his headband. It was too late. All the years of frustration, madhouses and prison cells, rubber chickens, Lamar, a scornful wife, took me by the elbow and gave me a formidable grip.

You can't spot a catfish fifteen points.

I scored on Paul. Sandpaper befuddled him, because his body was atuned to the kiss of sponge, and he heard nothing but scratch, scratch, scratch.

The crowd didn't stop loving him. He was their Paulito. And I was the sandpaper geek who slowed the champ down with chops from a bald piece of wood. The hombres jeered and called me a lazy chicken, a hen with tits. And Paul? His eyes filled with hate. I was the golem, a monster who stalked him in Houston and the Upper West Side. He'd won the Nationals before he was twelve. He took the European title, and arrived at Hong Kong like Genghis Khan, sweeping through the competition. And then he loses to gray Jerome.

Marty had to sneak me out the side exit, or the hombres would have thrown me under the ping-pong table and held me prisoner there.

"I didn't mean to hurt Paul's debut . . . but you know, Marty, I was always a devil with sandpaper."

He hugged me and went back to Paul. What a planet. The winner becomes a fucking thief. It was like Esau and Isaac. I'd robbed Paul's birthright somehow, crippled the thunder in his game. Imagine how my father would feel if I ever broke his violin. He'd wander across Houston in his slippers, looking for teddy bears.

THIRTY-ONE

Mississippi Ending

I.

SEVEN in the house.

Each one was feuding with the other. Fan screamed at Lamar. Jess fought with Lillian over who should have the bigger pillow on their bed. Mom was angry because I wouldn't continue her romance in night school. "You end a story with a candy box? Poof! That's it?"

My dad threatened to run away and leave us all.

We'd had it with Little John Woods. The porch was caving in. Cowbirds sat in a neighboring tree. Hundreds of them. Like props out of *Macbeth*. They were figuring somebody's doom. Ours, or the woods?

You couldn't scare the birds. I would come at them with a broom. They'd scatter and then resettle on the same tree.

Lamar didn't have to go bird-chasing with a broom.

"Baby, let's try San Antone."

"Hell," Fan said. "I'm taking Jess home to Louisiana. I don't need a husband here or there."

Jess had a tantrum. "I'm not going without my sister."

"You don't have a sister," Fan said.

"Yes I do! Lillian's my sis."

290   The Catfish Man

"Look," I said. "We're a family. The seven of us. We should stick together."

"Sure," Fan shot back. "Seven kooks. A dispossessed mayor. A nudie harpist. And a dead pony that we can mourn and mourn. You name it."

"So what? It's a family."

"Shut up with your family," she said. "A family can't exist without a real provider. Lamar? He's cracked without Bernice. Find him a pony and he might be sane enough to hold down a janitor's job."

"I'll provide," I said.

"How? With a story a month? All those prizes and we can't afford an orange juice squeezer."

Jess began to shriek. "Mama, mama, seven is a family."

"Then ask the big provider where he's taking us?"

"New York City."

Lamar shook his fist.

"I'm not going," he said. "No sir. Not New York . . . San Antone's got the cutest little river under the streets. Baby, it's like Venice, with canals and all."

Fan took the cowboy by his ear. "Venice? You haven't been north of Colorado . . . the rump of a pony is your map of the world."

The wife was fiercer than "Termite" Watkins these days. You couldn't touch her in a war of tongues. The cowbirds flew off their tree when Fan crossed into the yard, she had such a muscular walk. Hell seemed to break around her. She began to throw our junk into her ancient red Pinto. Sweaters, chairs. We were like a gang of squatters about to trade in one land of devastation for the next. Lamar was the first to climb in with the chairs. He gave up his dream of San Antone.

All the girls were up front. The two Fannies, and Jess on Lillian's lap. We had to leave the beds behind and Bernice's saddlery. Lamar carried her bit in his pocket. We were hunched in the back of the Pinto, Lamar, my dad, and me, with the family chairs, Lillian's monster harp, and dad's fiddle under the seat, locked inside a worn leather case. Dad wouldn't fiddle for us. Forty years old and I'd never watched him play!

Fan drove, while my mother sang of the history she remembered from night school: Washington on the Delaware in a dirty coat; Aaron Burr; the Tories and the Whigs; John Adams and his son Quincy, who went from the president's chair to a musty seat in Congress; Dolley Madison and the famous birthmark on her left shoulder that started seven duels and nearly brought down the White House. Ah, what a head for details my mother had! I would've loved to see the scratchings in her notebook. "George Washington, the Man Who Walked on Ice." She could weave a history of the United States that would make the best-seller lists. I was a common scrivener, with stories that snaked out of my guts. Mom had the humor. Not me.

Fan appointed Jerome the Scrivener to navigate our trip. I had to follow a map that went over my knees and dad's. When we arrived at Beaumont, I said, "We're making a stop in New Orleans. I want to see my old pal Sid."

"See him some other time," Fannie said.

"No. Let me out. I'll walk."

"We're going eighty . . . do you want to die? Goddammit, where is this pal of yours?"

"In the nuthouse at New Orleans."

Fannie bitched and bitched, but she drove me to that former bedlam of mine. "Well, what are you waiting for?"

"I can't get to Sid without a pass. He's the Ripper of Lake Charles."

"Lemme handle it," Lamar said. He had a badge he'd made for himself when he was chief magistrate of Little John Woods. The badge worked. The pony hadn't robbed him of all his wits. He chatted with the hospital supervisor, using plain country talk, and swore I was connected with the *Post.*

"A journalist?" the supervisor asked.

"Yessuh. Jerome Charyn."

And I got into the ward. It had those matrons with their .44's. And the usual geldings and convicts.

"Sid Cummings, please."

The matrons took me to his bunk. Old Sid, he still had 500 years to do. We'd be dancing on Mercury and Uranus long before his sentence ran out.

"You a writer fella?" he said. "I don't give interviews."

His eyes passed over my gray hair again. He fell on me and began to smile. "Morphy's little brother."

He told the matrons to beat it, and they listened to Sid. We had rum cakes smuggled in from the French Quarter. One of the convicts put up a kettle of tea to boil. We drank out of delicate Chinese cups.

"Oh Jesus," the Ripper said. "It must be wicked on the outside. Lawd, you look like a chicken."

"Ah, I've been in and out of jail."

"Jail can't punish a man's face. You got the crease of God on you . . . did you steal a horse? God don't like no horse thieves . . . come on back inside, Jerome. I'll fatten you up."

"Wish I could, Sid. Got a family. People to support."

I left the Ripper with his rum cakes, geldings, and teacups, and I had to reconsider things: he'll *do* those five hundred years. We can dance on Uranus, and my old pal Sid will be having his tea in bedlam's rear ward.

2.

MANHATTAN Island. March, 1978.

We had to find a place to live. "Try the Mississippi," Lillian said.

"You kidding? I won't bring my family into a single-room

hotel. Have my daughter grow up with winos and drug addicts?"

But the winos were already driven out of the Mississippi Hotel. That old whore had gone respectable again. The lions in the wall had been scrubbed with soap; men had come to scrape bits of patina from the roof, and you could see big copper freckles in the lovely green crust.

The renting manager accommodated our tribe of seven. He put us into a suite on the north side of the building. The question of two months' security came up. But Lillian rescued us with her harp.

"I'm Lillian Feld. My father once owned this place when it was a luxury hotel."

The manager was twenty-nine. What did he know about tales of the Korean War, how me and Lil slept in her father's room twenty-five years ago? But this young manager kept looking at Lillian's harp.

"Play something," he said.

Lil improvised. We gave her a chair. She rocked the monster back on her shoulder, warmed it up, and plucked five minutes of Debussy without having to take off her clothes. She wasn't nervous in front of the renting manager, who also noticed my father's violin.

"A musical family," he said, pleased with his tenants. He waived the security. But we still had a month's rent to deliver.

I ran down to that crazy wedge of stone on Twenty-third Street, the Flatiron Building, and besieged uncle Bob. He'd expanded his offices. He had connecting closets now.

"This isn't the old days, kid. Sure, our circulation goes up with 'The Red Candy Box,' but it's a bad time for adventure magazines. I'm going to publish books."

"Books? What Books? *The Pinkeye Kid Goes West?*"

"No, no. Something calmer than that. Let's say a biographical novel . . . on Paul Morphy."

"Bob, I'm finished with the little king."

"Then use Jeff Davis. A novel on the heroes of the Confederacy."

He scratched his name to a thousand-dollar check. "Call it option money."

"Where's the nephew? Johnny Broom. Did he move to Peking?"

The uncle wouldn't say. I took the thousand and returned to the Mississippi Apartments. We had a whole month's grace. Rent, food, little gifts for the daughter. And I had to search my brains for a book. The ideas wouldn't come. What could a catfish tell about Jefferson Davis? Did he swallow chicken heads? Did he play with a sandpaper racket? Did he love teddy bears? Why should I write about him?

3.

WALKING the Upper West Side, like a lost boy, clutching at book ideas, I met the champ. He was wearing a velvet jacket and one of Reisman's beebop caps. Seventeen, and he smoked little black cigars. He had his admirers with him. Ping-pong groupies. Girls from the Bronx High School of Science, housewives, and old men. He was the prince of Ninety-sixth Street. Where was the baby fat I remembered? I always imagined that shrimp growing up to be the best player in the world. But not as a fashionable brat with velvet on his shoulders.

I figured he'd walk past without a single twitch, and pretend there was no Charyn. But he dangled me instead to his pack of admirers. He wanted a bit of cat and mouse on Broadway.

"How are you, Jerome?"

That honey in his voice held more malice than any look of hate.

"Here's Jerome . . . he creamed me in the Houston Coliseum."

The girls from Bronx Science gaped at the catfish man with instant distrust.

"Tell them, Jerome, how you finished me off with sandpaper . . ."

"Fluke," I said. "The champ had sore feet."

"It wasn't a fluke. Jerome's the champ. We played together once upon a time . . . before his head got so gray. He wouldn't go to Boston with me . . . he was with the kosher chicken set, and he couldn't lose a day. Jerome doesn't like to travel. But he ran out to Texas. And now the champ's come home."

"Listen, Paul . . ."

"Don't apologize. You did me a favor, Charyn. I took the Nationals without you. And I didn't need a partner in Hong Kong."

He stepped around me with his entourage. They clattered up Broadway to Reisman's cellar, a thick flag of tee shirts and stockings, with a velvet jacket in the middle. I wondered about his mama. Did he still go marketing with Sarah of the painted cheeks? Or did he hire a groupie to carry her ketchup bottles, this champion of the world? But I couldn't devote myself to little Paul. I had to think and think. *A novel for uncle Bob.*

4.

WE had a reunion at the Mississippi. My natural brothers, Harvey and Marvin, arrived with their children and their wives. Miserable uncle, I couldn't remember all the children's names. Michael, Arthur, Sharon . . . but we were the Charyn brothers. A homicide detective, an engineer, and a writer in search of a novel. The three of us were gray against my father's dark, dark hair, as if his boys had been used up in America, and that fiddling had preserved him, put him out of harm's way. My mother said, "He's stingy, our Jerome. He doesn't have one story about the three brothers."

Ma, I wanted to tell her, Jeff Davis is paying for our bread, not a scrapbook of Marvin, Harvey, and Jerome.

We had some shindig in our suite. Lillian played the harp. The cowboy danced with Marvin's wife. Jessica had six new cousins to tease and admire. The renting manager showed up for a glass of beer. God was on our side, because the manager didn't say a word about next month's bill. I had sixty-seven dollars in my pocket.

My brothers must have sniffed the ragged edge to our life at the Mississippi. They took me into a corner and stuffed money into my shirt. "Ah, it's always harder at the beginning. We'll be all right."

The next morning the family woke me with a surprise. Dad was wearing a sea captain's uniform. He had epaulettes, striped pants, bars around his cuffs, and a silver bowtie.

"What's going on? Is he sailing with his fiddle on the *Queen Elizabeth?*"

"Don't be silly," my mother said. "Your father has a job."

He was starting work today as an usher at the Thalia movie theatre, and mom had sewn the trimmings onto his uniform.

I must have had a dybbuk in me, because I grabbed at my father and made him get out of his striped pants. "Mom, take it back . . . I didn't survive all those jails to see my dad a movie usher."

"It's a free country," dad said.

"Who says? I'm the boss around here."

They shrank from me and my shouting. Dad closed the door and returned to his fiddle. I dialed *Triton* magazine.

"Bob, I have a terrific idea . . . a novel . . . on Jefferson Davis . . . we'll picture him from childhood, right through the Confederacy and old age . . . but I'll need another thousand for a start."

5.

I wrote and wrote. It was flabby stuff. I took Davis up to the fall of the South and his imprisonment in a Yankee dungeon, with shackles on his feet and two ferocious guards stationed in his tiny cell. Here, in the dungeon, the book began to come alive. The dungeon overlooked a moat, and while his jailers cackled at him and called him rebel boy (he was fifty-seven and "skinny as a spear"), he would stand for hours with his eyes on that ditch of water, as if his body were in one place and his "heart had fled out onto the moat." Like a catfish he was.

History stopped, and I had him languish inside the dungeon at Ft. Monroe. The uncle pleaded with me. "Charyn, go on with it . . . get to the part where the Yankees bail him out."

But I didn't want to write about any reconstructed South, and Davis' retirement on the Mississippi Gulf Coast. He was a man who'd lost his country. He fared better in jail.

I would walk the streets, unable to go on with the novel. My Jeff Davis would always be a prisoner of war. Everywhere you looked you found posters of little Paul; he clutched that red hatchet of his, the monstrous handle of his sandwich bat. He was supposed to give exhibitions at Meadowland, Brooklyn College, and Madison Square Garden. The slyness had gone out of me. I wasn't going to track him to his various spots, and haunt him with a sheet of sandpaper. He'd have overcome the oddities of my style, send me into the roofs of Madison Square Garden with a forehand smash. But that wasn't the issue. Win or lose, I wasn't his personal golem. Whatever fate he captured would come without Jerome.

Harvey appeared. He was working on a Latino policy war that ranged from Brooklyn to the Bronx. One family of policy-makers had kidnapped and murdered the daughter of another. The second family struck back. A rash of bodies without heads had been found on City Island and the remoter regions of Pelham Bay Park. Harvey had the afternoon off. He took us on a family outing. Dad wanted to see that burnt-out part of the Bronx where the Poles had lived. Jess was at school. Lil was down at the manager's office, discussing music I suppose. Fan and the cowboy had gone for a stroll. So it was the four of us. Mom, dad, Harvey, and me.

We rode around the wastes of Crotona Park. It could have been a coal mine. The stubble on the ground was black. The few trees that survived the fire storm were all gray, like the Charyn boys. That dungeon of ours across from the park, the Crotona Y, was a rotting shell with rats scurrying out of the basement, rats with pink eyes and mousy white tails.

Then Harvey brought us over to the creek. It was a shallow trench with bugs hovering over it. The dry, cracked mud had footprints along the surface. The fish were gone, the frogs, the marvelous little water snakes. Who trafficked on this mud? Was it a playing field for some kind of imp from the housing projects in Hunts Point that had escaped the fire?

My father seemed impassive to the mud. That bit of Poland that had been rebuilt near Crotona Park and swept away with the fire couldn't stir him any longer. It was my mother who cried. The little queen. She must have felt orphaned ten times over. She'd come into the world without a recognizable dad, lost her landowning mother, Sarah the Wise, ran a slaughterhouse at three, became impoverished by the time she was seven, arrived in America, went to night school, where she discovered Dolley Madison's birthmark, married dad, moved to the Bronx, had her three sons, managed a whorehouse hotel, returned to Crotona Park until the great fire, lived in the Southwest, and made it to Manhattan. Where was home for ma? Could she settle into the Mississippi, or would she have to put on a gypsy's scarf, and cross yet another bayou? How many creeks did she carry in her chest? The orphan and the pioneer.

She looked into this hole that was once the umbilicus of an

entire enclave. The footprints weren't human for Fannie Charyn. "A monster," she said. "Harvey, hurry up . . . before he shows his teeth and pulls us down into the mud."

"Ah," my father assured her. "Give him a donation, and the monster goes away."

But we listened to my mother and drove out of the Bronx.

6.

REISMAN visited me.

"Charyn, we're in trouble."

"How? The champ has groupies on every block. He must be booked until 1985 with exhibitions in Miami and Singapore. Wasn't it the Garden last week?"

"He never showed up."

"Missed his own exhibition? Why's that?"

"His mama dropped dead."

"The crazy witch? Marty, why doesn't he live with you?"

"He's locked himself in her apartment, and he won't come out."

"Well, you're his manager. Talk to him, for God's sake."

"You think I haven't tried? I've knocked and knocked on the door. He says, 'Reisman, go away.'"

"What can I do? He hates my guts."

"Charyn, you were his partner . . . you could coax him out of there. I'm worried. A kid like that. He might not eat for days."

So I went down into the cellar of that old ratty brownstone on Ninety-first, where Paul would spend his nights with Sarah the witch, until he went on tour with Marty Reisman and became the number-one player in the world. Did he write postcards to the witch, and bunk somewhere with his groupies when he returned to New York?

The cellar was laden with banana peels, wormy bottles, and

crushed tins of evaporated milk. I stepped around the debris and waited outside a barred window. "Paul? It's Charyn. Come on . . . I've got a goddamn novel to write. My publisher is on my ass."

He came to the window. Where was the Paul of two weeks ago, smothered in velvet? He looked like a carnival geek. Welcome to the chicken head club! He had the dirtiest face I'd ever seen on a boy, the dirtiest hands, and the dirtiest hair.

"Are you going to sing a lullaby, huh Charyn? Comfort me for my mother? You fuck. If there wasn't bars on the window, I'd choke the air out of you."

"Choke me all you want, but let me in."

The dirty boy scuffled away from the window and opened his door. He tried to pounce on me, but he didn't have the strength to choke a bird. His arms had turned to sticks in his mama's house. I tapped him gently into a chair. He sat with a dark scowl, an unstrung Napoleon of ping-pong, with long ribbons of dirt on his arms. I felt sorry for the lunatic way he was mourning Sarah the witch. But what other way was there to mourn?

An anger grabbed hold of me, a harsh burning in my chest. I seized Paul by the roots of his filthy hair and dragged him over to the tub. I tore the clothes from his body. He still had those muscular worms in his thighs. The worms began to twitch. I sat him in the tub, found a decent washcloth and a bar of soap, and scrubbed him like a baby. I dug that cloth under his chin without mercy.

"Lemme go, you hear?"

"Squeal, squeal . . . what are you without your wonder bat, little Paul?"

"Gimme something to eat, and I'll show you."

"I'll give . . . you're coming home with me."

I expected him to rise out of the tub, scratching with his blue fingernails, but he started to blubber. His back shivered in deep shame.

"I left her all alone . . . I forgot about her. Yeah, I sent her money orders . . . Marty made me rich. You know how she died, Charyn? She was drinking whiskey, and she tripped down the stairs to the cellar and had a heart attack. She could have been lying there, screaming for days. Who the hell would have heard her? I was in Vermont."

What could I tell him? That he should have taken his mama along on his trips? She would have died on a different set of stairs.

"Sitting in your own stink isn't going to bring her back . . . Marty's worried about you."

"Let him worry. I'm finished with ping-pong."

"What will you do? Retire to a cellar at seventeen? That's some commemoration."

I went through his closets and picked a matching combination for him to wear. I was the champ's butler, Jerome. I packed a suitcase for him and then tossed him out into the light.

He blinked, shielded his eyes, and walked with feeble steps. I got him over to Broadway and up to the Mississippi.

"Mom, this is Paul . . . he's going to live with us for a while."

One look, and Paul fell in love with my mother. They must have smelled the orphan in each other, because they grew inseparable by the middle of the afternoon. He listened to her night school stories, George Washington, Aaron Burr, and the candy box that got her to marry my dad. He wasn't a boarder, this kid. He was another Charyn.

With my mother to make him laugh, and my father's violin, he turned from mourning to ping-pong.

"Reisman has me booked in New Jersey. I'll only be gone one night . . ."

It wasn't evil of me, I swear, to have sucked Paul into our family "bayou." I didn't want him to become like that other Paul, Morphy of New Orleans. Deranged and alone, in his sister's corset and shoes. He had a manager and mom's cooking, our little Paul.

7.

WE could help a ping-pong master, but things weren't perfect in our "bayou" on the eleventh floor. The family was beginning to slide. Lillian had a liaison with the renting manager. Jessie would awake without her sister in the bed and shriek for Lil. I had to comfort her. "Your sis will be up in a few hours, hon . . . she went downstairs to have tea with Joseph."

Joseph was the renting manager.

Jess didn't believe my little tea story.

"Unca Jerome, who drinks tea in the dark?"

"Ah, it's a custom we have in New York. This isn't Texas . . . hon, go back to sleep."

I had a visitor in my own bed, which stood in the hall, because that's where catfish like to sleep.

It was the wife. She wore a thin gown, and it was painful to see her breasts under that veil of cotton. I didn't have the nerve to touch this alien wife. She lived in back of the dining room, with Lamar. She hadn't come to me for a feud in the night. She put her arms around my neck, and we kissed like a pair of catfish. The crazy things that desire does to people. The two of us were suspended somewhere between love and hate. Kiss and scratch, kiss and scratch, was the language we understood.

Lamar was drowning, she said. This man who had ruled a little colony in Texas couldn't gather the wits to apply for a job. So I took the cowboy to see my brother Marvin. The kid brother was a sales engineer. He'd been the last to come along, the child of mom's middle years, and he struggled at school. I had to help him with his homework, the young author Jerome, whose sentences had poison in them most of the time. With such a helpmate, God knows how he finished junior high? Now he was a boss over other engineers. He got on the phone for Lamar and found him a job as a salesman in a camera supply shop. The cowboy could start right away.

I walked uptown, thinking of Jeff Davis. I had brothers everywhere on the map, in New York and New Orleans, and in a Yankee dungeon. Count them up. Harvey, Marvin, Sid Cummings, the cowboy, Jeff Davis, Johnny Broom, Morphy, and my own little Paul. And sisters, where were my sisters? Had I been cheated out of my share? Or was it that the catfish man couldn't have a sister in the house? Catfish are suspicious of women: mothers, sisters, wives. A blasted lot we are, wary of the female touch.

A man was carrying a sandwich board on Ninety-fifth Street. The board advertised a pair of old pirate movies: *Captain Blood* and *The Black Swan.* You could have your pick of Tyrone Power and Errol Flynn. Was it any wonder that I'd written of pirate after pirate, when Hollywood had destroyed my brains? . . . what little boy in 1945 wouldn't have fallen under the sway of that pirate ship, the Swan, and been marked for life? Who could be satisfied with anyone after you've had Maureen O'Hara's purple lips?

A head bobbed between the sandwich board. I recognized the owner of that head. My dad was the sandwich board. Son of a bitch. He'd taken that job at the Thalia. I grabbed him by the shoulder straps, raised the sandwich board with a tremendous shove, and pitched it to the ground. Tyrone Power's face ended with a clatter in the street.

My poor dad cringed in his sea captain's uniform. Bully bastard. I was the golem and he was the black-haired child. How could I dismiss the terror streaking under his eyes?

"Dad, I didn't mean it . . . I told you and mom, no ushers in our family. We're not mules and slaves any more. The Charyns don't need sandwich boards."

He followed me home at a distance. It was shame and anger, I think. I was the son who dismantled him, took away his wooden coat. Like a Cossack, or a Polish cavalry officer, I was something to be shunned.

8.

IT wasn't Lamar who sweated at night. Lamar found his niche. He was doing a tremendous volume at the camera shop. *I* dreamed of his pony. I was riding Bernice. She had a red froth in her mouth. Her flanks were heavy with a gray foam. I was the Polish rider, with his spurs and his nobleman's whip. I lashed the pony, cracked her sides with the wicked teeth of the spurs. She didn't hurl me out of the saddle. She didn't sit down. Her legs shot forward, but her body writhed and wouldn't go. I'd ridden the pony to her death. Her heart burst, with her legs still in the air. We tumbled over and over, and I slipped above her ears, turned, and landed with her raw mouth in my chest.

I was sitting in Lamar's lap.

"You screamed, boy . . . and fell off the bed. Change your pajamas. It feels like you were swimming in them."

"Thanks, Lamar. I'll be all right."

He went back in to Fan, clopping along in his bare feet.

I wasn't getting into bed after a dream like that. *The novelist who murdered Bernice.* It was four A.M. I dressed without disturbing the family and scuffled out the door. I didn't want to wake the elevator man, so I took the stairs. I crashed into Lillian on the seventh floor. She seemed embarrassed, coming up from the manager's office.

"Joseph's crazy about me," she said. "He'll die if I don't live with him . . . but my harp's upstairs. Jerome, what should I do?"

I wasn't her rabbi, for Christ's sake. I was the paterfamilias of my own lost tribe. I couldn't stop Lilly from moving her harp into Joseph's office. Let her pluck for him! I wouldn't hold her prisoner in our "creek." But parting with Lil would have been like losing a piece of the family flesh.

She stroked my face.

Could she tell the catfish's vulnerable spot, that need to never, never let go. Clutch the past, and twist it into time future. That first scrape of dad's Polish fiddle, will I hear it on the floor below? Blink once on Broadway and watch that three-year-old orphan, Fannie the Shrewd, bossing a whole village. And Lillian's brown nipples? I'll be smelling them tomorrow in my sleep, if I don't dream of horses again.

"Jerome, Jerome," she said. "You're always rescuing me. Joseph will have to suffer. I can't leave Jess, and you, and mom."

We kissed, and I went down into the street.

I could have gone to Reisman's cellar. But I wasn't in the mood. I'd have to sit under Marty's lights and watch boys and girls who'd copied Paul's style, and were thinking *Hong Kong* with every stroke. Future champions of the world. No, I didn't want to see their mechanical dance. Doll's with Paul's signature on them.

There were hawkers out at night, selling papers from Bolivia and Honduras, and for a minute you couldn't tell what city you'd entered from under the Mississippi's awning. Bahia? Or a spot on the Blue Nile?

I loped downtown, a wolf born in yellow mud. I had lots of spittle in my mouth. Who says Manhattan doesn't have a sky? The dawn was a pink mole that grew and grew on top of your head. The sun seemed to rise with a fierce gray shiver, like a goddamn delinquent who wanted to catch up on his sleep.

I was down in Chelsea, when I had my morning tea and got involved in a rent strike. Sitting in a diner on West Twenty-sixth, I saw a building hurl eggs and apples and rotting pies at a man in the street. It was a tenant crusade. People manned the windows and the fire escapes, and bombarded their landlord, who was appealing to them for rent long overdue. I would have laughed with the customers in the diner, cheered the falling apples and the explosion of eggs, but you see, the landlord was a friend of mine. Johnny Broom. He wasn't in Peking. He'd gone from his little brown books to becoming a slumlord in Chelsea. Chairman Mao was into real estate!

I called to him from the diner. "Jesus, John, get away from those windows." But the owner of the diner wouldn't let him through the door. John was notorious in the neighborhood. He sucked blood out of buildings until they went to pot.

So we had to disappear from Chelsea.

I didn't bother hiding my scowls.

"That's a big jump from a Navy scholarship, John . . . bleeding buildings. I ought to kick you in the ass. You ruined my kitchen gang at Diane's with your miserable brown book. You wouldn't let my men move a chicken wing. John and his labor songs! Now you're the Chelsea vampire."

"I'm going about my business, is all. Should I tell you how much it costs to heat one room?"

"I'd rather not hear it, John."

"Well, heat and water bills are gonna start hurting novelists one day. Who do you think got the uncle's mind off magazines? . . . I'm half owner of Triton Books."

Here I was, the slumlord's apprentice!

Goddamn. Maybe John was the original catfish, who could summon any ideology and scramble it with his tail, reverse himself whenever he liked, slough off identities and careers, so you couldn't tell what the catfish was wearing. Think about it. John had a Navy coat, but he was never a cadet. Was landlording another disguise? And now the catfish was a publisher! I didn't want any part of his tricks.

"Keep your option money. I'll ask my brother Marvin for a job."

"Don't be foolish. You're a Triton author . . . one of us. Can I say something? Your novel stinks. Shuck Jefferson Davis. That's my advice. Southern intrigue isn't your strong point, Jerome. You've got a head for the monstrous. Gargoyles and bumps. Old Mr. Jeff needs a softer touch. You took the man and made him into Monte Cristo. He'll sit in your Yankee jail until the year two thousand."

"Longer than that," I said. My pal Sid Cummings had 500 years to go. Why couldn't Davis do 150? It's my novel."

"You can treat history like a whore, flirt with her and bend her as much as you like. But you can't tear off all her skirts. She'll run amok, and people won't believe what you write."

"That's Chinese propaganda, John. You're still a fucking Maoist."

And we laughed that laugh of friends who'd gone their separate ways.

"Leave the South alone, buddy. Pick a new topic."

I could add another benefactor to my list. Commander Shirl, the sheriff of Harris County, and Johnny Broom. But it's the strangest thing. John was right. History's a whore that's got to have some of her skirts. You can't tarnish the old girl. She wasn't like Lilly, who could only perform in public without her clothes.

Went home and tore up my book. Fan didn't try to stop me. But she looked at the scattering of pages and shoved the hair out of her eyes. "You happy?" she asked. "How are we going to eat?"

"I'll write another book."

"On what?"

"I don't know."

"It's a madhouse here," she said. "We all should have moved in with your friend Sid . . . we have our own orchestra. Violins and harps. Lamar's a camera junkie. He's forgotten Bernice. And you? . . . I wish you'd never come into that canteen at the Grange. I had a reasonable life. A husband who paid the bills. I was fine until I met you, Jerome Charyn."

It must have been that dream of the pony and the talk with John, because I started to shiver. "I loved you on that hill, Fan. And I'm not sorry."

She fondled my gray head and picked at the tears with a

finger. "I'm not sorry either. My husband Maynard was a louse
. . . you're the most difficult man in creation. You can't trust
a soul, and you're always landing in jail . . . but you are a good
provider."

I crawled under her skirts, and we made love on the living
room floor, with the same proviso: she could only have one
husband at a time. And Lamar was her "husband" right now.
I was the in-between man, half lover, father, petulant son.

I retired to that closet where I wrote. It didn't have a window, but I could hear Lilly practice in the other room . . . and
dad scrape on his fiddle. They were comforting sounds and I
filled my mechanical pencil with a long strip of lead. You think
it's easy to scrap a novel and start again? Go search for a theme!
Marlon Brando? Frankenstein? Marcel Proust? I was sick of
pirates.

Catfish and ping-pong and a weightlifter's neck. Misplaced
Phi Beta Kappa keys. Rabbis with a blowtorch. They were my
themes. I wrote a first sentence and scratched it out. *Tell your
story, Jerome.* Who would want to hear about my obscure
birth? Streets of Polish Jews in the Bronx, destroyed by fire. I
wrote, scratched out, and wrote again. It was murderous to
begin. To get that feel on paper. It must have been 120 in the
closet. It was like the Sahara in there. The heck with it. I'd
catch my story by the tail and I wouldn't let go. I scribbled a
line that I could live with:

> The Bronx River is a wormy little stream famous for its
> catfish and the color of its mud.

Then I rolled the lead up into the bowels of the pencil to keep
it safe, put my notebook aside, and came out of the closet.

Mississippi Ending, Part Two

I.

So I was the little rabbi in a writing closet, retelling his life. Jerome the Scrivener had come to roost. The labor was enormous. What to put in? What to leave out? My mechanical pencil had become the catfish's forking tail. It was *À la Recherche du Temps Perdu,* featuring Crotona Park South. My "madeleine" was my mother's bananas and prunes. Ah, I had questions to ask. How come I was the good little boy who could eat with a knife and a fork when he was three, and mom had to stuff food into Harvey's cheeks at six and seven? Did Harvey want to stay the infant of the house? All the changing colors the past can fling at you. A million bits of camouflage. The catfish knows.

Sometimes I wouldn't come out of the closet for a day. The scrivener was disheveled. A gray beard would grow. My mother knocked on the closet door. Winter was coming. Dad had developed a cough. Mom worried about him. She and Sam were getting out. Dad's social security checks had arrived. They were going to Florida.

The scrivener went back into his closet. There was an inevitability to it: Polish boys have to lose their moms and dads to

Miami Beach. I was forty-one. I could throw mustard on a piece of bread and have the pluck of Lillian's harp to console me in my closet. But that familiar noise didn't come through the closet wall. In my blindness and neglect, the world pushed on around me. Lillian had married the renting manager. And with mom gone, Paul moved out to live with a girl from Bronx Science. Kids were setting up households at an early age in 1979. Why shouldn't little Paul have an independent life?

Lamar's camera supply shop was opening a branch in South Dakota. He was asked to be the manager over there. This was serious. It made me abandon the Crotona Y for a minute, and the story of mom's whorehouse hotel. I had to come out of the closet, scratch my beard. You get used to a daughter and a wife, even if the wife was "married" to Lamar. They were packing for South Dakota.

"Fan," I said, "they have blizzards, terrible storms. It snows into July."

"Shut up," she said, but she kissed me on the mouth and went out the door with Lamar and Jess. And I could suck wind in seven rooms.

All my struggles to hold on, to preserve Charyns under the same roof. A clan of one potato. Me.

The Mississippi became a prison house, another Ft. Monroe. I was Jerome Charyn as Jefferson Davis, captive to a different style of war: isolation, dread . . . a single-room-occupant in seven monstrous rooms.

I was less than a geek. I didn't have the stamina to do my chicken act. I couldn't have swallowed a goddamn thing.

Lillian was nice. She invited me to take my suppers with her and Joseph. Could have been their all-star boarder. I said no.

"Thanks, Lil, but the novel's chewing at me . . . I can't sit down for a regular meal."

I was in that confounded closet from morning til night, scratching away, like a ferocious bird trying to figure out its own history. It was in the closet that I had my only strength. I would swoop down on a word, peck at it on the page. Don't kid yourself. Orphans write the best sentences. But they don't know when to eat.

I looked more and more like a chicken, with my stooped back, the skin hanging from my neck, and a scalp of gray feathers.

I would quit working around nine and visit Reisman's cellar, not to play, but to share a candy bar with Reisman himself and kibbitz for half an hour.

"How's the shrimp?"

"Paul? He married his girlfriend. He's going to sit out the Internationals this year. He's too busy endorsing a line of ping-pong balls."

"The little capitalist," I said. But I was glad for the kid. How long can you play with that mad fever in your eye? He'd been hustling ping-pong since he was eight and a half.

I took a bite of candy and continued to reminisce. I wasn't Reisman's only customer. Marty had to make the rounds at his club. I returned to my closet with a furious sweat. Damp in the armpits, I tackled my days at Columbia College. The ignominy of being dropped from the NROTC, drummed out of the corps. I could have been an admiral by now if I'd listened to Shirl. Not a scribbler in a closet.

Charyn of the China Sea.

I crept into that bed I had in the hall. The wickedness of it: my dreams weren't wild and goosy. They were a nightbook, a companion to my novel. I dreamt of dad's violin. I was the fiddler in the story. I didn't have pinkeye, but I could play. Was it a Polish boy's composition? Who can tell? I brought the fiddle out of its cracked leather case. You could feel the indentations where the fiddle sat. It was blue velvet inside, going bald from the rub of the violin.

I dug the tail end into that wedge under my chin, and I

scratched on the fiddle with dad's bow of ancient horsehairs. I didn't have to adjust the pegs. The tune slid off the fiddle box. It was like ping-pong or chess. The rhythm came back at you, I swear. The fiddle had its own song. It gave my elbow a push. But it must have been in a fury, because the fiddle broke. The neck snapped off in my hands, and the belly split, exposing a pale wooden board. And I had a pathetic bunch of pegs, wires, and ribs.

It wasn't a dream you could wake to, and then rush off into a closet. A fiddle destroys itself, and who's to blame? The hell with Proust and the ravages of time. I had more immediate problems. A fiddle that murders its own song.

2.

SIX days in the closet.

A diet of crackers and milk.

I would ask while I scribbled: how come my family dissolved so soon? Did I hasten its end? Was I more golem than geek? A monster in the house named Jerome Charyn.

Then I got to Paul, "le petit Roi" of New Orleans. Thinking of myself, I wrote his sad story. The kid who overthrows his brother, his father, and his uncle at chess. *Another monster in the house.* He doesn't scream at people. He shows his rage on the chessboard, but it's always with a cool, cool fist.

And he ends up hiding in a closet, just like me.

I heard this shaking in my head, as if some wise guy were testing a mallet on different parts of my skull.

"Jerome, come out of there."

I opened the door, and a face peeked in. Blonde and clear. Someone who wasn't a woman or a child. She carried a pocketbook and wore high heels. Ah, it was a trick of geography. Jess had "aged" in South Dakota. She had her mother's gorgeous lips. The two of them stood over me, with their suitcases in the hall.

"You were right about Dakota," Fan said. "It does have blizzards in July."

Blizzards. July. I hugged the wife and Jess, hopped around them. The whole closet shook. No, I wasn't Jeff Davis, defeated man of the South, I was Catfish Jerome, with his two little girls. Fan understood what my squeezes were all about. But I couldn't pull off her clothes with the daughter there. We don't do that in Charyn's "creek."

I danced them across those seven rooms, until they were out of breath. They giggled and tugged at my gray beard. "Monte Cristo," I said. "The Count of Monte Cristo . . . coming out of his writing closet."

The wife mentioned Lamar. "He bought himself a new pony . . . Jocelyn. He took Jess for rides, but she's too big to sit with him on one pony. She kept asking, 'Where's my uncle Jerome?' . . . we missed you, I guess."

I chewed her blonde hair. I whirled Jess and Fan around again, and we landed on the floor, with my beard in the daughter's face. Light broke through the windows, shimmered on the Mississippi's walls. I tickled wife and daughter with the beard. And it wasn't a myth. I have my own creek that runs along seven rooms. The mud is gone, the beautiful yellow mud. No bullfrogs and tin cans. But there are two lady catfish. And whatever the cost, we'll have our delight. A Polish boy and his family. In a creek of seven rooms with sun on the walls.